BURNING BRIGHT

TRACY CHEVALIER is the *New York Times* bestselling author of four previous novels, including *Girl With a Pearl Earring*, which was translated into thirty-nine languages and made into an Oscar-nominated film. Born and raised in Washington, D.C., she lives in London with her husband and son.

Praise for *Burning Bright*

"If she succeeds in acquainting a new generation with the rapturous work of William Blake on the eve of the 250th anniversary of his birth, she can take pride in her accomplishment." —*The Boston Globe*

"[E]ighteenth-century London, from its shadier neighborhoods to its more elegant areas, arises from these pages in all its cacophony." —*Booklist*

"Chevalier brilliantly re-creates Georgian London . . . lovingly etched characters and polished prose." —*The Christian Science Monitor*

"Chevalier once again provides an irresistible evocation of a time and place where creativity flourished." —*More*

"Chevalier masterfully evokes a sense of working-class life . . . [in] French Revolution-era London." —*Entertainment Weekly*

"Chevalier's vivid descriptions and unusual mix of characters make this story an easy pleasure to read." —*Library Journal*

"Tracy Chevalier is a breath of fresh air. . . . *Burning Bright* is an ambitious, impressively researched novel." —*The Express*

"Vivid, romantic." —*Daily Mail*

"A wonderfully vivid portrait of eighteenth-century London." —*Time Out London*

Praise for *The Lady and the Unicorn*

"Richly imagined . . . a passionate, intricate novel." —*Los Angeles Times*

"Chevalier's grand and bawdy tale, once again, perfectly matches the scope and style of its inspiration . . . a lively, sexy, and thoroughly entertaining novel." —*Entertainment Weekly*

"Subtly rendered, surprisingly complex characters . . . a novel notable for its human warmth." —*The New York Times Book Review*

"Chevalier fashions in her radiant, quicksilver style an intimate tale of intrigue, passion, and deception." —*Elle*

Burning Bright

TRACY CHEVALIER

A PLUME BOOK

PLUME
Published by the Penguin Group
Penguin Group (USA) Inc., 375 Hudson Street, New York, New York 10014, U.S.A. •
Penguin Group (Canada), 90 Eglinton Avenue East, Suite 700, Toronto, Ontario,
Canada M4P 2Y3 (a division of Pearson Penguin Canada Inc.) • Penguin Books Ltd.,
80 Strand, London WC2R 0RL, England • Penguin Ireland, 25 St. Stephen's Green,
Dublin 2, Ireland (a division of Penguin Books Ltd.) • Penguin Group (Australia),
250 Camberwell Road, Camberwell, Victoria 3124, Australia (a division of Pearson Australia
Group Pty. Ltd.) • Penguin Books India Pvt. Ltd., 11 Community Centre, Panchsheel Park,
New Delhi – 110 017, India • Penguin Group (NZ), 67 Apollo Drive, Rosedale, North Shore
0632, New Zealand (a division of Pearson New Zealand Ltd.) • Penguin Books (South Africa)
(Pty.) Ltd., 24 Sturdee Avenue, Rosebank,
Johannesburg 2196, South Africa

Penguin Books Ltd., Registered Offices: 80 Strand, London WC2R 0RL, England

Published by Plume, a member of Penguin Group (USA) Inc.
Previously published in a Dutton edition.

First Plume Printing, March 2008
1 3 5 7 9 10 8 6 4 2

℗ REGISTERED TRADEMARK—MARCA REGISTRADA

The Library of Congress has catalogued the Dutton edition as follows:
Chevalier, Tracy.
Burning bright / by Tracy Chevalier.
p. cm.
ISBN 978-0-525-94978-7 (hc.)
ISBN 978-0-452-28907-9 (pbk.)
1. Blake, William, 1757–1827—Fiction. I. Title.
PS3553.H4367B87 2007
813'.54—dc22   2006026898

Printed in the United States of America
Original hardcover design by Nancy Resnick

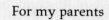

For my parents

PART I

March 1792

There was something humiliating about waiting in a cart on a busy London street with all your possessions stacked around you, on show to the curious public. Jem Kellaway sat by a tower of Windsor chairs his father had made for the family years ago, and watched aghast as passersby openly inspected the cart's contents. He was not used to seeing so many strangers at once—the appearance of one in their Dorsetshire village would be an event discussed for days after—and to being so exposed to their attention and scrutiny. He hunkered back among the family belongings, trying to make himself less conspicuous. A wiry boy with a narrow face, deep-set blue eyes, and sandy fair hair that curled below his ears, Jem was not one to draw attention to himself, and people peered more often at his family's belongings than at him. A couple even stopped and handled items as if they were at a barrow squeezing pears to see which was ripest—the woman fingering the hem of a nightdress that poked out of a split bag, the man picking up one of Thomas Kellaway's saws and testing its teeth for sharpness. Even when Jem shouted, "Hey!" he took his time setting it back down.

Apart from the chairs, much of the cart was filled with the tools of Jem's father's trade: wooden hoops used to bend wood for the arms and backs of the Windsor chairs he specialized in; a dismantled lathe for turning chair legs; and a selection of saws, axes, chisels, and augers. Indeed, Thomas Kellaway's tools took up so much room that the Kellaways had had to take turns walking alongside the cart for the week it took to get from Piddletrenthide to London.

The cart they had traveled in, driven by Mr. Smart, a local Piddle Valley man with an unexpected sense of adventure, was halted in front of Astley's Amphitheatre. Thomas Kellaway had had only a vague notion of where to find Philip Astley, and no idea of how big London really was, thinking he could stand in the middle of it and see the amphitheatre where Astley's Circus performed, the way he might back in Dorchester. Luckily for them, Astley's Circus was well known in London, and they were quickly directed to the large building at the end of Westminster Bridge, with its round, peaked wooden roof and front entrance adorned with four columns. An enormous white flag flying from the top of the roof read ASTLEY'S in red on one side and AMPHITHEATRE in black on the other.

Ignoring the curious people on the street as best he could, Jem fixed his eyes instead on the nearby river, which Mr. Smart had decided to wander along "to see a bit o' London" and on Westminster Bridge, which arched over the water and ran into the distant mass of square towers and spires of Westminster Abbey. None of the rivers Jem knew in Dorset—the Frome the size of a country lane, the Piddle a mere rivulet he could easily jump across—bore any resemblance to the Thames, a broad channel of rocking, choppy green-brown water pulled back and forth by the distant tide of the sea. Both river and bridge were clogged with traffic—boats on the Thames; carriages, carts, and pedestrians on the bridge. Jem had never seen so many people at once, even on market day in Dorchester, and was so distracted by the sight of so much movement that he could take in little detail.

Though tempted to get down from the cart and join Mr. Smart at the water's edge, he didn't dare leave Maisie and his mother. Maisie Kellaway was gazing about in bewilderment and flapping a handkerchief at her face. "Lord, it's hot for March," she said. "It weren't this hot back home, were it, Jem?"

"It'll be cooler tomorrow," Jem promised. Although Maisie was two years older than he, it often seemed to Jem that she was his younger sister, needing protection from the unpredictability of the world—though there was little of that in the Piddle Valley. His job would be harder here.

Anne Kellaway was watching the river as Jem had, her eyes fixed on a boy pulling hard on the oars of a rowboat. A dog sat opposite him, panting in the heat; he was the boy's only cargo. Jem knew what his mother was thinking of as she followed the boy's progress: his brother Tommy, who had loved dogs and always had at least one from the village following him about.

Tommy Kellaway had been a handsome boy, with a tendency to daydream that baffled his parents. It was clear early on that he would never be a chairmaker, for he had no affinity for wood and what it could do, or any interest in the tools his father tried to teach him to use. He would let an auger come to a halt midturn, or a lathe spin slower and slower and stop as he gazed at the fire or into the middle distance—a trait he inherited from his father, but without the accompanying ability to get back to his work.

Despite this essential uselessness—a trait Anne Kellaway would normally despise—his mother loved him more than her other children, though she could not have said why. Perhaps she felt he was more helpless and so needed her more. Certainly he was good company, and made her laugh as no one else could. But her laughter had died the morning six weeks before when she found him under the pear tree at the back of the Kellaways' garden. He must have climbed it in order to pick the one pear left, which had managed to cling on to its branch and hung just out of reach all winter, teasing them, even though they knew the cold would have ruined its taste. A branch had snapped, and he fell and broke his neck. A sharp pain pierced her chest whenever Anne Kellaway thought of him; she felt it now, watching the boy and the dog in the boat. Her first taste of London could not erase it.

~ *2* ~

Thomas Kellaway felt very small and timid as he passed between the tall columns outside the amphitheatre. He was a small, lean man, with tightly curled hair, like the pelt of a terrier, cut close to his scalp. His presence made little impression on such a grand entrance. Stepping inside and leaving his family out in the street, he found the foyer dark and empty, though he could hear the pounding of hooves and the cracking of a whip through a doorway. Following the sounds, he entered the theatre itself, standing among rows of benches to gape at the performing ring, where several horses were trotting, their riders standing rather than sitting on the saddles. In the center a young man stood cracking a whip as he called out directions. Though he had seen them do the same at a show in Dorchester a month earlier, Thomas Kellaway still stared. If anything it seemed even more astonishing that the riders could perform such a trick again. One time might be a lucky accident; twice indicated real skill.

Surrounding the stage, a wooden structure of boxes and a gallery had been built, with seats and places to stand. A huge three-tiered wagon-wheel chandelier hung above it all, and the round roof with open shutters high up also let in light.

Thomas Kellaway didn't watch the riders for long, for as he stood among the benches a man approached and asked what he wanted.

"I be wantin' to see Mr. Astley, sir, if he'll have me," Thomas Kellaway replied.

The man he was speaking to was Philip Astley's assistant manager. John Fox had a long mustache and heavy-lidded eyes, which he usually kept half-closed, only ever opening them wide at disasters—of which there had been and would be several in the course of Philip Astley's long run as a circus impresario. Thomas Kellaway's sudden appearance at the amphitheatre was not what John Fox would consider a disaster, and so he regarded the Dorset man without surprise and through drooping eyelids. He was used to people asking to see his boss. He also had a prodigious memory, which is always useful in an assistant, and remembered Thomas

Kellaway from Dorchester the previous month. "Go outside," he said, "an' I expect in the end he'll be along to see you."

Puzzled by John Fox's sleepy-looking eyes and lackadaisical answer, Thomas Kellaway retreated back to his family in the cart. It was enough that he'd got his family to London; he had run out of the wherewithal to achieve more.

No one would have guessed—least of all himself—that Thomas Kellaway, Dorset chairmaker, from a family settled in the Piddle Valley for centuries, would end up in London. Everything about his life up until he met Philip Astley had been ordinary. He had learned chair-making from his father, and inherited the workshop on his father's death. He married the daughter of his father's closest friend, a woodcutter, and except for the fumbling they did in bed together, it was like being with a sister. They lived in Piddletrenthide, the village they had both grown up in, and had three sons—Sam, Tommy, and Jem—and a daughter, Maisie. Thomas went to the Five Bells to drink two evenings a week, to church every Sunday, to Dorchester every month. He had never been to the seaside twelve miles away, or expressed any interest, as others in the pub sometimes did, in seeing any of the cathedrals within a few days' reach—Wells or Salisbury or Winchester—or of going to Poole or Bristol or London. When he was in Dorchester, he did his business—took commissions for chairs, bought wood—and went home again. He preferred to get back late rather than to stay over at one of the tradesmen's inns in Dorchester and drink his money away. That seemed to him far more dangerous than dark roads. He was a genial man, never the loudest in the pub, happiest when he was turning chair legs on his lathe, concentrating on one small groove or curve, or even forgetting that he was making a chair, and simply admiring the grain or color or texture of the wood.

This was how he lived, and how he was expected to live, until in February 1792, Philip Astley's Traveling Equestrian Spectacular came to spend a few days in Dorchester, just two weeks after Tommy Kellaway fell from the pear tree. Astley's Circus was touring the West Country, diverting there on its way back to London from a winter spent in Dublin and Liverpool. Though it was advertised widely with posters and handbills and puffs about the show in the *Western Flying Post*, Thomas Kellaway had not known the show was in town when he went on one of his trips there. He had come to deliver a set of eight high-back Windsor chairs, bringing them in his cart along with his son Jem, who was learning the trade, as Thomas Kellaway had done from his father.

Jem helped unload the chairs and watched his father handle the customer with that tricky combination of deference and confidence needed for business. "Pa," he began, when the transaction was complete and Thomas Kellaway had pocketed an extra crown from the pleased customer, "can we go and look at the sea?" On a hill south of Dorchester, it was possible to see the sea five miles away. Jem had been to the view a few times, and hoped one day to get to the sea itself. In the fields above the Piddle Valley, he often peered south, hoping that somehow the landscape of layered hills would have shifted to allow him a glimpse of the blue line of water that led to the rest of the world.

"No, son, we'd best get home," Thomas Kellaway replied automatically, then regretted it as he saw Jem's face shut down like curtains drawn over a window. It reminded him of a brief period in his life when he too wanted to see and do new things, to break away from established routines, until age and responsibility yanked him back into the acceptance he needed to live a quiet Piddle life. Jem no doubt would also come to this acceptance naturally. That was what growing up was. Yet he felt for him.

He said nothing more. But when they passed the meadows by the River Frome on the outskirts of town, where a round wooden structure with a canvas roof had been erected, he and Jem watched the men juggling torches by the roadside to lure customers in; Thomas Kellaway then felt for the extra crown in his pocket and

turned the cart off into the field. It was the first unpredictable thing
he had ever done, and it seemed, briefly, to loosen something in
him, like the ice on a pond cracking in spring.

It made it easier when he and Jem returned home later that
night with tales of the spectacles they'd seen, as well as an encounter they'd had with Philip Astley himself, for Thomas Kellaway to
face his wife's bitter eyes that judged him for having dared to have
fun when his son's grave was still fresh. "He offered me work,
Anne," he told her. "In London. A new life, away from—" He
didn't finish. He didn't need to—they were both thinking of the
mound of earth in the Piddletrenthide graveyard.

The Kellaways waited at the cart for half an hour before they were
visited by Philip Astley himself—circus owner, creator of spectacles,
origin of outlandish gossip, magnet to the skilled and the eccentric,
landlord, patron of local businesses, and oversized colorful character.
He sported a red coat he had worn years before during his service
as a cavalry officer; it had gold buttons and trim, and was fastened
only at the collar, revealing a substantial belly held in by a buttoned
white waistcoat. His trousers were white; his boots had chaps that
came to the knee; and in his one concession to civilian life, he wore
a black top hat, which he was constantly raising to ladies he recognized or would like to recognize. Accompanied by the ever-present
John Fox, he trotted down the steps of the amphitheatre, strode up
to the cart, raised his hat to Anne Kellaway, shook Thomas Kellaway's hand, and nodded at Jem and Maisie. "Welcome, welcome!"
he cried, brusque and cheerful at the same time. "It is very good to
see you again, sir! I trust you are enjoying the sights of London
after your journey from Devon?"

"Dorsetshire, sir," Thomas Kellaway corrected. "We lived near Dorchester."

"Ah, yes, Dorchester—a fine town. You make barrels there, do you?"

"Chairs," John Fox corrected in a low voice. This was why he went everywhere with his employer—to provide the necessary nudges and adjustments when needed.

"Chairs, yes, of course. And what can I do for you, sir, ma'am?" He nodded at Anne Kellaway a touch uneasily, for she was sitting ramrod straight, her eyes fixed on Mr. Smart, now up on Westminster Bridge, her mouth pulled tight like a drawstring bag. Every inch of her gave out the message that she did not want to be here or have anything to do with him; and that was a message Philip Astley was unused to. His fame made him much in demand, with too many people seeking his attention. For someone to display the opposite threw him, and immediately made him go out of his way to regain that attention. "Tell me what you need!" he added, with a sweep of his arm, a gesture lost on Anne Kellaway, who kept her eyes on Mr. Smart.

Anne Kellaway had begun to regret their decision to move from Dorsetshire almost the moment the cart pulled away from their cottage, the feeling deepening over the week they spent on the road picking their way through the early spring mud. By the time she sat in front of the amphitheatre, not looking at Philip Astley, she knew that being in London was not going to take her mind from Tommy as she'd hoped it might; if anything, it made her think of him even more, for being here reminded her of what she was fleeing. But she would rather blame her husband, and Philip Astley too, for her misfortune than Tommy himself for being such a fool.

"Well, sir," Thomas Kellaway began, "you did invite me to London, and I'm very kindly accepting your offer."

"Did I?" Philip Astley turned to John Fox. "Did I invite him, Fox?"

John Fox nodded. "You did, sir."

"Oh, don't you remember, Mr. Astley?" Maisie cried, leaning forward. "Pa told us all about it. He and Jem were at your show, an' during it someone were doing a trick atop a chair on a horse, an' the chair broke and Pa fixed it for you right there. An' you got to talking about wood and furniture, because you trained as a cabinetmaker, didn't you, sir?"

"Hush, Maisie," Anne Kellaway interjected, turning her head for a moment from the bridge. "I'm sure he doesn't want to hear about all that."

Philip Astley gazed at the slim country girl talking with such animation from her perch and chuckled. "Well, now, miss, I do begin to recall such an encounter. But how does that bring you here?"

"You told Pa if he ever wanted to, he should come to London and you would help him set himself up. So that's what we done, an' here we be."

"Here you be indeed, Maisie, all of you." He turned to Jem, judging him to be about twelve and of the useful age to a circus for running errands and helping out. "And what's your name, lad?"

"Jem, sir."

"What sort of chairs are those you're sitting next to, young Jem?"

"Windsors, sir. Pa made 'em."

"A handsome chair, Jem, very handsome. Could you make me some?"

"Of course, sir," Thomas Kellaway said.

Philip Astley's eyes slid to Anne Kellaway. "I'll take a dozen of 'em."

Anne Kellaway stiffened, but still did not look at the circus man despite his generous commission.

"Now, Fox, what rooms have we got free at the moment?" he demanded. Philip Astley owned a fair number of houses in Lambeth, the area around the amphitheatre and just across Westminster Bridge from London proper.

John Fox moved his lips so that his mustache twitched. "Only some with Miss Pelham at Hercules Buildings—but she chooses her own lodgers."

"Well, she'll choose the Kellaways—they'll do nicely. Take 'em over there now, Fox, with some boys to help unload." Philip Astley lifted his hat once more at Anne Kellaway, shook Thomas Kellaway's hand again, and said, "If you need anything, Fox'll see you right. Welcome to Lambeth!"

~ 4 ~

Maggie Butterfield noticed the new arrivals right away. Little escaped her attention in the area—if someone moved in or out, Maggie was nosing among their belongings, asking questions and storing away the information to relay to her father later. It was natural for her to be attracted to Mr. Smart's cart, now stopped in front of no. 12 Hercules Buildings.

Hercules Buildings was made up of a row of twenty-two brick houses, bookended by two pubs, the Pineapple and the Hercules Tavern. Each had three stories as well as a lower-ground floor, a small front garden, and a much longer garden at the back. The street itself was a busy cut-through taken by residents of Lambeth who wanted to cross Westminster Bridge but did not fancy their chances on the poor, ramshackle lanes along the river between Lambeth Palace and the bridge.

No. 12 Hercules Buildings boasted a shoulder-high iron fence, painted black, with spikes on top. The ground of the front garden was covered with raked pebbles, broken by a knee-high box hedge grown in a circle, with a bush severely pruned into a ball in the middle. The front window was framed by orange curtains pulled half to. As Maggie approached, a man, a woman, a boy her age, and a girl a little older were each carrying a chair into the house while a small woman in a faded yellow gown buzzed around them.

"This is highly irregular!" she was shouting. "Highly irregular! Mr. Astley knows very well that I choose my own lodgers, and always have done. He has no right to foist people on me. Do you hear me, Mr. Fox? No right at all!" She stood directly in the path of John Fox, who had come out of the house with his sleeves rolled up, followed by a few circus boys.

"Pardon me, Miss Pelham," he said as he sidestepped her. "I'm just doing what the man told me to do. I expect he'll be along to explain it himself."

"This is *my* house!" Miss Pelham cried. "I'm the householder. He's only the owner, and has nothing to do with what goes on inside."

John Fox picked up a crate of saws, looking as if he wished he hadn't said anything. Miss Pelham's tone seemed also to bother the unattended cart horse, whose owner was also helping to carry the Kellaways' possessions upstairs. It had been standing docilely, stunned into hoof-sore submission by the week-long journey to London, but as Miss Pelham's voice grew higher and shriller, it began to shift and stamp.

"You, girl," John Fox called to Maggie, "there's a penny for you to hold the horse steady." He hurried through the gate and into the house, Miss Pelham at his heels.

Maggie stepped up willingly and seized the horse's reins, delighted to be paid for a front-row view of the proceedings. She stroked the horse's nose. "There now, boy, you old country horse," she murmured. "Where you from, then? Yorkshire, is it? Lincolnshire?" She named the two areas of England she knew anything about, and that was very little—only that her parents had come from those parts, though they'd lived in London twenty years. Maggie had never been outside of London; indeed, she rarely enough went across the river to its center, and had never been a night away from home.

"Dorsetshire," came a voice.

Maggie turned, smiling at the singing, burring vowels of the girl who had carried her chair inside and come out again, and was now standing next to the cart. She wasn't bad-looking, with a rosy face and wide blue eyes, though she did wear a ridiculous frilly mop cap that she must have fancied would go down well in London. Maggie smirked. One glance told her this family's story: They were from the countryside, come for the usual reason—to make a better living here than they did back home. Indeed, sometimes country people did do better. Other times . . . "Where's home, then?" she said.

"Piddletrenthide," the girl answered, drawing out the last syllable.

"Lord a mercy—what did you say?"

"Piddletrenthide."

Maggie snorted. "Piddle-dee-dee, what a name! Never heard of it."

"It mean thirty houses by the River Piddle. 'Tis in the Piddle Valley, near Dorchester. It were a lovely place." The girl smiled at something across the road, as if she could see Dorsetshire there.

"What's your name, then, Miss Piddle?"

"Maisie. Maisie Kellaway."

The door to the house opened, and Maisie's mother reappeared. Anne Kellaway was tall and angular, and had her scrubby brown hair pulled back in a bun that hung low on her long neck. She gave Maggie a suspicious look, the way a chandler would someone he thought had stolen wares from his shop. Maggie knew such looks well.

"Don't be talking to strangers, Maisie," Anne Kellaway scolded. "Han't I warned you about London?"

Maggie shook the horse's reins. "Now, ma'am, Maisie's perfectly safe with me. Safer'n with some."

Anne Kellaway fastened her eyes on Maggie and nodded. "You see, Maisie? Even the locals say there be bad sorts about."

"That's right, London's a wicked place, it is," Maggie couldn't resist saying.

"What? What kind of wicked?" Anne Kellaway demanded.

Maggie shrugged, caught out for a moment. She did not know what to tell her. There was one thing, of course, that would clearly shock her, but Maggie would never tell that to Anne Kellaway. "D'you know the little lane across Lambeth Green, what runs from the river through the fields to the Royal Row?"

Maisie and Anne Kellaway looked blank. "It's not far from here," Maggie continued. "Just over there." She pointed across the road, where fields stretched almost unbroken to the river. The red-brick towers of Lambeth Palace could be seen in the distance.

"We only just arrived," Anne Kellaway said. "We han't seen much."

Maggie sighed, the punch taken out of her tale. "It's a little lane, very useful as a shortcut. It was called Lovers' Lane for a time 'cause—" She stopped as Anne Kellaway shook her head vehemently, her eyes darting at Maisie.

"Well, it was called that," Maggie continued, "but do you know what it's called now?" She paused. "Cut-Throat Lane!"

Mother and daughter shuddered, which made Maggie smile grimly.

"Tha' be no great thing," a voice chimed in. "We've a Dead Cat Lane back in the Piddle Valley." The boy who had been carrying the chair inside was standing in the doorway.

Maggie rolled her eyes. "A dead cat, eh? I suppose you found it, did you?"

He nodded.

"Well, I found the dead man!" Maggie announced triumphantly, but even as she said it she felt her stomach tighten and contract. She wished now that she'd kept quiet, especially as the boy was watching her closely, as if he knew what she was thinking. But he couldn't know.

She was saved from having to say more by Anne Kellaway,

who clutched the gate and cried, "I knew we should never have come!"

"There, now, Ma," Maisie murmured, as if soothing a child. "Let's get some things inside now. What about these pots?"

Jem let Maisie calm their mother. He had heard often enough of her worries during their journey. She had never betrayed such nerves in Dorsetshire, and her rapid transformation from capable countrywoman to anxious traveler had surprised him. If he paid too much attention to her, he began to feel anxious himself. He preferred instead to study the girl holding the horse. She was lively looking, with tangled black hair, brown eyes fringed with long lashes, and a V-shaped smile that made her chin as pointy as a cat's. What interested him most, however, was seeing the terror and regret that flashed across her face as she mentioned the dead man; when she swallowed, he felt sure she was tasting bile. Despite her cockiness, Jem pitied her. After all, it was certainly worse to discover a dead man than a dead cat—though the cat had been his, and he'd been fond of it. He had not, for instance, found his brother Tommy; that had been left to his mother, who had run into the workshop from the garden, a look of horror on her face. Perhaps that explained her anxiety about everything since then.

"What you doin' at Hercules Buildings, then?" Maggie said.

"Mr. Astley sent us," Jem answered.

"He invited us to London!" Maisie interjected. "Pa fixed a chair for him, and now he's come to make chairs in London."

"Don't say that man's name!" Anne Kellaway almost spat the words.

Maggie stared at her. Few people had a bad word to say about Philip Astley. He was a big, booming, opinionated man, of course, but he was also generous and good-natured to everyone. If he fought you, he forgot it a moment later. Maggie had taken countless pennies off of him, usually for simple tasks like holding a horse still for a moment, and had been allowed in free to see shows with a wave of his liberal hand. "What's wrong with Mr. Astley, then?" she demanded, ready to defend him.

Anne Kellaway shook her head, grabbed the pots from the cart, and strode up to the house, as if the man's name were physically propelling her inside. "He's one of the best men you'll meet in Lambeth!" Maggie called after her. "If you can't stomach him you won't find no one else to drink with!" But Anne Kellaway had disappeared upstairs.

"Is this all of your things?" Maggie nodded at the cart.

"Most of it," Maisie replied. "We left some with Sam—he's our older brother. He stayed behind. And—well—we'd another brother too, but he died not long ago. So I've only had brothers, you see, though I did always want a sister. D'you have sisters?"

"No, just a brother."

"Ours be marrying soon, we think, don't we, Jem? To Lizzie Miller—he been with her for years now."

"Come on, Maisie," Jem interrupted, reluctant to have his family's business made public. "We need to get these inside." He picked up a wooden hoop.

"What's that for, then?" Maggie asked.

"A chair mold. You bend wood round it to make it into the shape of a chair back."

"You help your pa make chairs?"

"I do," Jem answered with pride.

"You're a bottom catcher, you are!"

Jem frowned. "What d'you mean?"

"They call footmen fart catchers, don't they? But you catch bottoms with your chairs!" Maggie barked with laughter as Jem turned bright red. It didn't help that Maisie joined in with her own tinkling laugh.

Indeed, his sister encouraged Maggie to linger, turning back as she and Jem reached the door with the hoops looped around their arms. "What's your name?" she called.

"Maggie Butterfield."

"Oh, you be a Margaret too! In't it funny, Jem? The first girl I meet in London and she do have my name!"

Jem wondered how one name could be attached to two such different girls. Though not yet wearing stays the way Maisie did, Maggie was fuller and curvier, padded by a layer of flesh that reminded Jem of plums, while Maisie was slim, with bony ankles and wrists. Though intrigued by this Lambeth girl, he didn't trust her. She may even steal something, he thought. I'll have to watch her.

Immediately he felt ashamed of the thought, though it didn't stop him from glancing out of the open front window of their new rooms a few minutes later to make sure Maggie wasn't rummaging in their cart.

She wasn't. She was holding Mr. Smart's horse steady, patting its neck as a carriage passed. Then she was sniggering at Miss Pelham, who had come back outside and was discussing her new lodgers in a loud voice. Maggie seemed unable to keep still, hopping from one foot to the other, her eyes caught by passersby: an old woman walking along who cried out, "Old iron and broken glass bottles! Bring 'em to me!"; a young girl going the opposite way with a basket full of primroses; a man pulling the blades of two knives across each other, calling out above the clatter, "Knives sharpened, get your knives sharpened! You'll cut through anything when I'm done with you!" He pulled his knives close to Maggie's face and she flinched, jumping back as he laughed. She stood watching the man go and trembling so that the Dorsetshire horse bowed his head toward her and nickered.

"Jem, open that window wider," his mother said behind him. "I don't like the smell of the last lodgers."

Jem pushed up the sash window, and Maggie looked up and saw him. They stared at each other, as if daring the other to look away first. At last Jem forced himself to step back from the window.

Once the Kellaways' possessions were safely upstairs, they all went back out to the street to say good-bye to Mr. Smart, who would not stay the night with them, being anxious to make a start back to Dorsetshire. He'd already seen enough of London to provide weeks of anecdotes at the pub, and had no desire to be there still come nightfall, when he was sure the devil would descend on the inhabitants—though he didn't say so to the Kellaways. Each found it hard to let go of their last link to the Piddle Valley, and delayed Mr. Smart with questions and suggestions. Jem held on to the side of the cart while his father discussed which traveling inn to aim for; Anne Kellaway sent Maisie up to dig out a few apples for the horse.

At last Mr. Smart set off, calling "Good luck an' God bless'ee!" as he pulled away from no. 12 Hercules Buildings, muttering under his breath, "an' God help'ee too." Maisie waved a handkerchief at him even though he didn't look around. As the cart turned right at the end of the road, slipping in among other traffic, Jem felt his stomach twist. He kicked at some dung the horse had left behind, and though he could feel Maggie's eyes on him, he didn't look up.

A few moments later, he sensed a subtle shift in the sounds of the street. Although it continued to be noisy with horses, carriages, and carts, as well as the frequent cries of sellers of fish and brooms and matches, of shoe blackeners and pot menders, there seemed to be a quiet pause and a turning of attention that wound its way along Hercules Buildings. It reached even to Miss Pelham, who fell silent, and Maggie, who stopped staring at Jem. He looked up then, following her gaze to the man now passing. He was of medium height and stocky, with a round, wide face, a heavy brow, prominent gray eyes, and the pale complexion of a man who spends much of his time indoors. Dressed simply in a white shirt, black breeches and stockings, and a slightly old-fashioned black coat, he was most noticeable for the red cap he wore, of a sort Jem had never seen, with a peak flopped over; a turned-up rim; and a red, white, and blue rosette fixed to one side. It was made of wool, which in the unusual March heat caused sweat to roll down the man's brow. He held his head slightly self-consciously, as if the hat were new, or precious, and he must be careful of it; and as if he knew that all eyes would be on it—as indeed, Jem realized, they were.

The man turned in at the gate next to theirs, stepped up the path, and hurried inside, closing the door behind him without looking around. When he had disappeared, the street seemed to shake itself like a dog caught napping, and activity was renewed all the more vigorously.

"Do you see—that is why I must speak with Mr. Astley immediately," Miss Pelham declared to John Fox. "It's bad enough living next door to a revolutionary, but then to be forced to take in strangers from Dorsetshire—it's too much, really!"

Maggie spoke up. "Dorsetshire an't exactly Paris, ma'am. I bet them Dorseters don't even know what a *bonnet rouge* is—do you, Jem, Maisie?"

They shook their heads. Though Jem was grateful to Maggie for speaking up for them, he wished she wouldn't rub his nose in his ignorance.

"You, you little scamp!" Miss Pelham cried, noticing Maggie for the first time. "I don't want to see you round here. You're as bad as your father. You leave my lodgers alone!"

Maggie's father had once sold Miss Pelham lace he claimed was Flemish, but it unraveled within days and turned out to have been made by an old woman just down the road in Kennington. Though she hadn't had him arrested—she was too embarrassed that her neighbors would find out she'd been duped by Dick Butterfield— Miss Pelham spoke ill of him whenever she could.

Maggie laughed; she was used to people berating her father. "I'll tell Pa you said hallo," she simpered, then turned to Jem and Maisie. "Bye for now!"

"Z'long," Jem replied, watching her run along the street and disappear into an alley between two houses. Now she was gone, he wanted her back again.

"Please, sir," Maisie said to John Fox, who was just setting out with the circus boys to return to the amphitheatre. "What's a *bon-net rouge*?"

John Fox paused. "That'll be a red cap like what you just saw your neighbor wearing, miss. They wears it what supports the revolution over in France."

"Oh! We did hear of that, didn't we, Jem? Tha' be where they let all those people out of the Bastille, weren't it?"

"That's the one, miss. It don't have much to do with us here, but some folks like to show what they think of it."

"Who be our neighbor, then? Is he French?"

"No, miss. That'll be William Blake, born and bred in London."

Miss Pelham cut in. "You leave him be, you children. You don't want to get in with him."

"Why not?" Maisie asked.

"He prints pamphlets with all sorts of radical nonsense in them, that's why. He's a stirrer, that man is. Now, I don't want to see any *bonnets rouges* in my house. D'you hear me?"

~ 5 ~

Maggie came to see the Kellaways a week later, waiting until she judged they were well settled into their rooms. She had passed along Hercules Buildings a number of times, and always looked up at their front window, which they had quickly learned to keep shut so that the dust from the road wouldn't get inside. Twice she had seen Anne Kellaway standing at the window, hands pressed to her chest, looking down at the street. When she caught sight of Maggie, she stepped back, frowning.

This time no one was looking out. Maggie was about to throw a pebble at the window to get their attention when the front door opened and Maisie came out carrying a brush and dustpan. She opened the front gate and with a twist of her wrist emptied the pan full of wood shavings onto the road, looking around as she did. On spotting Maggie, she froze, then giggled. "Ar'ernoon, Maggie! Is't all right just to throw it in the road like that? I do see others throw worse."

Maggie snorted. "You can chuck what you like in the gutter. But what you doing throwin' out wood shavings? Anyone else'd burn them in the fire."

"Oh, we've plenty for that—too much, really. I throw away most of what I sweep up. Some of this be green too an' don't burn so well."

"Don't you sell the extra?"

Maisie looked puzzled. "Don't reckon we do."

"You should be sellin' that, you should. Plenty could do with shavings to light their fires with. Make yourself a penny or two. Tell you what—I could sell it for you, and give you sixpence out of every shilling."

Maisie looked even more confused, as if Maggie were talking too fast. "Don't you know how to sell things?" Maggie said. "You know, like that." She indicated a potato seller bellowing, "Lovely tatties, don't yer want some tatties!" vying with a man who was crying out, "You that are able, will you buy a ladle!"

"See? Everybody's got summat to sell."

Maisie shook her head, the frills on her mop cap fluttering around her face. "We didn't do that, back home."

"Ah, well. You got yourself sorted out up there?"

"Mostly. It do take some getting used to. But Mr. Astley took Pa and Jem to a timber yard down by the river, so they're able to start work on the chairs he wants."

"Can I come up and see?"

"Course you can!"

Maisie led her up, Maggie keeping quiet in case Miss Pelham

was hovering about. At the top of the stairs, Maisie opened one of two doors and called out, "We've a visitor!"

As they entered the back room that served as his workshop, Thomas Kellaway was turning a chair leg on a lathe, with Jem at his side, watching. He wore a white shirt and mustard-colored breeches, and over that a leather apron covered with scratches. Rather than frowning, as many do when they are concentrating, Thomas Kellaway was smiling a small, almost silly smile. When at last he did look up, his smile broadened, though to Maggie it seemed he was not sure what he was smiling at. His light blue eyes looked her way, but his gaze seemed to fall just beyond her, as if something in the hallway behind caught his attention. The lines around his eyes gave him a wistful air, even as he smiled.

Jem, however, did look directly at Maggie, with an expression half-pleased, half-suspicious.

Thomas Kellaway rolled the chair leg between his hands. "What'd you say, Maisie?"

"D'you remember Maggie, Pa? She held Mr. Smart's horse while we was unloading our things here. She lives—oh, where do you live, Maggie?"

Maggie shuffled her feet in the wood shavings that covered the floor, embarrassed by the attention. "Across the field," she mumbled, gesturing with her hand out of the back window, "at Bastille Row."

"Bastille Row? There be an odd name."

"It's really York Place," Maggie explained, "but we call it Bastille Row. Mr. Astley built the houses last year with money he made off a spectacle he put on of the storming of the Bastille."

She looked around, astonished at the mess the Kellaways had managed to make in the room after only a few days. It was as if a timber yard, with its chunks and planks and splinters and shavings of wood, had been dumped indoors. Scattered among the wood were saws, chisels, adzes, augers, and other tools Maggie didn't recognize. In the corner she could see tin pots and troughs, filled with liquid. There was a smell in the air of resin and varnish. Here and there she could find order: a row of elm planks leaning against the wall, a dozen finished chair legs stacked like firewood on a shelf, wood hoop frames hanging in descending size from hooks.

"Didn't take you long to make yourself at home! Does Miss Pelham know what you're doin' up here?" she asked.

"Pa's workshop were out in the garden back home," Jem said, as if to explain the disorder.

Maggie chuckled. "Looks like he thinks he's still outside!"

"We keep the other rooms tidy enough," replied Anne Kellaway, appearing in the doorway behind them. "Maisie, come and help me, please." She was clearly suspicious of Maggie.

"Look, here be the seat for the chair Pa's making specially for Mr. Astley," Maisie said, trying to put off leaving her new friend. "Extra wide to fit him. See?" She showed Maggie an oversized, saddle-shaped seat propped against other planks. "It has to dry out a bit more; then he'll add the legs and back."

Maggie admired the seat, then turned to look out of the open window, with its view over Miss Pelham's and her neighbors' back gardens. The gardens of Hercules Buildings houses were narrow—only eighteen feet across—but they made up for this deficiency with their length. Miss Pelham's garden was a hundred feet long. She made the most of the space by dividing it into three squares, with a central ornament gracing each: a white lilac in the square closest to the house, a stone birdbath in the central square, and a laburnum tree in the back square. Miniature hedges, graveled paths, and raised beds planted with roses created regular patterns that had little to do with nature but were more concerned with order.

Miss Pelham had made it plain that she did not want the Kellaways hanging about in her garden other than to use the privy. Every morning, if it wasn't raining, she liked to take a teacup full of broth—its dull, meaty smell visiting the Kellaways upstairs—and sit with it on one of two stone benches that faced each other sideways, halfway along the garden. When she got up to go inside again, she would dump the remains over a grapevine growing up the wall next to the bench. She believed the broth would make the vine grow faster and more robust than that of her neighbor's, Mr. Blake. "He never prunes his vine, and that is a mistake, for all vines need a good pruning or the fruit will be small and sour," Miss Pelham had confided to Jem's mother in a momentary attempt to reconcile herself to her new lodgers. She soon discovered, however, that Anne Kellaway was not one for confidences.

Apart from Miss Pelham's broth times and the twice-weekly visit from a man to rake and prune, the garden was usually deserted, and Jem went into it whenever he could, even though he could see little use for one like this. It was a harsh, geometrical place, with uncomfortable benches and no lawn to lie on. There was no space in which to grow vegetables, and no fruit trees apart from the grapevine. Of all the things Jem expected from the outdoors—fertile soil, large vibrant patches of growth, a solidity that changed daily and yet suggested permanence—only the varied ranges of green he craved were available in Miss Pelham's garden. That was why he went there—to feast his eyes on the color he loved best. He stayed as long as he could, until Miss Pelham appeared at her window and waved him out.

Now he joined Maggie at the window to look out over it.

"Funny to see this from above," she said. "I only ever seen it from there." She indicated the brick wall at the far end of the garden.

"What, you climb over?"

"Not over—I an't been in it. I just have a peek over the wall every now and then, to see what she's up to. Not that there's ever much to see. Not like in some gardens."

"What's that house in the field past the wall?" Jem indicated a large, two-story brick house capped with three truncated towers, set alone in the middle of the field behind the gardens of the Hercules Buildings houses. A long stable ran perpendicular to the house, with a dusty yard in front.

Maggie looked surprised. "That's Hercules Hall. Didn't you

know? Mr. Astley lives there, him an' his wife an' some nieces to look after 'em. His wife's an invalid now, though she used to ride with him. Don't see much of her. Mr. Astley keeps some of the circus horses there too—the best ones, like his white horse and John Astley's chestnut. That's his son. You saw him riding in Dorsetshire, didn't you?"

"I reckon so. It were a chestnut mare the man rode."

"He lives just two doors down from you, the other side o' the Blakes. See? There's his garden—the one with the lawn and nothin' else."

Hurdy-gurdy music was now drifting over from Hercules Hall, and Jem spotted a man leaning against the stables, cranking and playing a popular song. Maggie began to sing along softly:

> One night as I came from the play
> I met a fair maid by the way
> She had rosy cheeks and a dimpled chin
> And a hole to put poor Robin in!

The man played a wrong note and stopped. Maggie chuckled. "He'll never get a job—Mr. Astley's got higher standards'n that."

"What d'you mean?"

"People's always coming to perform for him over there, hopin' he might take 'em on. He hardly ever does, though he'll give 'em sixpence for tryin'."

The hurdy-gurdy man began the song again, and Maggie hummed along, her eyes scanning the neighboring gardens. "Much better view here than at the back," she declared.

Afterward Jem couldn't remember if it was the sound or the movement that first caught his attention. The sound was a soft "Ohh" that still managed to carry up to the Kellaways' window. The movement was the flash of a naked shoulder somewhere in the Blakes' garden.

Closest to the Blakes' house was a carefully laid out, well-dug kitchen garden partially planted, a garden fork now stuck upright

in the rich soil at the end of one row. Anne Kellaway had been following its progress over the last week, watching with envy the
solid, bonneted woman next door double-digging the rows and
sowing seeds, as Anne Kellaway would be doing herself if she were
in Dorsetshire or had any space to plant a garden here. It had never
occurred to her when they decided to move to London that she
might not have even a small patch of earth. However, she knew
better than to ask Miss Pelham, whose garden was clearly decora-
tive rather than functional; but she felt awkward and idle without
her own garden to dig in springtime.

The back of the Blakes' garden was untended, and filled with
brambles and nettles. Midway along the garden, between the orderly and the chaotic, sat a small wooden summerhouse, set up for
sitting in when the weather was mild. Its French doors were open,
and it was in there that Jem saw the naked shoulder and, following
that, naked backs, legs, bottoms. Horrified, he fought the temptation to step back from the window, fearing it would signal to Maggie that there was something he didn't want her to see. Instead he
pulled his eyes away and tried to direct her attention elsewhere.
"Where's your house, then?"

"Bastille Row? It's across the field—there, you can't quite see it
from here, what with Miss Pelham's tree in the way. What is that
tree, anyway?"

"Laburnum. You'll be able to tell easier in May when it flowers."

Jem's attempt to distract her failed, however, with the second
"Ohh" confirming that the sound came from the same place as the
movement. This time Maggie heard it and immediately located the
source. Jem tried but couldn't stop his eyes from being drawn back
to the summerhouse. Maggie began to titter. "Lord a mercy, what
a view!"

Then Jem did step back, his face on fire. "I've to help Pa," he muttered, turning away from the window and going over to his father,
who was still working on the chair leg and hadn't heard them.

Maggie laughed at his discomfort. She stood at the window for a few moments more, then turned away. "Show's over." She wandered over to watch Jem's father at the lathe, a heavy wooden frame with a half-carved leg clamped to it at chest height. A leather cord was looped around the leg, the ends attached to a treadle at his feet and a pole bent over his head. When Thomas Kellaway pumped the treadle, the cord spun the leg around and he shaved off parts of the wood.

"Can you do that?" Maggie asked Jem, trying now to smooth over his embarrassment, tempted though she was to tease him more.

"Not so well as Pa," he replied, his face still red. "I practice making 'em, an' if they be good enough he'll use 'em."

"You be doing well, son," Thomas Kellaway murmured without looking up.

"What do your pa make?" Jem asked. The men back in Piddletrenthide were makers, by and large—of bread, of beer, of barley, of shoes or candles or flour.

Maggie snorted. "Money, if he can. This an' that. I should find him now. That smell's making my head ache, anyway. What's it from?"

"Varnish and paint for the chairs. You get used to it."

"I don't plan to. Don't worry, I'll see myself out. Bye for now, then."

"Z'long."

"Come again!" Maisie called out from the other room as Maggie clattered down the stairs.

Anne Kellaway tutted. "What will Miss Pelham think of that noise? Jem, go and see she be quiet on the way out."

~ 6 ~

As Miss Pelham came up to her front gate, having spent a happy day visiting friends in Chelsea, she caught sight of some of the wood shavings Maisie had scattered in front of the house and frowned. At first Maisie had been dumping the shavings into Miss Pelham's carefully pruned, O-shaped hedge in the front garden. Miss Pelham had had to set her straight on that offense. And of course it was better the shavings were in the street than on the stairs. But it would be best of all if there were no shavings at all, because no Kellaways were there to produce them. Miss Pelham had often regretted over the past week that she'd been so hard on the family who'd rented the rooms from her before the Kellaways. They'd been noisy of a night and the baby had cried constantly toward the end, but at least they didn't track shavings everywhere. She knew too that there was a great deal of wood upstairs, as she'd watched it being carried through her hallway. There were smells as well, and thumping sometimes that Miss Pelham did not appreciate at all.

And now: Who was this dark-haired rascal running out of the house with shavings shedding from the soles of her shoes? She had just the sort of sly look that made Miss Pelham clutch her bag more tightly to her chest. Then she recognized Maggie. "Here, girl!" she cried. "What are you doing, coming out of my house? What have you been stealing?"

Before Maggie could reply, two people appeared: Jem popped out behind her, and the door to no. 13 Hercules Buildings opened and Mr. Blake stepped out. Miss Pelham shrank back. Mr. Blake had never been anything but civil to her—indeed, he nodded at her now—yet he made her nervous. His glassy gray eyes always made her think of a bird staring at her, waiting to peck.

"Far as I know, this is Mr. Astley's house, not yours," Maggie said cheekily.

Miss Pelham turned to Jem. "Jem, what is this girl doing here? She's not a friend of yours, I trust?"

"She—she's made a delivery." Even in the Piddle Valley, Jem had not been a good liar.

"What did she deliver? Four-day-old fish? Laundry that's not seen a lick of lye?"

"Nails," Maggie cut in. "I'll be bringing 'em by reg'lar, won't I, Jem? You'll be seein' lots more o' me." She stepped sideways off Miss Pelham's front path and into her front garden, where she followed the tiny hedge around in its pointless circle, running a hand along the top of it.

"Get out of my garden, girl!" Miss Pelham cried. "Jem, get her out of there!"

Maggie laughed, and began to run around the hedge, faster and faster, then leapt over it into the middle, where she danced around the pruned bush, sparring at it with her fists while Miss Pelham cried, "Oh! Oh!" as if each blow were striking her.

Jem watched Maggie box the leafy ball, tiny leaves showering to the ground, and found himself smiling. He too had been tempted to kick at the absurd hedge so different from the hedgerows he was used to. Hedges in Dorsetshire were made for a reason, to keep animals in fields or off of paths, and grown of prickly hawthorn and holly, elder and hazel and whitebeam, woven through with brambles and ivy and traveler's joy.

A tap on the window upstairs brought Jem back from Dorsetshire. His mother was glaring down at him and making shooing motions at Maggie. "Er, Maggie—weren't you going to show me something?" Jem said. "Your—your father, eh? My pa wanted me to—to agree on the price."

"That's it. C'mon, then." Maggie ignored Miss Pelham, who was still shouting and swatting ineffectively at her, and pushed through the ring of hedge without bothering to jump it this time, leaving behind a gap of broken branches.

"Oh!" cried Miss Pelham for the tenth time.

As Jem moved to follow Maggie into the street, he glanced at Mr. Blake, who had remained still and quiet, his arms crossed over his chest, while Maggie had her fun with the hedge. He did not seem bothered by the noise and drama. Indeed, they had all forgotten he was there, or Miss Pelham would not have cried "Oh!" ten times and Maggie would not have beaten the bush. He was looking at them with his clear gaze. It was not a look like that of Jem's father, who tended to focus on the middle distance. Rather Mr. Blake was looking at them, and at the passersby in the street, and at Lambeth Palace rising up in the distance, and at the clouds behind it. He was taking in everything, without judgment.

"Ar'ernoon, sir," Jem said.

"Hallo, my boy," Mr. Blake replied.

"Hallo, Mr. Blake!" Maggie called from the street, not to be outdone by Jem. "How's your missus, then?"

Her cry revived Miss Pelham, who had sunk into herself in Mr. Blake's presence. "Get out of my sight, girl!" she cried. "I'll have you whipped! Jem, don't you let her back in here. And see her to the end of the street—I don't trust her for a second. She'll steal the gate if we don't watch her!"

"Yes, ma'am." Jem raised his eyebrows apologetically at Mr. Blake, but his neighbor had already opened his gate and stepped into the street. When Jem joined Maggie, they watched as Mr. Blake walked down Hercules Buildings toward the river.

"Look at his cocky step," Maggie said. "And did you see the color in his cheeks? And his hair all mussed? We know what he's been up to!"

Jem would not have described Mr. Blake's pace as cocky. Rather he was flat-footed, though not plodding. He walked steadily and deliberately, as if he had a destination in mind rather than merely setting out for a stroll.

"Let's follow him," Maggie suggested.

"No. Let him be." Jem was surprised at his own decisiveness. He would have liked to follow Mr. Blake to his destination—not the way Maggie would do it, though, as a game and a tease, but respectfully, from a distance.

Miss Pelham and Anne Kellaway were still glaring at the children from their positions. "Let's be going," Jem said, and began to walk along Hercules Buildings in the opposite direction from Mr. Blake.

Maggie trotted after him. "You're really comin' with me?"

"Miss Pelham told me to see you to the end of the street."

"And you're goin' to do what that old stick in a dress wants?"

Jem shrugged. "She's the householder. We've to keep her happy."

"Well, I'm goin' to find Pa. You want to come with me?"

Jem thought of his anxious mother, of his hopeful sister, of his absorbed father, and of Miss Pelham waiting by the stairs to pounce on him. Then he thought of the streets he did not yet know in Lambeth, and in London, and of having a guide to take him. "I'll come with you," he said, letting Maggie catch up and match his stride so that they were walking side by side.

Dick Butterfield could have been in one of several pubs. While most people favored one local, he liked to move around, and joined drinking clubs or societies, where the like-minded met at a particular pub to discuss topics of mutual interest. These nights were not much different from other nights except that the beer was cheaper and the songs even bawdier. Dick Butterfield was constantly joining new clubs and dropping old ones as his interests changed. At the moment he belonged to a cutter club (one of his many occupations had been as a boatman on the Thames, though he had long ago lost the boat); a chair club, where each member took turns haranguing the others about political topics from the head chair at a table; a lottery club, where they pooled together on small bets that rarely won enough to cover the drinks, and where Dick Butterfield was always encouraging members to increase the stakes; and, by far his favorite, a punch club, where each week they tried out different rum concoctions.

Dick Butterfield's club and pub life was so complicated that his family rarely knew where he was of an evening. He normally drank within a half-mile radius from his home, but there were still dozens of pubs to choose from. Maggie and Jem had already called in at the Horse and Groom, the Crown and Cushion, the Canterbury Arms, and the Red Lion, before they found him ensconced in the corner of the loudest of the lot, the Artichoke on the Lower Marsh.

After following Maggie into the first two, Jem waited for her outside the rest. He had only been inside one pub since they arrived in Lambeth: A few days after they moved in, Mr. Astley called to see how they were getting on, and had taken Thomas Kellaway and Jem to the Pineapple. It had been a sedate place, Jem realized now that he could compare it with other Lambeth pubs, but at the time he'd been overwhelmed by the liveliness of the drinkers—many of them circus people—and Philip Astley's roaring conversation.

Lambeth Marsh was a market street busy with shops and stalls, and carts and people going between Lambeth and Blackfriars Bridge, toward the city. The doors to the Artichoke were open, and the sound poured across the road, making Jem hesitate as Maggie pushed past the men leaning in the doorway, and wonder why he was following her.

He knew why, though: Maggie was the first person in Lambeth to take any interest in him, and he could do with a friend. Most boys Jem's age were already apprenticed or working; he had seen younger children about, but had not yet managed to talk to any of them. It was hard to understand them, for one thing: He found London accents, as well as the many regional ones that converged on the city, sometimes incomprehensible.

Lambeth children were different in other ways too—more aware and more suspicious. They reminded him of cats who creep in to sit by the fire, knowing they are barely tolerated, happy to be inside but with ears swiveling and eyes in slits, ready to detect the foot that will kick them back out. The children were often rude to adults, as Maggie had been to Miss Pelham, and got away with it when he wouldn't have in his old village. They mocked and threw stones at people they didn't like, stole food from barrows and baskets, sang rude songs; they shouted, teased, taunted. Only occasionally did he see Lambeth children doing things he could imagine joining in with: rowing a boat on the river; singing while streaming out of the charity school on Lambeth Green; chasing a dog that had made off with someone's cap.

So when Maggie beckoned to him from the door of the Artichoke, he followed her inside, braving the wall of noise and the thick smoke from the lamps. He wanted to be a part of this new Lambeth life, rather than watching it from a window or a front gate or over a garden wall.

Although it was only late afternoon, the pub was heaving with people. The din was tremendous, though after a time his ears began to pick up the pattern of a song, unfamiliar but clearly a tune. Maggie plunged through the wall of bodies to the corner where her father sat.

Dick Butterfield was a small, brown man—his eyes, his wiry hair, the undertone of his skin, his clothes. A web of wrinkles extended from the outer corners of his eyes and across his forehead, forming deep furrows on his brow. Despite the wrinkles, he had a young, energetic air about him. Today he was simply drinking rather than attending a club. He pulled his daughter onto his lap, and was singing along with the rest of the pub when Jem finally reached them:

> And for which I'm sure she'll go to Hell
> For she makes me fuck her in church time!

At the last line, a deafening shout went up that made Jem cover his ears. Maggie had joined in, and she grinned at Jem, who blushed and stared at his feet. Many songs had been sung at the Five Bells in Piddletrenthide, but nothing like that.

After the great shout, the pub was quieter, the way a thunder-clap directly overhead clears the worst of a storm. "What you been up to, then, Mags?" Dick Butterfield asked his daughter in the relative calm.

"This an' that. I was at his house"—she pointed at Jem—"this is Jem, Pa—lookin' at his pa making chairs. They just come from Dorsetshire, an' are living at Miss Pelham's in Hercules Buildings, next to Mr. Blake."

"Miss Pelham's, eh?" Dick Butterfield chuckled. "Glad to meet you, Jem. Sit yourself down and rest your pegs." He waved at the other side of the table. There was no stool or bench there. Jem looked around: All of the stools in sight were taken. Dick and Maggie Butterfield were gazing at him with identical expressions, watching to see what he would do. Jem considered kneeling at the table, but he knew that was not likely to gain the Butterfields' approval. He would have to search the pub for an empty stool. It was expected of him, a little test of his merit—the first real test of his new London life.

Locating an empty stool in a crowded pub can be tricky, and Jem could not find one. He tried asking for one, but those he asked paid no attention to him. He tried to take one that a man was using as a footrest and got swatted. He asked a barmaid, who jeered at him. As he struggled through the scrum of bodies, Jem wondered how it was that so many people could be drinking now rather than working. In the Piddle Valley few went to the Five Bells or the Crown or the New Inn until evening.

At last he went back to the table empty-handed. A vacant stool now sat where Dick Butterfield had indicated, and he and Maggie were grinning at Jem.

"Country boy," muttered a youth sitting next to them who had watched the whole ordeal, including the barmaid's jeering.

"Shut your bonebox, Charlie," Maggie retorted. Jem guessed at once that he was her brother.

Charlie Butterfield was like his father but without the wrinkles or the charm; better-looking in a rough way, with dirty blond hair and a dimple in his chin, but with a scar through his eyebrow too that gave him a harsh look. He was as cruel to his sister as he could get away with, twisting burns on Maggie's arms until the day she was old enough to kick him where it was guaranteed to hurt. He still looked for ways to get at her—knocking the legs out from the stool she sat on, upending the salt on her food, stealing her blankets at night. Jem knew none of this, but he sensed something about Charlie that made him avoid the other's eyes, as you do a growling dog.

Dick Butterfield tossed a coin onto the table. "Fetch Jem a drink, Charlie," he commanded.

"I an't—" Charlie sputtered at the same time as Jem said, "I don't—" Both stopped at the stern look on Dick Butterfield's face. And so Charlie got Jem a mug of beer he didn't want—cheap, watery stuff men back at the Five Bells would spill onto the floor rather than drink.

Dick Butterfield sat back. "Well, now, what have you got to tell me, Mags? What's the scandal today in old Lambeth?"

"We saw summat in Mr. Blake's garden, didn't we, Jem? In their summerhouse, with all the doors open." Maggie gave Jem a sly look. He turned red again and shrugged.

"That's my girl," Dick Butterfield said. "Always sneakin' about, finding out what's what."

Charlie leaned forward. "What'd you see, then?"

Maggie leaned forward as well. "We saw him an' his wife at it!"

Charlie chuckled, but Dick Butterfield seemed unimpressed. "What, rutting is all? That's nothing you don't see every day you look down an alley. Go outside and you'll see it round the corner now. Eh, Jem? I expect you've seen your share of it, back in Dorsetshire, eh, boy?"

Jem gazed into his beer. A fly was struggling on the surface, trying not to drown. "Seen enough," he mumbled. Of course he had seen it before. It was not just the animals he lived among that he'd seen at it—dogs, cats, sheep, horses, cows, goats, rabbits, chickens, pheasants—but people tucked away in corners of woods or against hedgerows or even in the middle of meadows when they thought no one would pass through. He had seen his neighbors doing it in a barn, and Sam with his girl up in the hazel wood at Nettlecombe Tout. He had seen it enough that he was no longer surprised, though it still embarrassed him. It was not that there was so much to see—mostly just clothes and a persistent move- ment, sometimes a man's pale buttocks pistoning up and down or a woman's breasts jiggling. It was seeing it when he was not ex- pecting to, breaking into the assumed privacy, that made Jem turn away with a red face. He had much the same feeling on the rare occasion when he heard his parents argue—as when his mother demanded that his father cut down the pear tree at the bottom of their garden that Tommy had fallen from, and Thomas Kellaway had refused. Later Anne Kellaway had taken an axe and done it herself.

Jem dipped his finger into the beer and let the fly climb onto it and crawl away. Charlie watched with astonished disgust; Dick Butterfield simply smiled and looked around at the other custom- ers, as if searching for someone else to talk to.

"It wasn't just that they were doin' it," Maggie persisted. "They were—they had—they'd taken off all their clothes, hadn't they, Jem? We could see everything, like they were Adam an' Eve."

Dick Butterfield watched his daughter with the same appraising look he'd given Jem when he tried to find a stool. As easygoing as he appeared—lolling in his seat, buying drinks for people, smiling and nodding—he demanded a great deal from those he was with.

"And d'you know what they were doing while they did it?"

"What, Mags?"

Maggie thought quickly of the most outlandish thing two people could do while they were meant to be rutting. "They were reading to each other!"

Charlie chuckled. "What, the newspaper?"

"That's not what I—" Jem began.

"From a book," Maggie interrupted, her voice rising over the noise of the pub. "Poetry, I think it was." Specific details always made stories more believable.

"Poetry, eh?" Dick Butterfield repeated, sucking at his beer. "I expect that'll be *Paradise Lost*, if they were playing at Adam an' Eve in their garden." Dick Butterfield had once had a copy of the poem, in among a barrow full of books he'd got hold of and was trying to sell, and had read bits of it. No one expected Dick Butterfield to be able to read so well, but his father had taught him, reasoning that it was best to be as knowledgeable as those you were swindling.

"Yes, that was it. *Pear Tree's Loss*," Maggie agreed. "I know I heard them words."

Jem started, unable to believe what he'd heard. "Did you say 'pear tree'?"

Dick shot her a look. "*Paradise Lost*, Mags. Get your words right. Now, hang on a minute." He closed his eyes, thought for a moment, then recited:

> The world was all before them, where to choose
> Their place of rest, and providence their guide:
> They hand in hand with wandering steps and slow,
> Through Eden took their solitary way.

His neighbors stared at him; these were not the sort of words they normally heard in the pub. "What you sayin', Pa?" Maggie asked.

"The only thing I remember from *Paradise Lost*—the very last lines, when Adam an' Eve are leaving Eden. Made me sorry for 'em."

"I didn't hear anything like that from the Blakes," Jem said, then felt Maggie's sharp kick under the table.

"It was after you stopped looking," she insisted.

Jem opened his mouth to argue further, then stopped. Clearly the Butterfields liked their stories embroidered; indeed, it was the embroidery they wanted, and would soon pass on to everyone else, made even more elaborate, until the whole pub was discussing the Blakes playing Adam and Eve in their garden, even when that was not what Jem had seen at all. Who was he to spoil their fun— though Jem thought of Mr. Blake's alert eyes, his firm greeting, and his determined stride, and regretted that they were spreading such talk about him. He preferred to speak the truth. "What do Mr. Blake do?" he asked, trying instead to guide the subject away from what they had seen in the garden.

"What, apart from tupping his wife in the garden?" Dick Butterfield chuckled. "He's a printer and engraver. You seen the printing press through his front window, han't you?"

"The machine with the handle like a star?" Jem had indeed spied the wooden contraption, which was even bigger and bulkier than his father's lathe, and wondered what it was for.

"That's it. You'll see him using it now and then, him an' his wife. Prints books an' such on it. Pamphlets, pictures, that sort o' thing. Dunno as he makes a living from 'em, though. I seen a few of 'em when I went looking to sell him some copper for his plates when he first moved here from across the river a year or two ago." Dick Butterfield shook his head. "Strange things, they were. Lots o' fire an' naked people with big eyes, shouting."

"You mean like Hell, Pa?" Maggie suggested.

"Maybe. Not my taste, anyway. I like a cheerful picture, myself. Can't see that many would buy 'em from him. He must get more from engraving for others."

"Did he buy the copper?"

"Nah. I knew the minute I talked to him that he's not one to buy like that, for a fancy. He's his own man, is Mr. Blake. He'll go off an' choose his copper an' paper himself, real careful." Dick Butterfield said this without rancor; indeed, he respected those who would clearly not be taken in by his ruses.

"We saw him with his *bonnet rouge* on last week, didn't we, Jem?" Maggie said. "He looked right funny in it."

"He's a braver man than many," Dick Butterfield declared. "Not many in London show such open support for the Frenchies, however they may talk in the pub. PM don't take kindly to it, nor the King neither."

"Who's PM?" Jem asked.

Charlie Butterfield snorted.

"Prime Minister, lad. Mr. Pitt," Dick Butterfield added a little sharply, in case the Dorset boy didn't know even that.

Jem ducked his head and gazed into his beer once more. Maggie watched him struggling across the table, and wished now that she had not brought him to meet her father. He did not understand what Dick Butterfield wanted from people, the sort of quick, smart talk required of those allowed to sit with him on the stool he kept hooked around his foot under the table. Dick Butterfield wanted to be informed and entertained at the same time. He was always looking for another way to make money—he made his living out of small, dodgy schemes dreamt up from pub talk—and he wanted to have fun doing it. Life was hard, after all, and what made it easier than a little laughter, as well as a little business putting money in his pocket?

Dick Butterfield could see when people were sinking. He didn't hold it against Jem—the boy's confused innocence made him feel rather tender toward him, and irritated at his own jaded children. He pushed Maggie abruptly from his knee so that she fell to the floor, where she stared up at him with hurt eyes. "Lord, child, you're getting heavy," Dick said, jiggling his knee up and down. "You've sent my leg to sleep. You'll be needin' your own stool now you're getting to lady size."

"Won't nobody give her one, though, and I'm not talking 'bout just the stool," Charlie sneered. "Chicken-breasted little cow."

"Leave off her," Jem said.

All three Butterfields stared at him, Dick and Charlie leaning with their elbows on the table, Maggie still on the floor between them. Then Charlie lunged across the table at Jem, and Dick Butterfield put his arm out to stop him. "Give Maggie your stool and get another one," he said.

Charlie glared at Jem but stood up, letting the stool fall backward, and stalked off. Jem didn't dare turn around to watch him but kept his eyes on the table. He took a gulp of beer. He'd defended Maggie as a reflex, the way he would his own sister.

Maggie got up and righted Charlie's stool, then sat on it, her face grim. "Thanks," she muttered to Jem, though she didn't sound very grateful.

"So, Jem, your father's a bodger, is he?" Dick Butterfield said, opening the business part of the conversation since it seemed unlikely that Jem would entertain them further.

"Not a bodger, exactly, sir," Jem answered. "He don't travel from town to town, an' he makes proper chairs, not the rickety ones bodgers make."

"Course he does, lad, course he does. Where does he get his wood?"

"One of the timber yards by Westminster Bridge."

"Whose yard? Bet I can get it for him cheaper."

"Mr. Harris. Mr. Astley introduced Pa to him."

Dick Butterfield winced at Philip Astley's name. Maggie's father could negotiate good deals most places, but not when Mr. Astley had got in before him. He and his landlord kept a wide berth of each other, though there was a grudging respect on both sides as well. If Dick Butterfield had been a wealthy circus owner, or Philip Astley a small-time rogue, they would have been remarkably similar.

"Well, if I hear of any cheaper wood, I'll let you know. Leave it with me, lad," he added, as if it were Jem who'd approached him for advice. "I'll see what I can do. I'll call in one day, shall I, and have a word with your pa. I'm always happy to help out new neighbors. Now, you'll be expected back home, won't you? They'll be wonderin' what kept you."

Jem nodded and got up from the stool. "Thank'ee for the beer, sir."

"Course, lad." Dick Butterfield hooked his foot around Jem's stool and dragged it back under the table. Maggie grabbed Jem's half-drunk beer and took a gulp. "Bye," she said.

"Z'long."

On his way out, Jem passed Charlie standing with a crowd of other young men. Charlie glared at him and shoved one of his friends so that he knocked into Jem. The youths laughed and Jem hurried out, glad to get away from the Butterfields. He suspected, however, that he would see Maggie again, even if she had not said, "Bye for now," this time. Despite her brother and father, he wanted to. She reminded him of September blackberries, which looked ripe but could just as easily be sour as sweet when you ate them. Jem could not resist such a temptation.

PART II

April 1792

Anne Kellaway sometimes felt that a cord was tied at one end to her wrist and at the other to the window in the front room. She would be scrubbing potatoes, or washing clothes, or cleaning the ash from the fire, and find herself at the most inconvenient moment—hands smeared with dirt, sheets half-wrung, ash dusting the air—tugged to the window to look out. Often there was nothing unusual to see, but occasionally she was rewarded with something worthwhile: a woman wearing a hat trimmed with long peacock feathers; a man cradling a pineapple as if it were a newborn baby; a boy carrying an uprooted bay tree, its leaves trimmed into the shape of a dove. Maisie or Jem would have called to the others to come and see these unusual sights, but Anne Kellaway preferred to keep such little moments of pleasure to herself.

Today there were no potatoes or ash or laundry keeping her away from the window: It was Easter Monday and she was meant to rest. Maisie and Jem were clearing up after their midday meal, leaving Anne Kellaway to gaze down at the crowds of people moving along Hercules Buildings, many of the women dressed in new Easter gowns and bonnets. She had never seen so much color, such bright cloth, such daring cuts, and such surprising trim on the bonnets. There were the usual daffodils and primroses as you might see on hats outside the Piddletrenthide church, but there were also exotic feathers, bunches of multicolored ribbons, even fruit. She herself would never wear a lemon on a bonnet, but she rather admired the woman passing who did. She preferred something simpler and more traditional: a plait of daisies or a posy of violets, or one ribbon, like the sky blue one she'd just seen dangling down a girl's back almost to her knees. Anne Kellaway would happily wear that, though she would not have it be quite so long. London women seemed to push the length of a ribbon or the angle of a hat just that bit further than Anne Kellaway would dare to herself.

Among the traffic walked a man with a tray of white crosses on his head, calling, "Hot-cross buns! Four a penny, cheap for Easter, hot-cross buns! Buy 'em now, last day till next year!" He stopped in front of the house, just below Anne Kellaway, having found a customer. From the other direction strolled Miss Pelham, her bonnet festooned with tiny yellow ribbons. Anne Kellaway snorted, trying to mask the laugh that had begun to bubble up.

"What is't, Ma?" Maisie asked, looking up from wiping clean the table.

"Nothing. Just Miss Pelham in a silly hat."

"Let me see." Maisie came over to the window, peered down, and began to giggle. "She looks like she's had a pile of straw dumped on her head!"

"Shh, Maisie, she'll hear you," Anne Kellaway replied, though not very fiercely. As they watched, a gray horse pulling a peculiar two-wheeled vehicle trotted up the road, scattering bonnet wearers and potential bun buyers to the right and left. The cart had big wheels and peculiar dimensions, for though short and narrow, it had a high roof; on the side was a long vertical sign that proclaimed in black letters, ASTLEY'S ROYAL SALOON AND NEW AMPHITHEATRE PROUDLY ANNOUNCES ITS NEW SEASON BEGINNING TONIGHT! SPECTACULAR ACTS TO EXCITE AND STIMULATE! DOORS OPEN 5.30 P.M., PROMPT START 6.30 P.M.

Anne and Maisie Kellaway gaped as the gig drew up in front of Miss Pelham's house and a boy jumped down and said something to Miss Pelham, who frowned and pointed up at the Kellaways' window. Anne Kellaway shrank back, but was not quick enough at pulling Maisie out of sight as well.

"Wait, Ma, she's beckoning to us!" Maisie pulled Anne Kellaway forward again. "Look!"

Miss Pelham was still frowning—as she always did when any-thing to do with the Kellaways disturbed her—but she was indeed gesturing to them.

"I'll go down," Maisie declared, turning toward the door.

"No, you won't." Anne Kellaway stopped her daughter with a steely tone and a hand on her shoulder. "Jem, go and see what they want."

Jem left the pot he had been scouring and raced down the stairs. Maisie and Anne watched from the window as he exchanged a few words with the boy, who then handed him something white. He stared at whatever it was he held, while the boy jumped back into the gig and the driver tapped his whip lightly on the horse's neck and sped away up Hercules Buildings toward Westminster Bridge Road.

Jem returned a moment later, a puzzled look on his face.

"What is't, Jem?" Maisie demanded. "Oh, what have you got?"

Jem looked down at some bits of paper in his hand. "Four tick-ets for Mr. Astley's show tonight, with his compliments."

Thomas Kellaway looked up from the piece of beech he had been whittling.

"We're not going," Anne Kellaway declared. "We can't afford it."

"No, no, we don't have to pay. He's given them to us."

"We don't need his charity. We could buy our own tickets if we wanted."

"But you just said—" Maisie began.

"We're not going." Anne Kellaway felt like a mouse chased by a cat from one side of a room to the other.

Jem and Maisie looked at their father. Thomas Kellaway was gazing at them all but did not say anything. He loved his wife, and wanted her to love him back. He would not go against her.

"Have you finished that pot, Jem?" Anne Kellaway asked. "Once you do we can go for our walk." She turned away toward the win-dow, her hands shaking.

Maisie and Jem exchanged glances. Jem went back to the pot.

~ *2* ~

In the two weeks they'd been in Lambeth, the Kellaways had not gone much beyond the streets immediately surrounding their house. They did not need to—all the shops and stalls they needed were on Lambeth Terrace by Lambeth Green, on Westminster Bridge Road, or on the Lower Marsh. Jem had been with his father to the timber yards by the river near Westminster Bridge; Maisie had gone with her mother to St. George's Fields to see about laying out their clothes there to dry. When Jem suggested that they go for a walk on Easter Monday across Westminster Bridge to see Westminster Abbey, all were keen. They were used to walking a great deal in the Piddle Valley and found it strange not to be so active in Lambeth.

They set out at one o'clock, when others were eating or sleeping or at the pub. "How shall we go, then?" Maisie asked Jem, knowing better than to direct the question at her parents. Anne Kellaway was clutching on to her husband's arm as if a strong wind were about to blow her away. Thomas Kellaway was smiling as usual and gazing about him, looking like a simpleton waiting to go wherever was chosen for him.

"Let's take a shortcut to the river and walk along it up to the bridge," Jem said, knowing it had fallen to him to lead them, for he was the only Kellaway who had begun to become familiar with the streets.

"Not the shortcut that girl talked of, is't?" Anne Kellaway said. "I don't want to be going along any place called Cut-Throat Lane."

"Not that one, Ma," Jem lied, reasoning that it would take her a long time to work out that it was indeed Cut-Throat Lane. Jem had found it soon after Maggie told them about it. He knew his family would like the lane because it ran through empty fields; if

you turned your back to the houses and didn't look too far ahead
to Lambeth Palace or to the warehouses by the river, you could
more or less think you were in the countryside. One day Jem would
find the direction he needed to walk that would take him into countryside proper. Perhaps Maggie would know the way.

For now, he led his family up past Carlisle House, a nearby
mansion, to Royal Row and along it to Cut-Throat Lane. It was
very quiet there, with no one in the lane; and it being a holiday,
few were out working in the vegetable gardens that dotted the
fields. Jem was thankful too that it was sunny and clear. So often
in Lambeth the sky was not blue, even on a sunny day, but thick
and yellow with smoke from coal fires, and from the breweries and
manufactories for vinegar and cloth and soap that had sprung up
along the river. Yesterday and today, however, those places were
shut, and because it was warm, many had not lit fires. Jem gazed
up into the proper deep blue he knew well from Dorsetshire, coupled with the vivid green of the roadside grass and shrubs, and
found himself smiling at these colors that were so natural and yet
shouted louder than any London ribbon or dress. He began to walk
more slowly, at a saunter rather than the quick, nervous pace he'd
adopted since coming to Lambeth. Maisie paused to pick a few
primroses for a posy. Even Anne Kellaway stopped clutching her
husband and swung her arms. Thomas Kellaway began to whistle
"Over the Hills and Far Away," a song he often hummed when he
was working.

Too soon the lane made a sharp right and skirted along the
edges of the gardens surrounding Lambeth Palace. When they reached
the river their short idyll ended. In front of them stood a series of
dilapidated warehouses, flanked by rows of workmen's cottages.
The warehouses were shut today, which added to their menacing
atmosphere; normally the bustling action of the work made them
more welcoming. Anne Kellaway took her husband's arm again.

Though Jem and Thomas Kellaway had been down to the Thames
to buy wood and have it cut at the timber yards, the female Kella-

ways had only seen it briefly when they first arrived at Astley's Amphitheatre, and had not really taken it in. Now they had unwittingly chosen an unimpressive moment in which to get their first good look at the great London river. The tide was out, reducing the water to a thin, murky ribbon running through a wide, flat channel of gray silt that reminded Anne Kellaway of an unmade bed. Granted, even in its reduced state it was twenty times bigger than the Piddle, the river that ran alongside the Kellaways' garden in Piddletrenthide. Despite its small size, though, the Piddle still had the qualities Anne Kellaway looked for in a river—purposeful, relentless, cheerful, and cleansing, its sound a constant reminder of the world's movement.

The Thames was nothing like that. To Anne Kellaway it seemed not a river, but a long intestine that twisted each way out of sight. It did not have clear banks, either. The bed slid up toward the road, awash with pebbles and sludge, and it was easy enough to step straight from the road down into it. Despite the mud, children had done just that, and were running about in the riverbed, some playing, some picking out objects that had had been left exposed by the low tide: shoes, bottles, tins, bits of waterlogged wood and cloth, the head of a doll, a broken bowl.

The Kellaways stood and watched. "Look how dirty they're getting," Maisie said as if she envied them.

"Hideous place," Anne Kellaway stated.

"It looks better when the tide's in, like it were when we first arrived." Jem felt he had to defend the river, as if it were the embodiment of London and his family's decision to move there.

"Funny it has a tide," Maisie said. "I know our Piddle runs down to the sea somewhere, but it still always runs the same way. I'd feel topsy-turvy if it changed directions!"

"Let's go to the bridge," Jem suggested. They began to step more quickly now, past the warehouses and the workmen's cottages. Some of the workers and their wives and children were sitting out in front of their houses, talking, smoking, and singing. Most of them fell silent as the Kellaways passed, except for a man playing a pipe, who played faster. Jem wanted to step up their pace even more, but Maisie slowed down. "He's playing 'Tom Bowling,'" she said. "Listen!" She smiled at the man; he broke off playing and smiled back.

Anne Kellaway stiffened, then pulled at her daughter's arm. "Come along, Maisie!"

Maisie shook free and stood still in the middle of the road to join in singing the last verse in a high, clear voice:

> Yet shall poor Tom find pleasant weather,
> When He, who all commands,
> Shall give, to call life's crew together,
> The word to pipe all hands:
> Thus death, who kings and tars dispatches,
> In vain Tom's life has doffed,
> For though his body's under hatches,
> His soul has gone aloft,
> His soul has gone aloft.

She and the pipe player finished together, and there was a small silence. Anne Kellaway stifled a sob. Tommy and Maisie used to sing the song together in beautiful harmony.

"It be all right, Ma," Maisie said. "We has to sing it still, for we don't want to forget Tommy, do we?" She bobbed at the man and said, "Thank'ee, sir. Ar'ernoon."

~ *3* ~

On the approach to the bridge, the road curved briefly away from the river and passed the amphitheatre, with its grand pillared entrance where they had first met Philip Astley, and posters plastered on the wall in front announcing SHOW TONIGHT! It was only early afternoon and yet people were already milling about. Jem felt in his pocket and curled his hand around the tickets Philip Astley had sent them.

Anne Kellaway had a handbill thrust at her by a man running past calling, "Only a shilling and a pence to stand, two shillings tuppence a seat!" She stared at the crumpled paper, unsure what she was meant to do with it. Smoothing it against her skirt, she turned it over and over before at last starting to make out the words. When she recognized "Astley," she understood what it was and thrust it at her husband. "Oh, take it, take it, I don't want it!"

Thomas Kellaway fumbled and dropped the paper. It was Maisie who picked it up and brushed the dirt from it, then tucked it into the stays beneath her dress. "The show tonight," she murmured to Jem.

He shrugged.

"Do you have those tickets on you, Jem?" Anne Kellaway demanded.

Jem jerked his hand from his pocket as if he'd been caught touching himself. "Yes, Ma."

"I want you to take them to the theatre now and hand them back."

"Who's handin' back tickets?" called a voice behind them. Jem looked around. Maggie Butterfield jumped out from the wall she'd been idling behind. "What kind of tickets? You don't want to be handin' back any tickets. If they're good you can sell 'em for more'n you bought 'em for. Show 'em to me."

"How long have you been following us?" Jem asked, pleased to see her but wondering too if she had witnessed anything he'd rather she not see.

Maggie grinned and whistled a bit of "Tom Bowling." "Not half a bad voice you've got, Miss Piddle," she said to Maisie, who smiled and blushed.

"Away you go, girl," Anne Kellaway ordered. "We don't want

you hanging about." She glanced around to see if Maggie was on her own. They'd had a visit a few days before from Maggie's father, trying to sell Thomas Kellaway a load of ebony that he quickly spotted was oak painted black—though he was kind enough to suggest that Dick Butterfield had been hard done by someone else rather than trying to cheat the Kellaways. Anne Kellaway had disliked Dick Butterfield even more than his daughter.

Maggie ignored Jem's mother. "Have you got tickets for tonight, then?" she asked Jem coolly. "Which kind? Not for the gallery, I shouldn't think. Can't see her"—she jerked her head at Anne Kellaway—"standin' with them rascals. Here, show me."

Jem wondered himself, and couldn't resist pulling out the tickets to look. "'Pit,'" he read, with Maggie peering over his shoulder.

She nodded at Thomas Kellaway. "You must be makin' lots o' bum catchers to buy pit seats, and you only a couple o' weeks in London." A rare note of admiration crept into her voice.

"Oh, we didn't buy them," Maisie said. "Mr. Astley gave 'em to us!"

Maggie stared. "Lord a mercy."

"We're not going to see that rubbish," Anne Kellaway said.

"You can't give 'em back," Maggie declared. "Mr. Astley'd be insulted. He might even throw you out of his house."

Anne Kellaway started; she had clearly not thought of such a consequence from giving back the tickets.

"Course if you really don't want to go, you could let me go in your place," Maggie continued.

Anne Kellaway narrowed her eyes, but before she could open her mouth to say that she would never allow such an impudent girl to take her place, a deep drumbeat began to sound from somewhere over the river.

"The parade!" Maggie exclaimed. "It'll be starting. C'mon!" She began to run, pulling Jem along with her. Maisie followed, and fearful of being left alone, Anne Kellaway took her husband's arm once more and hurried after them.

Maggie raced past the amphitheatre and on toward Westminster Bridge, which was already crowded with people standing along the edges. They could hear a march being played at the other end, but they couldn't see anything yet. Maggie led them up the middle of the road and squeezed into a spot a third of the way along. The Kellaways crowded around her, trying to ignore the grumblings of those whose view they were now blocking. There was a fair bit of jostling, but eventually everyone could see, until the next lot of people stood in front of them and the crowd had to rearrange itself.

"What we waiting for?" Jem said to Maggie.

Maggie snorted. "Fancy standing in a crowd not even knowin' what you're there for. Dorset boy!"

Jem flushed. "Forget it, then," he muttered.

"No, tell us," Maisie insisted. "*I* want to know."

"Mr. Astley has a parade on the first day of the season," Maggie explained, "to give people a taste of the show. Sometimes he has fireworks, even in the daytime—though they'll be better tonight."

"You hear that, Ma?" Maisie said. "We can see fireworks tonight!"

"*If* you go." Maggie threw Anne Kellaway a look.

"We an't going tonight, and we an't staying for the parade now," Anne Kellaway asserted. "Come, Jem, Maisie, we're leaving." She began to push at the people in front of her. Fortunately for Jem and Maisie, no one wanted to move and give up a place, and Anne Kellaway found herself trapped in the dense crowd. She had never had so many people around her before. It was one thing to stand in the window and watch London pass beneath her, safe at her perch. Now she had every sort of person pressing into her— men, women, children, people with smelly clothes, smelly breath, matted hair, harsh voices. A large man next to her was eating a meat pie, and the flakes of pastry were dropping down his front as well as into the hair of the woman standing in front of him. Neither seemed to notice or care as much as Anne Kellaway did. She was tempted to reach over and brush the flakes away.

As the music drew closer, two figures on horseback appeared. The crowd shifted and pushed, and Anne Kellaway felt panic welling up like bile. For a moment she was so desperate to get away that she actually put a hand on the shoulder of the man in front of her. He turned briefly and shrugged it off.

Thomas Kellaway took her hand and tucked it into the crook of his arm. "There now, Anne, steady, girl," he said, as if he were talking to one of the horses they'd left behind with Sam in Dorsetshire. She missed their horses. Anne Kellaway closed her eyes, resisting the temptation to pull her hand away from her husband. She took a deep breath. When she opened her eyes again, the riders had drawn close. The horse nearest them was an old white charger, who walked sedately under its burden. The rider was Philip Astley.

"It's been a long winter, has it not, my friends?" he shouted. "You've had nothing to entertain you all these months since October. Have you been waiting for this day? Well, wait no more—Lent is over, Easter has come, and Astley's show has begun! Come and see *The Siege of Bangalore*, a sketch at once tragical, comical, and oriental! Feast your eyes on the splendid operatic ballet *La Fête de l'Amour*! Wonder at the talents of the Manage Horse, who can fetch, carry, climb a ladder, and even make a cup of tea!"

As he passed the Kellaways, his eyes fell on Anne Kellaway and he actually stopped in order to raise his hat to her. "Everyone is welcome to Astley's Royal Saloon and New Amphitheatre—especially you, madam!"

The people around Anne Kellaway turned to stare at her. The man with the pie dropped his mouth open so that she could see the meat and gravy mashed up in there. Sick from this sight and from the attention of so many, especially Philip Astley, she closed her eyes again.

Philip Astley saw her turn pale and shut her eyes. Pulling a flask from his coat, he signaled to one of the circus boys who ran alongside him to take it to her. He could not stop his horse any longer to see if she took a swig of brandy, however—the press of the procession behind pushed him on. He began his patter again: "Come and see the show—new acts of daring and imagination under the management of my son, John Astley, the finest equestrian rider in Europe! At little more than the price of a glass of wine, come for a full evening's entertainment that you'll remember for years to come!"

Beside him rode the son he spoke of. John Astley had as commanding a presence as his father, but in a completely different style. If Astley Senior was an oak—large and blunt, with a thick, strong center—Astley Junior was a poplar—tall and slender, with handsome, even features and clear, calculating eyes. He was educated, as his father had not been, and held himself more formally and self-consciously. Philip Astley rode his white charger like the cavalry man he once was and still thought himself to be, using the horse to get where he wanted to go and do what he wanted to do. John Astley rode his slim chestnut mare, with her long legs and nimble hooves, as if he and the horse were permanently attached and always on show. He jogged smoothly over Westminster Bridge, his horse capering sideways and slantways in a series of intricate steps to a minuet, played by musicians on trumpet, French horn, accordion, and drum. Anyone else in his seat would have been jolted over and over and dropped gloves, hat, and whip, but John Astley remained elegant and unruffled.

The crowd gazed at him in silence, admiring his skill rather than loving him as they did his father. All but one: Maisie Kellaway stood with her mouth open, staring up at him. She had never seen such a handsome man and, at fourteen, was ready to take a fancy to one. John Astley did not notice her, of course; he did not seem to see anyone, keeping his eyes fixed on the amphitheatre ahead.

Anne Kellaway had recovered herself without the aid of Philip Astley's brandy. That she had refused, to the disgust of Maggie, the meat pie man, the woman in front of him with the pastry flakes in her hair, the man whose shoulder she had touched, the boy who delivered the flask—in fact, just about everyone apart from the other Kellaways. Anne Kellaway didn't notice: Her eyes were fixed fast on the performers in the parade behind John Astley. First came a group of tumblers who walked along normally and then simultaneously fell into a series of forward rolls that turned into cartwheels and backflips. Then came a group of dogs who, at a signal, all got up onto their hind legs and walked that way for a good ten feet, then ran about jumping over one another's backs in a complicated configuration.

Surprising as these acts were, what finally captured Anne Kellaway's attention was the slack-rope dancing. Two strong men carried poles between which a rope hung, rather like a thick clothesline. Sitting in the middle of the rope was a dark-haired, moon-faced woman wearing a red and white striped satin dress with a tight bodice and a flared skirt. She swung back and forth on the rope as if it were a swing, then wrapped one part of the rope casually around her leg.

Maggie poked Jem and Maisie. "That's Miss Laura Devine," she whispered. "She's from Scotland, and is the finest slack-rope dancer in Europe."

At a signal, the men stepped away from each other, pulling the rope taut and making Miss Devine turn a graceful somersault, which revealed several layers of red and white petticoats. The crowd roared, and she did it again, twice this time, then three times, and then she turned constant somersaults, twirling round and round the rope so that her petticoats were a flashing blur of red and white.

"That's called Pig on a Spit," Maggie announced.

Then the men stepped toward each other, and Miss Devine came out of the last somersault into a long swing up into the sky, smiling as she did.

Anne Kellaway stared at Miss Devine, expecting to see her crash to the ground as her son Tommy had from the pear tree, reaching for that pear that was always—and now always would be—just out of his reach. But Miss Devine did not fall; indeed, she seemed incapable of it. For the first time in the weeks since her son's death,

Anne Kellaway felt the shard of grief lodged in her heart stop biting. She craned her neck to watch her even as Miss Devine moved far down the bridge and could barely be seen, even when there were other spectacles right in front of her—a monkey on a pony, a man riding his horse backward and picking up dropped handkerchiefs without leaving his saddle, a troupe of dancers in oriental costume turning pirouettes.

"Jem, what've you done with those tickets?" Anne Kellaway demanded suddenly.

"Here, Ma." Jem pulled them from his pocket.

"Keep 'em."

Maisie clapped her hands and jumped up and down.

Maggie hissed, "Put 'em away!" Already those around them had turned to look.

"Them for the pit?" the meat pie man asked, leaning over Anne Kellaway to see.

Jem began to put the tickets back in his pocket.

"Not there!" Maggie cried. "They'll have 'em off you in a trice if you keep 'em there."

"Who?"

"Them rascals." Maggie jerked her head at a pair of young boys who had miraculously squeezed through the crush to appear at his side. "They're faster'n you, though not faster'n me. See?" She snatched the tickets from Jem, and with a grin began to tuck them down the front of her dress.

"I can keep them," Maisie suggested. "You haven't got the stays."

Maggie stopped smiling.

"I'll keep them," Anne Kellaway announced, and held out her hand. Maggie grimaced but handed over the tickets. Anne Kellaway carefully tucked them into her stays, then wrapped her shawl tightly over her bosom. The stern, triumphant look on her face was armor enough to keep away any rogue fingers.

The musicians were passing them now, and behind them three men brought up the rear of the parade waving red, yellow, and white flags that read ASTLEY'S CIRCUS.

"What'll we do now?" Jem asked when they had passed. "Go on to the Abbey?"

He could have been speaking to a family of mutes, oblivious to the surging crowd around them. Maisie was staring after John Astley, who by now had become just a flash of blue coat over winking horse flanks. Anne Kellaway had her eye on the amphitheatre in the distance, contemplating the unexpected evening ahead. Thomas Kellaway was peering over the bridge's balustrade at a boat piled high with wood being rowed along the thin line of water toward the bridge.

"C'mon. They'll follow." Maggie took Jem's arm and pulled him toward the apex of the bridge, sidestepping the traffic of carriages and carts that had begun to cross it again, and making their way toward the Abbey.

Westminster Abbey was the tallest, grandest building in that part of London. It was the sort of building the Kellaways had expected to see plenty of in the city—substantial, ornate, important. Indeed, they had been disappointed by the shabbiness of Lambeth, even if they had not yet seen the rest of London. The filth, the crowds, the noise, the indifferent, casual, neglected buildings—none of it matched the pictures they'd conjured of London back in Dorsetshire. At least the Abbey, with its pair of impressive square towers, its busy detail of narrow windows, filigreed arches, jutting buttresses, and tiny spires, satisfied their expectations. It was the second time in the weeks they had been in Lambeth that Anne

Kellaway thought, *There* is a reason for us to be in London—the first time being only half an hour before, when she saw Miss Laura Devine performing the Pig on a Spit.

Just inside the arched entrance between the two towers, the Kellaways stopped, causing those behind them to grumble and push past. Maggie, who had continued on into the abbey, turned around and blew through her lips. "Look at those country fools," she muttered, as the four Kellaways stood in a row, eyes up, heads tilted at the same angle. She couldn't blame them, however. Although she had visited the Abbey many times, she too found it an astonishing sight on first entering and, indeed, throughout the building. At every turning, every chapel and tomb contained marble to be admired, carving to be fingered, elegance and opulence to be dazzled by.

For the Kellaways the sheer size was what pulled them up short. None had ever been in a place where the ceiling arched so high over their heads. They could not take their eyes off it.

Finally Maggie lost patience. "There's more to the Abbey than the ceiling," she advised Jem. "And there's better ceilings than this too. Wait till you see the Lady Chapel!"

Feeling responsible for their first proper taste of what London could offer, she led them through archways and in and out of small side chapels, casually throwing out the names of people buried there that she remembered from her father's guided tour of the place: Lord Hunsdon, the Countess of Sussex, Lord Bourchier, Edward I, Henry III. The string of names meant little to Jem; nor, once he grew accustomed to the size and lavishness of the place, did he really care for all of the stone. He and his father worked in wood, and he found stone cold and unforgiving. Still, he couldn't help marveling at the elaborate tombs, with the carved effigies in tan and beige marble of their inhabitants lying on top, at the brass reliefs of men on other slabs, at the black-and-white pillars ornamenting the headstones.

By the time they reached Henry VII's Lady Chapel at the other

end of the Abbey, and Maggie triumphantly announced, "Eliza-
beth I," Jem had stopped listening to her altogether and openly
gaped. He had never imagined a place could be so ornate.

"Oh, Jem, look at that ceiling," Maisie breathed, gazing up at
the fan vaulting, carved of stone so delicate it looked like lace spun
by spiders, touched in several places with gold leaf.

Jem was not studying the ceiling, however, but the rows of
carved seats for members of the royal court along both sides of the
chapel. Over each seat was an eight-foot-high ornamental tower
of patinated oak filigree. The towers were of such a complicated
interlocking pattern that it would not have been a surprise to hear
carvers had gone mad working on them. Here at last was wood
worked in a way the Kellaways would never see the likes of in
Dorsetshire, or Wiltshire, or Hampshire, or anywhere in England
other than in Westminster Abbey. Jem and Thomas Kellaway
gazed in awe at the carving, like men who make sundials seeing a
mechanical clock for the first time.

Jem lost track of Maggie until she rushed up to him. "Come
here!" she hissed, and dragged him away from the Lady Chapel to
the center of the Abbey and the Chapel of Edward the Confessor.
"Look!" she whispered, nodding in the direction of one of the tombs
surrounding Edward's massive shrine.

Mr. Blake was standing alongside it, staring at the bronze effigy
of a woman that lay along the top of it. He was sketching in a small
sand-colored notebook, never looking down at the paper and pen-
cil, but keeping his eyes fastened on the statue's impassive face.

Maggie put a finger to her lips, then took a quiet step toward Mr.
Blake, Jem following reluctantly. Slowly and steadily they rounded
on him from behind. He was so concentrated on drawing that he
noticed nothing. As the children got closer, they discovered that he
was singing under his breath, very soft and high, more like the
whining of a mosquito than of a man. Now and then his lips moved
to form a word, but it was hard to catch what he might be saying.

Maggie giggled. Jem shook his head at her. They were close

enough now that they were able to peek around Mr. Blake at his sketch. When they saw what he was drawing, Jem flinched, and Maggie openly gasped. Though the statue on the tomb was dressed in ceremonial robes, Mr. Blake had drawn her naked.

He did not turn around, but continued to draw and to sing, though he must have known now that they were just behind him.

Jem grabbed Maggie's elbow and pulled her away. When they had left the chapel and were out of earshot, Maggie burst out laughing. "Fancy undressing a statue!"

Jem's irritation outweighed his impulse to laugh too. He was suddenly weary of Maggie—of her harsh, barking laughter, her sharp comments, her studied worldliness. He longed for someone quiet and simple, who wouldn't pass judgment on him and on Mr. Blake.

"Shouldn't you be with your family?" he said abruptly.

Maggie shrugged. "They'll just be at the pub. I can find 'em later."

"I'm going back to mine." Immediately he regretted his tone, as he saw hurt flash through her eyes before she hid it with hard indifference.

"Suit yourself." She shrugged and turned away.

"Wait, Maggie," Jem called as she slipped out a side entrance he had not noticed before. As when he first met her, the moment she was gone, he wished she was back again. He felt eyes on him then, and looked across the aisle and through the door to Edward's Chapel. Mr. Blake was gazing at him, pen poised above his notebook.

~ 5 ~

Anne Kellaway insisted that they arrive early, so they found seats right at half past five, and had to wait an hour for the amphitheatre to fill and the show to begin. With tickets for the pit, they could at least sit on benches, though some in the pit chose to stand crowded close to the ring where the horses would gallop, the dancers dance, the soldiers fight. There was plenty to look at while they waited. Jem and his father studied the wooden structure of the boxes and the gallery, decorated with moldings and painted with *trompe l'œil* foliage. The three-tiered wagon-wheel chandelier Thomas Kellaway had seen on his first day was now lit with hundreds of candles, along with torches around the boxes and gallery; a round roof with open shutters high up also let in light until night fell. At one side of the ring a small stage had been built, with a backdrop painted with mountains, camels, elephants, and tigers—the oriental touch Philip Astley had referred to in describing *The Siege of Bangalore* pantomime.

The Kellaways also studied the audience. Around them in the pit were other artisans and tradesmen—chandlers, tailors, carpenters, blacksmiths, printers, butchers. The boxes held the middling sorts—merchants, bankers, lawyers—mostly from Westminster across the river. In the galleries stood the rougher crowd: the soldiers and sailors, the men who worked at the docks and in the warehouses along the Thames, as well as coalmen, coachmen, stablehands, brickmakers and bricklayers, nightsoil men, gardeners, street sellers, rag-and-bone men, and the like. There were also a fair number of servants, apprentices, and children.

Thomas Kellaway disappeared while they were waiting, then returned and, with a sheepish smile, held out four oranges. Jem had never had one: They were rare enough in London, and nonexistent in Piddletrenthide. He puzzled over the skin, then bit into it like an apple before realizing the peel was inedible. Maisie laughed at him as he spat out the peel. "Silly," she murmured. "Look." She nodded at those sitting nearby who deftly peeled their oranges and dropped the bits on the floor. As they trampled and shuffled over the remains throughout the evening, the peel released its sharp acid scent in waves, cutting through the various smells of horse dung, sweat, and smoke from the torches.

When the music struck up and Philip Astley stepped out onto the stage to address the audience, he stood for a moment, scanning the pit. Finding Anne Kellaway, he smiled, satisfied that with his charm he had turned an enemy into a friend. "Welcome, welcome to the Royal Saloon and New Amphitheatre for the 1792 season of Astley's Circus! Are you ready to be dazzled and distracted?"

The audience roared.

"Astonished and amazed?"

More roaring.

"Surprised and scintillated? Then let the show begin!"

Jem was happy enough before the show, but once it began he found himself fidgeting. Unlike his mother, he was not finding the circus acts a welcome distraction. Unlike his sister, he was not smitten with any of the performers. Unlike his father, he was not content because those around him were happy. Jem knew he was meant to find the novelty acts astonishing. The jugglers throwing torches without burning themselves, the learned pig who could add and subtract, the horse who could boil a kettle and make a cup of tea, Miss Laura Devine with her twirling petticoats, two tight-rope walkers sitting at a table and eating a meal on a rope thirty feet above the ground, a horseman drinking a glass of wine as he stood on two horses galloping around the ring—all of these spectacles defied some rule of life. People should tumble from standing on ropes strung up high or on galloping horses' backs; pigs shouldn't know how to add; horses can't make cups of tea; Miss Devine should become sick from so much spinning.

Jem knew this. Yet instead of watching these feats in awe, with the wide eyes and open mouth and cries of surprise of the people around him—his parents and sister included—he was bored precisely because the acts weren't like life. They were so far removed from his experience of the world that they had little impact on him. Perhaps if the horseman stood on the back of one horse and simply rode, or the jugglers threw balls instead of burning torches, then he too might have stared and called out.

Nor did the dramas interest him, with their oriental dancers, reenactments of battles, haunted houses, and warbling lovers— apart from the scenery changes, where screens of mountains and animals or rippling oceans or battle scenes full of soldiers and horses were suddenly whisked away to reveal starry night skies or castle ruins or London itself. Jem couldn't understand why people would want to see a replica of the London skyline when they could go outside, stand on Westminster Bridge, and see the real thing.

Jem only brightened when, an hour into the show, he noticed Maggie's face up in the gallery, poking out between two soldiers. If she saw him, her face showed no sign of it—she was enrapt by the spectacle in the ring, laughing at a clown who rode a horse backward while a monkey on another horse chased him. He liked watching her when she didn't know it, so happy and absorbed, the hard, shrewd veneer she cultivated dropped for once, the pulse of anxiety that drove her replaced by innocence, even if only temporarily.

"I'm just going out to the jakes," Jem whispered to Maisie. She nodded, her eyes fixed on the monkey, who had jumped from its horse to the horse carrying the clown. As Jem began to push through the dense crowd, his sister was laughing and clapping her hands.

Outside he found the entrance to the gallery around the corner, separating the rougher crowd from the more genteel audience in the pit. Two men stood in front of the staircase leading up. "Sixpence to see the rest of the show," one of them said to Jem.

"But I just been in the pit," Jem explained. "I'm going up to see a friend."

"You in the pit?" the man repeated. "Show me your ticket, then."

"My ma has it." Anne Kellaway had tucked the ticket stubs back into her stays, to be kept and admired.

"That'll be sixpence to see the rest of the show, then."

"But I don't have any money."

"Go away with you, then." The man turned away.

"But—"

"Get out or we'll kick you all the way to Newgate," the other
man said, and both laughed.

Jem went back to the main entrance, but he wasn't allowed
in there either without a ticket stub. He stood still for a moment,
listening to the laughter inside. Then he turned and went out to
stand on the front steps between the enormous pillars framing the
entrance. Lining the street in front of the amphitheatre, near where
he and his family had waited in Mr. Smart's cart the day they
arrived in London, were two dozen carriages, waiting to take
members of the audience home after the show, or down to Vauxhall Pleasure Gardens a mile south to continue their evening's
entertainment. The coach drivers slept in their seats or gathered
together to smoke and talk and flirt with the women who had wandered over to them.

Otherwise it was quiet, except for the occasional roar of the audience. Though the street outside the amphitheatre was well lit
with torches and lamps, the roads led away into darkness. Westminster Bridge itself was a shadowy hump over which two rows of
lamplights marched. Beyond them London hung like a heavy black
coat.

Jem found himself drawn back to the bridge and the river. He
walked up it, following the lamps from pool to pool of light. At the
apex of the bridge he stopped and leaned over the balustrade. It
was too high to see directly below, and so dark that he could make
out little anyway. Even so, he sensed that the Thames was a different river from what the Kellaways had seen earlier. It was full
now; Jem could hear it slopping and slurping and sucking at the
stone piers that held up the bridge. It reminded him of a herd of
cows in the dark, breathing heavily and squelching their hooves in
the mud. He took a deep breath—like cows, the river smelled of a
combination of fresh grass and excrement, of what came in and
what went out of this city.

Another scent enveloped him suddenly—like the orange peel

from his fingers, but far stronger and sweeter. Too sweet—Jem's throat tightened at the same time as a hand gripped his arm and another reached into his pocket. "Hallo, darling, looking for your destiny down there? Well, you've found her."

Jem tried to pull away from the woman but her hands were strong. She wasn't much taller than him, though her face was old under its paint. Her hair was bright yellow, even in the dim light, her dress dirty blue and cut low. She pushed her chest into his shoulder. "Only a shilling for you, darling."

Jem stared down into her exposed, creased bosom; a surge of desire and disgust coursed through him.

"Leave off him!" called a voice out of the dark. Maggie darted to them and in a quick movement peeled off the hand clamped on his arm. "He don't want you! 'Sides, you're too old and rank, you poxy cow—and you charged him too much!"

"Little bitch!" the whore shouted and struck out at Maggie, who easily dodged the blow and threw her off balance. As she staggered, Jem recognized the smell of gin mingled with the rancid orange. She reeled about, and he reached a hand out to try to help her regain her balance. Maggie stopped him. "Don't—she'll just latch on to you again! Rob you blind too. Probably already has. D'you have anything on you?"

Jem shook his head.

"Just as well—you'd never get it off her now. She'd have hidden it by her snatch." Maggie looked around. "There'll be more of 'em when the show lets out. That's their best time for business—when everybody's happy from the show."

Jem watched the woman totter into the dark along the bridge. In the next pool of light she grabbed on to another man, who threw her off without a glance. Jem shuddered and turned back to the river. "Tha' be what I hate about London."

Maggie leaned against the balustrade. "But you've got whores down in Piddle-dee-dee, don't you?"

"In Dorchester, yes. But they an't like that."

They stood still, looking out over the water. "Why'd you leave the show?" Maggie asked.

Jem hesitated. "I were poorly and come out for air. It were stuffy in there."

Her expression told him that Maggie didn't believe him, but she said nothing, only picked up a stone at her feet and let it drop over the side of the bridge. They both listened for the plop, but a carriage passed at that moment and its clatter obliterated the sound.

"Why'd *you* leave?" Jem asked when the carriage was gone.

Maggie made a face. "There's just the Tailor of Brentford left, and then the finale. I seen the Tailor too many times already. Finale's better from outside, anyway, what with the fireworks on the river."

From the amphitheatre they heard a roar of laughter. "That'll be them laughin' at the Tailor now," she said.

When the laughter died down it was quiet. No carriages passed. Jem stood awkwardly with Maggie by the balustrade. Though she had clearly been hurt earlier in the Abbey, she did not show it now. He was tempted to say something, but didn't want to ruin the fragile truce that seemed to have been established between them.

"I can show you some magic," Maggie said suddenly.

"What?"

"Go in there." She pointed to one of the stone alcoves that stood above the piers all along the bridge. The recess was semicircular and about seven feet high, designed so that passersby might shelter there out of the rain. A lamp was attached to the top of the alcove, and shone down around the recess, making it dark inside. To please Maggie, Jem stepped inside the dark space and turned to face her.

"No, stand with your back to me, with your face right up to the stone," Maggie ordered.

Jem obeyed, feeling foolish and vulnerable with his back to the world and his nose close to the cold stone. It was damp in the recess, and smelled of urine and sex.

He wondered whether Maggie was tricking him. Perhaps she had gone to get one of the whores and thrust her on him in the alcove where he wouldn't be able to get away. He was about to turn around and accuse her when he heard her seductive voice in his ear: "Guess where I'm talkin' from."

Jem whirled around. Maggie wasn't there. He stepped out of the alcove and searched around it, wondering if he had imagined the voice. Then she stepped out of the darkness of the alcove opposite his, on the other side of the road. "Go back in!" she called.

Jem stepped into the alcove again and turned to the wall, thoroughly confused. How could she have whispered in his ear and then run across the road so fast? He waited for her to do it again, thinking he would catch her at it this time. A carriage passed by. When it was quiet he again heard in his ear, "Hallo, Jem. Say summat nice to me."

Jem turned around again, but she wasn't there. He hesitated, then turned back to the wall.

"C'mon, Jem, an't you going to say nothing?" Her voice whispered around the stone.

"Can you hear me?" Jem asked.

"Yes! In't it amazing? I can hear you and you can hear me!"

Jem turned around and looked across at the other alcove. Maggie shifted slightly and he caught a flash of the white shawl over her shoulders.

"How'd you do that?" he said, but there was no answer. "Maggie?" When she still didn't answer, Jem turned to face the wall. "Can you hear me?"

"I can now. You have to face the wall, you know. It don't work otherwise."

Two carriages passed and drowned out the rest of what she said.

"But how can it be?" Jem asked.

"Dunno. It just works. One of the whores told me about it. The best is if you sing."

"Sing?"

"Go on, then—sing us a song."

Jem thought, and after a moment he began:

> The violet and the primrose too
> Beneath a sheltering thorny bough
> In bright and lively colors blow
> And cast sweet fragrance round.
>
> Where beds of thyme in clusters lay
> The heathrose opens its eyes in May
> And cowslips too, their sweets display
> Upon the heathy ground.

His voice was still high, though it would break before too long. Maggie, her face turned toward her own curved wall, was glad to be alone and in the dark so that she could listen to Jem's singing without feeling obliged to smirk. Instead she could smile, listening to his simple song and clear voice.

When he was done they were both silent. Another carriage passed. Maggie could have made a clever remark—teased him about singing about flowers, or accused him of missing the Piddle Valley. With others around, it would be expected of her. But they were alone, cupped in their standing stones, sheltered from the world on the bridge yet connected by the sounds bouncing back and forth, twisting into a cord that bound them together.

So she did not make a smart comment, but sang back her response:

> What though I be a country clown,
> For all the fuss you make,
> One need not be born in town
> To know what two and two make.

Then don't ye be so proud, d'ye see,
It weren't a thing that's suiting;
Can one than its opposite better be,
When both are on a footing?

She heard Jem chuckle. "I ne'er said the country were better'n the city," he said. "Dunno as they be opposites exactly, either."

"Course they are."

"Dunno," Jem repeated. "There be lanes in Lambeth where you find the same flowers as in the Piddle Valley—cowslip and celandine and buttercups. But then I've ne'er understood opposites anyway."

"Simple." Maggie's voice floated around him. "It's the thing exactly different from t'other. So the opposite of a room pitch black is a room lit bright."

"But you still have the room. That stays the same in both."

"Don't think of the room, then. Just think of black and white. Now, if you're not wet, you're what?"

"Dry," Jem said after a moment.

"That's it. If you're not a boy, you're a—"

"Girl. I—"

"If you're not good you're—"

"Bad. I know, but—"

"And you won't go to Heaven but to—"

"Hell. Stop! I know all that. I just think—" A coach rumbled past, drowning out his words. "It's hard to talk about it like this," Jem said when it was quieter.

"What, on *opposite* sides of the road?" Maggie's laughter rang around Jem's stone chamber. "Come over to me, then."

Jem darted across the road as Maggie came out of her alcove. "There," she said. "Now we're a boy and a girl on the same side of the road."

Jem frowned. "But that's not opposite us," he said, waving at where he'd just come from. "That's just t'other side. It don't mean it's different. This side of the road, that side of the road—they both be part of the road."

"Well now, my boy, they are what make the road the road," said one of two dark figures walking toward them from the Westminster side of the river. As they came into the pool of light, Jem recognized Mr. Blake's broad forehead and wide eyes that penetrated even in the darkness.

"Hallo, Mr. Blake, Mrs. Blake," Maggie said.

"Hallo, my dear," Mrs. Blake replied. Catherine Blake was a little shorter than her husband, with a similar stocky build. She had small, deep-set eyes, a broad nose, and wide, ruddy cheeks. The old bonnet she wore had a misshapen rim, as if someone had sat on it while it was wet with rain. She was smiling patiently; she looked tired, as if she were indulging her husband with a walk out at night rather than going because she wanted to herself. Jem had seen that look on other faces—usually women's, sometimes without the smile, waiting while their men drank at the pub, or talked to other men in the road about the price of seed.

"You see," Mr. Blake continued without even saying hello, for he was concentrated on making his point. "This side—the light side—and that side—the dark side—"

"There, that's an opposite," Maggie interrupted. "That's what Jem and me were talkin' about, weren't we, Jem?"

Mr. Blake's face lit up. "Ah, contraries. What were you saying about them, my girl?"

"Well, Jem don't understand 'em, and I was tryin' to explain—"

"I do understand them!" Jem interrupted. "Of course bad's the opposite of good, and girl the opposite of boy. But—" He stopped. It felt strange talking to an adult about such thoughts. He would never have such a conversation with his parents, or on the street in Piddletrenthide, or in the pub. There the talk was about whether there would be frost that night or who was next traveling to

Dorchester or which field of barley was ready for harvest. Something had happened to him since coming to London.

"What is it, my boy?" Mr. Blake was waiting for him to continue. That too was new to Jem—an adult seemed to be interested in what he thought.

"Well, it be this," he began slowly, picking his way through his thoughts like climbing a rocky path. "What's funny about opposites be that wet and dry both has water, boy and girl be about people, Heaven and Hell be the places you go when you die. They all has something in common. So they an't completely different from each other the way people think. Having the one don't mean t'other be gone." Jem felt his head ache with the effort of explaining this.

Mr. Blake, however, nodded easily, as if he understood and, indeed, thought about such things all the time. "You're right, my boy. Let me give you an example. What is the opposite of innocence?"

"Easy," Maggie cut in. "Knowing things."

"Just so, my girl. Experience." Maggie beamed. "Tell me, then: Would you say you are innocent or experienced?"

Maggie stopped smiling so suddenly it was as if she had been physically struck by Mr. Blake's question. A wild, furtive look crossed her face that Jem recalled from the first time he met her, when she was talking about Cut-Throat Lane. She frowned at a passerby and did not answer.

"You see, that is a difficult question to answer, is it not, my girl? Here is another instead: If innocence is that bank of the river"—Mr. Blake pointed toward Westminster Abbey—"and experience that bank"—he pointed to Astley's Amphitheatre—"what is in the middle of the river?"

Maggie opened her mouth, but could think of no quick response.

"Think on it, my children, and give me your answer another day."

"Will you answer us summat else, Mr. Blake?" Maggie asked, recovering quickly. "Why'd you draw that statue naked? You know, in the Abbey."

"Maggie!" Jem hissed, embarrassed she'd acknowledged their earlier spying. Mrs. Blake looked from Maggie to Jem to her husband with a puzzled expression.

Mr. Blake didn't seem bothered, however, but took seriously her question. "Ah, you see, my girl, I wasn't drawing the statue. I can't bear to copy from nature, though I did so for several years in the Abbey when I was an apprentice. That exercise taught me many things, and one of them was that once you know the surface of a thing, you need no longer dwell there, but can look deeper. That is why I don't draw from life—it is far too limiting, and deadens the imagination. No, earlier today I was drawing what I was told to draw."

"Who told you?"

"My brother Robert."

"He was there?" Maggie didn't remember seeing anyone with Mr. Blake.

"Oh, yes indeed, he was. Now, Kate, if you're ready, shall we go on?"

"Ready if you are, Mr. Blake."

"Oh, but—" Maggie cast about for something to keep the Blakes with them.

"Did you know about the echo in the alcoves, sir?" Jem interjected. He too wanted Mr. Blake to remain. There was something odd about him—distant yet close in his attention, an adult and yet childlike.

"What echo is that, my boy?"

"If you stand in the opposite alcoves, facing the wall, you can hear each other," Maggie explained.

"Can you, now?" Mr. Blake turned to his wife. "Did you know that, Kate?"

"That I didn't, Mr. Blake."

"D'you want to try it?" Maggie persisted.

"Shall we, Kate?"

"If you like, Mr. Blake."

Maggie stifled a giggle as she led Mrs. Blake into the alcove and had her stand facing the wall, while Jem led Mr. Blake to the alcove opposite. Mr. Blake spoke softly to the wall, and after a moment he and Mrs. Blake laughed. That much Jem and Maggie heard, but not the conversation—mostly one-sided, with Mrs. Blake occasionally agreeing with her husband. Their isolation left the children standing in the road on either side of the bridge, feeling a little foolish. Finally Jem wandered over to Maggie. "What do you think they be talking about?"

"Dunno. It won't be about the price of fish, that's sure. Wish they'd let us back in."

Did Mrs. Blake hear her? At that moment she stepped out and said, "Children, come and stand inside with me. Mr. Blake is going to sing."

Jem and Maggie glanced at each other, then squeezed into the alcove with Mrs. Blake. At close range she smelled of fried fish and coal dust.

They faced the wall once again, Jem and Maggie giggling a little at being so squashed together, but not trying to move apart either.

"We're ready, Mr. Blake," Mrs. Blake said softly.

"Very good," they heard his disembodied voice say. After a pause he began to sing in a high, thin voice very different from his speaking voice:

> When the green woods laugh with the voice of joy
> And the dimpling stream runs laughing by,
> When the air does laugh with our merry wit,
> And the green hill laughs with the noise of it.

When the meadows laugh with lively green
And the grasshopper laughs in the merry scene.
When Mary and Susan and Emily
With their sweet round mouths sing Ha, Ha, He.

When the painted birds laugh in the shade
Where our table with cherries and nuts is spread
Come live and be merry and join with me,
To sing the sweet chorus of Ha, Ha, He.

When he finished they were silent.

"Ha, ha, he," Maggie repeated then, breaking the spell. "Don't know that song."

"It's his own," Mrs. Blake explained. Jem could hear the pride in her voice.

"He makes his own songs?" he asked. He had never met anyone who wrote the songs people sang. He'd never thought about where songs came from; they were just about, to be pulled from the air and learned.

"Poems, and songs, and all sorts," Mrs. Blake replied.

"Did you like that, my boy?" came Mr. Blake's disembodied voice.

Jem jumped; he'd forgotten that Mr. Blake could hear them. "Oh, yes."

"It's in a book I made."

"What's it called?" Jem asked.

Mr. Blake paused. "*Songs of Innocence.*"

"Oh!" Maggie cried. Then she began to laugh, and Mr. Blake joined in from his alcove, then Mrs. Blake, and lastly, Jem. They laughed until the stone walls rang with it and the first fireworks of the circus finale rocketed up and exploded, burning bright in the night sky.

PART III

May 1792

Though she was meant to be ironing sheets and handkerchiefs—the only ironing her mother trusted her with—Maggie left the back door open and kept an eye out on Astley's field, which was just behind the house the Butterfields had rooms in. The wooden fence separating their garden from the field would normally block much of the view; it was old and rotting, though, and Maggie had slipped through it so often as a shortcut that she'd knocked it sideways and a gap had opened up. Every time the iron cooled, she shoved it into the coals in the fire and popped outside to poke her head through the gap so that she could watch the rehearsals taking place in Astley's yard. She also looked out for Jem, whom she was meant to meet in the field.

When she came back into the kitchen for the third time, she found her mother, barefoot and in a nightdress, standing over the ironing board and frowning at the sheet Maggie had half-finished. Maggie rushed to the fire, picked up the iron, wiped the ash from its surface, and stepped up to the sheet, nudging her mother with the hope that she would move aside.

Bet Butterfield paid no attention to her daughter. She continued to stand, flat-footed, her legs a little splayed, arms crossed over her substantial bosom that, free from stays at the moment, was slung low and wobbled under her nightdress. She reached out and tapped part of the sheet. "Look here, you scorched it!"

"It was there already," Maggie lied.

"Be sure and fold it so it's hidden, then," her mother said with a yawn and a shake of her head.

Bet Butterfield often declared that her blood ran with lye, for her mother, grandmother, and great-grandmother had all been

laundresses in Lincolnshire. It had not occurred to her to do anything different in her life, not even when Dick Butterfield—young
enough then that the map of wrinkles was not yet etched into
his forehead—passed through her village on his way from Yorkshire to London and charmed her into following him. She arrived
in Southwark, where they first lived, completely unimpressed by
novelty, and insisted first thing—even before marrying—on buying a new washtub to replace the one she still regretted leaving
back home. Bet didn't mind the low pay, or the hours—she started
her regular customers' monthly washes at four in the morning
and sometimes didn't finish till midnight—or even the state of
her hands, reduced to pigs' trotters by the time she was twenty.
Laundry was what she knew. Suggesting that she do something
else would be like saying she could change the shape of her face.
She continued to be astonished that not only was Maggie not
very good at laundry, she was also not interested in learning to
do it.

"Where've you been, then?" Bet Butterfield said suddenly, as if
she had just woken up.

"Nowhere," Maggie said. "Here, ironing."

"No, just now you were out back, while the iron was heating."
It was surprising, the little things Bet Butterfield noticed when so
often she seemed to be paying no attention.

"Oh. I was just in the garden for a minute, lookin' at Astley's
people."

Bet Butterfield glanced at the pile of sheets still to do; she'd
agreed to take them home to iron for an extra shilling. "Well, stop
spyin' and get ironin'—you only done two."

"And a half." Maggie banged her iron across the sheet on the
board. She only had to weather Bet Butterfield's scrutiny for a little longer before her mother would lose interest and shut off her
probing questions.

Indeed, Bet Butterfield's eyes suddenly dropped and her whole
face went slack, like a fist unclenching. She reached out for the

iron. Maggie set it down and her mother took it up and began ironing so naturally she might have been walking or brushing her hair
or scratching her arm. "Bring us some beer, would you, duck,"
she said.

"None here," Maggie announced, delighted with the errand,
and the timing—for Jem was just now peering through the gap in
the back fence. "I'll just pop to the Pineapple." She picked up a
tankard from the sideboard and headed for the back door.

"Don't push on that fence! Go round!" Bet Butterfield called.

But Maggie had already squeezed through the gap.

~ *2* ~

"Where you been?" she greeted Jem. "I been waitin' for you for
hours!"

"We was just bending a chair arm. It be easier with two. Anyway, I'm here now."

Since the night on Westminster Bridge, Jem and Maggie had
spent much of their free time together, with Maggie introducing
Jem to her favorite places along the river and teaching him how to
get about on the streets. While she irritated him sometimes with
her superior knowledge, he knew that Maggie was also giving him
the confidence to explore and extend the boundaries of his world.
And he found he wanted to be with her. Growing up in the
Piddle Valley he had played with girls, but never felt about them
the way he had begun to about Maggie—though he would never tell
her so.

"You know we missed Miss Devine," Maggie remarked as they
crossed Astley's field.

"I saw a bit of it. Ma were watching from our window."

"She didn't fall, did she?"

"No—and just as well, as there weren't a net or cushion. How do she do it, anyway? Walk up a rope like that, and so smooth?"

Miss Laura Devine's act included, apart from her celebrated twirls and swings, a walk up a rope left slack rather than pulled tight. She made it look as if she were strolling through a garden, pausing now and then to admire the flowers.

"D'you know, she's never fallen," Maggie said. "Not once. Everybody else made mistakes in their acts—I even saw John Astley fall off his horse once! But not Miss Devine."

They reached the wall at the bottom of Miss Pelham's garden, a sunny spot where they often met to sit and watch the goings-on around Philip Astley's house. Maggie set down the tankard and they squatted with their backs against the warm bricks. From there they had a perfect view of the circus acts.

Occasionally, when the weather was good, Philip Astley had his performers rehearse in the yard in front of Hercules Hall. It was a way not only of emptying the amphitheatre so that it could be cleaned, and refreshing stale acts by rehearsing them in a new location, but also of giving his neighbors an impromptu thanks for putting up with the disruption the circus's presence inevitably caused the area. The day was never announced, but the moment jugglers wandered into the field and began tossing flaming torches back and forth, or a monkey was placed on a horse's back and sent galloping around the yard, or, as today, a rope was strung between two poles and Miss Laura Devine stepped out onto it, word went out, and the field quickly filled with onlookers.

As Maggie and Jem settled into place, tumblers began turning backflips across the yard and building a human pyramid, first kneeling, then standing on one another's shoulders. At the same time, horses were led out into the field and several riders—not John Astley, however—began practicing a complicated maneuver in which they jumped back and forth between saddles. Jem enjoyed watching the acts in these informal surroundings more than at the amphitheatre, for the performers were not trying quite so hard, and they stopped to rework moves, breaking the illusion he had found so hard to accept during a performance. They also made mistakes he found endearing—the boy at the top of the human pyramid slipped and grabbed a handful of hair to stop himself, making the owner of the hair yelp; a rider slid right off the back of his saddle and landed on his bum; the monkey jumped from its horse and climbed to the roof of Hercules Hall, where it refused to come down.

While they watched, Jem answered questions about Piddletrent-hide, a place that seemed to fascinate Maggie. In true city fashion, she was particularly amused by the notion that there was so little choice in the village—just one baker, one tailor, one miller, one blacksmith, one vicar. "What if you don't like the vicar's sermons?" she demanded. "Or the baker's bread's too hard? Or you don't pay the publican in time an' he won't serve you any more beer?" The Butterfields had had plenty of experience with owing money and having shopkeepers banging on their doors demanding payment. There were several businesses in Lambeth—pie shops, taverns, chandlers—they could no longer go to.

"Oh, there be more'n one pub. There's the Five Bells, where Pa goes, the Crown and the New Inn—that be in Piddlehinton, next village along. And if you want a different sermon, there be a church in Piddlehinton too."

"Another Piddle! How many other Piddles are there?"

"A few."

Before Jem could list them, however, a disturbance broke in on their conversation. Wandering among the various performers in the Hercules Hall yard was a boy dragging a heavy log attached to his leg, of the sort used to keep horses from straying. A cry arose near him, and when Jem and Maggie looked over they saw Mr. Blake standing over him. "Who has put this hobble on you, boy?" he was shouting at the terrified lad, for in his anger—even though it was not meant for the boy—Mr. Blake could be frightening, with his heavy brow contorted, his prominent eyes glaring like a hawk's, his stocky body thrust forward.

The boy could not answer, and it was left to one of the jugglers to step forward and say, "Mr. Astley done it, sir. But—"

"Loose him at once!" Mr. Blake cried. "No Englishman should be subjected to such a misery. I would not treat a slave like this, no, nor even a murderer—much less an innocent child!"

The juggler, similarly intimidated by Mr. Blake's manner, melted into the crowd that had gathered, Maggie and Jem among them; and as no one else stepped forward to help, Mr. Blake himself knelt by the boy and began to fumble with the knots in the rope that attached the log to his ankle. "There you are, my boy," he said, throwing off the rope at last. "The man who has done this to you is not fit to be your master, and a coward if he does not answer for it!"

"Is someone calling me a coward?" boomed Philip Astley's unmistakable circus voice. "Stand and call me that to my face, sir!" With those words he pushed through the crowd and stepped up to Mr. Blake, who rose to his feet and stood so close to the other man that their bellies almost touched.

"You are indeed a coward, sir, and a bully!" he cried, his eyes blazing. "To do such a thing to a child! No, Kate," he growled at Mrs. Blake, who had joined the circle of spectators and was now pulling at her husband's arm. "No, I will not stand down to intimidation. Answer me, sir. Why have you shackled this innocent?"

Philip Astley glanced down at the boy, who was in tears by now with the unwanted attention, and in fact was holding on to the rope as if he did not want to let it go. A small smile played across Philip Astley's lips, and he took a step back, the flames of his anger quenched. "Ah, sir, it is the hobble you're objecting to, is it?"

"Of course I'm objecting to it—any civilized man would! No

one deserves such treatment. You must desist, and make amends, sir. Yes, apologize to the lad and to us too, for making us witness such degradation!"

Rather than reply in kind, Philip Astley chuckled—a response that made Mr. Blake bunch his fists at his side and lunge forward. "Do you think this is a jest, sir? I assure you it is not!"

Philip Astley held up his hands in a placatory gesture. "Tell me, Mr.—Blake, is it? My neighbor, I believe, though we have not met, for Fox collects the rent from you, don't you, Fox?" John Fox, watching the encounter from the crowd, gave a laconic nod. "Well, Mr. Blake, I should like to inquire: Have you asked the boy why he's wearing the log?"

"I don't need to ask," Mr. Blake replied. "It is clear as day that the child is being punished in this barbarous manner."

"Still, perhaps we should hear from the lad. Davey!" Philip Astley turned his foghorn toward the boy, who did not cower from it as he had from Mr. Blake's twisted brow and fiery eyes, for he was used to Astley's boom. "Why were you wearing the log, lad?"

" 'Cause you put it on me, sir," the boy replied.

"D'you see?" Mr. Blake turned to the crowd for support.

Philip Astley held up a hand again. "And why did I put it on you, Davey?"

"So's I could get used to it, sir. For the show."

"Which show is that?"

"The panto, sir. *Harlequin's Vagaries.*"

"And what part are you playing in this panto—which, by the way, will be the centerpiece of the new program and will feature John Astley as the Harlequin!" Philip Astley couldn't resist an opportunity to promote his show, and directed this last remark at the crowd.

"A prisoner, sir."

"And what are you doing now, Davey?"

"Rehearsin', sir."

"Rehearsing," Philip Astley repeated, turning with a flourish back to Mr. Blake, who was still glaring at him. "You see, Davey was rehearsing a part, sir. He was pretending. You, sir, of all people will understand that. You are an engraver, are you not, sir? An artist. I have seen your work, and very fine it is too, very fine. You capture an essence, sir. Yes, you do."

Mr. Blake looked as if he did not want to be affected by this flattery but was nonetheless.

"You create things, do you not, sir?" Philip Astley continued. "You draw real things, but your drawings, your engravings are not the thing itself, are they? They are illusions, sir. I think despite our differences"—he glanced sideways at Mr. Blake's plain black coat as against his own red one, with its gleaming brass buttons that his nieces polished daily—"we are in the same business, sir: We are both dealers in illusions. You make 'em with your pen and ink and graver, while I"—Philip Astley waved his hands at the people around him—"I make a world out of people and props, every night at the amphitheatre. I take the audience out of their world of cares and woes, and I give 'em fantasy, so they think they are somewhere else. Now, in order to make it look real, sometimes we have to *do* real. If Davey here is to play a prisoner, we get him to drag a prisoner's hobble. No one would believe in him as a prisoner if he were just dancing about, now, would they? Just as you make your drawings from real people—"

"That is not where my drawings come from," Mr. Blake interrupted. He had been listening with great interest, and now spoke more normally, the sting of anger drawn from him. "But I understand you, sir. I do. However, I see it differently. You are making a distinction between reality and illusion. You see them as opposites, do you not?"

"Of course," Philip Astley replied.

"To me they are not opposites at all—they are all one. Young Davey playing a prisoner *is* a prisoner. Another example: My brother Robert, standing over there"—he pointed to an empty patch of sunlight, which everyone turned to stare at—"is the same to me as someone whom I may touch." He reached out and flicked the sleeve of Philip Astley's red coat.

Maggie and Jem gazed at the empty spot, where dust from the yard was floating. "Him an' his opposites," Maggie muttered. Even a month later she still felt the sting of Mr. Blake's questions on Westminster Bridge, and her inability to answer them. She and Jem had not discussed their conversation with the Blakes; they were still trying to understand it.

Philip Astley was also not inclined to take on such heady topics. He gave the dusty spot a perfunctory glance, though clearly Robert Blake was not there, then turned back to Mr. Blake with a quizzical look, as if trying to think how to respond to this unusual observation. In the end, he decided not to probe and perhaps be drawn further into uncharted territory, which would take more time and patience than he had to navigate through. "So you see, sir," he said, as if there had been no digression, "Davey is not being punished with his log. I can understand your concern, sir, and how it must have looked to you. It is very humane of you. But I can assure you, sir: Davey is well looked after, aren't you, lad? Off you go, now." He handed the boy a penny.

Mr. Blake was not finished, however. "You create worlds each night at your amphitheatre," he announced, "but when the audience is gone and the torches have been blown out and the doors locked, what is left but the memory of them?"

Philip Astley frowned. "Very fine memories they are, sir, and nothing wrong with them—they see a man through many a cold, lonely night."

"Undoubtedly. But that is where we differ, sir. My songs and pictures do not become memories—they are always there to be looked at. And they are not illusions, but physical manifestations of worlds that do exist."

Philip Astley looked about himself theatrically, as if trying to catch sight of the back of his coat. "Where do they exist, sir? I have not seen these worlds."

Mr. Blake tapped his brow.

Philip Astley snorted. "Then you have a head teeming with life, sir! Teeming! You must find it hard to sleep for the clamor."

Mr. Blake smiled directly at Jem, who happened to be in his line of vision. "It is true that I have never needed much sleep."

Philip Astley wrinkled his brow and stood still in thought, a pose highly unusual for him. The crowd began to shift restlessly. "What you are saying, sir, if I understand you," he said at last, "is that you are taking ideas in your head and making them into something you can see and hold in your hand; while I am taking real things—horses and acrobats and dancers—and turning them into memories."

Mr. Blake cocked his head to one side, his eyes fastened on his opponent. "That is one way to consider it."

At that Philip Astley shouted with laughter, clearly pleased to have had such a thought all on his own. "Well then, sir, I would say that the world needs us both, don't it, Fox?"

John Fox's mustache twitched. "That may well be, sir."

Philip Astley stepped forward and extended his hand. "We will shake hands on it, Mr. Blake, won't we?"

Mr. Blake reached over and took the circus man's proffered hand. "We will indeed."

When Mr. Blake and Philip Astley had said their farewells, Mrs. Blake took her husband's arm and they walked toward the alley without speaking to Jem or Maggie or even acknowledging them.

Maggie watched them leave with a feeling of deflation. "Could've said hallo, or at least good-bye," she muttered.

Jem felt similarly, but did not say so. He walked with Maggie to sit back against the wall where they had been before Mr. Blake arrived. There was not much to see, however—the argument between Philip Astley and Mr. Blake seemed to be a signal to the performers to take a break. The tumblers and horse riders had stopped, and there was only a troupe of dancers rehearsing a scene from the upcoming pantomime. They watched for a few minutes before Maggie stretched, like a cat rearranging itself mid-nap. "Let's do summat else."

"What, then?"

"Let's go and see the Blakes."

Jem frowned.

"Why not?" Maggie persisted.

"You said yourself that he didn't say hallo to us."

"Maybe he didn't see us."

"What would he want with us, though? We wouldn't be any interest to him."

"He liked us well enough when we were up on the bridge. Anyway, don't you want to see inside? I bet he has strange things in there. Did you know he's got the whole house? The whole house! That's eight rooms for him and his wife. They han't any children, nor even a maid. I heard they had one, but she got scared off by him. He do stare with them big eyes, don't he?"

"I would like to see the printing press," Jem admitted. "I think I heard it the other day. A great creaking noise it made, like roof timbers when a thatcher's climbing on them."

"What's a thatcher?"

"Don't you—" Jem caught himself. Though he was constantly amazed by the things Maggie didn't know, he was careful not to say anything. Once, when he teased her for thinking that cowslips referred to animals falling, she wouldn't speak to him for a week. Besides, there was no thatch in London; how could she be expected to know what it was? "Dorset houses have thatched roofs," he explained. "Dried straw bound together all tight and laid over timbers."

Maggie looked blank.

"It's like if you took a bundle of straw and made it even and straight, then laid it on the roof instead of wood or slate," Jem elaborated.

"A straw roof?"

"Yes."

"How can that keep the rain out?"

"It do well, if the straw be tight and even. Have you not been out of London?" He waved his hand vaguely south. "It's not so far to proper countryside. There be thatched roofs just out of London— I remember when we first came. We could go out one day and see 'em."

Maggie jumped up. "I don't know the way out there."

"But you could find the way." Jem followed her along the wall. "You could ask."

"And I don't like bein' alone out on them little lanes, with no one round." Maggie shuddered.

"I'd be with you," he said, surprised by his protectiveness toward her. He had not felt that way about anyone but Maisie— though this was not exactly that brotherly feeling. "'Tis nothing to be afraid of," he added.

"I an't afraid, but I don't fancy it. It'd be boring out there." Maggie looked around and brightened. Stopping where the wall backed onto the Blakes' garden, she pulled her mop cap from her wavy dark hair and threw it over the wall.

"Why'd you do that?" Jem yelled.

"We need an excuse to go and see 'em. Now we have one. C'mon!" She ran along the back wall and through the alley to Hercules Buildings. By the time Jem caught up with her, she was knocking on the Blakes' front door.

"Wait!" he shouted, but it was too late.

"Hallo, Mrs. Blake," Maggie said when Mrs. Blake opened the door. "Sorry to trouble you, but Jem's thrown my cap over the wall into your garden. Is it all right if I fetch it?"

Mrs. Blake smiled at her. "Of course, my dear, as long as you don't mind a few brambles. It's gone wild back there. Come in." She opened the door wider and let Maggie slip inside. She gazed at Jem, who was hesitating on the step. "Are you coming in too, my dear? She'll need help finding her cap."

Jem wanted to explain that he had not thrown Maggie's cap, but he couldn't get the words out. Instead he simply nodded, and stepped inside, Mrs. Blake shutting the door behind them with a brisk slam.

He found himself in a passage that led back through an archway to a set of stairs. Jem had the odd feeling that he had been in this passage before, though it had been darker. A doorway to his left was open and threw light into the corridor. That shouldn't be open, he thought, though he didn't know why. Then he heard the rustle of Mrs. Blake's skirts behind him, and the sound reminded him of another place, and he understood: This house was the mirror image of Miss Pelham's; this was the passage, and that the set of stairs that he used every day. Hers were darker because she kept the door closed that led into her front room.

Maggie had already disappeared. Although he knew how to get to the garden—like Miss Pelham's, you passed through an archway, then jogged around the staircase and down a few steps—Jem felt he shouldn't be leading the way through someone else's house. He stepped into the doorway of the front room so that Mrs. Blake could pass, glancing inside as he did.

This was certainly different from Miss Pelham's, and from any room he'd seen in Dorsetshire too. On first coming to London the Kellaways had had to get used to different sorts of rooms: They were squarely built, with more right angles than an irregular Dorset cottage room, walls the thickness of a brick rather than as wide as your forearm, larger windows, higher ceilings, and small grates with marble mantelpieces rather than hearths with open fires. The smell of coal fires was new too—in Dorsetshire they had an abundant and free wood supply—and with it the constant smoke that fogged up the city and made his mother's eyes go red.

But the Blakes' front room was different from either a snug, crooked Piddle Valley kitchen or Miss Pelham's front parlor with its caged canary, its vases of dried flowers, its uncomfortable sofa stuffed with horsehair, and its low armchairs set too far apart. Indeed, here there was no place to sit at all. The room was dominated by the large printing press with the long star-shaped handle that Jem had seen from the street. It stood a little taller than Jem, and looked like a solid table with a small cabinet sitting on it. Above the smooth, waist-high plank hung a large wood roller, with another underneath. Turning the handle must move the rollers, Jem worked out. The press was made of varnished beech, apart from the rollers, which were of a harder wood, and was well worn, especially on the handles.

The rest of the room was organized around the press. There were tables full of metal plates, jugs, and odd tools unfamiliar to Jem, as well as shelves holding bottles, paper, boxes, and long thin drawers like those he had seen in a print shop in Dorchester. Lines of thin rope were strung across the room, though nothing hung from them at the moment. The whole room was laid out carefully, and was very clean. Mr. Blake was not there, however.

Jem stepped out of the front room and followed Mrs. Blake. The back room door was shut, and he sensed a muscular presence behind it, like a horse in a stable stall.

Maggie was down near the bottom of the garden, picking through a mass of brambles, nettles, thistles, and grasses. Her cap had got caught on a loop of bramble well off the ground and was signaling to her like a flag of surrender. She jerked it free and hurried back toward the house, stumbling over a bramble and scratching her leg. As she reached out to steady herself, she brushed against a nettle and stung her hand. "Damn these plants," she muttered, and slashed at the nettle with her cap, stinging her hand even more. "Damn damn damn." Sucking her hand, she stomped out of the wildness and into the patch of garden near the house, where there were orderly rows of seedlings planted—lettuce, peas, leeks, carrots, potatoes—and Jem inspecting them.

He looked up. "What's wrong with your hand?"

"Damned nettle stung me."

"Don't suck it—that don't help. Did you find some dock leaf?" Jem didn't wait for her answer, but pushed past and picked through the undergrowth to a bank of nettles growing near the summerhouse, where two chairs had been set just inside its open doors. "Look, it's this plant with the broad leaf—it grows next to nettles. You squeeze it to get some juice, then put it on the sting." He applied it to Maggie's hand. "Do that feel better?"

"Yes," Maggie said, both surprised that the dock leaf worked and pleased that Jem had taken her hand. "How'd you know about that?"

"Lots of nettles in Dorsetshire."

As if to punish him for his knowledge, Maggie turned to the summerhouse. "Remember this?" she said in a low voice. "Remember what we saw them doin'?"

"What'll we do now?" Jem interrupted, clearly discomfited by any talk of that day they saw the Blakes in their garden. He glanced at Mrs. Blake, who was standing in the grass by the back door, hands in her apron pockets, waiting for them.

Maggie gazed at him, and he went red. She paused a moment, enjoying the power she held over him even if she wasn't entirely sure what that power was, or why she had it with him and no one else. It made her stomach flutter.

Mrs. Blake shifted her weight from one hip to the other, and Maggie looked around for something that might keep them from having to leave. There was nothing unusual about the garden, however. Apart from the summerhouse, there was a privy by the door and an ash pit for the coal ash from the grates. The grapevine

Miss Pelham was competing with grew rampant along the wall. Next to it was a small fig tree with broad leaves like hands.

"Does your fig bear any fruit?" Maggie asked.

"Not yet—it's too young. We're hoping next year it will," Mrs. Blake answered. She turned to go inside, and the children reluctantly followed.

They passed by the closed door of the back room, and again Jem wished he could go in. The open door of the front room was more inviting, however, and he paused so that he could peek in once more at the printing press. He was just summoning up the courage to ask Mrs. Blake about it when Maggie said, "Mrs. Blake, could we see that song book of Mr. Blake's you told us about up on the bridge? We'd like to see it, wouldn't we, Jem?"

Jem started to shake his head but it came out as a nod.

Mrs. Blake stopped in the hallway. "Oh, would you, my dear? Well, now, let me just ask Mr. Blake if that will be all right. Wait here—I'll just be a moment." She went back to the closed door and tapped on it, waiting until she heard a murmur before she opened the door and slipped inside.

~ *4* ~

When the door opened again, Mr. Blake himself appeared. "Hallo, my children," he said. "Kate tells me you want to see my songs."

"Yes, sir," Maggie and Jem answered in unison.

"Well, that is good—children understand them better than everyone else. 'And I wrote my happy songs / Every child may joy to hear.' Come along." Leading them into the front room with the printing press, he went over to a shelf, opened a box, and brought out a book not much bigger than his hand, stitched into a mushroom-colored wrapper. "Here you are," he said, laying it on the table by the front window.

Jem and Maggie stood side by side at the table, but neither reached for the book—not even Maggie, for all her boldness. Neither had much experience with handling books. Anne Kellaway had been given a prayer book by her parents when she married, but she was the only family member to use it at church. Maggie's parents had never owned a book, apart from those that Dick Butterfield had bought and sold, and Bet Butterfield couldn't read— though she liked having her husband read old newspapers to her when he brought them back from the pub.

"Aren't you going to look at it?" Mr. Blake said. "Go on, my boy—open it. Anywhere will do."

Jem reached out and fumbled with the book, opening it to a place near the beginning. On the left-hand page was a picture of a large burgundy and mauve flower, and inside its curling petals sat a woman wearing a yellow dress with a baby on her lap. A girl stood next to them in a blue dress with what looked to Maggie like butterfly wings sprouting from her shoulders. There were words set out in brown under the flower, with green stems and vines twined around them. The right-hand page was made up almost entirely of words, with a tree of leaves growing up the right margin, vines snaking up the left, and birds flying here and there. Maggie admired the pictures, though she couldn't read any of the words. She wondered if Jem could. "What do it say?" she asked.

"Can't you read them, child?"

Maggie shook her head. "I only went to school a year, and forgot it all."

Mr. Blake chuckled. "I didn't go to school at all! My father taught me to read. Didn't your father teach you?"

"He's too busy for that."

"Did you hear that, Kate? Did you?"

"I did, Mr. Blake." Mrs. Blake was standing in the doorway, leaning against the jamb.

"I taught Kate to read, you see. Her father was too busy as well. All right, my boy, what about you? Can you read the song?"

Jem cleared his throat. "I'll try. I only had a little schooling." He placed a finger on the page and began slowly to read:

> I have no name
> I am but two days old.—
> What shall I call thee?
> I happy am
> Joy is my name—
> Sweet joy befall thee!

He read in such stops and starts that Mr. Blake took pity on him and joined in, strengthening and quickening his voice so that Jem was trailing him, echoing his words almost like a game:

> Pretty joy!
> Sweet joy but two days old,
> Sweet joy I call thee;
> Thou dost smile,
> I sing the while
> Sweet joy befall thee.

From the picture Maggie worked out that the song was about a baby, and Mr. Blake sounded like a doting father cooing, repeating phrases and sounding daft. She wondered that he would know this was how fathers sounded when he had no children of his own. On the other hand, he clearly knew little about babies or he'd not have one smiling when only two days old; Maggie had helped with enough babies to know the smile didn't come for several weeks, until the mother was desperate for it. She didn't tell him this, however.

"Here's one you'll remember." Mr. Blake turned over a few pages, then began to recite, "When the green woods laugh with the voice of joy," the song he'd sung to them on the bridge. This time he didn't sing it, but chanted quickly. Jem tried to follow along with the words on the page, chiming in here and there with a word he was able to read or could remember. Maggie frowned, annoyed that he and Mr. Blake shared the song in a way she couldn't. She looked at the picture that accompanied it. A group of people were sitting around a table with glasses of wine, the women in blue and yellow dresses, a man colored in mauve with his back turned, raising a cup of wine. She did remember one part of the song, so that when Mr. Blake and Jem got to the line, she joined in to shout "Ha, ha, he!" as if she were in a pub singing along with others.

"Did you make this book, sir?" Jem asked when they'd finished.

"From start to finish, my boy. Wrote it, etched it, printed it, colored it, stitched and bound it, then offered it for sale. With Kate's help, of course. I couldn't have done it without Kate." He gazed at his wife and she gazed back. To Jem it felt as if they were holding the ends of a rope and pulling it tight between them.

"Did you use this press?" he persisted.

Mr. Blake put a hand on one of the handles. "I did. Not in this room, mind. We were living in Poland Street then. Across the river." He gripped the handle and pulled it so that it moved a little. Part of the wood frame groaned and cracked. "The hardest part of moving to Lambeth was getting the press here. We had to take it apart, and get several men to move it."

"How do it work?"

Mr. Blake beamed with the look of a man who has found a fellow fanatic. "Ah, it's a beautiful sight, my boy. Very satisfying. You take the plate you've prepared—have you ever seen an etched plate? No? Here's one." He led Jem to one of the shelves and picked up a flat rectangle of metal. "Run your finger over it." Jem felt raised lines and swirls on the smooth, cold copper. "So. First we ink the plate with a dauber"—he held up a stubby piece of wood with a rounded end—"then wipe it, so that the ink is only on the parts we want printed. Then we put the plate on the bed of the press—here." Mr. Blake set the plate down on the table part of the press, near the rollers. "Then we take the piece of paper we've prepared and lay it over the plate, and then blankets over them. Then we pull the handles towards us"—Mr. Blake pulled the handle a little and the rollers turned—"and the plate and paper get caught up and pass between the rollers. That imprints the ink onto the paper. Once it's gone through the rollers, we take it out—very carefully, mind—and hang it to dry on those lines above our heads. When they're dry we color them."

While Jem listened intently, touching the different parts of the press as he had been longing to, and asking Mr. Blake questions, Maggie grew bored and turned away to flip through the book once more. She had not looked much at books—since she couldn't read, she had little use for them. Maggie had hated school. She'd gone when she was eight to a charity school for girls in Southwark, just over from Lambeth, where the Butterfields had lived before. To her it had been a miserable place, where the girls were crowded into a room together to trade fleas and lice and coughs, and where beatings occurred daily and indiscriminately. After roaming the streets, she had found it hard to sit still in a room all day, and could not take in what the schoolmistress was saying about letters and figures. It was all so much duller than being out and about in Southwark that Maggie either wriggled or fell asleep, and then was beaten with a thin stick that cut through skin. The only cheering sight in the school was the day Dick Butterfield came to school with his daughter after finding yet another set of welts on her back that he had not made himself, and walloped the schoolmistress. Maggie never went back after that, and until Jem and Mr. Blake recited the song together, she had never regretted not being able to read.

Mr. Blake's book of songs surprised her, for it didn't look like any book she had ever seen. Most books contained words with the odd picture thrown in. Here, though, words and pictures were entwined; at times it was hard to tell where the one ended and the other began. Maggie turned page after page. Most of the pictures were of children either playing or with grown-ups, and all of them seemed to be in the countryside—which according to Mr. Blake was not the big, empty, open space that she'd always imagined, but contained, with hedgerows as boundaries and trees to shelter under.

There were several pictures of children with their mothers—the women reading to them, or giving them a hand up from the ground, or watching them as they slept—their childhoods nothing like Maggie's. Bet Butterfield of course could never have read to her, and was more likely to shout at Maggie to pick herself up than reach out a hand to her. And Maggie doubted she would ever wake to find her mother sitting by her bed. She looked up, blinking rapidly to rid her eyes of tears. Mrs. Blake was still leaning in the doorway, her hands in her apron. "You must have sold a lot o' these to stay in this house, ma'am," Maggie said, to hide her tears.

Maggie's statement appeared to bring Mrs. Blake out of a reverie. She pushed herself off of the doorjamb and ran her hands down her skirt to straighten it. "Not so many, my dear. Not so many. There's not many folk understand Mr. Blake, you see. Not even these songs." She hesitated. "Now I think it's time for him to work. He's had a fair few interruptions today, haven't you, Mr. Blake?" She said this tentatively, almost fearfully, as if frightened of her husband's response.

"Of course, Kate," he answered, turning away from the printing press. "You're right, as ever. I'm always getting distracted by one thing or another, and Kate's always having to pull me back." He nodded to them and stepped out of the room.

"Damn," Maggie said suddenly. "I forgot Mam's beer!" She left *Songs of Innocence* on the table and hurried to the door. "Sorry, Mrs. Blake, we've to go. Thanks for showing us your things!"

~ 5 ~

After fetching the tankard where she'd left it by the wall in Astley's field, Maggie ran to the Pineapple at the end of Hercules Buildings, Jem at her side. As they were about to go in, he looked around, and to his surprise spied his sister, pressed against the hedge across the road and stepping from one foot to the other. "Maisie!" he cried.

Maisie started. "Oh! Ar'ernoon, Jem, Maggie."

"What you doin' here, Miss Piddle?" Maggie demanded as they crossed over to her. "Weren't you goin' to say hallo?"

"I'm—" Maisie broke off as the door to the Pineapple opened and Charlie Butterfield stepped out. Her bright face fell.

"Damn," Maggie muttered as Charlie caught sight of them and wandered over. He scowled when he recognized Jem. "What you hangin' about for, country boy?"

Maggie stepped between them. "We're just gettin' Mam some beer. Jem, would you go in and get it for me? Tell 'em it's for the Butterfields and Pa'll pay for it at the end of the week." Maggie preferred to keep Jem and Charlie separate if she could; they'd hated each other from the start.

Jem hesitated—he didn't much like going into London pubs on his own—but he knew why Maggie was asking him. Grabbing the tankard, he ran across to the Pineapple and disappeared inside.

When he was gone Charlie turned his attention to Maisie, taking in her guileless face, her silly frilled cap, her slim form and small breasts pushed up by her stays. "Who's this, then?" he said. "An't you goin' to introduce us?"

Maisie smiled a Piddle Valley smile. "I'm Maisie—Margaret, like Maggie. I'm Jem's sister. Are you Maggie's brother? You two look just alike, except that one be dark and t'other fair."

Charlie smiled at her in a way that Maggie didn't trust. She could see him guzzling Maisie's innocence. "What you doin' in the street, Maisie?" he said. "You waitin' for me?"

Maisie giggled. "How could I do that when I ne'er saw you before? No, I be waiting—for someone else."

Her words seemed to make the pub door open, and John Astley stepped out, accompanied by a girl who made costumes for the circus. They were laughing, and his hand was giving her a little push in the small of her back. Without looking at the trio, they turned and walked down a path that skirted the Pineapple and led back to the Astley stables. Maggie knew there was an empty stall at the end where he often brought his women.

"Oh!" Maisie gulped, and stepped into the street to follow them.

Maggie took hold of her elbow. "No, Miss Piddle."

"Why not?" Maisie seemed to ask this innocently as she tried to pull her elbow free. Maggie glanced at Charlie, who raised his eyebrows.

"C'mon, now, Maisie. They'll be busy and won't want you hangin' about."

"He must be showing her his horse, don't you think?" Maisie said.

Charlie snorted. "Showin' her summat, that's sure."

"Best leave it," Maggie advised. "You don't want to be spyin' on him—he wouldn't like that."

Maisie turned her large blue eyes on Maggie. "I hadn't thought of that. D'you think he'd be angry with me?"

"Yes, he would. You go home, now." Maggie gave Maisie a little push. After a moment Maisie started up Hercules Buildings. "Nice to meet you," she called to Charlie over her shoulder.

Charlie chuckled. "Good Lord a day, where'd you find her?"

"Leave her be, Charlie."

He was still watching Maisie, but flicked his eyes at his sister. "What makes you think I'm goin' to do summat to her, Miss Cut-Throat?"

Maggie froze. He had never called her that before. She tried not to show her panic, keeping her eyes fixed on his face, taking in the bristles on his chin and the beginnings of a skimpy blond moustache. He was her brother, though, and knew her well, catching the flash in her eyes and the sudden stillness of her breathing.

"Oh, don't worry." He smiled his dubious smile. "Your secret's safe with me. Fact is, I didn't think you had it in you."

Jem appeared at the pub door and started over, walking carefully so that he wouldn't jog the full tankard. He frowned when he saw Maggie's tense, miserable face. "What's the matter?" He turned on Charlie. "What'd you do to her?"

"You goin' home now?" Charlie said, ignoring Jem.

Maggie frowned. "What d'you care?"

"Mam and Pa have a little surprise for you, is all." In one movement he grabbed the tankard from Jem and pulled a long drink from it, emptying a third before he thrust it back and ran off, laughter floating behind him.

~ 6 ~

When Maggie returned, Bet Butterfield was by the fire, dumping fistfuls of chopped potatoes into a pot of water. Charlie was already at the table, his long legs spread in front of him. "Chop up the onions, would you, duck," Bet Butterfield said, taking the tankard from Maggie without comment on its late arrival or the missing beer. "You cry less'n me."

"Charlie don't cry at all," Maggie retorted. Charlie did not take the hint, but continued to lounge at the table. Maggie glared at him as she began to peel the onions. Bet Butterfield cut some of the fat off the meat and dropped it into a frying pan to heat. Then she stood over her daughter, watching her work.

"Not rings," she said. "Slivers."

Maggie paused, the knife biting into half an onion. "Stop it, Mam. You said onions make you cry, so go 'way."

"How can I go 'way when you an't chopping 'em right?"

"What difference does it make how I chop 'em? Rings or slivers, they taste the same. Onions is onions."

"Here, I'll do it." Bet Butterfield grabbed at the knife. Maggie held on to it.

Charlie looked up from his contemplation of nothing and watched mother and daughter grapple with the knife. "Careful, Mam," he drawled. "Maggie's handy with a knife, an't you, Maggie?"

Maggie let go. "Shut it, Charlie!"

Bet Butterfield glanced from one to the other of her children. "What you talkin' about?"

"Nothing, Mam," they answered in unison.

Bet Butterfield waited, but neither said anything more, though Charlie smirked at the fire. Their mother began chopping the onions just as she had done the ironing—automatically, methodically, repeating an act so familiar that she didn't have to waste any thought on it.

"Mam, the fat's smokin'," Maggie announced.

"Put the meat in, then," Bet Butterfield ordered. "Don't let it burn. Your pa don't like it burnt."

"I'm not going to burn it."

Maggie burnt it. She did not like cooking any more than ironing. Bet Butterfield finished chopping the onions, scooped them up and dropped them into the pan before grabbing the spoon from her daughter. "Maggie!" she cried when she turned the meat and saw the black marks.

Charlie chuckled.

"What'd she do this time?" Dick Butterfield spoke from the doorway. Bet Butterfield flipped the meat back over and stirred the onions vigorously. "Nothing, nothing—she's just gettin' back to the ironing, an't you, duck?"

"Mind you don't scorch it," Dick Butterfield commented. "What? What?" he added as Charlie began to laugh and Maggie kicked at her brother's legs. "Listen, girl, you need to treat your family with a little more respect. Now, help your mother." He hooked a stool with his foot and pulled it under him as he sat down, a movement he had perfected from years of pub stool sitting.

Maggie scowled, but pulled the iron from the fire and went back to the pile of sheets. She could feel her father's eyes on her as she ran the iron back and forth, and for once she concentrated on smoothing the cloth systematically rather than haphazardly.

It was rare for all four Butterfields to be in the same room together. By the nature of their different work, Dick and Bet were often out at odd times, and Charlie and Maggie had grown up dipping in and out of the house as they liked, eating from pie shops or taverns or street sellers. The kitchen felt small with them all there, especially with Charlie's legs taking up so much space.

"So, Mags," Dick Butterfield said suddenly, "Charlie tells us you was out with the Kellaway boy when you was meant to be gettin' beer for your mam."

Maggie glowered at Charlie, who smiled.

"You spend all your time runnin' round with Dorset boys," her father continued, "while your mam an' me is out workin' to put food in your mouth. It's time you started to earn your keep."

"I don't see Charlie working," Maggie muttered into her ironing.

"What's that?" Charlie growled.

"Charlie don't work," Maggie repeated more loudly. "He's years older'n me and you're not sendin' him out to work."

Dick Butterfield had been batting a piece of coal back and forth on the table, and Bet Butterfield was holding the pan over the pot and pushing the meat and onions in to join the potatoes. Both paused what they were doing and stared at Maggie. "What you mean, gal? Course he works—he works with me!" Dick Butterfield protested, genuinely puzzled.

"I meant that you never had him apprenticed, to a trade."

Charlie had been looking smug, but now he stopped smiling.

"He *is* apprenticed, to *me*," Dick Butterfield said quickly, with a glance at his son. "And he's learned plenty about buying and selling, han't you, boy?"

It was a sore point with Charlie. They'd not had the fee needed to have him apprenticed at thirteen, for Dick Butterfield had been in prison then. He'd done two years for trying to pass off pewter as silver, and by the time he'd come out and recovered his business, Charlie was a fifteen-year-old boor who slept till noon and spoke in grunts. The few tradesmen who might have been prepared to take on an older boy spent just a minute in his company and made their excuses. Dick Butterfield was only able to call in one favor, and Charlie lasted all of two days at a blacksmith's before he burnt a horse while playing with a hot poker. The horse dispatched him for the blacksmith by kicking him unconscious; he bore the scar through one eyebrow from that blow.

"It an't Charlie we're talkin' about here, anyway," Dick Butterfield declared. "It's you. Now, your mam says it's no good you doin' the laundry with her, as you haven't got the knack of it, have you? So I've asked about, and got you a place with a friend of mine in Southwark, makes rope. You start tomorrow morning at six. Best get a good night's sleep tonight."

"Rope!" Maggie cried. "Please, Pa, not that!" She was thinking of a woman she'd seen in a pub once whose hands were rubbed raw from the scratchy hemp she had to handle all day.

"Surprise," Charlie mouthed at her.

"Bastard!" Maggie mouthed back.

"No arguments, gal," Dick Butterfield said. "It's time you grew up."

"Mags, run next door and ask 'em for some turnips," Bet Butterfield ordered, trying to defuse the growing anger in the room.
"Tell 'em I'll get some more down the market tomorrow."

Maggie banged the iron into the coals and turned to go. If she'd
simply gone out, got the turnips, and come back, the moment might
have passed. But as she went toward the door, Charlie stretched
out a foot to trip her, and Maggie sprawled forward, banging
her shins on the table and knocking Dick Butterfield's arm so
that the piece of coal he'd been playing with flew from his hands
and dropped into the stew. "Damn, Mags, what you doing?" he
shouted.

Even then the situation could have been repaired if only her
mother had scolded Charlie for tripping her up. Instead Bet Butterfield cried, "What's the matter with you, you clumsy clod! You
tryin' to ruin my stew? Can't you do anything right?"

Maggie staggered up from the floor to come face-to-face with
Charlie's sneer. The sight made something in her snap, and she
spat in her brother's face. He jumped up with a roar, his chair flung
backward. As Maggie hopped across the room to the door, she
shouted over her shoulder, "Fuck you, the lot of you! You can take
your turnips and shove 'em straight up your arse!"

Charlie chased her out of the house and down the street, bellowing "Bitch!" all the way, and would have caught her but for a
coach rumbling along Bastille Row that she darted in front of and
that he was forced to stop for. This gave her the crucial seconds she
needed to get him off of her heels, race across Mead Row, and dive
down an alley that ran along the backs of gardens and came out
eventually across from the Dog and Duck. Maggie knew every
hidey-hole and alley in the area much better than her brother.
When she looked back, Charlie was no longer following her. He
was the sort of boy who never bothered to chase someone unless
he was sure he could catch them, for he hated being seen to lose.

Maggie hid behind the Dog and Duck for a while, listening to
the noise inside the pub and watching out for her brother. When

she felt sure that he was no longer looking for her, she crept out and began to make her way through the streets in a wide semicircle around Bastille Row. It was quiet now; people were at home eating, or in the pub. Street sellers had packed up their wares and gone; the whores were just beginning to emerge.

Eventually Maggie ended up at the river by Lambeth Palace. She sat on the bank for a long time, watching the boats going up and down in the early evening sunlight. She could hear, up along the river, the distinct sounds of Astley's Circus—music and laughter and occasional cheers. Her heart was still pounding and she was still grinding her teeth. "Damned rope," she muttered. "Piss on that."

Though she was hungry, and she would need somewhere to sleep, she didn't dare go home to face her parents and Charlie, and rope. Maggie shivered, though it was a balmy evening yet. She was used to spending time away from the house, but she'd never slept anywhere else. Perhaps Jem will let me sleep at his house, she thought. She couldn't think of another plan, and so she leapt up and ran along Church Street past Lambeth Green to Hercules Buildings. It was only when she was standing in the road across from Miss Pelham's house that Maggie faltered. No one was standing in the windows of the Kellaways' rooms, though they were propped open. She could call out or throw a pebble up to get someone's attention, but she didn't. She just stood and looked, hoping that Jem or Maisie would make it easy by spotting her and beckoning for her to come up.

After a few minutes of standing and feeling foolish, she stepped into the road again. It was getting dark now. Maggie walked down the alley between two Hercules Buildings houses that led to Astley's field. Across it was her parents' garden, where she could see a faint light through the gap in the fence. They would have eaten the stew by now. She wondered if her mother had saved any for her. Her father might have slipped to the pub to bring back more beer and perhaps an old paper or two that he would be reading out to

Bet and Charlie, if Charlie hadn't already gone to the pub himself. Perhaps the neighbors had popped around and they were catching up on the local gossip or talking about how difficult daughters could be. One of their neighbors played the fiddle—perhaps he'd brought it with him and Dick Butterfield had drunk enough beer to sing "Morgan Rattler," his favorite bawdy song. Maggie strained her ears, but couldn't hear any music. She wanted to go back, but only if she could slip in and sit with her family and not have a fuss made, and not have to say sorry, and take the beating she knew waited for her, and go the next morning and make rope for the rest of her life. That was not going to happen, and so she had to stand and watch from afar.

Her gaze fell then on the wall at the end of the Blakes' garden just to her left. She contemplated it, gauging how high it was, and what was behind it, and whether or not climbing over it was what she wanted to do.

Not far from the wall was a wheelbarrow one of Astley's nieces had been using in the kitchen garden. Maggie looked around. For once the yard was deserted, though there were figures moving about inside Hercules Hall—servants preparing a late supper for their master. She hesitated, then ran in a crouch over to the barrow and pushed it to the end of the wall, wincing at the squeak the wheel made. Then, when she was sure no one was watching, she climbed onto the barrow, pulled herself to the top of the wall, and jumped down into the darkness.

PART IV

June 1792

It was a treat for Anne and Maisie Kellaway to be able to sit out in Miss Pelham's garden to make their buttons. Miss Pelham had gone the day before to visit friends in Hampstead, taking her maid with her, and was staying the week for the air—Lambeth was unseasonably hot and the hills just north of London were likely to be cooler. In her absence the Kellaway women were taking advantage of the sunshine and the empty garden. They had brought chairs out and were sitting in the square with the white lilac in the center, surrounded by pinks. Lilac was Maisie's favorite flower; she'd longed to sniff it but had only been able to watch over it longingly from their windows as its white blossoms began to appear. Whenever she went to the privy, she wondered if she could dash across the gravel path, bury her nose in the flowers, then run back before Miss Pelham saw her. But her landlady always seemed to be lingering at the back window or in the garden itself, pacing with her cup of beef broth, and Maisie never dared. Now, though, she could sit by it for a whole morning and get her fill of its scent until next year.

Maisie leaned back in her chair and sighed as she stretched her neck, tilting her head to the left and right.

"What is't?" her mother asked, still bent over the button—a Blandford Cartwheel—she was making. "Tired already? We've hardly begun. You've only made two."

"It's not that. You know I like making buttons." Indeed, Maisie had once made fifty-four Blandford Cartwheels in one day, a record for the Piddle Valley—though a girl to the east in Whitchurch was known to make a gross of buttons a day, as Mr. Case, the button agent who came monthly to Piddletrenthide, often reminded the women who brought their finished buttons to him. Maisie was sure the girl made simpler buttons that could be done faster—Singletons and Birds' Eyes, or Dorset Crosswheels, which weren't as fiddly as Cartwheels. "It be just that I—I miss our lilac back home."

Anne Kellaway was silent for a moment, examining her finished button and using her thumbnail to distribute rows of thread more evenly so that the button resembled a tiny spider's web. Satisfied, she dropped the button in her lap with the others she had made, and picked up a new metal ring, which she began wrapping with thread right the way around the rim. Then she addressed Maisie's comment. "Lilac smells the same here, don't it?"

"No, it don't. It be smaller and has fewer flowers, and it an't so perfumed, and there be dirt all over it."

"The bush be different, but the flowers still smell the same."

"No, they don't," Maisie insisted.

Anne Kellaway did not pursue the argument; though she had—with the help of regular visits to the circus—grown more accepting of their new life in London, she understood what her daughter meant. "I wonder if Lizzie Miller's picked any elderflowers yet," she said instead. "I han't seen any out here yet. Don't know if they come out here earlier or later'n Dorsetshire. I hope Sam shows her where the early patch be up Dead Cat Lane."

"What, near the top?"

"Yes." Anne Kellaway paused, thinking about the spot. "Your father carved me a whistle from the wood of that tree when we was young."

"That were sweet. But you can't still have the whistle, Ma, can you? I never seen it."

"I lost it not long after, in the hazel wood near Nettlecombe Tout."

"How tragic!" her daughter cried. Recently Maisie had grown more sensitive to the goings-on between couples, loading them with a depth of emotion that Anne Kellaway herself felt she could never match.

She glanced sideways at her daughter. "It weren't so tragic as all that." She would never tell Maisie, but she'd lost it during a tumble with Thomas Kellaway—"priming the pump for the marriage bed," as he'd put it. Now, so many years later, it was hard to imagine why they'd done such a thing. Though she knew she must still love her husband, she felt old and numb.

"D'you think Sam has married Lizzie by now?" Maisie asked. "She got the ring in the Michaelmas pie last year, didn't she? It be time for her to marry."

Anne Kellaway snorted. "That old tale. Anyway, Sam said he would send word if he did."

"I wish we were there to see it. Lizzie'd look so pretty with flowers in her hair. What would she wear, d'you think? I'd wear white lilac, of course."

Anne Kellaway frowned as she wound the thread rapidly around the button ring. She and Maisie had been making buttons for years in their spare time, and she had always enjoyed sitting with her daughter, chatting about this and that or simply being quiet together. These days, however, she had little to add to Maisie's remarks about love and beauty and men and women. Such thoughts were far from her life now—if they had ever been close. She couldn't recall being interested in things like that when she was fourteen. Even Thomas Kellaway's courting her at nineteen had surprised her; sometimes when she'd walked with him along lanes and across fields, or lain with him in the woods where she lost her whistle, she had felt as if it were someone else in her place, going through the motions of flirting and blushing and kissing and rubbing her hands along her lover's back, while Anne Kellaway herself stood off to one side and studied the ancient furrows and dikes that underpinned the surrounding hills. Maisie's intent interest embarrassed her.

However, she too wished that she could see her eldest son married. They'd only had one letter from Sam, at the beginning of May, though Maisie, who could read and write better than the rest of the Kellaways, had set herself the task of writing to him weekly, and began her letters with a paragraph full of questions and speculation about all that might be going on in the Piddle Valley—who would be shearing their sheep, who was making the most buttons, who had been to Dorchester or Weymouth or Blandford, who'd had babies. However, though he could read and write a little—all the Kellaway children had gone for a bit to the village school—Sam was not a letter writer, or very talkative. His letter was short and poorly written, and did not answer Maisie's questions. He told them only that he was well, that he'd carved the arms for a new set of pews for the church at Piddletrenthide, and that it had rained so much that the stream running through Plush had flooded some of the cottages. The Kellaways devoured these bits of news, but there had not been enough of them, and they were still hungry.

Since they got little news from home, Anne and Maisie Kellaway could only speculate over their buttons. Had the publican sold the Five Bells as he was always threatening to do? Had the headstock holding the treble bell at the church been mended in time for the Easter Sunday peal? Had the maypole been set up in Piddletrenthide or Piddlehinton this year? And now, as they bent over their buttons: Would Lizzie Miller pick the choicest elderflowers for cordial and wear lilac in her hair at the wedding the Kellaways would miss? Anne Kellaway's eyes blurred with tears for not knowing. She shook her head and focused on her Blandford Cartwheel. She had finished wrapping the ring with thread and was now ready to create spokes to make it look like the wheel of a cart.

"What's that sound?" Maisie said.

Anne Kellaway heard a chop-chop-chopping next door. "Tha' be Mrs. Blake with her hoe," she said in a low voice.

"No, not that. There it be again—someone knocking on Miss Pelham's door."

"Go on and see who it is," Anne Kellaway said. "It may be tickets for the circus." She'd heard that the program was to change again soon, and Mr. Astley had sent them tickets every time it did. She had already begun to anticipate a knock on the door and another set of tickets thrust at her. Anne Kellaway knew that she was becoming greedy for the circus, and was perhaps relying too readily on Mr. Astley's continuing generosity with complimentary tickets. "Seats for seats!" he'd said once, delighted with the chairs Thomas Kellaway had made him.

As she went to answer the door, Maisie was smoothing her hair, biting her lips, and pulling at her dress to make it sit properly over her stays. Although a circus boy usually brought them the tickets, Maisie nursed a fantasy that John Astley himself might deliver them. She'd had a special thrill the last time the Kellaways went to the circus, when John Astley had played the Harlequin in *Harlequin's Vagaries*, and Maisie had been treated to a whole half hour of gazing at him as he sang, courted Columbine—played by newcomer Miss Hannah Smith—and danced upon his chestnut mare. Maisie had watched him with a lump in her throat—a lump that got stuck when at one point she was certain he looked at her.

When she was thinking sensibly, Maisie knew very well that John Astley was not a man she could ever expect to be with. He was handsome, cultured, wealthy, urbane—as different as could be from the sort of man she would marry in the Piddle Valley. Although she loved her father and brothers—especially Jem—they were awkward and dull next to John Astley. Besides, he provided a distraction from London, which still scared her, and from her brother Tommy's death, which she seemed to feel more acutely four months on. It had taken that long for her to acknowledge that he was not still in Piddletrenthide and might appear at any time

at Miss Pelham's door, whistling and boasting of the adventures
he'd had on the road to London.

For a brief moment, Maisie stood by the front door of no. 12
Hercules Buildings and listened to the knock, which had grown
persistent and impatient, and wondered if it could be John Astley.

It was not, but rather a woman she had not seen before. She was
of medium height, but seemed taller because of her bulk; for
though she was not fat, she was well endowed, and her arms were
like legs of lamb. Her face was round, with bright cheeks that
looked as if they'd seen too much heat. Her brown hair had been
shoved under a cap, from which it had escaped in several places
without the woman appearing to have noticed. Her eyes were both
lively and tired; indeed, she yawned in front of Maisie without
even covering her gaping mouth.

"Hallo, duck," she said. "You're a lovely one, an't you?"

"I-I'm sorry, but Miss Pelham an't here," Maisie stuttered,
flustered by the compliment but disappointed that the woman
wasn't John Astley. "She'll be back in a week."

"I don't want to see any Miss Pelham. I'm after my daughter—
Maggie, that is—and wanted to ask you lot about her. Can I
come in?"

~ 2 ~

"Ma, this be Mrs. Butterfield," Maisie announced, arriving back in
the garden. "Maggie's mother."

"Call me Bet," the woman said. "It's Maggie what I come
about."

"Maggie?" Anne Kellaway repeated, half rising from her seat
and clutching the buttons she had made. Then she realized whom
Bet meant and sank back down. "She's not here."

Bet Butterfield did not seem to have heard. She was staring into Anne Kellaway's lap. "Are them buttons?"

"Yes." Anne Kellaway had to fight the urge to cover the buttons with her hands.

"We do buttony," Maisie explained. "We used to make 'em all the time back in Dorsetshire, and Ma took some of the materials with us when we came here. She thinks maybe we can sell 'em in London."

Bet Butterfield held out her hand. "Let me see."

Anne Kellaway reluctantly dropped into Bet's rough, red hand the delicate buttons she had made so far that morning. "Those be called Blandford Cartwheels," she couldn't resist explaining.

"Lord, an't they lovely," Bet Butterfield murmured, pushing them around with a finger. "I see these on ladies' nightgowns and am always careful with 'em when I wash 'em. Is that a blanket stitch you've used on the rim?"

"Yes." Anne Kellaway held up the button she was working on. "Then I wrap the thread across the ring to make spokes for the wheel, and then backstitch round and round each spoke, so the thread fills in the space. At the end I gather it in the center with a stitch, and there be your button."

"Lovely," Bet Butterfield repeated, squinting at the buttons. "Wish I could make summat like this. I an't bad at repairs and that, but I don't know as I could manage summat this small and delicate. I'm better at washin' what's already made than makin' it. Is these the only kind of buttons you make?"

"Oh, we do all sorts," Maisie broke in. "Flat ones like these— the Dorset Wheels—we do in cartwheel, crosswheel, and honeycomb patterns. Then we do the High Tops, and the Knobs—those are for waistcoats—and the Singletons and Birds' Eyes. What others do we do, Ma?"

"Basket Weaves, Old Dorsets, Mites and Spangles, Jams, Yannells, Outsiders," Anne Kellaway recited.

"Where you going to sell 'em?" Bet Butterfield asked.

"We don't know yet."

"I can help you with that. Or my Dick can. He knows everybody, could sell eggs to a chicken, that man could. He'll sell your buttons for you. How many you got ready?"

"Oh, four gross at least," Maisie replied.

"And how much you get per gross?"

"It depends on what sort and how good they be." Maisie paused. "Won't you sit down, Mrs. Butterfield?" She gestured to her own chair.

"I will, duck, thanks." Bet Butterfield lowered herself onto the hoop-back Windsor chair that, even after ten years of daily use, did not creak when her substantial mass met its elm seat. "Now, there's a nice chair," she said, leaning back against the spindles and running her finger along the smooth curved arm. "Plain, not fussy, and well made—though I never seen chairs painted blue before."

"Oh, we paint all our chairs back in Dorsetshire," Maisie declared. "That's how folk like 'em."

"Mags told me Mr. Kellaway's a bodger. He make this one, Mrs.—?"

"Anne Kellaway. He did. Now, Mrs. Butterfield—"

"Bet, love. Everybody calls me Bet."

"Like Bouncing Bet!" Maisie exclaimed, sitting down on one of Miss Pelham's cold stone benches. "I've just thought of it. Oh, how funny!"

"What's funny, duck?"

"Bouncing Bet—it be what we call soapwort. Back in Dorsetshire, at least. And you use soapwort for your washing, don't you?"

"I do. Bouncing Bet, eh?" Bet Butterfield chuckled. "I'd not heard o' that one. Where I'm from we called it Crow Soap. But I like that—Bouncing Bet. My Dick'll start calling me that if I tell him."

"What were it you've come for?" Anne Kellaway interjected. "You said it were something to do with your daughter."

Bet Butterfield turned to her soberly. "Yes, yes. Well, you see,

I'm lookin' for her. She an't been round for a while and I'm startin' to wonder."

"How long has she been gone?"

"Two weeks."

"Two weeks! And you're only now looking for her?" Anne Kellaway couldn't imagine losing Maisie for one night in this city, much less two weeks.

Bet Butterfield shifted in her chair. This time it creaked. "Well, now, it an't as bad as that. Maybe it's been a week. Yes, that's right, just a week." At Anne Kellaway's continuing look of horror, she blustered on. "And maybe not even that long. I'm often not at home, see; what with my washing, I work sometimes through the night at people's houses and sleep during the day. There's days go by I don't see my Dick or Charlie or no one 'cause I'm out."

"Has anyone else seen her?"

"No." Bet Butterfield shifted in the chair again; again it creaked. "I'll tell you truly, we had a bit of a row and she run off. She's got a temper on her, has Mags—like her father. She's a slow fuse but once she goes off—watch out!"

Anne and Maisie Kellaway were silent.

"Oh, I know she's round," Bet Butterfield added. "I leave food out for her and that disappears right enough. But I want her back. It an't right for her to stay away so long. Neighbors are startin' to ask questions, and look at me funny—like you lot are doing."

Anne and Maisie Kellaway bowed their heads and began stitching at their Blandford Cartwheels.

Bet Butterfield leaned forward to watch their fingers at work. "Mags has been spendin' a lot of time with your boy—Jem, is it?"

"Yes, Jem. He's helping his father." Anne Kellaway nodded toward the house.

"Well, then, I come to ask if he—or any of you—has seen Maggie in the last while. Just round the streets, or by the river, or here, if she's come to visit."

Anne Kellaway looked at her daughter. "Have you seen her, Maisie?"

Maisie was holding her button and letting the thread dangle, with the needle on the end of it. The motion of the stitching tended to twist the thread so much that now and then she had to stop and let it unwind itself. They all watched as the needle spun, then slowed, and finally stopped, swinging lightly at the end of the thread.

~ *3* ~

On the other side of the wall, Maggie was lounging on the steps of the Blakes' summerhouse, looking through *Songs of Innocence*, when she heard her mother next door and sat up as if a whip had been cracked. It was a shock to hear Bet Butterfield's town crier of a voice after being lulled by the Kellaway women's Dorset accents and dull talk about the Piddle Valley.

She felt peculiar eavesdropping when the talk was about Maggie herself. Bet Butterfield sounded like someone in the market comparing the price of apples, and it took Maggie a few minutes to realize that the Kellaways and her mother were discussing *her*. She wrapped her arms around her knees and pulled them to her chest, resting her chin on them and lightly rocking back and forth in the entrance of the summerhouse.

Maggie was still surprised that the Blakes hadn't thrown her out of their garden, as she was sure her own parents would do if they found a stray girl in theirs. Indeed, Maggie tried hard to hide the first days she was there. She had a miserable time of it, though. The night she first pitched over the wall, she didn't sleep at all, shivering back among the brambles she'd tumbled into, even though it was a balmy night, and jumping at every rustle and snap as rats and foxes and cats went about their business around her. Maggie was not afraid of the animals, but their sounds made her think that people might be about, even though the Blakes' garden was well removed from the shouts from the pubs, the comings and goings around Hercules Hall, the drunken quarrels, the ruttings up against the back wall. She hated not having four walls and a roof to protect her, and toward the end of the night she crept into the summer-house, where she slept fitfully until dawn, waking with a yelp when she thought someone was sitting in the doorway. It was only a neighbor's cat, however, watching her curiously.

The next day she went across Westminster Bridge and dozed in the sun in St. James's Park, knowing the Butterfields were unlikely to go there. That night she hid in the summerhouse, this time with a blanket she'd stolen from home when no one was in, and slept much better—indeed, so well that she woke late, with the sun in her eyes and Mr. Blake sitting out on the steps of the summer-house, a bowl of cherries beside him.

"Oh!" Maggie cried, sitting up and pushing her tangled hair from her eyes. "Sorry, Mr. Blake! I—"

One look from his bright gray eyes silenced her. "Would you like some cherries, my girl? First of the season." He set the bowl next to her, then turned to look back out over the garden.

"Thanks." Maggie tried not to gobble them, though she had eaten little the last two days. As she reached toward the bowl for the fourth time, she noticed that Mr. Blake had his notebook on his knee. "Was you goin' to draw me?" she asked, trying to re-cover some of her spirit under awkward circumstances.

"Oh no, my girl, I never draw from life if I can help it."

"Why not? An't it easier than to make it up?"

Mr. Blake half turned toward her. "But I don't make it up. It's in my head already, and I simply draw what I see there."

Maggie spat a stone into her hand to join the others she held, hiding her disappointment behind the gesture. She would have liked Mr. Blake to draw her. "So what d'you see in your head, then? Children like them pictures in your book?"

Mr. Blake nodded. "Children, and angels, and men and women speaking to me and to each other."

"An' you draw 'em in there?" She pointed at the notebook.

"Sometimes."

"Can I see?"

"Of course." Mr. Blake held out his notebook. Maggie threw the cherry stones into the garden and wiped her hand on her skirt before she took the notebook, knowing without having to be told that it was important to him. He confirmed this by adding, "That is my brother Robert's notebook. He allows me to use it."

Maggie leafed through it, paying more attention to the drawings than the words. Even if she had been able to read, she would have found it hard to make out his scrawl, full of words and lines scratched out and written over, verses turned upside down, sometimes written so quickly they seemed more like black marks than letters. "Lord, what a mess," she murmured, trying to untangle the jumble of words and images on a page. "Look at all that crossin' out!"

Mr. Blake laughed. "What comes out first is not always best," he explained. "It needs reworking to shine."

Many of the drawings were rough sketches, barely recognizable. Others, though, were more carefully executed. On one page a monstrous face carried a limp body in its mouth. On another a naked man stretched across the page, calling out anxiously. A bearded man in robes and with a mournful expression spoke to another man bowing his head. A man and woman stood side by side, naked, and other naked bodies were drawn twisted and contorted. Maggie chuckled at a sketch of a man peeing against a wall, but it was a rare laugh; mostly the pictures made her nervous.

She stopped on a page filled with small drawings, of angels with folded wings, of a man carrying a baby on his head, of faces with bulging eyes and gaping mouths. At the top was a striking likeness of a man with beaded eyes, a long nose, and a crooked smile, his curly hair mussed about his head. He looked so different from the other figures—more concrete and unique—and the drawing done with such care and delicacy that Maggie knew immediately he was someone real. "Who's this, then?"

Mr. Blake glanced at the page. "Ah, that's Thomas Paine. Have you heard of him, my child?"

Maggie dredged up memories of evenings half-asleep with her family at the Artichoke. "I think so. My pa talks about him at the pub. He wrote summat what got him into trouble, didn't he?"

"*The Rights of Man.*"

"Hang on—he supports the Frenchies, don't he? Like—" Maggie cut herself off, remembering Mr. Blake's *bonnet rouge*. She had not seen him wear it recently. "So you know Tom Paine?"

Mr. Blake tilted his head and squinted at the grapevine snaking along the wall. "I have met him."

"Then you do draw real people. This an't just from your head, is it?"

Mr. Blake turned around to look at Maggie fully. "You're right, my girl. What is your name?"

"Maggie," she replied, proud that someone like him wanted to know.

"You're right, Maggie, I did draw him as he sat across from me. That was indeed one instance of drawing from life. Mr. Paine seemed to demand it. I suppose he's that sort of fellow. But I don't make a practice of it."

"So—" Maggie hesitated, not sure she should push such a man as Mr. Blake. But he looked at her inquiringly, eyebrows raised, his face open to her, and she felt that here, in this garden, she could ask things she wouldn't elsewhere. It was the beginning of her education. "In the Abbey," she said, "you was drawin' summat you saw for real. That statue—except without the clothes."

Mr. Blake gazed at her, small movements in his face accompanying his thoughts from puzzlement to surprise to delight. "Yes, my girl, I did draw the statue. But I was not drawing what was there, was I?"

"No, that's certain." Maggie chuckled at the memory of his sketch of the naked statue.

Lesson over, Mr. Blake picked up his notebook and stood, shaking his legs as if to loosen them.

The rasping scrape of a window being opened made Maggie look up. Jem was hauling up the back window next door. He saw her and Mr. Blake and froze, staring. Maggie raised a finger to her lips.

Mr. Blake did not look up at the sound the way most people would, but started toward the door. He seemed to Maggie to be interested in the world around him only when he chose to; and now he had lost interest in his garden, and in her. "Thanks for the cherries, Mr. Blake!" Maggie called. He lifted a hand in reply but did not turn around.

When he was inside, Maggie beckoned to Jem to join her. He frowned, then disappeared from the window. A few minutes later his head appeared above the wall—he had climbed up Miss Pelham's bench and was standing on its back. "What you doing there?" he whispered.

"Come over—the Blakes won't mind!"

"I can't—Pa needs me. What you doing there?" he repeated.

"I left home. Don't tell anyone I'm here—promise?"

"Ma and Pa and Maisie will see you from the window."

"You can tell Maisie, but no one else. Promise?"

"All right," Jem said after a moment.

"I'll see you later, down by Lambeth Palace."

"Right." Jem started to scramble down.

"Jem?"

He stopped. "What is it?"

"Bring us summat to eat, eh?"

And so Maggie stayed in the Blakes' garden. The Blakes said nothing about her being there—not even when she continued to stay. At first she spent most of the day out and about in Lambeth, avoiding the places her parents and brother might be, meeting up with Jem and Maisie when she could. After a while, when it became clear that the Blakes didn't mind her remaining, she began to hang about their garden more, sometimes helping Mrs. Blake with her vegetables, once with the laundry, and even doing a bit of mending, which she would never have offered to do for her mother. Today Mrs. Blake had brought *Songs of Innocence* to her and sat with her for a bit, helping to sound out words, then suggested Maggie look through it on her own while she got on with her hoe. Maggie offered to help, but Mrs. Blake smiled and shook her head. "You learn to read that, my dear," she said, "and Mr. Blake'll be more pleased with you than with my lettuces. He says children understand his work better than adults."

Now when she heard Bet Butterfield ask Anne and Maisie Kellaway if they'd seen her daughter, Maggie held her breath as she waited for Maisie's reply. She had little faith in the girl's ability to lie—she was no better than Jem at it. So when Maisie said after a pause, "I'll just ask Jem," Maggie let out her breath and smiled. "Thanks, Miss Piddle," she whispered. "London must be teachin' you summat, anyway."

When Maisie arrived upstairs, Jem and Thomas Kellaway were bending a long ash pole to make the hoop for the back of a Windsor chair. Jem didn't yet have the strength or skill to do the bending himself, but he could secure the iron pegs that held the ash his father bent around the hoop frame. Thomas Kellaway grunted and strained against the pole he had earlier steamed to make more supple; if he bent it too far it would split and be ruined.

Maisie knew better than to speak to them at this crucial stage. Instead she busied herself in the front room, rustling about in Anne Kellaway's box of buttony materials filled with rings of various sizes, chips of sheep horn for the Singletons, a ball of flax for shaping round buttons, bits of linen for covering them, both sharp and blunt needles, and several different colors and thicknesses of thread.

"One last peg, lad," Thomas Kellaway muttered. "That's it—well done." They carried the frame, with the pole wrapped around and pegged to it, over to the wall and leaned it there, where it would dry into shape.

Maisie then let a tin of horn bits drop; when it hit the floor the lid popped open and exploded, scattering a shower of rounds of horn all over the floor. "Oh!" she exclaimed, and went down on her knees to gather them up.

"Help her, Jem, we be done here," Thomas Kellaway said.

"Maggie's mother's come asking if we've seen her," Maisie whispered as Jem crouched beside her. "What do we say?"

Jem rubbed a polished gray disk of sheep horn between his finger and thumb. "It's taken her long enough to come looking, han't it?"

"Tha' be what Ma said. I don't know, Jem. Maggie seems happy where she is, but she should be with her family, shouldn't she?"

Jem said nothing, but stood up and went to the back window to look out. Maisie joined him. From there they had a clear view into the Blakes' summerhouse, where Maggie was sitting, just the other side of the wall from Anne Kellaway and Bet Butterfield.

"She's been listening to us!" Maisie cried. "She heard it all!"

"Maybe she'll go back now she knows her mother wants her."

"Dunno—she's awfully stubborn." Maisie and Jem had tried to talk Maggie into returning home, but she was adamant that she would live at the Blakes' all summer.

"She should go back," Jem decided. "She can't stay there forever. It's not fair on the Blakes, is't, having her there. We should tell Mrs. Butterfield."

"I suppose." Maisie clapped her hands. "Look, Jem, Ma's showing Mrs. Butterfield how to make buttons!"

Indeed, while Maisie was upstairs, Bet Butterfield had leaned over to watch enviously as Anne Kellaway's deft fingers wound thin thread around a tiny ring. Seeing such delicacy tempted her to rebel, just to show everyone Bet Butterfield's worn hands could do more than wring water from sheets. "Let me try one o' them fiddly things," she declared. "It'll keep me out of mischief."

Anne Kellaway started her on a straightforward Blandford Cartwheel, trying not to laugh at the laundress's fumbling fingers. Bet Butterfield had managed only to sew around the ring, however, when her buttony lesson was cut short by an unexpected sound: a sudden explosion booming through the houses on Bastille Row, across Astley's field and through the back wall. Bet Butterfield felt her chest thud, as if someone had thumped her with a cushion. She dropped the button, which immediately unraveled, and stood up. "Dick!" she cried.

The boom made Anne Kellaway's teeth chatter the way they did when she had a high fever. She too stood up, but she had the presence of mind to hang on to the buttons in her lap.

The rest of the Kellaways froze where they were in the workshop when they heard the explosion, which rattled the panes of the sash windows. "Good Lord, what was that?" Maisie cried. She and Jem peered out of the window, but could see nothing unusual apart from the reaction of others. Mrs. Blake, for instance, paused with her hoe among her lettuces and turned her head toward the sound.

Maggie jumped up immediately, though she then sat right down again—her mother might spot the top of her head if she stood, and Maggie didn't want to be discovered. "What can it be? Oh, what can it be?" she muttered, craning her neck in the direction of the blast. She heard Bet Butterfield go farther down the garden, saying, "Where'd it come from, then? Damn that laburnum—it's blockin' the view! Look, if we go down to the end of the garden we might see it. There! What did I tell you? I never seen such smoke since a house caught fire over in Southwark where we used to live—burnt so clean there weren't a trace of it afterwards. Lord, I hope Dick an't mixed up in it. I'd better get back home."

Philip Astley knew immediately what the sound was. Not normally a slugabed, he'd had vinegary wine the night before and suffered later from a rotten gut. He was lying in bed in a fitful doze, his legs tangled up in sheets, his belly resembling a shrouded barrel, when the explosion woke him right into a standing position. He registered the direction of the blast and bellowed, "Fox! Saddle my horse!"

Moments later a circus boy—there were always boys hanging about Hercules Hall waiting to run errands—was sent to rouse John Astley, who ought to have been up by now rehearsing the new program that would soon open, but had been distracted by other things and was still at home, and, indeed, naked.

Philip Astley came rushing out of his house, pulling on his coat, his trousers not fully buttoned, John Fox at his heels. At the same time another boy led out his white charger and held him while Philip Astley mounted. There was no need to ride his horse; for where he was going it would be quicker to slip around the back of Hercules Hall and across the field to an alley between some of the Bastille Row houses. That indeed was what John Fox and the circus boys would do. But Philip Astley was a circus man, and always aware of the impact he made in public. It wouldn't do for a circus owner and ex–cavalry man to appear on foot at the scene of a disaster—even one only a few hundred yards away. He was expected to be a leader, and it was better to lead from atop a horse than on the ground, puffed and red-faced from running with a belly such as his.

As part of the Astley showmanship, another circus boy brought out John Astley's chestnut mare and led her down the alley to stand in front of her owner's house. Astley Senior soon joined them outside no. 14 Hercules Buildings, and when his son did not immediately appear, he shouted at the open windows, "Get up, you bloody fool, you idiot son of mine! Do you not realize what that sound was? Tell me you care a tinker's damn about your own circus that you're meant to be managing! Show me just this once that it means more to you than your drinking and rutting!"

John Astley appeared in the doorway of his house, his hair ruffled but looking otherwise unhurried. Philip Astley's words appeared to have no effect on him. He deliberately took his time shutting the door, inflaming his father further. "Damme, John, if this is how you feel about the business, I'll cut you out of it! I will!"

At that moment there was another, smaller explosion, then a series of pops and crackles, some loud, some soft, and whooshings and high-pitched shrieks. Those noises had the effect that none of Philip Astley's words did: John Astley ran to his horse and leapt into the saddle even as the horse jumped ahead in answer to his call. He took off up Hercules Buildings at a gallop, leaving his heavier father to trot more sedately behind.

None of them looked back or they would have seen the head of Miss Laura Devine, Europe's finest slack-rope dancer, poke out of the first-floor window of John Astley's house and watch them clatter up the road and turn right onto Westminster Bridge Road. Only an old woman with a basket of strawberries saw Miss Devine's moon face hovering above the street. She held up a berry. "Nice sweet juicy strawb for you, my dear? You've already given in to temptation once. Go on, have a bite."

Miss Devine smiled and shook her head; then, with a glance up and down the street, she withdrew from sight.

At no. 6 Bastille Row, Dick and Charlie Butterfield were sitting in the kitchen, a pan of bacon between them, fishing out slices with their knives and dipping hunks of bread in the pan fat. They both jumped at the first enormous bang, coming from just the other side of the Asylum for Female Orphans, which faced the houses on Bastille Row. Moments later there was a tinkle of glass all up and down the street, as each window in the row of houses fell to the ground. Only no. 6 was spared, as it had no glass in its windows at present: Charlie had broken them one drunken evening when he'd thrown his shoes at the cat.

Now, without a word, both set down their knives, pushed back their chairs, and went out into the street, Charlie wiping at his greasy chin with his sleeve. They stood side by side in front of their door.

"Where'd it come from?" Dick Butterfield asked.

"There." Charlie pointed southeast toward St. George's Fields.

"No, it was that way, I'm sure." Dick Butterfield gestured east.

"Why'd you ask then if you're so sure?"

"Watch yourself, lad. A little respect for your pa and his hearing."

"Well, *I'm* sure it was that way." Charlie waved emphatically toward St. George's Fields.

"There's nothing could blow up that way."

"What's your way, then?"

"Astley's fireworks laboratory."

They were saved from arguing further by the sight of a cloud of smoke rising from the direction Dick Butterfield had chosen, about two hundred yards away. "Astley's," he confirmed. "He'll be in a right state. This'll be a sight to see." He hurried toward the smoke, Charlie following more slowly. Dick Butterfield looked back at his son. "Come on, lad!"

"Couldn't we finish the bacon first?"

Dick Butterfield stopped short. "Bacon! Bacon at a time like this! Christ amighty, I'm ashamed to call you a Butterfield! How often have I told you, lad, about the importance of speed? We'll get nothing from this if we dawdle and grease our lips with bacon and let others get there before us! What is it about that idea that escapes you, lad? Tell me." Dick Butterfield gazed at his son, taking in his seemingly permanent sneer, his fidgety hands, his badly wiped chin slick with grease, and worst of all, his eyes like a fire laid but unlit, not even by an explosion he ought to be curious about. Not for the first time, Dick Butterfield found himself thinking, Maggie should be here—she'd learn from this, and wishing she were a boy. He wondered where she was now. The explosion surely would flush her out and bring her running. Then he would wallop her good for running away—though he might hug her too. He turned his back on Charlie and stumped off toward the smoke. After a moment Charlie followed, still thinking of the bacon congealing in the pan at home.

The blast indeed flushed Maggie out in the end. When she heard the ruckus from Hercules Hall—circus boys running back and forth, Philip Astley shouting, John Fox giving directions—and then the crackles and shrieks began from the site of the explosion, she could stand it no longer: She was not going to miss out on the neighborhood drama, no matter if her parents saw her. She ran to the back of the Blakes' garden and hoisted herself up and over the wall, dropping to a run across Astley's field, joined there by other curious residents heading toward the smoke and the noise.

Jem watched her make her escape and knew he couldn't remain at home. "Come on, Maisie!" he shouted, pulling his sister after him down the stairs. Out in the street they heard a clattering, and first John Astley and then Philip Astley passed by on horseback. "Oh!" Maisie cried, and began to run after them. Her frilly mop cap flew off, and Jem had to stop and snatch it up before hurrying to catch up with her.

5

Every year on the fourth of June, Philip Astley provided a fireworks display for the King's birthday, setting them off from barges in the Thames at half-past ten at night, when the circus had finished. No one had asked him to take on this responsibility; he had simply begun it twenty years before, and it had become a tradition. Astley sometimes used fireworks on other occasions—at the beginning and end of the season to promote his circus, and during performances when someone important was attending. He set up a fireworks laboratory in a house on Asylum Place, down a short lane from the Asylum for Female Orphans.

The Asylum was a large, formidable building, not unpleasant to look at, on a site where Hercules Buildings, Bastille Row, and Westminster Bridge Road all met. It provided a home for two hundred girls, who were taught to read a little, and to clean, cook, wash, and sew—everything that would prepare them for lives as servants once they left the Asylum at age fifteen. They might have been stunned by losing their families, but the Asylum was a respite of sorts between that sorrow and the long drudgery that their lives were to become.

The Asylum yard was surrounded by a six-foot-high black iron fence. It was up against these bars in a corner of the yard that many of the girls and their minders were crowded, their faces all turned like sunflowers toward the fireworks house, which was now spitting and crackling and burning bright. For the girls it was as if this unusual entertainment had been laid on especially for them, with a fine spot from which to view it.

Inhabitants from surrounding houses were watching the fire too, but they were not so exhilarated by the spectacle. Indeed, those whose properties were very close to the laboratory feared their own houses would catch fire. Men were shouting; women were weeping. More people arrived all the time from neighboring streets to see what was happening. No one did anything, however: They were waiting for the right person to take charge.

He arrived on horseback with his son. By this time rockets were exploding, most of them heading sideways and smashing into the walls of the laboratory house, but one escaping up through the flames—which by now had eaten open a section of the roof—and shooting into the sky. Fireworks are impressive even in daylight, and especially when you have never seen them, as many of the orphans had not, for they were locked in at night well before any of Astley's fireworks displays on the river. A sigh arose from them as the rocket shed green sparks.

For the Astleys, however, the sparks were green tears. They dismounted from their horses at the same moment as John Fox, his half-lidded eyes opened wide on this occasion, arrived at their side. "Fox!" Philip Astley bellowed. "Have the men all got out?"

"Yes, sir," he reported, "and no injuries but for John Honor, who hurt himself escaping out of a window."

"How bad is he?"

John Fox shrugged.

"Have a boy fetch Honor's wife, and a doctor."

Philip Astley looked around and took in the situation quickly. As a military man as well as a circus owner, he was used to crises and to directing large numbers of people, many of them temperamental or under strain. A crowd of gaping men and hysterical women proved no challenge to him. He stepped naturally into his position of authority. "Friends!" he shouted over the pops of firecrackers and the hiss of fiery serpents. "We have need of your services, and quickly! Women and children, run home and fetch every bucket you can find. Quick as you can, now!" He clapped his hands, and the women and children scattered like dust blown from a mantelpiece.

"Now, men! Form a chain from the fire to the nearest well. Where is the nearest well?" He looked around and descended on a surprised man idling across the street from the blazing house. "Sir, where is the nearest well? As you can see, we need quantities of water, sir—quantities!"

The man thought for a moment. "There's one down by Shield's Nursery," he said, not quite matching Astley's sense of urgency with one of his own. He thought again. "But the closest is in there." He pointed through the fence along which the orphan girls ranged in a mass of dark brown serge.

"Open the gates, ladies, and have no fear—you are doing us a great service!" Philip Astley cried, ever the showman.

As the gates swung back, a line of men—and soon women and children, and even a few of the braver orphans—strung out across the yard to the well near the Asylum building, and began passing buckets of water along toward the fire. Philip and John Astley themselves stood at the front of the line and threw the water onto the flames, then handed the empty buckets to children who raced with them back to the beginning of the line.

It was organized so quickly and effectively, once Philip Astley had taken charge, that it was impossible for anyone standing nearby not to want to join in. Soon there were enough people for two lines and twice the buckets. Along those lines could be found Dick and Charlie Butterfield, Jem and Maisie Kellaway, Bet and Maggie Butterfield, and even Thomas and Anne Kellaway who, like Jem, had found it impossible to remain at home with so much noise going on, and had come over to see the blaze. All of them passed buckets till their arms ached, none of them knowing that there were other family members there doing the same.

The Astleys threw hundreds of buckets of water onto the flames. For a time it seemed to be helping, as the fire on one side of the ground floor was extinguished. But other flames kept finding stores of fireworks and, igniting them, sent them blasting and rocketing all over and starting fires again. Then too, the fire had spread quickly upstairs, and burning parts of the ceiling and roof kept raining downward and reigniting the bottom. Nothing could stop the destruction of the house. Eventually the Astleys admitted defeat and concentrated the contents of the buckets on either side of the house to keep the fire from spreading to other properties.

At last Philip Astley sent word to those at the well to stop drawing water. The last bucket moved along each line, and when people turned to their neighbor for the next one, as they had been doing for the last hour, they found none was being swung at them. They looked around, blinked, then began to move toward the house to see the effect of all of their work. It was dispiriting to find the building in ruins, a wrecked gap among the other houses, like a rotted tooth splintered and pulled from its neighbors. Although the fire was now out, smoke still billowed from the charred remains, darkening the air so that it seemed like dusk rather than midmorning.

~ 6 ~

There was an awkward pause after the energized organization of the firefighting. Then Philip Astley once again stepped up to the responsibility of raising spirits. "Friends, you have come to the aid of Astley's Circus, and I am forever in your debt," he began, standing as straight as he could, though the physical exertion of the last hour had taken its toll on him. "This has been a grievous, calamitous accident. Stored here were the fireworks meant for the celebration of the birthday of His Majesty the King in two days' time. But we can thank God that only one man has been injured, and because of your heroic efforts, no other properties have caught fire. Nor will Astley's Circus be affected; indeed, the show will take place this evening at the usual time of half-past six, with tickets still available at the box office. If you haven't seen it, you will have missed an event far more spectacular than this fire. I am tremendously grateful to you, my neighbors, who have worked tirelessly to keep this unfortunate incident from becoming a tragedy. I am . . ."

He went on in the same vein. Some listened to him; some didn't. Some needed to hear the words; others wanted only to sit down, to have a drink or a meal or a gossip or a sleep. People began to mill about, looking for family and friends.

Dick Butterfield stood close behind Philip Astley so that he might

overhear what the situation called for. For instance, when he heard
Philip Astley tell a man who lived in the street that he would re-
build the house immediately, Dick Butterfield began thinking of a
load of bricks he knew of down in Kennington that were just waiting to be used. In a few hours he would go down to the pub where
the brickmaker took his dinner and speak with him. There were a
few timber merchants along the river he would call on in the
meantime. He smiled to himself—though the smile disappeared
quick enough when he saw Charlie Butterfield kicking burning
embers about in the street with some other lads. Dick Butterfield
grabbed his son and pulled him out of the makeshift game. "Use
your head, you idiot! How does that look to a man who's just lost
his property for you to be making sport of it!"

Charlie scowled and slunk to a less crowded spot, away from his
father and the boys he had been with. Though he had never admitted it to anyone, he hated helping his father. The line of business
that Dick Butterfield pursued required a certain charm that even
Charlie knew he didn't have and would never develop.

Once they'd finished with the buckets, Maisie dragged Jem to
the crowd gathered around Philip Astley so that she could watch
John Astley, who stood close by, his face black with ash. Some in
the crowd who liked to speculate before the smoke had even dis-
persed were already muttering to one another that, as John Astley
was the general manager of the circus, he ought to be making the
rousing speeches rather than his father. Old Astley couldn't stay
away and let his son run the show, they whispered. Until he truly
let go, his son would continue to drink and rut his way through the
circus women, as he just had with Miss Laura Devine, Europe's
finest slack-rope dancer. That sighting at the window by the strawberry seller had already jumped beyond one set of old eyes. Gossip
spread quickly in Lambeth. It was a kind of currency, with coins
newly minted every hour. The strawberry seller held that particular coin with Miss Devine's head stamped on it, and even as she

passed buckets, the old woman was spending the coin on her neighbors.

Maisie had not heard this gossip, however, and could still look passionately on John Astley as he gazed into the distance, while his father spilled over with gratitude. The charitable might say that behind his charcoal-colored mask he was stunned by what had happened to the King's fireworks and the Astley laboratory; others would say that he simply looked bored.

When Philip Astley finished, and people were coming up to give their condolences or put forward theories as to how the fire might have started, Maisie took a gulp of air and pushed through the crowd toward John Astley.

"Maisie, what're you doing?" Jem called.

"Leave her," a voice said. "If she will make a fool of herself, there's nought you can do about it."

Jem turned to find Maggie standing beside him. "Mornin'," he said, forgetting for an instant about his foolish sister. He was still surprised at how glad he always was to see Maggie, though he tried to hide both pleasure and surprise. "We saw you leave the garden. You all right?"

Maggie rubbed her arms. "I'll be feeling them buckets in my sleep tonight. Exciting, though, wan't it?"

"I feel bad for Mr. Astley."

"Oh, he'll be all right. By Monday night he'll have added to his show a spectacle based on the explosion, with a backdrop of this"— Maggie gestured around her—"and fireworks going off to make it feel real. And John Astley will ride up and dance on his horse."

Jem had his eye on his sister standing near John Astley, her back set very straight, as it did when she was nervous. Maisie was blocking his view of John Astley's face, so he had no idea what the horseman's response to his sister was. He could only guess by the glow on Maisie's face as she turned and skipped back to him and Maggie.

"He's such a brave man!" she declared. "And so gentlemanly

with me. D'you know, he's burnt his arm from getting too near
the flames when he were throwing water, but he didn't even stop
to look at it and has only just discovered it? I"—Maisie flushed
scarlet with the thought of her daring—"I offered to bandage it for
him, but he told me not to worry, that I should find my family as
they'd be concerned for me. Weren't that nice of him?"

Jem could now see John Astley's face. He was studying Maisie's
slim form, his blue eyes glowing almost supernaturally from his
sooty face in a way that made Jem uneasy. Jem glanced at Maggie,
who shrugged and took Maisie's arm. "That's very well, Miss Piddle, but we should be gettin' you home. Look, there are your parents. You don't want 'em to see you settin' your eyes at Mr. Astley,
do you?" She pulled Maisie toward Thomas and Anne Kellaway,
who had emerged from the smoke, which was now as thick as a
winter fog. Anne Kellaway's hair was flying in every direction,
and her eyes were streaming so that she had to hold a handkerchief
to them.

"Jem, Maisie, you been here as well?" Thomas Kellaway asked.

"Yes, Pa," Jem answered. "We was helping with the buckets."

Thomas Kellaway nodded. "Tha' be the neighborly thing to do.
Reminds me of when the Wightmans' barn burnt down last year
and we did the same. Remember?"

Jem did remember that fire on the edge of Piddletrenthide, but
it was different from this one. He recalled how little effect their
buckets had on the flames, which grew as high as the nearby oak
trees once they reached the hay; after that there was little anyone
could do to stop them. He remembered the screams of the horses
trapped behind the flames and the smell of their burning flesh, and
of Mr. Wightman screaming in response and having to be held
back to keep him from running like a fool into the fire after his animals. He remembered Mrs. Wightman weeping during all the
crackles and cries. And Rosie Wightman, a girl he and Maisie had
played with sometimes in the River Piddle, catching eels and picking watercress: She watched the fire with wide, shocked eyes, and

ran away from the Piddle Valley soon after when it was discovered she'd been playing with candles out in the barn. She had not been heard of since, and Jem sometimes thought of her, wondering what became of a girl like Rosie. Mr. Wightman lost his barn, his hay and his horses, and he and his wife ended up in the workhouse at Dorchester.

Mr. Astley's fire destroyed only fireworks, whereas the Wightman fire had been an inferno that destroyed a family. The King would still be a year older whether his London subjects saw fireworks on his birthday or not. Indeed, Jem sometimes wondered how Philip Astley could spend so much time and energy on something that contributed little to the world. If Thomas Kellaway and his fellow chairmakers did not make chairs and benches and stools, people could not sit down properly, and would have to perch on the ground. If Philip Astley did not run his circus, would it make any difference? Jem could not say such a thing to his mother, however. He would never have guessed that she would come to love the circus so much. Even now she was staring through glistening eyes at the Astleys.

In a pause in conversation, Philip Astley felt her gaze on him and turned. He couldn't help smiling at the concern etched on her face—this from the woman who would not even look at him a few months ago. "Ah, madam, there is no need to cry," he said, pulling a handkerchief from his pocket and offering it to her, though it was so filthy with soot that it would not have been much use. "We Astleys have been through worse in our time."

Anne Kellaway did not accept his handkerchief, but wiped her eyes with her sleeve. "No, no, it's the smoke affects my eyes. London smoke do that." She took a step back from him, for his presence had that effect of crowding people out of their own space.

"Fear not, Mrs. Kellaway," Philip Astley said, as if she had not spoken. "This is merely a temporary setback. And I thank God that only my carpenter was hurt. He's sure to be back on his feet very soon."

Thomas Kellaway had been standing beside his wife, his eyes on the smoking wreck of the house. Now he spoke up. "If you need any help in the meantime, sir, with the wood and that, I and my boy would be happy to give a hand, wouldn't we, Jem?"

His innocent offer to a neighbor in need, made in his soft voice without any underlying calculation, had more impact than he could ever have imagined. Philip Astley looked at Thomas Kellaway as if someone had just turned up the lamps very bright. The pause before he answered was not from rudeness, but because he was thinking in this new light. He glanced at John Fox, who as ever stood at his elbow, his eyes once more half-lidded now that the fire was out. "Well, now," he began. "That is a very kind offer, sir, a very kind offer indeed. I may well take you up on that. We shall see. For the moment, sir, madam"—he bowed to Anne Kellaway— "I must take my leave of you, as there is so much to be getting on with. But I will see you again very soon, I expect. Very soon, indeed, sir." He turned away with John Fox to rejoin his son and begin giving orders to those who awaited them.

Jem had listened to his father and Philip Astley in stunned silence. He couldn't imagine himself and his father working for someone else rather than for themselves. Maisie's face lit up, however, for she was already picturing herself finding reasons to visit her father and brother at the amphitheatre and staying to see John Astley. Anne Kellaway too wondered if this meant she might be able to escape to the circus even more often.

During this discussion, Dick Butterfield had spotted Maggie standing with the Kellaways and began stealing toward her. He had been gathering himself to pounce—if he didn't get a firm grip on the girl, she was likely to run off—when Thomas Kellaway's offer to Philip Astley pulled him up short. Dick Butterfield thought of himself as the master of the honeyed phrase and timely suggestion, pitched to draw the right response and drop the coin into his pocket. He was good at it, he thought, but Thomas Kellaway had just outmaneuvered him. "Damn him," he muttered, then lunged for Maggie.

Caught unawares, she yelled and tried to pull away from her father. "You got her, then?" Bet Butterfield called, pushing through the crowd to her husband's side. "Where in hell have you been, you little minx?" she roared at her struggling daughter, and slapped her. "Don't ever run away from us again!"

"Oh, she won't," Dick Butterfield declared, renewing his grip on Maggie. "She'll be too busy working, won't you, Mags? Rope not to your liking, eh? Not to worry—I found another place for you, see. Mate o' mine runs the mustard manufactory down by the river. You'll be working there come Monday. Keep you out of mischief. It's time you started bringin' in a wage—you're old enough now. Till then, Charlie'll keep an eye on you. Charlie!" he shouted, casting his eye about.

Charlie sauntered over from the wall he'd been squatting against. He tried to glare at Jem and smile at Maisie at the same time, but it came out as a confused smirk. Jem glared back at him; Maisie studied her toes.

"Where you been, boy?" Dick Butterfield cried. "Get hold of your sister and don't let her out of your sight till you take her to the mustard works Monday morning."

Charlie grinned and grabbed Maggie's other arm with both hands. "Sure, Pa." When no one was looking, he twisted her skin so that it burnt.

With her parents there, Maggie couldn't kick him. "Damn you, Charlie!" she cried. "Mam!"

"Don't talk to me, girl," Bet Butterfield huffed. "I want nothing to do with you. You been one hell of a worry to us."

"But—" Maggie stopped when Charlie made the sign of slitting his throat with his finger. She closed her eyes and thought of the attention she'd had from the Blakes, and of the peace she'd known briefly in their garden, where she could put from her mind thoughts of Charlie and what had gone on in the past. She'd known it was too good to last, that eventually she would have to leave the garden and return to her parents. She just wished she'd had the chance to decide for herself when that would happen.

Tears seeped from the corners of her eyes, and though she rubbed them away quickly with finger and thumb, the Kellaway children spotted them. Maisie gazed at Maggie sympathetically, while Jem dug his fingernails into his palms. He had never felt so much like hitting someone as he did Charlie Butterfield.

Bet Butterfield glanced about, suddenly aware of her family's public display of disunity. "Hallo again," she said, spying Anne Kellaway and trying to get back to safe neighborly chitchat. "I'll be coming round to finish that Blandfield Wagon Wheel one o' these days."

"Cartwheel," Anne Kellaway corrected. "Blandford Cartwheel."

"That's right. We'll be seeing you. Shall we, Dick?" She took her husband's arm.

"Dog and Duck, I think, gal."

"That'll do me."

The Butterfields went one way, the Kellaways the other. Jem caught Maggie's eye as Charlie pulled her along, and they held each other's gaze until she was yanked out of sight by her brother.

None of them noticed Mr. Blake sitting on the steps of one of the houses across from the fire; Mrs. Blake stood behind him, leaning against the house. He had his little notebook resting on his knee and was scribbling rapidly.

~ 7 ~

At five on Sunday morning, John Honor, head carpenter for Astley's Circus, died of injuries sustained from the fireworks laboratory explosion. After paying his condolences to the widow, Philip Astley caught the Kellaways as they were leaving for the early church service at St. Mary's, and offered Thomas Kellaway a position as carpenter for his circus.

"He will," Anne Kellaway answered for the family.

PART V

September 1792

"Friends, gather round now—I want to have a word with you. That's all of you, in the ring, please." Philip Astley's thundering voice could be heard throughout the amphitheatre. Jem and Thomas Kellaway glanced at each other and laid down the tools they had been gathering up—it was Saturday noon and they were just finishing their work for the day. They made their way with the other carpenters from backstage to the ring, where they were joined by grumbling acrobats, riders, costume girls, grooms, circus boys, musicians, dancers, and all the rest of the circus workers. It was not unheard of for Philip Astley to call a meeting of the company, but he did not normally choose to do so when they were about to have an afternoon off before the evening performance. His timing suggested that the news would not be good.

Thomas Kellaway did not join in the grumbling. Though he had now been working for the circus for three months, and was glad of the regular wages, he still felt too new to say anything unless asked directly. Instead he simply stood next to the stage with Jem and the other carpenters and kept quiet.

John Fox leaned against the barrier that separated the pit seats from the circus ring, and continued to chew on something so that his long mustache wriggled. His eyelids were so low that he seemed to be asleep where he stood; he could also conveniently avoid eye contact with anyone. John Astley was sitting in the pit with some of the other horsemen, his riding boots—cleaned and polished daily by one of his cousins—propped up on a railing, as he picked at a thumbnail.

"Fox, is everyone here? Good. Now, friends, listen to me." Philip Astley batted his hands up and down to quiet the noises of discontentment. "Boys and girls, first I would like to say that you have been doing an impressive job—a most impressive job. Indeed, I believe this season will go down as one of our very best. For sheer professionalism as well as dazzling entertainment, no one can touch us.

"Now, my friends, I must share some news with you that will affect us all. As you are aware, these are trying times. Dangerous times, we might say. Revolutionary times. Over the summer there has been growing turbulence in France, has there not? Well, good people of the circus, it may well be reaching a bloody climax. Perhaps some of you have heard the news today from Paris, where there are reports of twelve thousand citizens killed. Twelve thousand royalists, friends—people loyal to king and family! People like you and me! Not twelve, not twelve hundred, but twelve thousand! Do you have any idea how many people that is? That is twelve nights' audience, sir." He gazed at the singer Mr. Johannot, who stared back at him with wide eyes. "Imagine twelve audiences piled up in the streets around us, ladies." Philip Astley turned toward a group of seamstresses who had been giggling in their seats, and who froze when he glared at them. "Slaughtered mercilessly, men, women, and children alike—throats cut, bellies slashed open, their blood and entrails pouring down the gutters of Westminster Bridge Road and Lambeth Marsh." One of the girls burst into tears, and two others followed.

"Well may you cry," Philip Astley continued over their sobs. "Such actions so close to our own shores pose a grievous threat to us all. Grievous, dear colleagues. The imprisonment of the French king and his family is a challenge to our own royal family. Watch and weep, friends. It is an end to innocence. England cannot let this challenge to our way of life pass. Within six months we will be at war with France—my instincts as a cavalryman tell me so. Kiss your fathers and brothers and sons good-bye now, for they may soon be off to war."

During the pause that followed as Philip Astley let his words

sink in, irritated looks and grumbles were replaced with solemn
faces and silence, apart from the weeping from the costume bench.
Thomas Kellaway looked around in wonder. The revolution in
France was certainly discussed more in London pubs than at the
Five Bells in Piddletrenthide, but he had never thought it would
ever affect him personally. He glanced at Jem, who had just turned
thirteen. Though too young for cannon fodder, his son was old
enough to feel the threat of being press-ganged into the army.
Thomas Kellaway had seen for himself a press-gang in action at a
Lambeth pub, drawing in a gullible youth with promises of free
pints, and then frogmarching him to a nearby barracks. Tommy
would have been a prime target, Thomas Kellaway thought. It
should be Tommy he'd be concerned about rather than Jem. But
then, if Tommy were alive to worry about, they'd still be a close,
loving family safely tucked away in the Piddle Valley, far from the
danger of press-gangs. Thomas Kellaway had not considered such
threats when he and his wife decided to come to London.

"I have been taking the measure of our audiences," Philip
Astley continued, and Thomas Kellaway pulled himself out of his
thoughts to listen. "Public entertainers must be ever vigilant to
public moods. Vigilant, my friends. I am aware that, though audiences like to be kept abreast of the state of the world, they also
come to the amphitheatre to forget—to laugh and rejoice at the
superlative wonders before their eyes, and to put out of their minds
for one evening the worries and threats of the world. This world"—
he gestured around him, taking in the ring, the stage, the seats,
and the galleries—"becomes their world.

"Even before today's terrible news, I had reached the inevitable
conclusion that the current program places perhaps too much emphasis on military spectacle. The splendid and realistic enactment
of soldiers striking camp at Bagshot Heath, and the celebration of
peace during the East India Military Divertissement—these are
scenes of which we can be justly proud. But perhaps, friends, given
the present state of affairs in France, they are *de trop*—particularly

for the ladies in the audience. We must think of their sensitive na-
tures. I have seen many members of the gentler sex shudder and
turn away from these spectacles; indeed, three have fainted in the
last week!"

"That were from the heat," the carpenter next to Thomas Kellaway muttered, though not loud enough for Philip Astley to hear.

"And so, boys and girls, we are going to replace the Bagshot
Heath spectacle with a new pantomime I have penned. It will be a
continuation of the adventures of the Harlequin my son played
earlier this season, and will be called *Harlequin in Ireland*."

A groan arose from the assembled company. Astley's Circus
had been playing to good crowds and, after several changes in program, had settled down into a happy routine that many had expected would take them right through early October to the end of
the season. They were tired of change, and content to repeat themselves each night without learning a new show, which would re-
quire a great deal of unexpected extra work. Saturday afternoon
off would certainly be canceled, for a start.

Even as Philip Astley reiterated that *Harlequin in Ireland* would
be a tonic for revolution-weary audiences, the carpenters were already heading backstage to ready themselves for immediate set
building. Thomas Kellaway followed more slowly. Even three
months into his job with the circus, he found working with so
many others overwhelming at times, and sometimes longed for
the quiet of his workshop in Dorsetshire or at Hercules Buildings,
where there had only been him and his family to make noise. Here
there was a constant parade of performers, musicians, horses, sup-
pliers of timber and cloth and oats and hay, boys running in and
out on the endless errands supplied by Philip Astley, and general
hangers-on creating chaos along with the rest of them. Above all
there was Philip Astley himself, bellowing orders, arguing with
his son about the program or Mrs. Connell about ticket sales or
John Fox about everything else.

Noise was not the only thing Thomas Kellaway had had to adjust to in his new position. Indeed, the work couldn't be more different from his chairs, and he sometimes thought he ought to tell Philip Astley that he was not suitable for the demands made on him, and admit that he had really taken the job only to satisfy his circus-obsessed wife.

Thomas Kellaway was a chairmaker—a profession which required patience, a steady hand, and an eye for the shape wood would best take. Building the sorts of things needed for Astley's Circus was a completely different use of wood. To expect Thomas Kellaway to be able do such work was like asking a brewer to trade jobs with a laundress, simply because both used water. In making chairs, the choice of wood used for each part was critical in creating a strong, comfortable, long-lasting chair. Thomas Kellaway knew his elm and ash, his yew and chestnut and walnut. He knew what would look and work best for the seat (always elm), the legs and spindles (he preferred yew if he could get it), the hoop for the back and arms (ash). He understood just how much he could bend ash before it splintered; he could sense how hard he had to chop at an elm plank with his adze to shape the seat. He loved wood, for he had been using it all his life. For scenery, however, Thomas Kellaway had to use some of the cheapest, poorest wood he had ever had the misfortune to handle. Knotty oak, seconds and ends of beech, even scorched wood salvaged from house fires—he could barely stand to touch the stuff.

Harder even than that, though, was the idea behind what he was meant to make. When he made a chair, he knew it was a chair—it looked like one, and it would be used as one. Otherwise there was no reason for him to make it. The scenery, however, was not what it was meant to be. He constructed sheets of board cut into the shapes of clouds, painted white, and hung up in the "sky" so that they looked like clouds—yet they were not clouds. He was building castles that were not castles, mountains that were not mountains, Indian pavilions that were not Indian pavilions. The only function of what he now made was to resemble something else rather than to be it, and to create an effect. Certainly it looked good, from a distance. Audiences often gasped and clapped when the curtain went up and the carpenters' creations set the scene—even if up close they were clearly just bits of wood nailed together and painted for effect. Thomas Kellaway was not used to something looking good from far away but not up close. That was not how chairs worked.

His first weeks at Astley's were not the disaster they so easily could have been, however. Thomas Kellaway was rather surprised by this, for he had never in his life worked as part of a group. The first time he appeared at the amphitheatre, the day after Philip Astley hired him, carrying his tools in a satchel, no one even noticed him for an hour. The other carpenters were busy building a shed at the back in which to store the few bits and pieces that had been salvaged from the laboratory fire. Thomas Kellaway watched them for a time; then, noting one of the carpenters going around the gallery of the theatre, tightening handrails, he found some nails and bits of wood, took up his tools, and set about making repairs in the boxes. When he'd finished, having gained in confidence, he went back to the half-built shed and quietly inserted himself into the scrum of men, handing over the right-sized plank just when it was needed, scrounging up nails when no one else could find any, catching a loose board before it hit a man. By the time the last plank for the slanted roof had been hammered into place, Thomas Kellaway had become a natural part of the team. To celebrate his arrival, the carpenters took him at noon to their favored pub, the Pedlar's Arms, just across the road from the timber yards north of Westminster Bridge. They all got drunk except for Thomas Kellaway, drinking toasts to their late head carpenter, the unfortunate John Honor. He left them to it, finally, and returned to work alone on a wood volcano that was to spew fireworks as part of the drama *Jupiter's Vengeance*.

Since then Thomas Kellaway had spent the summer keeping

quiet and working hard. It was easier, keeping quiet, for when he did open his mouth the men laughed at his Dorset accent.

Now he began to sort through his tools. "Jem, where be our compass saw?" he called. "One o' the men needs it."

"At home."

"Run and get it, then, there's a good lad."

~ *2* ~

When needed, as today, Jem helped his father in the amphitheatre; other times he joined the other circus boys hanging about to run errands for Philip Astley or John Fox. Usually they were to places in Lambeth or nearby Southwark. The few times he was asked to go farther afield—to a printer's by St. Paul's, or a law office at Temple, or a haberdasher's off St. James's—Jem passed on the honor to other boys, who were always looking for the extra penny that came with trips across the river.

Often Jem didn't know where he was meant to go. "Run to Nicholson's Timber Yard and tell them we need another delivery of beech, same size as yesterday's," John Fox would say, then turn away before Jem could ask him where the yard was. It was then that he most missed Maggie, who could have told him in a flash that Nicholson's was just west of Blackfriars Bridge. Instead he was forced to ask the other boys, who teased him equally for his ignorance and his accent.

Jem didn't mind being sent home; indeed, he was pleased to get out of the amphitheatre. September was a month he associated with being outside even more than the summer months, for it was often balmy but not stifling. September light in Dorsetshire was glorious, the sun casting its gold aslant across the land rather than beating straight down as it did in midsummer. After the frantic haying that kept the countryside constantly moving in August, September was quieter and more reflective. Much of his mother's garden was ready to eat, and the flowers—the dahlias, the Michaelmas daisies, the roses—flourished. He and his brothers and Maisie gorged on blackberries till their fingers and lips were stained bright purple—or until Michaelmas at the end of September, when the devil was meant to have spat on brambles and the berries went sour.

Yet beneath all of the golden September abundance, an inevitable current was also pulling the other way. There might still be plenty of green about, but the undergrowth was slowly accumulating dried leaves and withered vines. The flowers were at their brightest, but they also faded quickly.

September in London was less golden than in Dorsetshire, but it was still very fine. Jem would have lingered if he could; but he knew that if he delayed fetching the compass saw, the waiting carpenter would go to the pub, and then would be unable to work, leaving more for him and his father to do. So he hurried through the back streets between Astley's Amphitheatre and Hercules Buildings without stopping to enjoy the sunshine.

Miss Pelham was hovering in the front garden of no. 12 Hercules Buildings, wielding a pair of pruning shears, the sun lighting up her yellow dress. Next door at no. 13, a man was leaving William Blake's house whom Jem had not seen before, though he seemed familiar, leaning forward as he walked with his hands tucked behind his back, his gait deliberate and almost flat-footed, his wide brow furrowed. It was only when Miss Pelham whispered, "That's Mr. Blake's brother," however, that Jem recognized the family resemblance. "Their mother's died," she continued in her hiss. "Now, Jem, you and your family are not to make noise, do you hear? Mr. Blake won't want you hammering and banging and moving whatnot about. You be sure to tell your parents."

"Yes, Miss Pelham." Jem watched Mr. Blake's brother walk up

Hercules Buildings. That must be Robert, he thought—the one Mr. Blake had mentioned a few times.

Miss Pelham snipped savagely at her box hedge. "The funeral's tomorrow afternoon, so don't you get in the way."

"Will the procession be going from here?"

"No, no, from across the river. She's to be buried at Bunhill Fields. But you stay out of Mr. Blake's way anyway. He won't want you or that girl hanging about in his moment of sorrow."

In fact, Jem had seen nothing of Mr. Blake all summer, and little enough of Maggie either. It seemed a year since Maggie had hidden at the Blakes', their lives had changed that suddenly.

This made it even more surprising when a few minutes later Jem spied her, of all places, in the Blakes' garden. He had looked out of the back window to see if his mother was in Mr. Astley's kitchen garden. Indeed she was, showing an Astley niece how to tie tomato plants to stakes without damaging the stems. Thomas Kellaway had got up his courage to ask Philip Astley if his wife might use a bit of the field for her own vegetable patch in return for helping out the Astley niece, who seemed not to know a turnip from a swede. Anne Kellaway had been overjoyed when he agreed, for though it was mid-June by then, and too late to plant much, still she had managed to put in some late lettuces and radishes, as well as leeks and cabbage for later in the year.

Jem was about to turn away to head downstairs, compass saw in hand, when a flash of white inside the Blakes' summerhouse caught his eye. At first he feared he might be seeing a repeat of the naked display he'd witnessed a few months back, and which still made him blush when he thought of it. Then he saw a hand flung out in the shadow of the doorway, and a boot he recognized, and gradually he made out Maggie's still form.

No one else was in the Blakes' garden, though Miss Pelham was now in her back garden, deadheading her roses. Jem hesitated briefly, then clattered downstairs, hurried along Hercules Buildings, into the alley leading to Hercules Hall, and then left at the end to skirt along the back garden walls. Anne Kellaway was still with her tomato plants, and Jem crept past her. He reached the Blakes' back wall, where an old crate was still hidden under a clump of long grass from the two weeks when Maggie climbed back and forth over it rather than trampling through the Blakes' house. He stood by it, watching his mother's back. Then, in a rush, he climbed the wall and hopped over.

Picking his way quickly through the wild back garden, Jem stole toward Maggie, keeping the summerhouse between him and the Blakes' windows so that they wouldn't see him. Once next to her, he could see her shoulders and chest moving up and down with her breath. Jem looked around, and when he was certain the Blakes were not in sight, he sat down to watch Maggie as she slept. Her cheeks were flushed, and there was a smear of yellow along her arm.

Since the fire, Maggie had vanished. Jem and his father worked hard at Astley's, but they did not put in the hours that Maggie did at the mustard manufactory, where she started at six in the morning and worked until evening, six days a week. On Sundays, when the Kellaways were at church, Maggie was still asleep. Sometimes she slept all of Sunday. When she did that, Jem didn't see her from one week to the next.

If she did get up on a Sunday afternoon, they would meet by the wall in Astley's field, and go down to the river together—sometimes by Lambeth Palace, other times to walk over Westminster Bridge. Often they didn't do even that, but simply sat against the wall. Jem watched as Maggie's liveliness drained from her; with each passing Sunday she looked more exhausted, and thinner, the curves that attracted him hardening. The lines on her palms and fingers and the spaces under her nails were seamed with yellow. A fine dust settled on her skin as well—on her cheeks, her neck, her arms—that did not wash away entirely, a yellow ghost lingering. Her dark hair went dull gray because of the powdered mustard dust it collected. At first Maggie had washed it out every day, but she soon gave up—washing took up time when she could be sleeping, and why bother to have clean hair when the next morning it would just go mustardy again?

She smiled less. She talked less. Jem found that for once he was leading the conversation. Most of the time he entertained her with stories of the goings-on at Astley's: the fight between Philip Astley and Mr. Johannot over the bawdy words in "The Pieman's Song" that brought the house down each night; the disappearance of one of the costume girls, later found at Vauxhall Gardens, drunk and pregnant; the night when Jupiter's volcano was knocked over by the force of the fireworks ignited from it. Maggie loved these stories, and demanded more.

Jem felt an ache, looking at her now. He wanted to reach over and run his finger through the mustard dust on her arm.

Finally he whispered her name.

Maggie sat up with a shout. "What? What is it?" She looked around wildly.

"Shhh." Jem tried to calm her, cursing himself for frightening her. "Miss Pelham be close by. I just saw you here, from our window, and thought—well, I wanted to see if you was all right."

Maggie rubbed her face, recovering her composure. "Course I'm all right. Why wouldn't I be?"

"No reason. It's just—shouldn't you be at the factory?"

"Oh, that." She sighed, a grown-up sound Jem hadn't heard from her before, and ran her fingers through tangled curls. "Too tired. I went this morning, then run off at dinnertime. All I want is a little sleep. You got anything to eat on you?"

"No. Did you not get any at the factory?"

Maggie laced her fingers together and stretched so that her shoulders humped back. "Nah, left while I could. Never mind, I'll eat later."

They sat awhile in silence, listening to the snipping of Miss Pelham at work on her roses. Jem's eyes kept straying to Maggie's arm, which was now hugging her knees.

"What you lookin' at?" she said suddenly.

"Nothing."

"Yes, you are."

"I just wondered—what it tastes like." He nodded at the dusty smear on her arm.

"Mustard? Like mustard, fool. Why—d'you want to lick it?" Maggie teasingly held it out.

Jem turned red, and Maggie pressed her advantage. "Go on," she murmured. "I dare you."

Though he wanted to, Jem didn't want to admit it. He hesitated, then leaned over and ran the flat of his tongue a few inches through the mustard dust, the soft hairs that grew on her arm tickling his tastebuds. He felt dizzy with the sensation of tasting her warm, musky skin for just a moment before the harsh mustard exploded in his mouth, prickling at the back of his throat and making him cough. Maggie laughed, a sound he hadn't heard enough of these days. He sat back, so ashamed and aroused that he didn't notice the hairs on Maggie's arms standing on end.

"Did you hear? Mr. Blake's ma died," he said, trying to find his way back to solid ground.

Maggie shivered, wrapping her arms around her knees again. "Has she? Poor Mr. Blake."

"Funeral be tomorrow. Bunhill Fields, Miss Pelham said."

"Really? I been there once, with Pa. Shall we go to it? Tomorrow's Sunday, so we're not workin'."

Jem looked sideways at his friend. "We can't do that—we didn't even know her."

"Don't matter. You've not been over that way, have you?"

"Where?"

"Past St. Paul's, by Smithfield's. The older bit of London."

"Don't reckon I have."

"You even been across the river?"

"Course I have. Remember when we went to Westminster Abbey?"

"That's all? You been here six months and you been across the river just once?"

"Three times," Jem corrected. "I went back to the Abbey once. And I've been across Blackfriars Bridge." He didn't tell Maggie that he'd gone across but not got off the bridge on the other side. He had stood and watched the chaos of London, and couldn't bring himself to step into it.

"Go on—you'd like it," Maggie persisted.

"What—the way you'd like the countryside?"

"Hah! It's not the same." When Jem continued to look dubious, Maggie added, "C'mon, it'll be an adventure. We'll follow Mr. Blake, like we've always wanted to do. What, you afraid?"

She sounded so much like her old self that Jem said, "All right. Yes."

~ *3* ~

Jem did not tell his parents or Maisie where he was going. Anne Kellaway would forbid him to go so far into London; Maisie would want to come along. Normally Jem didn't mind if his sister was with him and Maggie. Today, however, he was nervous, and didn't want to be responsible for Maisie too. So he simply said he was going out, and though he didn't meet Maisie's eye, he could feel her pleading gaze.

Perhaps it was because she'd had extra sleep the previous day, but Maggie was more sparkling than she had been for many a Sunday. She had washed herself, hair as well, so that, except for the creases in her hands, her skin was a more normal color. She had put on a clean shift over her gown, tied a light blue neckerchief around her neck, and even wore a slightly crumpled straw hat with a broad brim, trimmed with a navy blue ribbon. Her shape was

different too—her waist and chest sharper, more defined—and
Jem realized she was wearing stays for the first time.

She took Jem's arm with a laugh. "Shall we step into town,
then?" she said, sticking her nose up in the air.

"You look nice."

Maggie smiled and smoothed her shift over her stays, a gesture
Maisie often made but that clearly was new to Maggie, as it had
little effect on the wrinkles and bunches under her arms and at her
waist. Jem suppressed an urge to run his own hands down her sides
and squeeze her waist.

He glanced down at his patched, dusty breeches, coarse shirt,
and plain brown coat that had once been his brother Sam's. It
hadn't occurred to him to keep on his good church clothes for going into London; apart from worrying that they would be damaged
or get dirty in the city, he would have had to explain to his family
why he was wearing them. "Should I put on a better coat?" he
asked.

"Don't matter. I just like to dress up when I get the chance.
Neighbors'd make fun of me if I wore this round here. C'mon,
we'd best get back to the Blakes'. I been keeping an eye on the
house but no one's come out yet."

They set themselves up to wait across from no. 13 Hercules
Buildings, behind the low hedge that separated the field across the
road from the road itself. It was not as sunny as the day before;
still warm, but hazy and close. They lay in the grass, and now and
then one of them would pop up to look over and see if there was
any sign of Mr. Blake. They saw Miss Pelham leave with a friend,
heading for the Apollo Gardens on Westminster Bridge Road, as
she often did on a Sunday afternoon, to drink barley water and
look at the flower displays. They saw John Astley ride out on his
horse. They saw Thomas and Anne Kellaway and Maisie leave
no. 12 and walk past them on their way down to the Thames.

Just after the Kellaways passed, the door to no. 13 opened and
Mr. and Mrs. Blake stepped out, turning into Royal Row to make

their way through back streets to Westminster Bridge. They were dressed as they always were: Mr. Blake wore a white shirt, black breeches buckled at the knee, worsted stockings, a black coat, and a black broad-brimmed hat like a Quaker's; Mrs. Blake wore a dark brown dress with a white neckerchief, her creased bonnet, and a dark blue shawl. Indeed, they looked more like they were going for a Sunday afternoon stroll than to a funeral, except that they walked a little more quickly than usual, and with more purpose, as if they knew exactly where they were going, and that end point was more important than the journey there. Neither looked grim or upset. Mrs. Blake's face was perhaps a little blank, and Mr. Blake's eyes more firmly fixed on the horizon. As they seemed so ordinary, no one said anything or took off a hat as people might have done had they known the Blakes were mourners.

Maggie and Jem scrambled over the hedge and began to follow them. At first they stayed well behind them. But the Blakes never looked back, and by the time they crossed Westminster Bridge, the children had drawn close enough that they would be able to hear them speak. The Blakes did not talk, however; only Mr. Blake hummed to himself, and occasionally sang snatches of songs in a high-pitched voice.

Maggie nudged Jem. "Those an't hymns, like what you'd expect him to be singing today. I think those are his songs what he'd got in his book. Them *Songs of Innocence*."

"P'raps." Jem was paying less attention to the Blakes and more to the scenery around him. They had passed Westminster Hall and the Abbey—where crowds were milling about after the end of one service or before the beginning of another—and continued straight along the road from the bridge. Soon it ran into a large green space dotted with trees, with a long narrow body of water in the middle.

Jem stopped to gape. People were strolling along the raked gravel paths dressed in far finer clothing than anything he had seen in Lambeth. The women wore gowns so structured that the clothes seemed almost to be alive themselves. Their wide skirts were in bright colors—canary yellow, burgundy, sky blue, gold— and sometimes striped or embroidered, or decorated with tiers of ruffles. Elaborately trimmed petticoats filled out the women's figures, while their hair, piled high on their heads like towers and capped with huge creations in cloth that Jem was reluctant to call hats, made them look like top-heavy ships that might blow over easily with a passing wind. These were the sorts of clothes that you could never wear if you wanted to do any work.

If anything the men's clothes surprised him more, for they were meant to be closer to what Jem himself wore; there was a nod toward utility, though clearly these men did no work either. He studied a man passing by, who wore a coat of brown and gold silk that cut away elegantly to reveal breeches of the same pattern, a cream and gold waistcoat, and a shirt with ruffles at the neck and cuffs. His stockings were white and clean, the silver buckles on his shoes highly polished. If Jem or his father wore these clothes, nails would snag the silk, wood shavings would be caught in the ruffles, the stockings would get dirty and torn, and the silver buckles would be stolen.

In such well-dressed company, Jem felt even more ashamed of his patched breeches and frayed coat sleeves. Even Maggie's attempts at dressing up—her battered straw hat, her wrinkled neckerchief—looked ludicrous here. She felt it too, for she smoothed down her dress once more, as if defying others to look down on them. When she lifted her arms to straighten her hat, her stays creaked.

"Wha' be this place?" Jem said.

"St. James's Park. See, there's the palace over there, what it's named for." She pointed across the park to a long, redbrick building, crenellated towers flanking its entrance and a diamond-shaped clock suspended in between that read half-past two. "C'mon, the Blakes will get away from us."

Jem would have liked to linger longer to take in the scene—not only the costume parade, but the sedans being carried about by footmen wearing red; the children dressed almost as lavishly as their parents, feeding ducks and chasing hoops; the dairy maids calling out, "A can of milk, ladies! A can of milk, sirs!" and squirting milk into cups from cows tethered nearby. Instead he and Maggie hurried to catch up.

The Blakes headed north, skirting the east side of the park. At the beginning of a wide avenue planted with four rows of elms— "The Mall," Maggie explained—which ran down past the palace, they veered into a narrow lane that led out to a street lined with shops and theatres. "They'll be going up the Haymarket," Maggie said. "I'd best take your arm."

"Why?" Jem asked, though he didn't pull his elbow away when she tucked her hand into it.

Maggie chuckled. "We can't have London girls taking advantage of a country lad."

After a minute he saw what she meant. As they walked up the wide street, women began to nod at him and say hello, when no one had paid him any attention before. These women were not dressed as the women in St. James's Park had been, but were in cheaper, shinier gowns, with more of their bosom revealed, and their hair bundled under feathered hats. They were not as rough as the whore he had met on Westminster Bridge, but that may have been because it was daylight and they were not yet drunk.

"An't you a lovely lad," said one, walking arm in arm with another woman. "Where you from, then?"

"Dorsetshire," Jem replied.

Maggie yanked his arm. "Don't talk to her!" she hissed. "She'll get her claws into you and never let go!"

The other whore wore a floral print gown and matching cap, which could have looked elegant if she didn't have so much cleavage on show. "Dorsetshire, eh?" she said. "I know a girl or two round here from Dorsetshire. Want to meet 'em? Or would you rather have London-bred?"

"Leave him alone," Maggie muttered.

"What, got your own already?" the floral one said, grabbing Maggie's chin. "Don't think she'll give you what I can."

Maggie jerked her chin away and let go of Jem's arm. The whores laughed, then turned to latch on to a better prospect while Maggie and Jem stumbled off, silent with embarrassment. The haze had grown thicker, and the sun had disappeared, poking through only briefly now and then.

Luckily Haymarket was a short street, and they soon passed into quieter, narrower lanes, where buildings were crowded, making the way darker. Though the houses were closer together, they were not shabby, and the people in the streets were a little more prosperous than Jem and Maggie's Lambeth neighbors.

"Where are we?" Jem asked.

Maggie skirted some horse dung. "Soho."

"Is Bunhill Fields near here?"

"No, it's a ways yet. They'll be going to his mam's house first, and take her from there. Look, they've stopped. There." The Blakes were knocking at the door of a shop where black cloth had been hung in the windows.

"James Blake, Haberdasher," Jem read aloud from the sign above the shop. The door opened and the Blakes stepped inside, Mr. Blake turning to lock the door behind him. Jem thought he glanced up for a moment, but not long enough to recognize them. Nonetheless, they backed down the street until they were out of sight of the shop.

There were no carriages waiting near the door, or any sign of movement inside once the Blakes had disappeared. After leaning against the side of some stables a few doors down and attracting sharp looks from the people passing in and out of nearby houses, Maggie pushed herself off of the wall and began to walk back toward the shop. "What you doing?" Jem said in a low voice as he caught up with her.

"We can't stand there waitin'—attracts too much attention. We'll walk round and keep an eye out for the undertaker's carriage."

They walked past the shop windows and up and down the neigh-boring streets, soon finding themselves at Golden Square, whose name a posy seller told them. As London squares go, it was not particularly elegant, but the house fronts were wider, and it was lighter than the surrounding streets. The square itself was fenced off with iron railings, so Jem and Maggie strolled all around the outside of it, studying the statue of George II in the center.

"Why'd they do that to me?" Jem asked as they walked.

"Who do what?"

"Those . . . women in the Haymarket. Why'd they ask me those things? Can't they see that I be young for—for that?"

Maggie chuckled. "Maybe boys start earlier in London."

Jem turned red and wished he hadn't said anything, especially as Maggie seemed to relish teasing him about it. She was smiling at him in a way that made him kick at the gravel path. "Let's go back," he muttered.

By the time they arrived, a cart was stopped in front of the shop and the door was open. Neighbors began to open their own doors and stand in the street, and Jem and Maggie hid among them. Mr. Blake appeared with the undertakers and two brothers—one of them the man Jem had seen at Hercules Buildings the day before. Mrs. Blake followed with another woman who had the same thick brow and chunky nose as the Blake men, and must be a sister. As the men carried the coffin out of the door and placed it in the cart, the gathered crowd in the street bowed their heads and the men removed their hats.

When the coffin had been loaded, two of the undertakers climbed onto the box seat and, touching the horses with their reins, set off slowly, the mourners following on foot, with the neighbors behind them. The procession moved up the street until it nar-rowed; there the neighbors stopped, and stood watching until the cart doglegged into an even smaller street and disappeared.

Jem halted. "P'raps we should go back to Lambeth," he sug-gested, swallowing to try to move the lump lodged in his throat.

Seeing the coffin in the cart and the neighbors removing their hats had reminded him of his own brother's funeral, where neighbors had stood in their doorways with heads bowed as the cart carrying his coffin passed, guided to the graveyard by the tolling of a single bell at the Piddletrenthide church. People had openly cried, for Tommy had been a popular boy, and Jem had found it hard to make that short walk between cottage and church in front of every-one. Though he thought of his brother less now, there were still moments when he was ambushed by memories. London had not completely buried Tommy, for any of the Kellaways. At night Jem still heard his mother crying sometimes.

Maggie did not stop with Jem, however, but ran up the street the moment the neighbors turned away to go back to their houses. At the intersection where the procession had disappeared she looked back at Jem and gestured urgently. After a moment, he followed.

They soon arrived at Soho Square, a little larger than Golden Square, but with similar iron railings, grass plots, gravel walks, and a statue of Charles II on a pedestal in the center. Unlike Golden Square, it was open to the public, and while the funeral procession passed around the north side, Jem and Maggie walked directly through it, mingling with other Londoners out looking for a bit of fresh air and light—though the air was thicker here than in Lam-beth, and full of the smells of people living close together: coal fire smoke, sour, mildewed clothes, boiled cabbage, fish on the turn. And although Soho Square was much more open than the sur-rounding streets they had walked through, the sky had clouded over completely now, so that there was no longer any golden September light, but a weak, diffuse gray that made Jem think of endless November afternoons. It seemed late, almost evening, and he felt he had been away from Lambeth for hours; yet he had not heard the bells strike four o'clock.

"Here." Maggie thrust a piece of gingerbread at him that she'd bought from a seller walking past with a tray on his head.

"Thank'ee." Jem crunched the hard, spicy bread guiltily. He had not brought any money to buy things with, for he had thought it might be taken from him.

On the other side of the square they rejoined the back of the procession, and a few turnings later passed a square church topped with a tall tower. Maggie shivered. "St. Giles," was all she said, as if the name should conjure up its own associations without her having to explain. Jem did not ask. He knew St. Giles was the patron saint of outcasts, and it was clear enough from the surrounding buildings that the church was aptly named. Though they did not advance down them, Jem could glimpse the filth on the cramped streets, smell them from afar, and see the misery marked on the faces around him. It was not his first encounter with London slums. He and Maggie had explored some of the streets by the river in Lambeth, not far from where she now worked making mustard, and he had been shocked that people could live in such dank, dark conditions. Then, as now, his heart was squeezed tight with longing for Dorsetshire. He wanted to stop a man who passed them in rags, his face drawn and dirty, and tell him to walk out of London, and to keep going until he reached the beautiful green hills etched with furrows and washed in sunlight that formed the backdrop of Jem's childhood.

He did not stop the man, however. Jem followed Maggie, who followed the Blakes. He did notice that Mr. Blake turned his head to look down those slummy streets even as he continued his march behind his mother's coffin.

Where there were slums in London, there were whores; St. Giles was full of them. They had the manners not to call out to the members of the funeral procession. Jem, however, was at a distance behind it, and not wearing black, and so was considered a fair target. They began calling to him, as those on the Haymarket had, though these whores were a very different breed. Even Jem, who'd had no experience of women like this, could see that the St. Giles whores were in a much more desperate state than their better dressed, healthier Haymarket equivalents. Here faces were gaunt and pockmarked, teeth black or missing, skin yellow, eyes red from drink or exhaustion. Jem could not bear to look at them, and stepped more quickly, even at the risk of catching up with the Blakes. But he could hear them. "Sir, sir," they insisted on calling him, running alongside and tugging at his sleeve. "Have a go, sir. Give us sixpence, sir. We'll make you smile, sir." Their accents were primarily Irish, like most of the St. Giles population, but there were others too—Lancashire, Cornish, Scottish, even a Dorset burr piping up.

Jem walked faster; but not even Maggie swearing at them could shake the women. He drew so close to the funeral procession, with his human gaggle of geese honking noisily at his elbow, that one of Mr. Blake's brothers—the one Jem thought might be Robert—turned around and frowned at the whores, who at last dropped back.

"We're coming up to High Holborn," Maggie announced as the street began to widen. Then she stopped.

Jem stopped too. "What is't?"

"Shh. I'm listening."

He thought he could hear nothing but the normal sounds of London life: carriages rumbling past; a man calling, "Cotton laces, ha'penny a piece, long and strong!"; another playing a sad tune on a pipe and interrupting it to shout, "Give a penny to a poor man and I'll change my tune to a merry one!"; a couple quarreling over a mug of beer. These were all sounds he'd grown used to after six months in Lambeth.

Then he did hear something; underneath all of these growls and rumbles and shouts came a voice of a different timbre—a Dorset voice. "Jem! Jem! Come back!"

Jem whirled about and peered through the crowded street. "There," Maggie said, and darted toward a frilly white cap.

Maisie was standing with another girl near a stall selling cockles. Though Maisie's age, she was much smaller, with a hank of straw-colored hair and a pale thin face rouged with two great dots on her cheeks and a smear across her lips, like a young girl's idea of how to paint her face. Her eyes were pinched and red, as if she'd been crying, and she looked about as if expecting a blow to come at her from anywhere. She wore no chemise, but simply her leather stays, dark and greasy with use, and a red satin skirt over dirty petticoats. She had torn a strip from the bottom of the skirt and tied it in her hair.

"Jem! Jem!" Maisie cried, rushing up to him. "Here be Rosie Wightman. Didn't you recognize her when you passed? Rosie, it's Jem."

Jem would not have given the girl a second look, but when she turned her red-rimmed eyes up to him he saw—under the rouge, the grime, and the pathetic attempt at seductiveness—the face of the girl he used to catch eels with in the River Piddle, and whose parents lost their barn to fire because of her. "Ar'ernoon, Jem," she said, revealing the familiar gap between her front teeth.

"Lord—you know this girl?" Maggie said.

"She be from home," Maisie answered.

"And what in the name of God's green earth are *you* doing here, Miss Piddle?"

Maisie looked as shifty as it was possible for a girl wearing a frilly mop cap to look. "I were—I were following you. I saw you set out after the Blakes, so I told Ma and Pa my head ached, and I come after you. Followed you all the way," she added proudly.

"You got a penny for us, Jem?" Rosie asked.

"Sorry, Rosie—I han't any money on me."

"Give her your gingerbread," Maisie ordered.

Jem handed the half-eaten piece to Rosie, who crammed it into her mouth.

"Damn, the Blakes!" Maggie muttered, and turned to look for the procession. After moving so slowly through the back streets, the cart was now picking up speed on the larger road. It was almost out of sight among the traffic along High Holborn. "I'll just run and see which way they're going—wait here and I'll come back for you." Maggie disappeared into the crowd.

"What you doing here?" Jem asked Rosie.

Rosie looked around, as if to remind herself of where she was. "I do work here," she said through a mouth full of ginger sludge.

"But why did you run off an' come to London?"

Rosie swallowed. "You know why. I couldn't have my parents and the neighbors all pointin' fingers at me about the fire. So I made my way up here, didn't I."

"But why don't you go home?" Maisie said. "Your parents would—" She stopped as she remembered that the Wightmans were in the workhouse at Dorchester, information she was not about to pass on to Rosie. "Anyway, surely Dorsetshire be better than this!"

Rosie shrugged and wrapped her arms around herself, as if comforting herself with a hug.

"We can't just leave her here, Jem," Maisie said. "Let's bring her back to Lambeth with us."

"But then Ma and Pa'd know we come into town," Jem argued, trying not to let his distaste show. It seemed that whores were following him everywhere.

"Oh, they won't mind, not when they do see we've brought Rosie."

"I dunno."

While the Kellaways discussed what to do, Rosie stood docile, licking her fingers for stray ginger crumbs. It might be expected that she would take some interest in what was to happen to her, but she did not. Since arriving in London the year before, she had been raped, robbed, and beaten; she owned nothing but what she wore, and was constantly hungry; and though she didn't know it yet, she had the clap. Rosie no longer expected to have any say over her life, and so she did not say anything.

She'd only managed to attract one man so far today. Now, though, perhaps because a bit of attention was being paid to her, men suddenly took more notice of her. Rosie caught the eye of a slightly better dressed man and brightened.

"You busy, love?" he asked.

"No, sir. Anything for you, sir." Rosie wiped her hands on her dress, smoothed her straw hair and took his arm. "This way, sir."

"What're you doing?" Maisie cried. "You can't leave us!"

"Nice to see you," Rosie said. "Z'long."

"Wait!" Maisie grabbed her arm. "Come—come and find us. We can help you. We live in Lambeth. Do you know where tha' be?"

Rosie shook her head.

"What about Westminster Bridge?"

"I been there," Rosie said.

The man pulled his arm from her grasp. "Are you coming or do I have to find company elsewhere?"

"Course I am, sir." Rosie grabbed his arm again and walked away with him.

"Go to Westminster Bridge, Rosie," Maisie called, "and at the end of it you'll see a big building that has a white flag with red and black letters flying from it. Tha' be Astley's Circus. Go there during the day and ask for Thomas Kellaway—all right?"

Rosie did not look back but led her customer down a side street, pulling him out of sight into an alley.

"Oh, Jem, I think she nodded," Maisie said. "She heard me and she nodded. She'll come—I'm sure of it!" Her eyes were full of tears.

Maggie ran up to them. "It's all right," she panted. "They're held up by two coaches scraped each other and the drivers arguin'. We've a minute or two." She looked around. "Where's the other Miss Piddle?"

"Gone off," Jem said.

"She's going to meet us at Astley's tomorrow," Maisie added.

Maggie looked from one to the other and raised her eyebrows.

~ 5 ~

As the children followed the funeral procession down High Holborn, Jem sensed a change in the city the farther east they went, into the older part of London. The streets of Soho had been laid out in a kind of grid pattern. Now, however, streets led away from High Holborn less predictably, curving out of sight, dead-ending abruptly, narrowing into lanes a cart could barely squeeze through. They looked as though they simply grew into their shape and size rather than being planned. This part of London was what it was, and made no attempt to be grand or elegant or ordered, as Soho and Westminster did. There were still plenty of houses and shops and pubs about, but these were broken up with larger buildings—factories and warehouses. Jem could smell beer, vinegar, starch, tar, lye, tallow, wool. And when they at last turned off High Holborn, he smelled blood.

"Lord a mercy, I can't believe they're going through Smithfield's!" Maggie cried, wrinkling her nose. "Couldn't they take another route?"

"What's Smithfield's?" Maisie asked.

"Cattle market. We're on Cow Lane now."

The street led uphill toward a series of low buildings, where the smells of manure, urine, and cow sweat mingled with the darker metallic odors of blood and flesh. Though the market was shut on a Sunday, there were still people cleaning out stalls. As they passed, a woman threw a bucket of water across their path, sloshing a pink wave around their shoes. Maisie froze in the puddle and put her hand to her mouth.

"C'mon, Miss Piddle," Maggie ordered, grabbing her by the arm and marching her through the bloody water—though she herself had gone pale at the sight of blood. "Don't stop now—we can't have you being sick on us, can we? Now, you haven't told us how you managed to follow us so far without being seen. I didn't see her back there, did you, Jem?" As she spoke, she was gulping air, making Jem study her.

Maisie giggled, recovering more quickly than Maggie. "It weren't easy—especially all that time when you was waiting for the undertakers to arrive. Once you doubled back on yourselves and I had to turn away and look in a clockmaker's window till you'd passed. I were so sure you'd see me then, but you didn't. And then in the second square when I were looking at the statue and you come up, I had to jump behind it! Oh, but Jem, you do think Rosie will come to Astley's, don't you? She has to. And we'll help her, won't we?"

"I don't see what we can do, really. We can't send her back to Dorsetshire—not with her parents in the workhouse, and her like she be now."

"She could stay with us, couldn't she? Ma and Pa wouldn't turn her away."

"Miss Pelham would."

"Not if we say she be our sister, come from Dorsetshire. Miss Pelham won't know we han't a sister."

"She'd have to change her clothes, that's sure," Maggie interjected. "Couldn't wear those clothes and call her a Piddle girl. The old stick would see her for what she is in a minute."

"I'll lend her clothes. And she could get a job—at the mustard factory, for instance. She could work with you."

Maggie snorted. "I wouldn't wish that even on an enemy. Look what happens when you work there." She pulled a handkerchief from her stays, blew into it, and showed them. The contents were bright yellow, streaked with blood. "D'you know that feeling when you take too much mustard sauce on your beef or your fish, and it hurts your nose? Well, that's what it feels like every day at the factory. When I was first there I sneezed all the time, and my eyes and nose ran. They said they'd let me go if it kept up. Wish they had. I got used to it finally, but I can't smell anything now, and I taste mustard whenever I eat. Even that gingerbread tasted of mustard. So don't go suggesting your friend work there."

"P'raps we could find her work at the circus," Maisie suggested.

"Or the Asylum for Female Orphans might take her, if we lie and say her parents be dead," Jem said. "Which they do be, in a way, to her."

"There's better'n that for her," Maggie said. "She could go to the Magdalen Hospital in St. George's Fields. They take whores there"—Maisie flinched at the word—"and turn 'em into proper girls, teach 'em to sew an' that, find 'em places as servants."

Maisie broke in. "Rosie can sew. I know she can. She used to make buttons with me. Oh, I know we can help her!"

During all this talk, they had been walking steadily, turning here and there to follow the mourners. Suddenly the funeral cart stopped in front of a gate behind which rows of gravestones loomed. They had arrived at Bunhill Fields Burying Ground.

~ 6 ~

Jem had not really considered what it was he had come all this way for. He had supposed Bunhill Fields would be grand, being in London—the Westminster Abbey equivalent of a graveyard, something you walked miles to see. To his surprise, it seemed to him not so different from the Piddletrenthide church graveyard. It was, of course, much bigger. Ten Piddle church grounds could have fit comfortably into this field. Moreover, there was no church or chapel for services or spiritual comfort, but simply row upon row of gravestones, broken up here and there by larger monuments, and by a few trees—oak, plane, mulberry. Nor was it sheltered from the outside world as a place for quiet contemplation, for a large brewery jutted into the field, filling it with the worldly, lively smell of hops, and doubtless very busy during the week.

Yet as he stared at the gravestones through the iron railings, waiting with the girls for Mr. Blake's mother to be carried to her resting place, and later, as a few graveside words were spoken and they idled among the stones, Jem felt Bunhill Fields send him into the silent reverie—part tranquil, part melancholic—so familiar to him from when he used to wander around the Piddletrenthide church graveyard. Now that village graveyard included Tommy's grave, though, and Jem knew he would feel different there. "Pear tree's loss," he murmured, making Maggie turn her head and stare.

The funeral was over quickly. "They didn't have a church service," Jem whispered to Maggie as they leaned against a large rectangular monument and watched from a distance while Mr. Blake and his brothers shoveled earth into the grave, then handed the spade over to professional gravediggers.

"They don't here," Maggie explained. "This is a Dissenters' graveyard. They don't use prayer books or nothing, and the grounds han't been blessed. Mr. Blake's a proper radical. Didn't you know that?"

"Do that mean he'll go to Hell?" Maisie asked, plucking at a daisy growing at the base of the grave.

"Dunno—maybe." With her finger Maggie traced the name on the tombstone, though she could not read it. "We're all going to Hell, I expect. I'll wager there is no Heaven."

"Maggie, don't say that!" Maisie cried.

"Well, maybe there's a Heaven for you, Miss Piddle. You'll be awfully lonely there, though."

"I don't see why there has to be just the one or t'other," Jem said. "Can't there be something that's more a bit of both?"

"That's the world, Jem," Maggie said.

"I suppose."

"Well said, my girl. Well said, Maggie."

The children jumped. Mr. Blake had detached himself from the funeral party and come up behind them. "Oh, hallo, Mr. Blake," Maggie said, wondering if he was angry with them for following him. He did not seem angry, though—after all, he was praising her for something.

"You have answered the question I posed you on Westminster Bridge," he continued. "I wondered when you would."

"I did? What question?" Maggie searched her memory, but couldn't recall much of the heady conversation they'd had with Mr. Blake on the bridge.

"I remember," Jem said. "You were asking what was in the middle of the river—between its opposite banks."

"Yes, my boy, and Maggie has just said what it is. Do you understand the answer?" He turned his intense gaze on Jem, who looked back at him, though it hurt, the way staring at the sun does, for the man's glittering eyes cut through whatever mask Jem had donned to go this deep into London. As they looked at each other, he felt stripped naked, as if Mr. Blake could see everything inside him—his fear of all that was new and different about London; his concern for Maisie and his parents; his shock at the state of Rosie Wightman; his new, surprising feelings for Maggie; his deep sorrow for the death of his brother, of his cat, of everyone who was lost and would be lost, himself included. Jem was confused and exhilarated by his afternoon with Maggie, by the odors of life and death at Smithfield's, by the beautiful clothes in St. James's Park and the wretched rags of St. Giles, by Maggie's laughter and the blood from her nose.

Mr. Blake saw all of this in him. He took it in, and he nodded to Jem, and Jem felt different—harder and clearer, as if he were a stone that had been burnished by sand.

"The world," he said. "What lies between two opposites is us."

Mr. Blake smiled. "Yes, my boy; yes, my girl. The tension between contraries is what makes us ourselves. We have not just one, but the other too, mixing and clashing and sparking inside us. Not just light, but dark. Not just at peace, but at war. Not just innocent, but experienced." His eyes rested for a moment on the daisy Maisie still held. "It is a lesson we could all do well to learn, to see all the world in a flower. Now, I must just speak with Robert. Good day to you, my children."

"Z'long, sir," Jem said.

They watched him thread his way through the graves. He did not stop at the funeral party as they'd expected, however, but continued on until he knelt by a grave.

"What were that all about?" Maisie asked.

Jem frowned. "You tell her, Maggie. I'll be back in a minute." He picked his way through stone slabs until he could crouch behind one near Mr. Blake. His neighbor was looking very animated, his eyes glinting, though there was little light to make them so— indeed, the clouds had grown thicker, and Jem felt a raindrop on his hand as he hid and listened.

"I feel it pushing at me from all sides," Mr. Blake was saying. "The pressure of it. And it will get worse, I know it, with this news from France. The fear of originality will stifle those who speak with different voices. I can tell only you my thoughts—and Kate, bless her." After a pause, he continued, "I have seen such things, Robert, that would make you weep. The faces in London streets are marked by Hell."

After another, longer pause, he began to chant:

I wander through each chartered street
Near where the chartered Thames does flow
And mark in every face I meet
Marks of weakness, marks of woe.

In every cry of every man
In every infant's cry of fear
In every voice, in every ban
The mind-forged manacles I hear.

"I've been working on that one. I am writing all new, for things have changed so. Think on it, until we meet again, my brother." He got to his feet. Jem waited until he had gone back to the group in black, then went around to look at the headstone Mr. Blake had knelt by. Doing so confirmed what he had begun to suspect about the brother Mr. Blake spoke of so much: The stone read "Robert Blake, 1762–1787."

~ 7 ~

The undertakers with their cart moved off in one direction, the Blakes in the other, down the long tree-lined avenue that led to the street. The infrequent spots of rain were beginning to fall more persistently. "Oh dear," Maisie said, pulling her shawl closely around her shoulders. "I never thought it would rain when I came out. And we be such a long way from home. What do we do now?"

Maggie and Jem did not have a plan beyond reaching Bunhill Fields. It was enough to have done that. Now it was dim with rain, and there was no longer a goal to reach, other than getting home.

Out of habit, Maggie followed the Blakes, with Jem and Maisie falling in behind her. When the family reached the street, they did not turn down it and retrace their steps. Instead, the group got into a carriage that sat waiting for them. It set off briskly, and though the children ran after it, it soon left them behind. They stopped running and stood in the street, watching the carriage race far away from them until it turned right and disappeared. The rain was coming down faster now. They hurried along the street until they came to the crossroads, but the carriage could not be seen. Maggie looked about. She didn't recognize where they were; the carriage was taking a different route back.

"Where are we?" Maisie asked. "Shouldn't we try to follow them?"

"Don't matter," Maggie answered. "They'll just be goin' back to Soho when we want Lambeth. We can find our own way back. C'mon." She set out as confidently as she could, without telling the others that in the past she'd always come to this part of London with her father or brother, and had let them lead the way. However, there were plenty of landmarks Maggie had been to and could surely find her way back from: Smithfield's, St. Paul's, the Guildhall, Newgate Prison, Blackfriars Bridge. It was just a matter of finding one of them.

For example, ahead of them and across a green was a massive U-shaped building, three stories high and very long, with towered sections in the middle and at the corners where the wings began.

"What's that?" Maisie said.

"Dunno," Maggie answered. "Looks familiar. Let's see it from the other side."

They walked parallel to the railings that enclosed the green and then past one wing of the building. At the back a high, crumbling stone wall covered with ivy ran alongside, and another, even higher wall had been built closer to the building, clearly designed to keep people in.

"There be bars on the windows," Jem announced, squinting up through the rain. "This a jail?"

Maggie peered at the windows high up in the walls. "Don't think so. I know we're not near Fleet, nor Newgate neither—I been there for hangings and it don't look like this. There's not this many criminals in London, not behind bars."

"You've seen someone hanged?" Maisie cried. She looked so horrified that Maggie felt ashamed to confirm it.

"Just the once," she said quickly. "That was enough."

Maisie shuddered. "I couldn't bear to see someone killed, no matter what they've done."

Maggie made a garbled noise. Jem frowned. "You all right?"

Maggie swallowed hard, but before she could say anything, they heard a wail from one of the high barred windows. It began low in pitch and volume, then ascended the scale, growing louder and higher until it became a scream so forceful it must have torn its owner's throat. The children froze. Maggie felt goose bumps sweep up and down her.

Maisie clutched Jem's arm. "What's that? Oh, what is't, Jem?"

Jem shook his head. The sound stopped suddenly, then began again in its low range, to climb higher and higher. It reminded him of cats fighting.

"A lying-in hospital, maybe?" he suggested. "Like the one on Westminster Bridge Road. Sometimes you hear screams coming from it, when the women are having their babies."

Maggie was frowning at the ivy-covered stone wall. Suddenly her face shifted with recognition and disgust. "Oh Lord," she said, taking a step back. "Bedlam."

"What's—" Jem stopped. He was remembering an incident one day at Astley's. One of the costume girls had seen John Astley smiling at Miss Hannah Smith and begun to cry so hard that she sent herself into a fit. Philip Astley had thrown water in her face and slapped her. "Pull yourself together, my dear, or it's Bedlam for you!" he'd said before the other costume girls led her away. He'd turned to John Fox, tapped his temple, and winked.

Jem looked up at the windows again and saw a hand fluttering between the bars, as if trying to grasp at the rain. When the scream began the third time, he said, "Let's go," and turned on his heel to walk what felt like west to him, toward Soho and, eventually, Lambeth.

Maggie and Maisie followed. "That's London Wall, you know," Maggie said, gesturing at the stone wall to their right. "There's bits of it all round. It's the old wall to the city. That's what made me recognize Bedlam. Pa brought me past here once."

"Which way do we go, then?" Jem said. "You must know."

"Course I do. This way." Maggie turned left at random.

"Who . . . who stays at Bedlam?" Maisie faltered.

"Madmen."

"Oh dear. Poor souls." Maisie stopped suddenly. "Wait—look!" She pointed at a figure in a red skirt ahead of them. "There's Rosie! Rosie!" she called.

"Maisie, we're nowhere near St. Giles," Maggie said. "She won't be over here."

"She might be! She said she works all over. She could've come here!" Maisie broke into a run.

"Don't be an idiot!" Maggie called after her.

"Maisie, I don't think—" Jem began.

Jem's sister was not listening, but running faster, and when the girl turned suddenly into an alley, Maisie dived after her and disappeared.

"Damn!" Maggie ran, Jem matching her stride for stride.

When they reached the turning, both Maisie and the red skirt were gone. "Dammit!" Maggie muttered. "What a silly fool!"

They hurried down the alley, looking at each turning for Maisie. Down one they saw a flash of red in the doorway of a house. Now that they could see her face, it was clear that indeed the girl was not Rosie, or a whore either. She shut the door behind her, and Jem and Maggie were left alone among a few houses, a church, a copper shop, and a draper's.

"Maisie must have kept going," Maggie said. She ran back to

the original alley, Jem at her heels, and continued along it, ducking into other alleys and lanes. At a dead end, they turned; at another they turned again, getting wound more and more tightly into the maze of streets. Jem said little, except to stop Maggie once and point out that they'd come in a circle. Maggie thought he must be furious with her for getting them so lost, but he seemed to show neither anger nor fear—just a grim determination.

Maggie tried not to think beyond finding Maisie. When for a moment she let her mind picture the three of them, lost in these tiny streets in an unknown part of a huge city, with no knowing how to get home, she began to feel so breathless with fear that she thought she would have to sit down. She had only ever felt this frightened once before, when she'd met the man in what would become Cut-Throat Lane.

As they ran along another alley, they passed a man who turned and leered at them. "What you runnin' from, then?"

Maggie shrieked, and shied like a spooked horse, startling Jem and the man, who shrank back and disappeared into a passageway.

"Maggie, what is't?" Jem grabbed his friend by the shoulders, but she threw him off with a shudder and turned away, her hand against the wall, trying to steady herself. Jem stood watching her and waiting. At last she took a deep, shaky breath and turned back to him, rain dripping from her crushed straw hat into her eyes. Jem searched her unhappy face and saw there a distant, haunted look that he had caught a few times before—sometimes when she didn't know he saw it, others like now when she desperately tried to hide it. "What is't?" he said again. "What happened to you?"

She shook her head; she would not say what it was.

"It be about that man in Cut-Throat Lane, don't it?" Jem guessed. "You was always funny about that. You went funny back at Smithfield's too."

"It was Maisie what looked sick, not me," Maggie retorted.

"You did too," Jem insisted. "You looked sick because you saw so much blood back in Cut-Throat Lane. Maybe you even—" Jem paused. "You saw it happen, didn't you? You saw him get killed." He wanted to put his arm around her to comfort her, but knew she wouldn't let him.

Maggie turned her back on him and started down the alley again. "We have to find Maisie," she muttered, and would say nothing more.

Because of the rain, there were few people about. As they searched, the rain fell even harder in a last attempt to drench anyone outside, then suddenly stopped altogether. Immediately doors began to open. It was a close, cramped area of London, with small, dark houses that had survived change from fire and fashion and poverty only because they were so solid. The people who emerged were similarly sturdy and settled. There were no Yorkshire or Lancashire or Dorsetshire accents here, but the sound of families who had lived for many generations in the same place.

In such a neighborhood, strangers stick out like early-budding crocuses. Hardly had the streets begun to fill with Sunday evening strollers than a woman passing pointed behind herself. "You'll be wanting the girl with the frilly cap, will you? She's back there, by Drapers' Gardens."

A minute later they came out into an open space where there was yet another enclosed garden, and saw Maisie standing by the iron railings, waiting, her eyes shiny with tears. She said nothing, but threw her arms around Jem and buried her face in his shoulder. Jem patted her gently. "You be all right now, do you, Maisie?"

"I want to go home, Jem," she said, her voice muffled.

"We will."

She pulled back and looked in his face. "No, I mean back to Dorsetshire. I be lost in London."

Jem could have said, "Pa makes more money working for Mr. Astley than he ever did as a chairmaker in Piddletrenthide." Or, "Ma prefers the circus to Dorset buttons." Or, "I'd like to hear more of Mr. Blake's new songs." Or even, "What about John Astley?"

Instead he stopped a boy his own age, who was whistling as he passed. "Excuse me, sir—where be the Thames?"

"Not far. Just there." The boy pointed, and the children linked arms before heading in the direction he'd indicated. Maisie was trembling and Maggie was pale. To distract them, Jem said, "I know a new song. D'you want to learn it?" Without waiting for them to reply, he began to chant:

> I wander through each chartered street
> Near where the chartered Thames does flow
> And mark in every face I meet
> Marks of weakness, marks of woe.

They had chanted the two verses he knew three times together when they slipped into a stream of traffic heading onto London Bridge. "It be all right now," Jem said. "We're not lost. The river will lead us back to Lambeth."

PART VI

October 1792

Maisie watched John Astley rehearse from her favorite seat. She had tried all of the different seats in the amphitheatre, and knew which she liked best. When they attended shows, the Kellaways normally sat in the pit, close to the ring where the horses ran, the armies marched, the tumblers tumbled, and Miss Laura Devine spun and swooped. However, for those who wanted a view from above, the boxes were the best seats. Located on either side of the stage over the pit, they raised their viewers above the action of both circus and audience.

Today Maisie was sitting in a box to the right of the stage. She liked it there because it was snug and private, and she had a clear view of everything John Astley did, whether with his horse in the ring or with Miss Hannah Smith on stage. Miss Smith was petite, with the turned-out feet of a trained dancer, fair hair, and a delicate face like an orchid. She had played a fetching Columbine opposite John Astley's Harlequin, and was popular with audiences. Maisie hated her.

This afternoon John Astley was rehearsing on horseback with Miss Smith for a surprise finale that would mark the end of the season. At the moment they were sitting together on their horses—he on his chestnut mare and wearing a bright blue coat, she in a white gown that stood out against her black stallion—discussing some part of their act. Maisie sighed; though she hated Miss Smith, she could not take her eyes off of her or John Astley, for they seemed to fit perfectly together. After a few minutes of watching, Maisie found she was grinding her fists in her lap.

She did not leave, however, though her mother could have done with her help at home, where she was pickling cabbage. Soon

Maisie would not see John Astley at all: The day after the last performance of the season, the company would travel directly by coach to Dublin, to spend the winter season there and at Liverpool. The rest of the show—the scenery, the props, the cranes and pulleys and hoists, the horses—would follow by ship. Her father and brother were even now rushing to pack up scenery from the earlier shows in the season, readying it for transport that had not even been secured yet. Maisie knew this because Philip Astley was sitting in the box next to hers, conducting business, and she had just heard him compose with John Fox an advertisement for a newspaper:

> WANTED, A VESSEL TO CARRY MACHINERY TO DUBLIN
> She must sail the 13th, 14th, or 15th instant.
> Apply to Mr. Astley, Astley's Amphitheatre,
> Westminster Bridge Rd.

Maisie knew little about shipping, but even she was sure they needed more than three days to find passage to Ireland. It made her catch her breath and squeeze her hands together in her lap. Perhaps during the delay Mr. Astley would at last ask Thomas Kellaway and his family to travel to Dublin, as she had been praying he would during the last month.

Applause broke out from all around the amphitheatre, for Miss Hannah Smith was now standing on one foot on the saddle of her horse, the other leg held out behind her. They all had stopped what they were doing to watch. Even Jem and Thomas Kellaway had come out from backstage along with the other carpenters and were clapping. Not wanting her silence to stand out, Maisie clapped too. Miss Smith smiled tightly, trying not to let her extended leg wobble.

"Brava, my dear!" Mr. Astley shouted from his box next to Maisie's. "She reminds me of Patty," he said to John Fox. "I must get the wife along to the finale to see this. Shame so few women are willing to perform on horseback."

"They got more sense'n men," John Fox pointed out. "Looks like she's lost hers."

"That girl will do anything for John," Philip Astley said. "That's why she's up there now."

"Anything?"

"Well, not anything. Not yet." Both men laughed.

"She knows what she's doing," Philip Astley continued. "She's handling him as well as any horse. Brava, my dear!" he shouted out once more. "We've got our grand finale now!"

Miss Smith slowed her horse and lowered her leg. When she'd maneuvered herself back into the saddle, John Astley leaned over and kissed her hand, to more applause and laughter, and blushes from Miss Smith.

It was then that Maisie felt the silence rippling out from the box on the other side of the ring. She peered across and saw there the one person who wasn't clapping: From the shadows emerged the round white face of Miss Laura Devine, gazing down at Miss Smith with even more hatred than Maisie herself felt for the ingenue. Miss Devine's face was no longer so smooth and welcoming as it had once been. Instead it was haggard, underlined with a disgusted wince, as if she had just tasted something she didn't care for. She looked wretched.

When Miss Devine looked up and met Maisie's eyes, her expression did not change. They gazed at each other, until Miss Devine let herself sink back into the shadows, like the moon disappearing behind clouds.

~ 2 ~

Next door, Philip Astley was running through a list of names with John Fox. "Mr. and Mrs. De Castro. Mr. Johannot. Mr. Lawrence.

Mrs. Henley. Mr. Davis. Mr. Crossman. Mr. Jeffries. Mr. Whitmore. Monsieur Richer. Mr. Sanderson."

"He's coming later."

"Damme, Fox, I need him now! The Irish will want new songs and they'll want 'em straightaway. I was expecting to ride with him in the coach and compose 'em then."

"He's writing for a show that's to open on the Haymarket."

"I don't care if he's writing for the King himself! I want him in that coach on the thirteenth!"

There was silence from John Fox.

"Any other surprises for me, Fox? Any others I should know about? Tell me now. Next you'll be saying the carpenters have laid down their tools and become sailors."

John Fox cleared his throat. "We han't got a carpenter agreed to come, sir."

"What? Why not?"

"Most o' them's got jobs elsewhere, and don't fancy the trip. They know what it's like."

"There's nothing wrong with Dublin! Have we asked everyone?"

"All but Kellaway."

Maisie had been only half-listening to the conversation, but now she sat up.

"Send Kellaway up, then."

"Yes, sir." There was a pause. "You'll want to speak to her too."

"Who?"

"Her. Across the way. Can't you see her?"

"Ah. Yes."

"Does she know about Monsieur Richer?" John Fox asked.

"No."

"She'll need to know, sir. So's they can rehearse."

Philip Astley sighed. "All right, I'll talk to her after Kellaway. Get him now."

"Yes, sir."

"It's not easy being manager, Fox."

"I expect not, sir."

When her father appeared before Mr. Astley, Maisie remained as still as she could in her box, feeling guilty already for eavesdropping, before words had even been exchanged.

"Kellaway, my good man, how are you?" Philip Astley called out, as if Thomas Kellaway were on the other side of the ring rather than standing in front of him.

"Well enough, sir."

"Good, good. You still packing up the scenery?"

"Yes, sir."

"There's so much to do to get the company on the road, Kellaway. It requires an enormous amount of planning and packing, packing and planning, don't it?"

"Yes, sir. It be a bit like moving from Dorsetshire to London."

"Well, now, I suppose you're right, Kellaway. So it'll be easy for you this time, now you've had the practice."

"Practice for what, sir?"

"On my word, I'm jumping ahead of myself, an't I, Fox? I mean packing up and going to Dublin."

"To Dublin?"

"You do know we're going to Dublin, don't you, Kellaway? After all, that's what you're packing the scenery for."

"Yes, sir, but—"

"But what?"

"I—I didn't think that meant me, sir."

"Of course it means you! Did you think we wouldn't need a carpenter in Dublin?"

"I be a chairmaker, sir, not a carpenter."

"Not for me you're not. Do you see any chairs around here that you've made, Kellaway?"

"Besides," Thomas Kellaway added, as if Philip Astley had not spoken, "there be carpenters in Dublin could do the job just as well."

"Not ones who know the scenery as you do, Kellaway. Now, what's bothering you? I thought you'd welcome a trip to Dublin. It's a roaring city—you'll love it, I'm sure. And it's milder than London in winter. Liverpool too, after. Come now, Kellaway, you wanted to get away from Dorsetshire and see a bit of the world, didn't you? Here's your chance. We leave in three days—that's enough time to pack your things, eh?"

"I—what about my family?"

The seat creaked as Philip Astley shifted his weight. "Well, now, Kellaway, that's tricky. We've to tighten our belts on the road, you see—a smaller company, with no room for extras. A wife's extra. Even Patty don't go to Dublin, do she, Fox? So I'm afraid it's just you, Kellaway."

Maisie gasped. Luckily the men didn't hear her.

"But you'll be back soon, Kellaway—it's only till March."

"Tha' be five months, sir."

"And you know, Kellaway, your family will be that glad to see you when you get back. Works like a tonic for Patty and me. Absence makes the heart fonder, you know."

"I don't know, sir. I'll have to talk to Anne about it an' give you an answer tomorrow."

Philip Astley started to say something, but for once Thomas Kellaway interrupted him. "I have to get back to work now. Excuse me, sir." Maisie heard the door open and her father leave.

There was chuckling from next door. "Oh, don't you start, Fox!"

The chuckling continued.

"Damme, Fox, he got the better of me, didn't he? He actually thinks he has a choice in the matter, don't he? But I'm the one making decisions here, not a carpenter."

"Shouldn't your son be making those decisions, sir? Seeing as he's the manager."

Philip Astley heaved another sigh. "You would think so, wouldn't you, Fox? But look at him." Maisie glanced down: John Astley was on his horse, dancing sideways across the ring while

Miss Hannah Smith watched. "That's what he does best, not sitting up here making hard decisions. Speaking of which—go and fetch Miss Devine."

John Fox made his way around the gallery to the boxes on the other side. Though Miss Laura Devine must have seen him approaching, she did not move to meet him, or answer the door to his knock, but sat and stared across at Philip Astley. Finally John Fox answered his own knock, opening the door and entering the box, where he leaned over to whisper something in Miss Devine's ear. He then stood in the doorway and waited.

For a long time she did not move; nor did John Fox. At last, however, she gathered her shawl around her shoulders and stood, shaking out her skirts and patting at her dark hair, which was pulled back into a bun at the nape of her neck, before she took the arm John Fox offered. He then escorted her around the gallery as if it were full of its usual rough customers he must protect her from. When he deposited her at Philip Astley's box, she said, "Stay, John," as if his gallantry might soften the blow that was to come. For she knew the blow would come. She had been expecting it for weeks.

Maisie also knew what was to come. She and her mother had watched Miss Devine perform more slowly and clumsily at a recent show and guessed what was wrong. She knew too that John Fox's presence would make little difference to the outcome—only, perhaps, to the manner in which it was relayed by Mr. Astley.

"Miss Devine, welcome," Mr. Astley said in a tone completely different from the jocularity he had used with Thomas Kellaway. "Sit down, my dear, sit here next to me. You're looking a touch pale—don't she, Fox? We'll get Mrs. Connell to make you some broth. That's what she gives me when I'm under the weather, and Patty swears by it, don't she, Fox?"

Neither John Fox nor Miss Devine responded to his solicitations, which made him burble on even more. "You've been watching the rehearsals, have you, my dear? Very exciting, the last night upon us already. And then the move to Dublin once more. On my word, how many more times will we pack up and cross the Irish Sea, eh, Fox?" He cut himself off then, as he realized this was not the most tactful thing to be saying just now.

Indeed, Philip Astley seemed to be momentarily at a loss for words. It only lasted that moment, but it was enough for all the listeners to understand that it was a struggle for him to say what he was to say. Miss Laura Devine had been with Astley's Circus for ten years, after all, and was—now he found the words—"like a daughter you are to me, my dear, yes, like a daughter. That's why I know when things have changed, because I know you as well as a father knows his daughter. And things have changed, my dear, han't they?"

Miss Devine said nothing.

"Did you think I wouldn't notice, Laura?" Philip Astley asked, allowing some of his natural impatience to creep back into his voice. "Half the audience has guessed! Did you really think we wouldn't notice you getting fatter and slower? Why, you're making 'Pig on a Spit' into the real thing!"

Maisie caught her gasp before it could ring out into the appalled silence that followed his cruel remark. It was a silence that spurred Philip Astley to fill it. "Come, now, girl, what were you thinking? How could you let that happen to you? I thought you were smarter than that." After a pause he added more gently, "He's not the man for you, Laura. Surely you knew that."

At last Miss Devine spoke, though she gave an answer to a different question. "It's because my family's not good enough for you, isn't it?" she said in her soft Scottish lilt—so soft that Maisie had to lean forward almost out of her box to hear. "I expect her family's more to your liking."

Miss Smith was now jogging sedately around the ring on her stallion while John Astley rode in the opposite direction; each time they passed, one handed the other a glass of wine to drink from and pass back the next time around.

"Laura, I have never had any jurisdiction over my son's women. That is his own affair. I don't want to get into an argument over why he does what he does. That is for you to take up with him. My only concern is for the show and its performers. And when I see a member of the company who can no longer perform in her condition, then I must take action. First of all, I have hired Monsieur Richer from Brussels to join the show."

There was a short silence. "Monsieur Richer is a wobbler," Miss Devine said with disdain. "A clown on the rope." It was true that the two slack-rope artists had very different styles. Miss Laura Devine made it a matter of honor, as well as of taste, not to wobble when she walked along the rope. Her performance was as smooth as her dark hair and pale skin.

"When John and Miss Smith finish in the ring," Philip Astley continued as if she had not spoken, "you are to rehearse a routine with Monsieur Richer for the final show, which will introduce his talents to the audience and prepare them for his *solo* return next year. For you won't be coming with us to Dublin, Miss Devine, nor joining us when we return. I'm sorry, my dear, truly I am, but there it is. Of course, you may stay in your accommodation for another month." Philip Astley got to his feet, clearly ready for this chat to be over, now that the meat of the matter had been laid out. "Now, I must see to a few matters. If there is anything else I can do for you," he added as he opened the door, "you need only ask John Fox, eh, Fox?"

He almost got away, but Miss Devine's soft voice carried farther and with more force than might have been expected. "You seem to forget that the bairn will be your grandchild."

Philip Astley stopped short and made a choking noise. "Don't you dare try that with me, girl!" he roared. "That baby will have nothing to do with the Astleys! Nothing! He'll be no grandson of mine!"

His unchecked voice, so accustomed to needing to carry over the noise of the show and audience, was heard in every corner of the amphitheatre. The costume girls, wrapping up bundles of clothes in a room offstage, heard it. Thomas and Jem Kellaway, building big wooden supports to sandwich pieces of scenery in between and protect them for the journey to Dublin, heard it. Mrs. Connell, counting the takings from ticket sales in the front of house, heard it. Even the circus boys, waiting outside for John Astley and Miss Hannah Smith to finish with their horses, heard it.

Maisie heard it, and it completed a puzzle she'd been worrying at in her head—the last piece being what she'd expected but hoped wasn't so, as it meant she really ought to hate Miss Devine too.

Miss Hannah Smith certainly heard it. Though she continued to ride around the ring, she turned her face toward the box and stared, noticing for the first time the drama that was playing out at a level just above her head.

John Astley alone seemed not to have noticed his father's outburst. He was used to Philip Astley's bellows and rarely listened to their content. As Miss Smith was still holding out her hand for the glass, he passed it to her. She was now looking elsewhere, however, and thinking elsewhere as well, so she did not grasp it, and the glass fell to the ground between them. Despite the cushioning sawdust, it smashed.

John Astley immediately pulled up his horse. "Glass!" he shouted. A boy who had been waiting alongside to sweep up horse dung ran into the ring with his broom.

Miss Hannah Smith did not stop her horse, however. She kept riding around the ring, whipping her head around to keep her eyes on Philip Astley and Miss Laura Devine. Indeed, she would have run down the sweeping boy if John Astley hadn't grabbed the reins of her horse and stopped it himself. "Hannah, what's the matter with you?" he cried. "Careful where you let your horse step—that glass could do injury!"

Miss Smith sat on her horse and pulled her eyes from Miss Laura Devine to fix them on John Astley. She had gone very pale, and no longer displayed the pretty smile she had maintained throughout the rehearsal. Instead she looked as if she might be sick.

John Astley stared at her, then glanced up at the box where Miss Laura Devine sat with fiery eyes and his father still huffed like a winded horse.

Next Maisie heard something she could never have imagined issuing from Miss Hannah Smith's mouth. "John Astley, you shit sack!" She was not as loud as Philip Astley, but loud enough for Maisie and everyone in the adjacent box to hear. The boy sweeping up the glass snorted. John Astley opened his mouth, but was unable to think of an appropriate reply. Miss Smith then jumped down from her horse and ran off, her turned-out feet making her retreat even more pathetic.

When she was gone, John Astley glared up at the box, where Miss Laura Devine still sat, triumphant for just one moment in this bleak farce. He looked as if he wanted to say something, but the giggling boy at his feet made him think the better of dragging out the scene in public. Instead he quickly dismounted, flung the reins of both horses at the boy, straightened the sleeves of his blue coat, and hurried after Miss Smith.

"Well, I hope you're happy, my dear," Philip Astley hissed. "Is that what you wanted?"

"It is you who makes a public drama of everything," Laura Devine replied. "You have never known how to be calm or quiet."

"Get out! I can't stand the sight of you!" Though Philip Astley shouted this at her, he himself barged out of the box, calling for John Fox to follow.

After they were gone, Miss Laura Devine continued to sit in

the box, with Maisie quiet in hers next door. Her hands were trembling in her lap.

"Come and see me a moment," Maisie heard Miss Devine murmur, and started when she realized the command was directed at her, and that Miss Devine had seen her sitting in her box before, and would know that she had heard it all. Maisie got up and slipped into the adjacent box, trying not to bring attention to herself—though apart from the boy, who had led off the horses and now come back to sweep up the rest of the glass and horse dung, there was no one about.

Miss Devine did not look up at Maisie's arrival. "Sit with me, pet" was all she said. Maisie sank into the chair that Philip Astley had not long vacated next to the slack-rope dancer; indeed, the seat was still warm. Together they looked out over the ring, which for once was quiet, but for the boy's broom. Maisie found its even, scraping sound a comfort. She knew she did not hate Miss Devine, whatever had happened. Instead she pitied her.

Miss Laura Devine seemed to be in a dreamy state. Perhaps she was thinking about all of the ropes she had walked along or spun around or dangled from or swung on in this ring. Or she was thinking about the extraordinary finale she would perform in three nights' time. Or she may have been listening to her body in that silent private dialogue pregnant women sometimes have with themselves.

"I'm sorry, Miss Devine," Maisie said at last.

"I'm not—not for myself. For you, perhaps. And for her." Miss Devine nodded at the memory of Miss Hannah Smith riding in the ring. "She'll be stuck with the worry over him and his women all her life now. I'm done with that." She glanced at Maisie. "How old are you, Miss—"

"Maisie. I be fifteen."

"No longer so innocent, then. But not yet experienced, are you?"

Maisie wanted to protest—who on the verge of adulthood likes to be reminded of their lingering innocence?—but Miss Devine's weary face demanded honesty. "I've little experience of the world," she admitted.

"Then let me teach you something. What you want is not worth half the value of what you've still got. Remember that."

Maisie nodded, though she did not yet understand the words. She tucked them away for later, when she would take them out and study them. "What will you do now, Miss Devine?" she asked.

Miss Laura Devine smiled. "I am going to fly out of here, pet. That's what I'm going to do."

Normally Maisie would have stayed longer at the amphitheatre, watching rehearsals all afternoon if she could, but after Miss Laura Devine spoke to her she was eager to leave. She did not want to stay and see the slack-rope dancer rehearse with her own replacement. Moreover, John Astley had disappeared, and Maisie doubted he would be able to convince Miss Hannah Smith to get back on her horse. Besides, she should be helping her mother with the cabbage, or getting on with the sewing the Kellaway women were taking in to replace the buttons they used to make. For Bet Butterfield had bought all of their buttons and materials off them, and got them to show her how to make several sorts. Maisie had expressed surprise when her mother agreed to give up the buttons, but Anne Kellaway had been adamant. "We live in London now, not Dorsetshire," she'd said. "We have to leave Dorset things behind." At first Maisie had been glad of the change, but lately she had begun to miss her Dorset buttons. Mending others' clothes was not as satisfying as the thrill of making something entirely new out of nothing—a delicate, cobwebbed button out of a ring and a piece of thread, for instance.

Now she stood on the front steps of the amphitheatre and peered out into the fog engulfing London. The Kellaways had heard much about this thick, choking blanket, but had been lucky enough not to experience it fully until now, for the spring and summer had been breezy, which kept the fog from settling. In the autumn, however, coal fires in houses were lit all day, billowing smoke into the streets, where it hung in the stillness, muffling light and sound. It was only midafternoon, but street lamps were already lit—Maisie could see them disappearing up into the gloom on Westminster Bridge. From habit she studied the people appearing out of the fog as they walked over the bridge toward her, looking in each figure for Rosie Wightman. Maisie had been watching for her this past month, but her old friend had not come.

She hesitated on the steps. Since getting lost in London the month before, Maisie had stopped taking the back-street route between the amphitheatre and home, even though she knew the way and several of the people and shops along it as well. Instead she usually walked along Westminster Bridge Road, where there were more people and the route was clear. It had grown so foggy since she'd come to the amphitheatre earlier, however, that she wondered if she should walk even there. She was just turning to go back in and ask Jem if he would accompany her when John Astley pushed through the door and ran straight into her.

"Oh!" Maisie cried.

John Astley bowed. "My apologies, miss." He was going to pass her but happened to glance at her face, and stopped. For John Astley saw there a look that balanced out the fire of Miss Laura Devine and the tears of Miss Hannah Smith. Maisie was gazing at him with the complete earthy adoration of a Dorset girl. She would never glare at him, or call him a shit sack, or slap him—as Miss Hannah Smith had just done when he followed her backstage.

Maisie would not criticize him, but support him; not make demands on him, but accept him; not spurn him, but open herself to him. Though not as refined as Miss Hannah Smith—this was after all a raw country girl with a red nose and a frilly mop cap—yet she had bright eyes and a fine slight figure that a part of his body was already responding to. She was just the tonic a man needed after being the target of rage and jealousy.

John Astley put on his kindest, most helpful face; most importantly, he appeared interested, which was the most seductive quality of all to a girl like Maisie. He studied her as she hesitated on the edge of the dense, sulfuric, all-enveloping fog. "May I be of assistance?" he asked.

"Oh thank'ee, sir!" Maisie cried. "It's just—I need to get home, but the fog do scare me."

"Do you live nearby?"

"That I do, sir. I be just two doors away from you at Hercules Buildings."

"Ah, so we are neighbors. I thought you looked familiar."

"Yes, sir. We met at the fire in the summer—do you remember? And—well, my father and brother work here for the circus. I be here often, bringing them their meals and such."

"I am going towards Hercules Buildings myself. Allow me to escort you." John Astley held out an arm to her. Maisie stared at it as if he were offering her a jewel-encrusted crown. It was rare in the life of a modest girl such as Maisie to be given exactly what she had been dreaming of. She reached over and touched his arm tentatively, as though expecting it to melt. But the cloth of his blue coat, with its flesh underneath, was real, and a thrill visibly shook her.

John Astley laid his other hand over hers and squeezed it, encouraging Maisie to tuck her hand in the crook of his elbow. "There we are, miss—"

"Maisie."

"I am at your service, Maisie." John Astley led her down the steps and left into the murk of Stangate Street rather than right into the marginally brighter fog of Westminster Bridge Road. Maisie was in such a warm fog of her own that without a murmur she allowed him to take her along the shortcut she had avoided for a month. Indeed, Maisie didn't even notice where they were going. To be able to walk with—and even to touch—the handsomest, ablest, and most elegant man she knew was beyond a dream. It was the most important moment in her life. She stepped lightly alongside him as if the fog had got under her feet and cushioned her from the ground.

John Astley was fully aware of the effect he was having on Maisie, and he knew enough to say little as they first went along. To start with he only spoke to direct her through the fog—"Careful of that cart"; "Let's get you out of the gutter, shall we?"; "Just step to your right a moment to avoid that dung." John Astley had grown up with London fog and was used to navigating through it, allowing his other senses to take over—his nose sniffing out horses or pubs or rubbish, his feet sensing the slope of the gutter on the sides of the road or the cobbles in mews. Though the fog muffled sound, he could still tell whether one, two, or four horses were coming along, and distinguish a gig from a chaise. And so he walked confidently through the fog—slowly too, for Hercules Buildings wasn't far, and he needed time.

Once he had gained Maisie's physical confidence, he began gently to lead her along in conversation. "Did you bring dinner to your father and brother today?" he suggested.

"Yes, sir."

"And what did you bring them? Wait, let me guess. A meat pie?"

"Yes, sir."

"Did you buy it or make it yourself?"

"I helped Ma. I made the crust."

"I'm sure you make a very fine crust, Maisie, with your delicate fingers—the finest in Lambeth."

Maisie giggled. "Thank'ee, sir."

They walked a little farther, passing the Queen's Head at the corner where Stangate Street ran into Lambeth Marsh, the yellow light from the pub staining the fog the color of phlegm. No one was outside drinking in such weather, but as they passed, the door burst open and a man reeled out, laughing and cursing at the same time. "Oh!" Maisie clutched John Astley's arm.

He put his other hand over hers again and squeezed it, pulling her arm through his so that they were closer together. "There, now, Maisie, there's no need to worry. You're with me, after all. He wouldn't lay a finger on you." Indeed, the man hadn't noticed them, but began weaving one way up Lambeth Marsh while John Astley and Maisie turned down the other. "I expect he's gone up the Marsh to buy vegetables for his wife. What do you think he'll buy—swedes or turnips?"

Maisie chuckled, despite her nerves. "Oh, swedes, I do think, sir. They be much nicer."

"And leeks or cabbages?"

"Leeks!" Maisie laughed as if she had made a joke, and John Astley joined in.

"That is an unsavory pub, that one," he said. "I should not have brought you past it, Maisie. I do apologize."

"Oh, don't worry, sir. I be perfectly safe with you."

"Good. I am glad, my dear. Of course, not all pubs are like that one. Some are very nice. The Pineapple, for instance. Even ladies can go there and feel quite at home."

"I suppose so, sir, though I never been in." At the mention of that pub, Maisie's face lost its clear brightness as she was reminded of waiting outside it to see John Astley come out with one of the costume girls. Without quite meaning to, she pulled her hand a little way out of the tight grip of his elbow. He felt the shift and inwardly cursed. Not the Pineapple, then, he thought—she clearly didn't like it. Perhaps it was not the best place, anyway—though it was handy for Astley's stables where he intended to end up, it was also likely to be full of circus folk who might know her.

Before John Astley's mention of the Pineapple, Maisie had been able to float along happily on their mild, flirtatious chat and her imagination. Naming the pub, however, forced her to acknowledge to herself his intentions. After all, a visit to a pub with John Astley was a concrete event. She hesitated. "I watched you riding with Miss Smith just now," she said. "You looked so fine together."

This was not where John Astley intended their conversation to go. He wanted to get it back to laughing over vegetables. "Miss Smith rides very well," he answered simply, wondering how much Maisie had seen during the rehearsal. Had she heard what his father shouted at Miss Laura Devine?

For her part, Maisie was also thinking about what she had seen and heard, the piece of the puzzle that linked John Astley with Miss Devine. She thought about it, and found that his actual presence at her side—his broad shoulders and tapered waist under his well-cut blue coat, his gay eyes and ready smile, his light, sure step and firm grip, even the meaty smell of horse sweat on him—was far more potent to her than anything he had done to anyone else. With only a twinge of guilt for the kindness Miss Devine had shown and the warning she had given her, Maisie shut her mind to John Astley's history and thought only of this moment. He might pay attention to many women, but why shouldn't she have a share of that attention? She wanted it.

She even made it easy for him. When they emerged from the lane into Hercules Buildings, with the Kellaways' rooms just to the right of them, Maisie said, "Here so soon!" in as sad a tone as she could manage.

John Astley immediately took her up. "My dear, I thought you would be pleased to arrive home safely! Are you expected?"

"No," Maisie answered. "Not yet. I'll help Ma with the cabbage, but really she's not so busy."

"What, no leeks or swedes for you?"

Maisie smiled, but he was leading her across the street now, and her stomach churned with the thought that he would soon deposit her at her door and she might never again talk to him or touch him.

"It has been such a pleasure escorting you home, Maisie, that I am loath to give up the sensation," John Astley announced, stopping short of Miss Pelham's house. "Perhaps we might take a drink together before I leave you at home."

"That—that would be—very nice."

"Perhaps the tavern at the top of the road would suit. It is close—we wouldn't want to go far in this fog—and it has a snug little corner that I think you will like."

"All—all right, sir." Maisie could barely utter the words. For a moment she felt dizzy with a heady mix of guilt and fear. But she gripped John Astley's arm tightly again, turned her back on her barely visible home, and walked in the direction he—and she—wanted to go.

~ 5 ~

Hercules Tavern completed the line of houses along Hercules Buildings just where it met Westminster Bridge Road, with the Pineapple shoring up the other end. It was bigger and more crowded than the Pineapple, with booths and bright lights. John Astley had drunk there a few times but preferred to conduct his seductions in quieter, darker places. However, at least there were no circus people here; nor did anyone look up as they came in.

John Astley paid a couple to move, and sat Maisie in a corner booth screened with shoulder-high wood panels that gave them a little privacy from their neighbors in the booths on either side, but with a clear view of the room. Then he went to the bar and got her a rum punch, with a glass of wine for himself. "Make it sweet and strong," he said of the punch. The barman glanced at Maisie in her seat, but made no comment.

Once they were sitting together with their drinks, John Astley did not take the lead in conversation as he had out on the street. In fact, he felt little desire to talk at all. He had achieved his first aim—to get Maisie sitting in a pub with a drink in front of her. He felt he had done enough, and the rum and his physical presence would do the rest to bring him his second aim. He did not really enjoy talking with women, and felt he had little now to say to Maisie. She was a pretty girl, and he simply wanted solace from the more trying women in his life.

Maisie said nothing at first because of the novelty of sitting with a handsome man in a London pub. She had been to pubs in the Piddle Valley, of course, but they were dark, smoky, and poor compared to this. Though Hercules Tavern was itself only a shabby local pub, its wooden tables and chairs were better made than the rough, half-broken ones at the Five Bells in Piddletrenthide, where the landlord bought secondhand chairs from traveling bodgers rather than pay for Thomas Kellaway's superior work. Hercules Tavern was warmer too, for despite the larger room, its coal fire drew better, and there were more customers to heat it as well. Even the pewter mugs for beer were not so dented as in Piddletrenthide, and the glasses for wine and punch were of a better quality than she'd seen in Dorsetshire.

Maisie had never been in a room with so many lamps, and was fascinated by the detail she could now make out—the patterns on women's dresses, the wrinkles on a man's brow, the names and initials carved into the wood panels. She watched people passing to and fro much as a cat might spy on a tree full of birds—hungrily following one, then being distracted by another, her head whipping back and forth. The other customers seemed to be in high spirits. When a group across the room guffawed, Maisie smiled. When two men began to shout at each other, she raised her eyebrows, then sighed in relief as they suddenly laughed and thumped each other's back.

She had no idea what the punch cup John Astley set in front of her contained—she'd only ever drunk weak beer—but took it up gamely and sipped. "Oh, it do have something in it—makes it spicy." She licked her lips. "I didn't think drinks would be different in London. But so many things are. This pub, for instance—it be so much livelier than the Five Bells!" She sipped once more—though she didn't actually think much of the drink, she knew it was expected of her.

John Astley wasn't really listening, but calculating how much rum he would need to buy her before she was pliable enough to agree to anything. He glanced at her red cheeks and silly smile. Two should do it, he thought.

While Maisie didn't look closely enough to recognize any of the customers, one of them recognized her. In the crowd of men gathered at the bar, she did not see Charlie Butterfield waiting for drinks, even when he began to stare at her. Once John Astley was sitting with her and she was well into her rum punch, Charlie turned away in disgust. However, he couldn't resist saying as he set down beer in front of his parents, "Guess who's sitting in the next booth. No, don't, Mam!" He pulled Bet Butterfield down as she started to get up so that she could peer over the screen. "Don't let 'em see you!"

"Who's there, boy?" Dick Butterfield asked as he brought the beer to his lips and took a dainty sip. "Ah, lovely."

"That nan-boy Astley with little Miss Dorset."

"Dorset? Not Maisie?" Bet Butterfield said. "What's she doing here, then? This an't the place for her." She turned an ear toward the neighboring booth to listen. Maisie was growing louder with each sip of rum punch, so the Butterfields could hear at least one side of the conversation—John Astley's voice was low, and he said little.

"Ma and me goes to the circus twice a week," she was saying.

"So I've seen everything you've done, several times. I do love your horse, sir. You sit her so beautifully."

John Astley merely grunted. He never talked about work at the pub, nor did he need to hear compliments from her; but Maisie was not experienced enough to sense this. In truth, he was beginning to tire of her. He had spotted a couple of women in the room who he expected would have given him a better time than Maisie. She was clearly a virgin, and in his experience he'd found that virgins were better in theory than in practice. Deflowering them required a certain patience and responsibility that he was not always keen to take on; often they cried, and he would prefer a woman to take some pleasure in being with him. Only Miss Laura Devine had shown any virginal sophistication, laughing rather than crying during the act, and aware of the ways a woman might please a man without his having to teach her. He had been surprised that she was still a virgin; surprised too that she then displayed a virgin's other characteristic besides tears—the belief that she now had some claim on him. After a few pleasurable meetings he had shaken her off, and refused to believe she was carrying his child until Miss Hannah Smith slapped the knowledge into him earlier today.

Still, whatever John Astley thought of Maisie, he had already made his claim to her by seating her in the booth and plying her with punch in full view of the other drinkers. The women in the room could see full well what he was up to and had no interest in being second choice of the day.

He would at least make this quick. The moment she finished her rum punch, he got up to renew it and his wine. On his way back to their seats, a drink in each hand, he stepped aside to let a boy with a scarred eyebrow pass. The boy stepped to the same side as him, then stepped back as John Astley did, sneering all the while. After blocking John Astley's passage for a moment more, he bumped his shoulder, jolting the horseman's glass of wine so that half of it slopped onto the floor. "Nan-boy," he hissed as he passed.

John Astley had no idea who he was, but was familiar with the type: The boy had probably been to the show and was jealous of Astley's fame and skill. Men sometimes stopped him in the street or at the pub and taunted him; occasionally a fight would break out as jealousy flared into action. John Astley tried to avoid this when possible, as it was undignified for someone in his superior position to be brawling with common folk. But he did defend himself very ably, and fought off attacks in particular to his handsome face. Despite several falls and kicks from horses, he had managed to keep his face clear of damage and scarring, and he had no intention of losing his looks to a mere punch-up with a drunk working lad.

Maisie had not noticed the exchange, for she was now listening to a buxom woman with chapped cheeks and beefy arms leaning over the partition from the adjacent booth.

"I been meanin' to drop in on you and your mam both," the woman was saying. "I've a lady wants a different kind of button, for waistcoats she's making. Do you know how to make a High Top?"

"Course I do!" Maisie cried. "I be from Dorsetshire, don't I? Dorset buttons from a Dorset maid!" The punch made her voice loud and a bit shrill.

Bet Butterfield frowned—she had caught a whiff of rum. "Your mam knows you're here, does she?"

"Of course she does," John Astley interrupted. "But it's not your business, is it, Madam Nosy?"

Bet Butterfield bristled. "It is too my business. Maisie's my neighbor, she is, and we look out for our neighbors round here— some of 'em, anyway." She cut her eyes sideways at him.

John Astley considered how to handle her: He could flatter her, or he could treat her with disdain and indifference. It was not always easy to judge which method would work with which type of woman, but he had to decide before he lost Maisie to her neighbors. Now that there was a chance that he could not have her, he wanted her more. Setting down the drinks and turning his back on the laundress, he slid onto the bench next to Maisie and boldly put his arm around her. Maisie smiled, snuggled back against his arm, and took a gulp of rum punch.

Bet Butterfield watched this cozy display with suspicion. "Maisie, are you—"

"I be fine, Mrs. Butterfield, really. Ma knows I be here."

"Do she, now?" Though Maisie was becoming more adept at lying, it took some doing to convince Bet Butterfield.

"Leave it, Bet," Dick Butterfield grumbled, with a tug at her skirt. It was the week's end and he was tired, wanting nothing more than to sink into a few drinks with family and friends. He often felt his wife interfered too much in others' dramas.

Bet Butterfield satisfied herself by saying, "I'll come and see you later about those High Tops, shall I?" as if to warn John Astley that Maisie should be at home soon to receive her.

"Yes, or tomorrow. Best make it soon, as we may be leaving shortly."

"Leaving? To go where—back to Dorsetshire?"

"Not Dorsetshire." Maisie waved her hand about. "To Dublin with the circus!"

Even John Astley looked surprised—if not horrified—at this news. "You are?"

"I heard your father ask mine to come. And of course you can convince him to let Pa bring all of us." She sipped her punch and banged the glass down. "We'll all be together!"

"Will you, now." Bet Butterfield frowned at John Astley. "Perhaps I'd best go with you now to your mam, then."

"Bet, sit down and finish your drink." Dick Butterfield used a commanding tone Bet Butterfield did not often hear, and she obeyed, sinking slowly into her seat, the frown still glued to her face.

"Somethin' an't right there," she muttered. "I know it."

"Yes, and it an't your business, is it. You leave those Kellaways be. You're as bad as Maggie, lookin' out that Kellaway boy every chance she gets. Maybe you should be more worried about her than that girl in the next booth. Miss Dorset is old enough to know what she's about. She'll get what she wants from Astley. Now, when you do go round to see Mrs. Kellaway, be sure and ask what her husband's goin' to do with all his wood if they're off to Ireland. Tell him I'll take it off him for very little—chairs too, if he's got any. Now I think on it, perhaps I'll come with you when you pay your visit."

"Now who's buttin' into Kellaway business?"

Dick Butterfield stretched, then took up his mug. "This an't Kellaway business, my chuck—this is Butterfield business! This is how I keep that roof over your head."

Bet Butterfield snorted. "These are what keep it." She held out her chafed, wrinkled hands, which had been handling wet clothes for twenty years and looked much older than Bet was herself. Dick Butterfield seized one and kissed it in a combination of pity and affection. Bet Butterfield laughed. "You old sausage, you. What am I going to do with you?" She sat back and yawned, for she had just finished an overnight wash and not slept in more than a day. She settled into her seat like a rock set into a stone wall and allowed Maisie to slip from her mind. She would not be moving for several hours.

John Astley, in the meantime, was pondering Dublin. One of Maisie's attractions was that he would be leaving her here in a few days and not have to wrestle with any virginal claim she made on him. "What's this about Dublin, then?" he said. "Your father is going to do what?"

"Carpentry. He be a chairmaker, but Mr. Astley asked him to

join the circus to build all sorts of things." Maisie slurred the last words, the rum taking effect. She wanted to lay her spinning head on the table.

John Astley relaxed—his father would certainly never allow a carpenter's family to join them in Dublin. He drained his glass and stood up. "Come, let's go."

Not a moment too soon, either. The surly lad who had made him spill his wine was now with a group across the room and had begun to sing:

> A loving couple met one day
> Bonny Kate and Danny
> A loving couple met one day
> Together both to sport and play
> And for to pass the time away
> He showed her little Danny!

Maisie's cheeks were fiery red now, and she looked a little dazed. "Come, Maisie," John Astley repeated, glaring at the singers. "I'll see you home."

Around the room others had taken up the song:

> He took her to his father's barn
> Bonny Kate and Danny
> He took her to his father's barn
> There he pulled out his long firearm
> It was as long as this my arm
> And he called it little Danny!

Maisie was taking her time arranging her shawl around her shoulders. "Quick, now!" John Astley muttered. Pulling her to her feet, he put an arm around her and led her to the door. Over the singing, Bet Butterfield called out, "Don't forget, now, duck—I'll be comin' to your mam's shortly!"

He took her to the river's side
Bonny Kate and Danny
He took her to the river's side
And there he laid her legs so wide
And on her belly he did ride
And he whipped in little Danny!

John Astley shut the door behind them to bellows of laughter. Maisie did not seem to notice, however, though the fresh air made her stand straight and shake her head as if to clear it. "Where we going, sir?" she managed to say.

"Just for a little stroll, then I'll get you home." John Astley kept his arm around her and led her, not left along Hercules Buildings, but right into Bastille Row. There was a gap that way between two of the houses that led to Hercules Hall and its stables.

The cold air made Maisie progress instantly from happy drunk to sick drunk. A little way along Bastille Row she began to moan and hold her stomach. John Astley let go of her. "Idiot girl," he muttered as Maisie sank to her knees and vomited into the gutter. He was tempted to leave her now to find her own way. It was not far back to the pub, though the fog was so dense that there was no sign of it.

At that moment a figure came pattering out of the fog toward them. They were only a few steps from the Butterfields' rooms, where Maggie had stopped briefly after work to change her clothes. She was now working at a vinegar manufactory near the river, by the timber yards north of Westminster Bridge, and though she smelled acidic, at least her nose no longer hurt and her eyes were clear. The owner even let them off early on a Saturday afternoon.

Maggie started when she saw John Astley. For a year now she had not liked going through the fog on her own, though she did it when she had to. She had walked back from the factory with another girl who lived nearby, and the pub was so close to the

Butterfields' that she had not thought to worry. Seeing the horseman so suddenly almost made her scream, until she spied the huddled form at his feet, still retching into the gutter. Then she chuckled,
for she recognized John Astley with one of his conquests. "Having
fun, are you, sir?" she jeered, and ran on before he could reply.
Her relief that this was a familiar scene and John Astley no threat
to her, coupled with her haste to get to the pub out of the fog and
the cold, made her give Maisie no more than a glance before she
hurried on to Hercules Tavern.

~ 6 ~

"There you are, Mags," Dick Butterfield called. "Come and sit."
He stood up. "You'll be wantin' a beer, will you?" These days he
was more solicitous of his daughter; handing over her wages to
him every week had bought her better treatment.

"And a pie, if there's any left," Maggie called after him as she
took his vacated place next to her mother. "Hallo, Mam."

"Hallo, duck." Bet Butterfield yawned. "You all done, then?"

"I am—and you?"

"For the moment." Mother and daughter sat side by side in
weary companionship.

"Is Charlie here?" Maggie asked, trying not to sound hopeful.
"Oh, never mind, there he is." Though her brother bothered her
less than before—another bonus from her wages was that Dick Butterfield reined in Charlie—she was always more at ease when she was
alone with her parents.

"Anything happenin' here?" she asked her mother.

"Nah. Oh—did you know that the Kellaways are going to Dublin?" Bet Butterfield had a habit of changing the possible into the
definite.

Maggie snapped upright. "What?"

"'Tis true. They're leaving this week."

Maggie narrowed her eyes. "Can't be. Who told you?"

Bet Butterfield shifted in her seat, Maggie's disbelief making her nervous. "Maisie Kellaway."

"Why didn't Jem tell me? I saw him the other night!"

Bet Butterfield shrugged.

"But they're mad to go! They're not travelers. It was hard enough for them to come here from Dorsetshire—and they're just startin' to settle. Why would Jem hide it from me?" Maggie tried to keep the note of hysteria from rising in her words, but Bet Butterfield heard it.

"Calm yourself, duck. Didn't know you cared so much. Pity you weren't here five minutes ago—you could've asked Maisie herself."

"She was here?"

"She was." Bet Butterfield fiddled with an end of her shawl, picked up her glass of beer, then set it down.

"Maisie don't go to pubs. What was she doing here, Mam?" Maggie persisted.

Bet Butterfield frowned into her beer. "She was with that circus man. You know." She waved her hand in the air. "The one what rides the horses. John Astley."

"John Astley?" Even as she shouted his name, Maggie shot to her feet. Neighboring drinkers looked up.

"Careful, Mags," Dick Butterfield said, halting in front of her with two full glasses and a pie balanced on their rims. "You don't want to lose your beer 'fore you've even tasted it."

"I just saw John Astley outside! But he was with a—" Maggie stopped, horrified that she hadn't looked closely enough at the figure in the gutter to recognize her as Maisie. "Where were they going?"

"Said he was takin' her home," Bet Butterfield muttered, her eyes lowered.

"And you believed him?" Maggie's voice rose.

"Stay out of it, gal," Dick Butterfield said sharply. "It an't your business."

Maggie looked from her mother's bent head to her father's set face, and knew then that they had already had this argument.

"You can have my beer," she said to Dick Butterfield, and pushed through the crowd.

"Maggie! You get back here, gal!" Dick Butterfield barked, but Maggie had pulled open the door and plunged into the fog.

It was dark now, with only the street lamps cutting through the dense mist, casting weak, yellowy green pools of light at their bases. Maggie ran past the spot—now deserted—where she had last seen John Astley and Maisie, and headed down Bastille Row. She passed her own house, then stopped a neighbor just going inside two doors down. He had not seen the couple. When he shut the door behind him, Maggie was alone on the street in the fog.

She hesitated, then ran on. In a minute she reached the gap between the houses, where an alley led to the field around Hercules Hall and its stables. She stood looking down the dark passageway, for there were no lights on at Philip Astley's house to guide her through it. She could not go around and enter by the Hercules Buildings alley on the opposite side of the field, however—it was a long way around and just as dark. As she stood, undecided, the fog swirled around her, leaving a shiny, sulfurous film of sweat on her face. Maggie gulped. She could hear the sound of her heavy breath thrown back at her.

Then a figure stepped out of the fog behind her, and Maggie gasped—it was so like the man looming out at her from another fog on another night. The scream got caught in her throat, though, and she was grateful for that—for the figure was her brother, who would have teased her ever after for screaming in his face.

Maggie grabbed his arm before he could speak. "Charlie, c'mon, we have to go down here!" She tried to pull him along the passage.

Despite his lean frame, when Charlie planted his feet, it was impossible to move him, and Maggie's arm-pulling had no effect. "Hang on a minute, Miss Cut-Throat. Where do you think you're takin' me?"

"Maisie," Maggie hissed. "He's taken Maisie down here, I'm sure of it. We have to get to them before he . . . he . . ."

"He what?" Charlie seemed to enjoy drawing this out.

"You know what he's goin' to do. D'you really want him to ruin her?"

"Didn't you hear Pa say it was none of our business? The rest of the pub did."

"Course it's our business. It's your business. You like her. You know you do."

Charlie's face hardened. He did not want others—particularly his sister—thinking he had such feelings.

"Charlie, please."

Charlie shook his head.

Maggie dropped his arm. "Then why'd you follow me here? Don't tell me you didn't follow me—no one'd be out here just for a wander."

"Thought I'd see what you're so bothered about."

"Well, now you know. And if you're not goin' to help me, then go away." To make clear that she would do this on her own if she had to, Maggie stepped into the darkness, though beads of sweat broke out once again on her upper lip and brow.

"Hang on a minute," Charlie said. "I'll come with you, if you tell me something first."

Maggie turned back. "What?" Even as she said it, her stomach clenched, for she knew there was only one thing about her that interested her brother.

"What was it like?"

"What was what like?" she said, playing his game of drawing it out, giving him the time and space he craved for the line he was now to deliver.

"What was it like to kill a man?"

Maggie had not heard these words spoken aloud, and they had the effect of taking her clenched stomach and twisting it, knocking the wind out of her as effectively as if Charlie had punched her.

There was a pause while she recovered her voice. It gave her the time to think of something that would satisfy him quickly and move them on. "Powerful," she answered, saying what she thought he wanted to hear, though it was the opposite of what she had actually felt. "Like I could do anything."

What she had really felt that night a year ago was that she had actually killed a part of herself rather than someone else, for she felt sometimes that she was dead now rather than alive. She knew, though, that Charlie would never understand that; she herself didn't. Mr. Blake might understand it, though, she thought, for it fell into his realm of opposites. One day maybe she would get him to explain it to her so that she would know where she was. "Nothing was the same after that," she added truthfully. "I don't know as it ever will be."

Charlie nodded. His smile made Maggie shudder. "All right," he said. "Where we going?"

~ 7 ~

Maisie felt much better after being sick, for it cleared the rum from her. She was sober enough to say to John Astley as the stables appeared out of the fog, "You taking me to see your horse?"

"Yes."

He did, in fact, lead her to the stall where his chestnut mare was stabled, lighting a candle first so that they could see. After the rehearsal at the amphitheatre the mare had been brought here and groomed, watered, and fed, and was standing stolidly, chewing,

waiting for a circus boy to come and get her for the evening performance. She snorted when she saw John Astley, who reached
over and patted her neck. "Hallo there, my darling," he murmured,
with considerably more feeling than he used with people.

Maisie also reached out a timid hand to stroke the horse's nose.
"Oh, she be lovely!"

"Yes, she is." John Astley was relieved that Maisie was no longer quite so drunk. "Here," he said, stooping to fill a ladle from a
bucket of water. "You'll want a drink."

"Thank'ee, sir." Maisie took the ladle, drank, and wiped her
lips.

"Come here a moment." John Astley led the way past other
horses—Miss Hannah Smith's stallion among them—to a stall on
the end.

"Which horse—oh!" Maisie peeked in to see nothing but a pile
of straw. John Astley set the candle down on an upturned bucket
and pulled a blanket from the corner, which he spread out over
the straw. "Come and sit with me for a moment." The stench of
horses all around had aroused him, and the bulge of his groin was
prominent.

Maisie hesitated, her eyes drawn to the bulge. She had known
this moment would arrive, though she had not allowed herself to
think about it. What girl nearing womanhood does not know, after
all? The whole world seems to wait and watch for it, a girl's move
from one side of the river to the other. It seemed strange to Maisie
that it should come down to a blanket that stank of horse on a bed
of straw, in a dim puddle of light, surrounded by fog and dark and
London. She had not pictured it that way. But there was John Astley holding out his hand, and she reaching across and taking it.

By the time Maggie and Charlie reached the stall John Astley
had her chemise off, and her stays loosened and pulled down so
that her pale breasts had popped out. He had a nipple in his mouth,
a hand up her skirt, and the other holding her hand over his groin
and teaching her to stroke him. Maggie and Charlie stared. It was

agonizing to Maggie how long it took for the couple to realize the Butterfields were there and stop what they were doing—plenty of time for her to ponder just how embarrassing and inappropriate it was to watch lovers unawares. She had not felt that seven months before when she and Jem had seen the Blakes in their summer-house, but that somehow had been different. For one thing, they had been farther away, not right under her nose. And since Maggie hadn't known them well, she could look on them more objectively. Now hearing Maisie groan flooded her with shame. "Leave off her!" she shouted.

John Astley leapt back and to his feet in one movement, and Maisie sat up in a daze of pleasure and confusion, so befuddled that she did not immediately cover her breasts, though Maggie made frantic gestures at her. Charlie Butterfield kept looking from John Astley to Maisie's exposed flesh, until at last Maisie pulled up her stays.

To Maggie's surprise, no one responded as she'd expected them to. John Astley did not show remorse or shame; nor did he run away. Maisie did not cry and hide her face, or scramble away from her seducer and go to Maggie. Charlie did not challenge John Astley, but stood gaping, his hands at his sides. Maggie herself was frozen in place.

John Astley didn't know who Maggie was—he was not in the habit of noticing neighborhood children—but he recognized Charlie as the boy who had bumped into him in Hercules Tavern, and wondered if he was sufficiently drunk or angry to act.

The horseman would have to do something to take charge. He had not thought lying with this girl could possibly be so difficult, but now that he had been with her on the straw, he was determined to return to it. He didn't have much time, either—the circus boys would come soon for the horses for the evening's performance. However, obstacles always strengthened John Astley's resolve. "What in hell's name are you doing here? Get out of my stables!"

At last Maggie found her voice, though it came out feebly. "What you doin' to her?"

John Astley snorted. "Get out of my stables," he repeated, "or I'll have you sent to Newgate so fast you won't have time to wipe your arse!"

At the mention of Newgate, Charlie shifted from one foot to the other. Dick Butterfield had spent time in that prison and advised his son to avoid it if at all possible. He was also uneasy being in a stables at all, with horses all about waiting to kick him.

Now Maisie began to cry—the sensation of swinging from one extreme emotion to its opposite was too much for her. "Why don't you go!" she moaned.

It took Maggie a moment to realize that the words were directed at her. It was gradually dawning on her that perhaps no one else thought that what had been happening was wrong. John Astley of course thought nothing of lying with a girl in the stables; he'd done it dozens of times. To Charlie a man was simply having what he wanted and a girl was giving it to him; indeed, he was beginning to look sheepish for interrupting them. Maisie herself was not protesting and—Maggie admitted—had seemed to be enjoying herself. Only Maggie linked the act to the man in the fog on Lovers' Lane. Now she, rather than the man, was being made out to be the criminal. All of her indignation suddenly fled, leaving her without the energy she needed to fight.

There was no Charlie to back her, either. Much as he hated John Astley, he was also cowed by his authority, and quickly lost what little confidence he possessed to stand up to such a man, alone, in a stable in the fog, surrounded by hateful horses, and with no friends about to encourage him. If only Jem were here, Maggie thought. He would know what to do.

"C'mon, Maggie," Charlie said, and began to shuffle out of the stall.

"Wait." Maggie fixed her eyes on the other girl. "Come with us, Miss Piddle. Get up and we'll go and find Jem, all right?"

"Leave her alone," John Astley commanded. "She's free to do as she likes, aren't you, my dear?"

"That means she's free to go with us if she wants to. C'mon, Maisie—are you comin' with us or stayin' here?"

Maisie looked from Maggie to John Astley and back again. She closed her eyes so that she could say it more easily, though taking her sight away gave her the sensation of falling. "I want to stay."

Even then, Maggie might have remained, for surely they wouldn't continue as long as she was there. But John Astley pulled a whip out from the straw and said, "Get out," and that decided matters. Maggie and Charlie backed away—Maggie reluctant, Charlie in his relief pulling her after him. The horses whinnied when they passed, as if commenting on the Butterfields' lack of courage.

~ 8 ~

When they got out to the yard, Charlie turned toward the passage they had first come down. "Where you going?" Maggie demanded.

"Back to the pub, of course. I've wasted too much time out here already, Miss Cut-Throat. Why, an't you?"

"I'm going to find someone with more guts'n you!"

Before he could grab her, Maggie ran down the other alley to Hercules Buildings. The fog no longer frightened her; she was too angry to be scared. When she reached the street, she looked both ways. Figures huddled in wraps hurried past her—the fog and dark discouraged lingering. She ran after one, calling out, "Please, help me! There's a girl in trouble!"

It was an old man, who shook her off and grumbled, "Serves her right—shouldn't be out in this weather."

Passing close enough to hear this exchange was a small woman in a yellow bonnet and shawl. When Maggie saw her little face peeking out, she shouted, "What you lookin' at, you old stick!" and Miss Pelham scuttled toward her door.

"Oh, please!" Maggie cried to another man passing in the other direction. "I need your help!"

"Get off, you little cat!" the man sneered.

Maggie stood helplessly in the street, on the verge of tears. All she wanted was someone with the moral authority to stand up to John Astley. Where was he?

He came from the direction of the river, striding out of the fog with his hands tucked behind him, his broad-brimmed hat jammed low over his heavy brow, and a brooding expression on his face. He had stood up to Philip Astley when he'd felt injustice was being done to a child; he would stand up to Astley's son.

"Mr. Blake!" Maggie cried. "Please help me!"

Mr. Blake's expression immediately cleared, focusing intently on Maggie. "What is it, my girl? What can I do?"

"It's Maisie—she's in trouble!"

"Show me," he said without hesitation.

Maggie ran back down the alley, Mr. Blake following close behind. "I don't think she knows what she's doin'," she panted as she ran. "It's like he's cast a spell over her."

Then they were in the stables, and in the stall, and John Astley looked up from where he was crouched next to a weeping Maisie. When Maisie saw Mr. Blake she buried her face in her hands.

"Mr. Astley, stand up, sir!"

John Astley stood swiftly, with something like fear on his face. He and Mr. Blake were the same height, but Mr. Blake was stockier, his expression stern. His direct gaze pinned John Astley, and there was an adjustment in the stall, with one man taking in and acknowledging the other. It was what Maggie had thought would happen with the combined forces of her and Charlie; they did not have the weight of experience behind them, however. Now, in Mr. Blake's presence, John Astley lowered his eyes and fixed them on a mound of straw in the corner.

"Maggie, take Maisie to my wife—she will look after her." Mr. Blake's tone was gentle but commanding too.

Maisie rubbed her face to get rid of her tears and stood, brushing the straw from her skirt and carefully avoiding John Astley's eyes. She needn't have worried—he was staring fixedly at the ground.

Maggie wrapped Maisie's shawl tightly around her shoulders, then put her arm around the girl and led her from the stall. As they left, Mr. Blake was saying, "For shame, sir! Revolted spirit!"

Out in the fog Maisie collapsed and began to weep.

"C'mon, Miss Piddle, don't cry," Maggie cajoled, holding her up. "Let's get you back, shall we—then you can cry all you like. Come now, pull yourself together." She gave Maisie a little shake.

Maisie took a deep breath and straightened her shoulders.

"That's it. Now, this way. It's not far."

As they stumbled up Hercules Buildings, the fog discharged a welcome surprise—Jem was hastening toward them. "Maisie, where you been? I just heard that—" He stopped at Maggie's frown and shake of her head, and did not go on to say that he had been suspicious when he heard that John Astley had accompanied Maisie, and came out to search for his sister. "Let's go home. Ma'll be expecting you."

"Not yet, please, Jem," Maisie said in a small voice, without looking at him. She was shivering, her teeth chattering. "I don't want them to know."

"I'm takin' her to Mrs. Blake," Maggie declared.

Jem followed them up to the Blakes' door. As they waited after knocking, there was a flicker in Miss Pelham's curtains before she saw Maggie and Jem glaring at her and let them fall back into place.

Mrs. Blake did not seem surprised to see them. When Maggie said, "Mr. Blake sent us, ma'am. Can you get Maisie warmed up?"

she opened the door wide and stood aside to let them pass as if she did this every day for them. "Go downstairs to the kitchen, my dears—there's a fire's lit there," she said. "I'll just get a blanket and then come and make you a cup of tea."

~ *9* ~

The Kellaways did not attend the final performance of the season of Astley's Circus. Despite Mrs. Blake's ministrations, Maisie came down with a fever, and was still in her sickbed that night, with Anne Kellaway tending her. Thomas and Jem Kellaway spent the evening clearing out the workroom, which had been neglected over the months while they were working for Philip Astley. It would need to be in order now, for Thomas Kellaway had told Philip Astley that he would not be accompanying him to Dublin. Maisie was too ill to travel, and though he did not know what had caused it, he had a vague suspicion—a feeling he could not pin down or articulate—that the circus, if not Astley himself, had something to do with it. In truth, though Thomas Kellaway was of course horrified by his daughter's illness, he was relieved to have a concrete excuse not to go to Dublin.

Maggie did see the final show, and later described it to Jem, for it was quite eventful in its own way. Miss Laura Devine decided to make a private drama very public indeed. She performed the new routine with Monsieur Richer, as promised, the two of them turning in opposite Pigs on Spits, Monsieur Richer spinning rapidly in his black tailcoat, Miss Devine more slowly with her rainbow petticoats not quite the blur of color they normally were. As she came out of her spin into the swoop up that had so captivated Anne Kellaway when she first saw it on Westminster Bridge, this time Miss Devine simply let go and flew through the air. She landed in the pit, breaking her ankle but not bringing on the miscarriage she so desired. As they carried her out through the audience she kept her eyes squeezed shut.

Miss Laura Devine's fall caused such an uproar that the debut of Miss Hannah Smith on horseback was something of an anticlimax, the applause lukewarm. This may also have been due to the rare sight of John Astley making a mistake. As he and Miss Smith were passing the wineglass back and forth while riding in opposite circles around the ring—for they had made up after their fight— John Astley happened to glance down and see Mr. and Mrs. Blake sitting in the pit. They had never been to the circus, and Anne Kellaway had insisted on giving them her tickets, as thanks for finding Maisie in the fog. Mr. Blake was watching John Astley with his fierce eyes. When Miss Smith then held out the glass to him as she passed, John Astley fumbled with it, and it fell to the ground and shattered.

PART VII

December 1792

It was rare for Maggie to be given the afternoon off. In manufactory jobs you began at six in the morning, worked till noon, when you had an hour to eat, then worked again until seven at night. If you didn't work your hours, you were let go, as she had been from the mustard factory after she'd gone for her nap in the Blakes' garden. So when the owner, Mr. Beaufoy, announced that the workers at his vinegar manufactory would not have to stay after dinner, Maggie did not cry "Huzzah" and clap along with the others. She was sure he was not telling them something. "He'll take it from our wages," she muttered to the girl next to her.

"I don't care," the other replied. "I'm going to put my feet up by the fire and sleep all afternoon."

"And not eat all the next day for losin' that sixpence," Maggie retorted.

It turned out that they lost both the sixpence and the sleep by the fire. At noon, Mr. Beaufoy made another announcement as the workers were sitting down to dinner. "You are doubtless aware," he said, addressing the long tables full of men and women attacking plates of sausages and cabbage, "of the continuing atrocities being committed across the Channel in France, and the poison issuing forth to pollute our shores. There are those here who can hardly call themselves Englishmen, for they have heeded this reckless revolutionary call, and are spreading seditious filth to undermine our glorious monarchy."

No one looked up or took much notice of his oration: They were far more interested in finishing their food so that they could leave before Mr. Beaufoy changed his mind about granting them a half day's holiday. Mr. Beaufoy paused, gritting his teeth so that his jaw flexed. He was determined to make his workers understand that, though his surname was French, he was English through and through. He dropped his complicated language. "Our King is in danger!" he boomed, causing forks to pause. "The French have imprisoned their King and offered to help those who wish to do the same here. We cannot allow such treason to spread. Finish eating quickly so that you may follow me—we are going to give up our afternoon's wages to attend a public meeting and demonstrate our loyalty to King and country. Anyone who doesn't come," he added in a raised voice over protests, "anyone who doesn't come will not only lose their work and wages, but will be placed on a list of those suspected of sedition. Do you know what sedition is, good people? It is incitement to disorder. More than that, it is the first step on the road to treason! And do you know what the punishment for sedition is? At the very least, a good strong whipping, but more likely, a long visit to Newgate. And, should you continue along that road toward treason, your visit will end with the hangman."

He waited till the roaring died down. "It is a simple choice: follow me to Vauxhall to declare your loyalty to our King, or walk out now and face prison or worse. Who would like to leave? I am not standing in your way. Go, and let us shout traitor to your back!"

Maggie looked around. No one moved, though a few were frowning into their plates at Mr. Beaufoy's bullying. She shook her head, baffled that something happening in France could have the effect of taking away her wages. It made no sense. What a funny world, she thought.

And yet she found herself walking with three dozen others through the frozen streets that ran along the Thames, past Westminster Bridge and Astley's Amphitheatre—now boarded up and lifeless—past the brick towers of Lambeth Palace, and on down to Cumberland Gardens in Vauxhall, just next to a rival's vinegar works. Maggie was surprised by the large crowd that had gathered, wondering that so many were willing to stand in the cold and listen to a lot of men talk about their love of the King and hatred of the French. "I'll bet he smells his own farts!" Maggie whispered of each speaker to her neighbor, sending them both into giggles each time.

Luckily Mr. Beaufoy lost all interest in his workers once they were installed at Cumberland Gardens and had served their purpose in swelling the numbers of the meeting. He hurried off to join the group of men running the meeting so that he might add his own florid voice to those eager to try out their expressions of loyalty. Eventually his foreman also disappeared, and once the Beaufoy vinegar workers realized that no one was watching them, they began to disperse.

Though she hated losing her afternoon wages, Maggie was glad of the change, and delighted with her luck—for she might find Jem down this way with her father. Dick Butterfield was today taking the Kellaway men to see a man at a timber yard in Nine Elms, just along the river from Vauxhall. They were hoping to find cheaper wood there, as well as a market for their chairs—the timber merchant being also a furniture dealer. For the only time in his life, and at his wife's insistence, Dick Butterfield was providing this introduction for free. The laundress had visited the Kellaways several times while Maisie was ill, prompted by unvoiced guilt that she had done nothing to stop the girl from going out into the fog with John Astley. On a recent visit she had glimpsed the tower of unsold chairs and Anne Kellaway's thin soup, and afterward had ordered her husband to help the family. "You've got to get over that gal, chuck," Dick Butterfield had said. He had not said no, however. In his way, Dick Butterfield too felt badly about Maisie.

Maggie suspected they would have finished their business at the timber yard by now, and would round out the visit with a drink at a pub, where Dick Butterfield would no doubt take as many pints off of Thomas Kellaway as he could. She slipped out of the crowd to the road, and ducked first into the Royal Oak, the nearest pub to the gathering. As expected, it was jammed with people come in from the meeting to warm up, but her father and the Kellaways were not there. She then headed toward Lambeth, calling in at the White Lion and the Black Dog before finding them sucking pints at a table in a corner of the King's Arms. Her heart pounded harder when she spotted Jem, and she took the moment before they saw her to study his hair curling around his ears, the pale patch of skin visible at the back of his neck, and the strong span of his shoulders that had broadened since they first met. Maggie was so tempted to go up behind him, put her arms around his neck, and nuzzle his ear that she actually took a step forward. Jem looked up then, however, and she stopped, her nerve lost.

He started at the sight of her. "Ar'ernoon. You all right?" Though he said it casually, he was clearly pleased to see her.

"What you doin' here, Mags?" Dick Butterfield said. "Beaufoy catch you nickin' a bottle of vinegar and send you packing?"

Maggie folded her arms over her chest. "Hallo to you too. I suppose I'm going to have to get my own beer, will I?"

Jem gestured to his own seat and mug of beer. "Take it—I'll get another."

"No, Pa, I did not get the boot from Beaufoy," Maggie snapped, dropping onto Jem's stool. "If I wanted to steal his poxy vinegar I know how to do it without getting caught. No, we had the afternoon off to go to that loyalist meeting down the road." She described the gathering at Cumberland Gardens.

Dick Butterfield nodded. "We saw 'em when we was passing. Stopped for a minute, but we'd worked up a thirst by then, hadn't we, sir?" He aimed this at Jem's father. Thomas Kellaway nodded, though his pint was barely touched. He was not much of a daytime drinker.

"'Sides, those meetings don't mean nothing to me," Dick Butterfield continued. "All this talk about the threat from France is nonsense. Them Frenchies has their hands full with their own revolution without tryin' to bring it over here too. Don't you think, sir?"

"Dunno as I understand it," Thomas Kellaway answered—his usual response to such questions. He had heard talk of the French revolution when he worked with the other carpenters at the circus, but, as when serious matters were discussed at the Five Bells in Piddletrenthide, he usually listened without supplying his own opinion. It was not that Thomas Kellaway was stupid—far from it. He simply saw both sides of an argument too readily to come down on one side or the other. He could accept that the King was a con-crete manifestion of the English soul and spirit, uniting and glori-fying the country, and thus essential to its well-being. He could also agree when others said King George was a drain on the coun-try's coffers, an unstable, fickle, willful presence that England would be better off without. Torn by conflicting views, he preferred to keep quiet.

Jem came back with another drink and a stool, and squeezed in next to Maggie so that their knees were touching. They smiled at each other, at the rarity of sitting together in the middle of a Monday afternoon, and remembering too the first time they had been to a pub together, when Jem met Dick Butterfield. His stool-finding and pub presence had improved greatly in the nine months since.

Dick Butterfield watched this exchange of smiles with a small cynical smile of his own. His daughter was young to be locking eyes with this boy—and a country boy at that, even one who was learning a good trade.

"You sell your chairs, then?" Maggie asked.

"Maybe," Jem said. "We left one with him. And he's going to get us some yew cheaper than we had from the other yard, in't he, Pa?"

Thomas Kellaway nodded. Since Philip Astley's departure to Dublin, he had been making Windsor chairs again, but had fewer commissions now that the circus man was no longer around to

send customers his way. He filled his days making chairs anyway,
using leftover bits of wood scrounged from the circus. Their back
room was filling with Windsor chairs that awaited buyers. Thomas
Kellaway had even given two to the Blakes, a gift for helping
Maisie on that foggy October afternoon.

"Oh, you'll do much better with this man at Nine Elms, lad,"
Dick Butterfield put in. "I could have told you that months ago
when you went to see that friend of Astley's about wood."

"He were all right for a time," Jem argued.

"Let me guess—until the circus left town? Astley's little deals
only last while he's got his eye on 'em."

Jem was silent.

"That's always the way with him, boy. Philip Astley showers
you with attention, gets you customers, bargains, jobs, and free
tickets—until he leaves. And he's gone five months—that's almost
half the year, boy, half your life where he pulls out and leaves you
stranded. You notice how quiet Lambeth is without him? It's like
that every year. He comes and helps you out, brings in business,
gets people settled and happy, and then comes October and poof!—
in a day he's gone, leaving everybody with nothing. He builds a
castle for you, and then he tears it down again. Grooms, pie makers, carpenters, coachmen, or whores—it happens to 'em all. There's
a great scramble to pick up work, then people drift off—the whores
and coachmen go to other parts of London; some of the country
folk go back home." Dick Butterfield brought his beer to his lips
and took a long draw. "Then come March it'll start all over again,
when the great illusionist builds his castle once again. But some of
us knows better than to do business with Philip Astley. We know
it don't last."

"All right, Pa, you made your point. He do go on, don't he?"
Maggie said to Jem. "Sometimes I fall asleep with my eyes open
when he's talkin'."

"Cheeky gal!" Dick Butterfield cried. Maggie dodged and laughed
as he swatted at her.

"Where's Charlie, then?" she asked as they settled back down.

"Dunno—said he had summat to do." Dick Butterfield shook his head. "Someday I'd like that boy to come home and tell me he's done a deal, and show me the money."

"You may be waitin' a long time, Pa."

Before Dick Butterfield could respond, at the bar a tall man with a broad square face spoke up in a deep, carrying voice that silenced the pub. "Citizens! Listen, now!" Maggie recognized him as one of the plainer speakers at the Cumberland Gardens rally. He held up what looked like a black ledger book. "The name's Roberts, John Roberts. I've just come from a meeting of the Lambeth Association—local residents who are loyal to the King and opposed to the trouble being stirred up by French agitators. You should have been there as well, rather than drinking away your afternoon."

"Some of us was!" Maggie shouted. "We already heard you."

"Good," John Roberts said, and strode over to their table. "Then you'll know what I'm doing here, and you'll be the first to sign."

Dick Butterfield kicked Maggie under the table and glared at her. "Don't mind her, sir, she's just bein' cheeky."

"Is she your daughter?"

Dick Butterfield winked. "For my sins—if you know what I mean."

The man showed no sign of a sense of humor. "You'd best see that she controls her tongue, then, unless she fancies a bed in Newgate. This is nothing to laugh about."

Dick Butterfield raised his eyebrows, turning his forehead into its field of furrows. "Perhaps you could trouble to tell me what the matter is that I'm not to laugh at, sir."

John Roberts stared at him, puzzling over whether or not Dick Butterfield was making fun of him. "It is a declaration of loyalty to the King," he said finally. "We're going from pub to pub and house to house asking the residents of Lambeth to sign it."

"We need to know what we're signin', don't we?" Dick Butterfield said. "Read it to us."

The pub was silent now. Everyone watched as John Roberts opened the ledger. "Perhaps you would like to read it aloud, for everyone's benefit, since you're so interested," he said, sliding it toward Maggie's father.

If he thought his demand would humiliate the other man, however, he had miscalculated; Dick Butterfield pulled the book to him and read reasonably fluidly, and even with feeling that he may not have actually felt, the following:

> We, the Inhabitants of the Parish of Lambeth, deeply sensible of the Blessings derived to us from the present admired and envied Form of Government, consisting of King, Lords and Commons, feel it a Duty incumbent on us, at this critical Juncture, not only to declare our sincere and zealous Attachment to it, but moreover to express our perfect Abhorrence of all those bold and undisguised Attempts to shake and subvert this our invaluable Constitution, which the Experience of Ages has shewn to be the most solid Foundation of national Happiness.
>
> Resolved unanimously,
> That we do form ourselves into an Association to counteract, as far as we are able, all tumultuous and illegal Meetings of ill designing and wicked Men, and adopting the most effectual Measures in our Power for the Suppression of seditious Publications, evidently calculated to mislead the Minds of the People, and to introduce Anarchy and Confusion into this Kingdom.

When Dick Butterfield finished reading, John Roberts set a bottle of ink on the table and held out a pen. "Will you sign, sir?"

To Maggie's astonishment, Dick Butterfield took the pen, uncorked the ink, dipped it in, and began to sign at the bottom of the list of signatures. "Pa, what you doing?" she hissed. She hated the hectoring attitude of John Roberts and her employer, Mr. Beaufoy, indeed of all of the men who'd spoken at the meeting, and had assumed her father would as well.

Dick Butterfield paused. "What d'you mean? What's wrong with signing? I happen to agree—though them words is a bit fancy for my taste."

"But you just said you didn't think the Frenchies were a threat!"

"This an't about the Frenchies—it's about us. I support old King George—I done all right by him." He applied pen to paper again. In the silence, the entire pub concentrated on its scratching across the page. When he finished, Dick Butterfield looked around and feigned surprise at the attention. He turned to John Roberts. "Anything else you want?"

"Write down where you live as well."

"It's no. 6 Bastille Row." Dick Butterfield chuckled. "But p'raps York Place'd be better for such a document, eh?" He wrote it next to his name. "There. No need to visit, then, eh?"

Now Maggie recalled several crates of port that had appeared from nowhere a few days earlier and were hidden under her parents' bed, and smiled: Dick Butterfield had signed so readily because he didn't want these men paying any visits to Bastille Row.

Once he had captured Dick Butterfield's details, John Roberts slid the open book across to Thomas Kellaway. "Now you."

Thomas Kellaway gazed down at the page, with its carefully composed declaration—its rhetoric-laden, almost incomprehensible wording decided on at an earlier, smaller meeting, its messengers with their books fanning out across Lambeth's pubs and markets even before the Cumberland Gardens meeting was over—and its ragtag signatures, some confident, others wavering, along with several Xs with names and addresses scrawled after them in

John Roberts's hand. It was all too complicated for him. "I don't understand—why must I sign this?"

John Roberts leaned over and rapped his knuckles on the table next to the ledger. "You're signing in support of the King! You're saying you want him to be your King, and you'll fight those who want to get rid of him." He peered at the chairmaker's puzzled face. "What, are you a fool, sir? Do you not call the King your King?"

Thomas Kellaway was not a fool, but words worried him. He had always lived by a policy of signing as few documents as possible, and those only for business. He did not even sign the letters Maisie wrote to Sam, and discouraged her from writing anything about him. This way, he thought, there was little trace of him in the world, apart from his chairs, and he would not be misunderstood. This document before him, he felt with a clarity that surprised him, was open to misunderstanding. "I am not sure the King be in danger," he said. "There be no French here, do there?"

John Roberts narrowed his eyes. "You would be surprised at what an ill-informed Englishman is capable of."

"And what d'you mean by publications?" Thomas Kellaway continued without appearing to have heard John Roberts. "I don't know anything about publications."

John Roberts looked around. The goodwill that Dick Butterfield's signature had garnered with the rest of the pub was rapidly diminishing with every ponderous word Thomas Kellaway uttered. "I haven't time for this," he hissed. "There are plenty of others here waiting to sign. Where do you live, sir?" He flipped to another page and waited with pen poised to note down the address. "Someone will visit you later to explain."

"No. 12 Hercules Buildings," Thomas Kellaway replied.

John Roberts stiffened. "You live at Hercules Buildings?"

Thomas Kellaway nodded. Jem felt a knot tighten in his stomach.

"Do you know a William Blake, who is a printer in that street?"

Jem, Maggie, and Dick Butterfield caught on at the same time, partly thanks to Thomas Kellaway's mention of publications. Maggie kicked Thomas Kellaway's stool and frowned at him, while Dick Butterfield feigned a coughing fit.

Unfortunately, Thomas Kellaway could be a bit of a terrier when it came to making a point. "Yes, I know Mr. Blake. He's our neighbor." And, because he did not care for the unfriendly look on John Roberts's face, he decided to make his feelings clear. "He be a good man—he helped out my daughter a month or two back."

"Did he, now?" John Roberts smiled and slammed shut the book. "Well, we were planning to pay a visit to Mr. Blake this evening, and can call on you as well. Good day to you." He scooped up the quill and ink bottle and went on to the next table. As he made his way around the pub collecting signatures—Jem noticed that no one other than his father refused to sign—John Roberts glanced over now and then at Thomas Kellaway with the same sneer. It made Jem's stomach turn over. "Let's go, Pa," he said in a low voice.

"Let me just finish my beer." Thomas Kellaway was not going to be rushed by anyone, not when he had half a pint left to finish, even if the beer was watery. He sat squarely on his stool, hands resting on the table on each side of his mug, his eyes on its contents, his mind on Mr. Blake. He was wondering if he had got him into trouble. Though he did not know him well the way his children seemed to, he was sure Mr. Blake was a good man.

"What should we do?" Jem said in a low voice to Maggie. He too was thinking about Mr. Blake.

"Leave it be," Dick Butterfield butted in. "Blake'll probably sign it," he added, glancing sideways at Thomas Kellaway. "Like most people."

"We'll warn him," Maggie declared, ignoring her father. "That's what we'll do."

~ 2 ~

"Mr. Blake is working, my dears," Mrs. Blake said. "He can't be disturbed."

"Oh, but it's important, ma'am!" Maggie cried, in her impatience darting to one side as if to get around her. But Mrs. Blake comfortably blocked the doorway, and did not move.

"He is in the middle of making one of his plates, and he likes to do that all in one sitting," Mrs. Blake explained. "So we mustn't stop him."

"I'm afraid it be important, ma'am," Jem said.

"Then you may tell me, and I'll pass it on to Mr. Blake."

Jem looked around, for once wishing there were a deadening fog about that would hide them from curious passersby. Since their earlier encounter with John Roberts, he'd felt as if there were eyes on them everywhere, watching them as they walked up the road. He expected any moment that Miss Pelham's yellow curtains would twitch. As it was, a man driving past on a cart loaded with bricks glanced at the little group in the doorway, his gaze seeming to linger.

"Can we come in, ma'am? We'll tell you inside."

Mrs. Blake studied his serious face, then stood aside and let them pass, shutting the door behind them without looking around, as others might. She put her finger to her lips and led them down the passage, past the front room with the printing press, past the closed door of Mr. Blake's workroom and down the stairs to the basement kitchen. Jem and Maggie were already familiar with the room, for they had sat there with Maisie to warm her up after her encounter with John Astley. It was dark and smelled of cabbage and coal, with only a bit of light coming in from the front window, but the fire was lit and it was warm.

Mrs. Blake gestured for them to sit at the table; Jem noted that the chairs were his father's Windsors. "Now, what is it, my dears?" she asked, leaning against the sideboard.

"We heard something in the pub," Maggie said. "You're to have a visit tonight." She described the meeting at Cumberland Gardens and their encounter with John Roberts, leaving out that her father had signed the declaration.

A deep line appeared between Mrs. Blake's eyebrows. "Was this meeting run by the Association for the Preservation of Liberty and Property Against Republicans and Levellers?" She rattled off the name as if she were very familiar with it.

"They was mentioned," Maggie answered, "though they just called the local branch the Lambeth Association."

Mrs. Blake sighed. "We'd best go up and tell Mr. Blake, then. You were right to come." She wiped her hands on her apron as if she had just been washing something, though her hands were dry.

Mr. Blake's workroom was very tidy, with books and papers in various stacks on one table, and Mr. Blake at another table by the room's back window. He was hunched over a metal plate the size of his hand, and did not look up immediately when they came in, but continued dabbing a brush in a line from right to left across the surface of the plate. While Maggie went to the fire to warm herself, Jem stepped up and watched him at work. It took him a minute to make out that Mr. Blake was writing words by painting them with the brush onto the plate. "You're writing backwards, an't you, sir?" Jem blurted out, though he knew he shouldn't interrupt.

Mr. Blake did not answer until he had reached the end of the line. Then he looked up. "That I am, my lad, that I am."

"Why?"

"I'm writing with a solution that will remain on the plate when the rest gets eaten away by acid. Then when I print them the words will be going forwards, not backwards."

"Opposite to what they are now."

"Yes, my boy."

"Mr. Blake, I'm sorry to trouble you," his wife interrupted, "but Jem and Maggie have told me something you ought to hear." Mrs. Blake was wringing her hands now, whether from what Jem and Maggie had told her or because she felt she was disturbing her husband, Jem was not sure.

"It's all right, Kate. While I've stopped, could you get me some more turps? There's some next door. And a glass of water, if you don't mind."

"Of course, Mr. Blake." Mrs. Blake stepped out of the room.

"How did you learn to write backwards like that?" Jem asked. "With a mirror?"

Mr. Blake glanced down at the plate. "Practice, my boy, practice. It's easy once you've done it enough. Everything engravers do gets printed opposite. The engraver has to be able to see it both ways."

"From the middle of the river."

"That's it. Now, what did you want to tell me?"

Jem repeated what Maggie had said down in the kitchen. "We thought we should warn you that they be coming to see you tonight," he finished. "Mr. Roberts weren't nice about it," Jem added, when Mr. Blake did not seem to react to the news. "We thought they might give you trouble."

"Thank you for that, my children," Mr. Blake replied. "I am not surprised by any of this. I knew it would come."

He was not responding at all the way Maggie had expected him to. She'd thought he would jump up and do something—pack a bag and leave the house, or hide all of the books and pamphlets and things he'd printed, or barricade the front windows and door. Instead he simply smiled at them, then dipped his brush into a dish of something resembling glue, and began to write more backwards words across the metal plate. Maggie wanted to kick his chair and shout, "Listen to us! You may be in danger!" But she didn't dare.

Mrs. Blake came back with a bottle of turps and a glass of water, which she set down by her husband. "They told you about the Association coming tonight, did they?" She at least seemed anxious about what Jem and Maggie had told them.

"They did, my dear."

"Mr. Blake, why do they want to visit you specially?" Jem asked.

Mr. Blake made a little face and, setting down his brush, twisted around in his chair to face them fully. "Tell me, Jem, what do you think I write about?"

Jem hesitated.

"Children," Maggie offered.

Mr. Blake nodded. "Yes, my girl—children, and the helpless, and the poor. Children lost and cold and hungry. The government does not like to be told it is not looking after its people. They think I am suggesting revolution, as there has been in France."

"Are you?" Jem asked.

Mr. Blake waggled his head in a movement that could have meant yes or no.

"Pa says that the Frenchies have gone bad, with all that killing of innocent people," Maggie said.

"That is not surprising. Doesn't blood flow before judgment? Only look to the Bible for instances of it. Look at the Book of Revelation for blood flowing in the streets. This Association that intends to come tonight, though, wants to stop anyone who questions those in power. But power unchecked leads to moral tyranny."

Jem and Maggie were silent, trying to follow his words.

"So you see, my children, that is why I must continue making my songs and not run from those who would have me silenced. And so that is what I am doing." He turned his chair back around so that he faced the desk, and picked up his brush once more.

"What is that you're working on?" Jem asked.

"Is it another song they won't like?" Maggie added.

Mr. Blake looked back and forth between their eager faces and smiled. Setting down his brush once more, he leaned back and began to recite:

> In the Age of Gold
> Free from winters cold
> Youth and maiden bright
> To the holy light
> Naked in the sunny beams delight.
>
> Once a youthful pair
> Filled with softest care
> Met in garden bright
> When the holy light
> Had just removed the curtains of the night.
>
> There in rising day
> On the grass they play
> Parents were afar
> Strangers came not near
> And the maiden soon forgot her fear.
>
> Tired with kisses sweet
> They agree to meet,
> When the silent sleep
> Waves o'er heavens deep
> And the weary tired wanderers weep.

Maggie felt her face sweep with heat from a deep blush. She could not look at Jem. If she had, she would have seen that he was not looking at her either.

"Perhaps it's time to go, my dears," Mrs. Blake interrupted before her husband could continue. "Mr. Blake's very busy just now, aren't you, Mr. Blake?" He jerked his head and sat back; clearly it was rare for her to break in on him when he was reciting.

Maggie and Jem stepped backward toward the door. "Thank you, Mr. Blake," they said together, though it was not at all clear what they were thanking him for.

Mr. Blake seemed to recover himself. "It is we who should be thanking you," he said. "We are grateful for the warning about this evening."

As they left his study, they heard Mrs. Blake murmur, "Really, Mr. Blake, you shouldn't tease them like that, reciting that one rather than what you were working on. They're not ready yet. You saw how they blushed." They did not hear his reply.

While the Kellaway men were at the timber yard with Dick Butterfield, the Kellaway women had remained at Hercules Buildings. With the arrival of winter, Anne Kellaway no longer worked in the garden, but stayed indoors, cooking, cleaning, sewing, and trying to find ways to keep out the cold. As the Kellaways had not experienced proper cold weather in London until now, they'd hadn't realized how poorly heated the Lambeth house was, nor appreciated how snug a Dorsetshire cottage could be, with its thick cob walls, small windows, and large hearth. The Hercules Buildings' brick walls were half the thickness; the fireplaces in each room were tiny and took expensive coal rather than wood they could cut and haul for free in Dorsetshire. Anne Kellaway now hated the large Lambeth windows she had spent so much time looking out of earlier in the year; she stuffed bits of cloth and straw in the cracks to keep out drafts, and double-lined the curtains.

The fog often kept kept her inside as well. Now that coal fires were burning all day in most houses in London, fog was inevitable. Of course the Piddle Valley had had occasional fogs, but not such thick, dirty ones that settled in for days like an unwanted guest. On foggy days there was so little light that Anne Kellaway drew the curtains against it and lit the lamps, in part for Maisie, who sometimes grew agitated when she looked out at the murk.

Maisie was almost always indoors. Even on clear sunny days, she did not go out. In the two months since losing her way in the fog—for that is what she and Maggie and Jem allowed her parents to think had happened—she had been out of no. 12 Hercules Buildings only twice, to church. At first she had been too ill: The cold and damp had settled on her chest, and she was in bed for two weeks before she was strong enough even to go downstairs to the privy. When she did get up at last, she was no longer fresh as she had been, but rather like a white-washed wall that has begun to yellow—still bright, but without the glow of the new. She was quieter as well, and did not make the cheerful remarks the Kellaways had not even realized they relied on.

Anne Kellaway had gone out earlier to pick a cabbage and pull up some late carrots from Philip Astley's now-deserted garden, and had got a bone from the butcher for a soup. She'd boiled the bone, chopped and added the vegetables, and cleared up after herself. Now she wiped her hands on her apron and took a seat opposite Maisie. Anne Kellaway knew something was different about her daughter, even apart from her recent illness, but she had put off for weeks asking Maisie, until she seemed strong enough and less skittish. Now she was determined to discover what it was.

Maisie paused as her mother sat, her needle hovering above a button she was working on for Bet Butterfield, who had hired her to make Dorset High Tops. There was little in it for Bet, but it was the least she could do for the girl.

"It be a lovely day," Anne Kellaway began.

"Yes, it do," Maisie agreed, gamely glancing out of the window at the bright street below. A cart passed carrying a huge pig, which sniffed daintily at the Lambeth air. Maisie smiled despite herself.

"Not like that fog. If I'd known it be so foggy in London I'd never have come here to live."

"Why did you then, Ma?" One of the changes Anne Kellaway had noticed in Maisie was that her questions now occasionally contained a sharp sliver of judgment.

Rather than chiding her daughter, Anne Kellaway tried to answer honestly. "Once Tommy died I thought the Piddle Valley were ruined for us, and perhaps we'd be happier here."

Maisie made a stitch in her button. "And are you?"

Anne Kellaway dodged the question by responding to a different one. "I'm just glad you be less poorly now." She began to twist a knot in her apron. "In the fog that day—were you frightened?"

Maisie stopped stitching. "I were terrified."

"You never told us what happened. Jem said you was lost and Mr. Blake found you."

Maisie looked at her mother steadily. "I were at the amphitheatre and decided to come home to help you. But I couldn't find Jem to see me home, and when I looked out at the fog it seemed to be a little clearer, and I thought I could get home by myself. So I walked along Westminster Bridge Road, and I were fine, as there were people along there and the street lamps were lit. It were just that when I got to the turning for Hercules Buildings I didn't turn sharp enough and went down Bastille Row instead, so that Hercules Tavern were on my right rather than my left." Maisie deliberately mentioned Hercules Tavern, as if by naming it she could dismiss it too, and Anne Kellaway would never suspect that she had been inside the pub. Her voice only wavered a tiny bit when she said the name.

"After a bit I knew I weren't on Hercules Buildings, so I turned back, but the fog were so thick and it were getting dark and I didn't know where I were. And then Mr. Blake found me and brought me home." Maisie told her story a little mechanically, except for Mr. Blake's name, which she said reverentially, as if referring to an angel.

"Where did he find you?"

"I don't know, Ma—I were lost. You'll have to ask him." Maisie said this with confidence, sure that Anne Kellaway would never ask Mr. Blake—she was too daunted by him. He and Mrs. Blake had visited Maisie once she was improving, and Anne Kellaway had been disturbed by his bright, piercing eyes and the familiarity he'd had with both Maisie and Jem. Then too, he had said something very odd to her when she thanked him for finding Maisie. "'Heaven's last best gift,'" he had replied. "'Oh much deceived, much failing, hapless Eve.'"

At Anne Kellaway's blank stare, Catherine Blake had leaned forward to say, "That's *Paradise Lost*, that is. Mr. Blake is very fond of quoting from it, aren't you, Mr. Blake? Anyway, we're glad your daughter is on the mend."

Even stranger, Jem had murmured under his breath, "Pear tree's loss," and Anne Kellaway had felt the familiar shard in her heart that signaled Tommy Kellaway's death—a feeling she had managed to suppress for months, until the departure of the circus. It was back, though, as strong as ever, catching her out when she wasn't looking, making her draw in her breath sharply with grief for her son.

Now Anne Kellaway looked at her daughter and knew that she was lying about the fog. Maisie returned her gaze. How had she come to grow up so quickly, Anne Kellaway wondered. After a moment she stood. "I must check that the bread an't stale," she said. "If it be I'll pop out for more."

Thomas Kellaway said nothing to the Kellaway women about what had gone on between him and John Roberts when he and Jem returned, with Maggie in tow. Rather than go home, Maggie spent the rest of the afternoon with the Kellaways, learning how to make High Tops with Maisie by the fire while Jem and his father worked on a chair seat in the workshop and Anne Kellaway sewed and swept and kept the fire bright. Though Maggie was not especially good at button-making, she preferred to be busy with this family rather than idle in the pub with her own.

They worked, and waited, even those who didn't know they were waiting for anything, and time pressed down like a stone. Once it began to get dark and Anne Kellaway had lit the lamps, Jem kept coming in from the workshop and going to the front window until his mother asked him what he was looking for. Then he stayed in the back, but listened keenly, stealing glances at Maggie through the open door, wishing they had a plan.

It began as a low hum that at first wasn't noticeable because of more immediate sounds: horses clopping past, children shouting, street criers selling candles and pies and fish, the watchman calling the hour. Soon, though, the sound of a company of feet crunching along the road and voices murmuring to one another became more distinct. When he heard it Jem left the workshop and went to the window again. "Pa," he called after a moment.

Thomas Kellaway paused, then laid down the adze he had been using to carve a saddleback shape into the chair seat, and joined his son at the window. Maggie jumped up, scattering the High Tops she had accumulated in her lap.

"What is't, Tom?" Anne Kellaway said sharply.

Thomas Kellaway cleared his throat. "I've some business downstairs. I won't be long."

Frowning, Anne Kellaway joined them at the window. When she glimpsed the crowd gathering in the street in front of the Blakes' door—and growing bigger all the time—she turned pale.

"What do you see, Ma?" Maisie called from her chair. A few months ago she would have been the first out of her seat and to the window.

Before anyone could respond, they heard a rap at Miss Pelham's front door, and the crowd in the street broadened its attention to include no. 12 Hercules Buildings. "Tom!" Anne Kellaway cried. "What's happening?"

"Don't you be worrying, Anne. It'll be all right in a minute."

They heard the door open downstairs and Miss Pelham's querulous voice ring out, though they could not make out what she said.

"I'd best go down," Thomas Kellaway said.

"Not on your own!" Anne Kellaway followed him from the room, turning at the top of the stairs to call back, "Jem, Maisie, stay here!"

Jem ignored her; he and Maggie clattered down after them. After sitting alone in the room for a moment, Maisie got up and followed.

As they reached the front door, Miss Pelham was signing a book similar to John Roberts's ledger. "Of course I'm happy to sign if it's going to do any good," she was saying to an older man with a crooked back who held out the book for her. "I can't bear the thought of those revolutionaries coming here!" She shuddered. "However, I don't at all appreciate a mob in front of my house—it paints me in a poor light among my neighbors. I would like you to take your . . . your associates elsewhere!" Miss Pelham's frizzy curls quivered with indignation.

"Oh, the rabble an't for you, ma'am," the man replied reassuringly. "It's for next door."

"But my neighbors don't know that!"

"Actually, we do want to see"—he referred to his book—"a Thomas Kellaway, who was a little reluctant earlier to sign. I believe he lives here." He looked past Miss Pelham's head into her hallway. "That will be you, will it, sir?"

Miss Pelham whipped her head around to glare at the Kellaways gathered behind her.

"You were reluctant earlier?" Anne Kellaway hissed at her husband. "When were that?"

Thomas Kellaway stepped away from his wife. "Pardon, Miss Pelham, if you do just let me pass I'll go an' straighten this out."

Miss Pelham continued to glare at him as if he had brought great shame on her household. Then she caught sight of Maggie. "Get that girl out of my house!" she cried. Thomas Kellaway was forced to squeeze past his landlady so that he could stand on the doorstep next to the man with the humpback.

"Now, sir," the man said, with more politeness than John Roberts had shown earlier. "You are Thomas Kellaway, is that right? I believe you were read earlier the declaration of loyalty we are asking each resident of Lambeth to sign. Are you prepared now to sign it?" He held out the book.

Before Thomas Kellaway could respond, a cry went up from the crowd, who had turned their attention back to no. 13 Hercules Buildings. The man with the hump stepped away from Miss Pelham's door so that he might see what was, after all, the main attraction. Thomas Kellaway and Miss Pelham followed him onto the path.

William Blake had opened his door. He did not say a word—not a hallo, or a curse, or a "What do you want?" He simply stood filling his doorway in his long black coat. He was hatless, his brown hair ruffled, his mouth set, his eyes wide and alert.

"Mr. Blake!" John Roberts stepped up to the door, his jaw flexing as if he were chewing on a tough piece of meat. "You are requested by the Lambeth Association for the Preservation of Liberty

and Property Against Republicans and Levellers to sign this declaration of loyalty to the British monarchy. Will you sign it, sir?"

There was a long silence, during which Jem, Maggie, Anne
Kellaway, and Maisie pushed out of the house so that they might
see and hear what was happening. Anne Kellaway joined her husband, while the others crept to the end of the path.

Maggie and Jem were stunned by how big the crowd had grown,
filling the street completely. There were torches and lanterns dotted
about, and the street lamps had been lit, but still most of the faces
were in shadow and looked unfamiliar and frightening, even though
they were probably neighbors Jem and Maggie knew, and there
out of curiosity rather than meaning to cause trouble. Nonetheless,
there was a tension among the people that threatened to erupt into
violence.

"Oh, Jem, what we going to do?" Maggie whispered.

"I dunno."

"Is Mr. Blake in trouble?" Maisie asked.

"Yes."

"Then we must help him." She said it so firmly that Jem felt
ashamed.

Maggie frowned. "C'mon," she said finally, and, taking Jem's
hand, she opened Miss Pelham's gate and slipped into the crowd.
Maisie took his other hand, and the three snaked through the
onlookers, pushing their way closer to Mr. Blake's front gate. There
they discovered a gap in those gathered. The men, women, and
children on the street were simply watching, while on the other
side of the Blakes' fence a smaller group had bunched together
in the front garden, all of them men, most recognizable from the
Cumberland Gardens meeting. To Maggie's astonishment, Charlie
Butterfield was among them, though standing on the edge of the
group, as if he were a hanger-on not yet completely accepted by
the others. "That bastard! What's he doing there?" Maggie muttered. "We have to distract 'em," she whispered to Jem. She looked

around. "I've an idea. This way!" She plunged into the crowd, pulling Jem after her.

"Maisie, go back to Ma and Pa," Jem called. "You shouldn't be out here."

Maisie did not answer him; she may not even have heard him. She was watching Mr. Blake, who stood silent in his doorway, not answering any of the questions John Roberts was putting to him: "You are a printer, Mr. Blake. What sort of things do you print? Do you write about the French revolution, Mr. Blake? You have worn the *bonnet rouge*, have you not, Mr. Blake? Have you read Thomas Paine, Mr. Blake? Do you own copies of his works? Have you met him? In your writing, do you question the sovereignty of our King, Mr. Blake? Are you or aren't you going to sign this declaration, Mr. Blake?"

Throughout this interrogation, Mr. Blake maintained an impassive expression, his eyes set on the horizon. Though he appeared to be listening, he did not seem to feel that he must answer, or indeed even that the questions were directed at him.

His silence riled John Roberts more than anything he said would have. "Are you going to answer, or are you going to hide your guilt behind silence?" he roared. "Or will we have to smoke it out of you?" With those words he threw the torch he'd been holding into Mr. Blake's front garden. The dramatic gesture turned into a slightly less dramatic smolder as bits of dry grass and leaves caught alight and then died away into thin streams of smoke.

Thomas Kellaway's eyes followed the smoke from next door as it unfurled above them into the evening sky. It decided him. He had seen what could happen to a family when its livelihood burnt to the ground. Whatever the different sides of the argument, no man had the right to set light to another's property. That much he was clear about. He turned to the humpback man, who was still holding out the ledger. "I won't sign anything," he announced.

~ 6 ~

Maisie, still standing in the street just across the gap from the Association men, also looked above her into the sky, now darkened into an inky blue. It was the time of night when the first stars appeared. She found one burning bright directly above her. Then she began to recite:

> I wander through each chartered street
> Near where the chartered Thames does flow
> And mark in every face I meet
> Marks of weakness, marks of woe.

Though she had spent much of the past two months in bed or sitting by the fire, her voice was strong, and carried through the crowd in the street, who stepped back from her so that she was now standing alone. Her voice carried to the group gathered at Mr. Blake's door, among them Charlie Butterfield, who started when he saw who was speaking. It carried to her parents in the garden next door, and to Miss Pelham, quivering with nerves on her doorstep. It carried to Mr. Blake, who set his eyes on Maisie's face like a benediction and gave a tiny nod, which encouraged her to take a deep breath and begin the second verse:

> In every cry of every man
> In every infant's cry of fear
> In every voice, in every ban
> The mind-forged manacles I hear.

Now her voice carried to Jem and Maggie, who had detached themselves from the crowd and were squatting behind the hedge on the other side of the road from no. 13 Hercules Buildings. Maggie popped up to look. "Damn! What's she doing?"

Jem joined her and peered at his sister. "God help her," he muttered.

"What's this? Quiet, girl! Someone stop her!" John Roberts shouted.

"Leave her be!" a man countered.

"Quick," Maggie whispered. "We'd better do it now. Careful who you hit, and be ready to run." She reached to the ground and fumbled about until she found a chunk of frozen horse dung—street sweepers often dumped their findings over the hedge there. She aimed carefully, then flung it hard so that it flew over the heads of the crowd, over Maisie, and landed in the group of men surrounding Mr. Blake.

"Ow!" one of them cried. A chuckle rose from the crowd watching.

Jem threw another clod, hitting one of the men in the back.

"Hey! Who's doing that?"

Though they couldn't see the men's faces, they knew they'd had some effect, for there was a rippling out of the group as they turned away from Mr. Blake and peered into the dark. They threw more dung, and gnarled carrots, but these fell short, into the gap between the men and the street, while a bit of dung thrown too hard hit the Blakes' window, though it didn't break. "Careful!" Jem hissed.

Now Mr. Blake began to speak, taking over from Maisie in a sonorous voice that froze the men at his door:

> How the chimney sweeper's cry
> Every blackening church appals
> And the hapless soldier's sigh
> Runs in blood down palace walls.

But most through midnight streets I hear
How the youthful harlot's curse
Blasts the new-born infant's tear
And blights with plagues the marriage hearse.

Maggie struck lucky, heaving a half-rotted cabbage that hit John Roberts in the head just as Mr. Blake finished the last line. Guffaws and shouts of "Huzzah!" arose from the crowd at the sight. John Roberts staggered from the blow, shouting, "Get them!"

A group detached itself from the Assocation men and began pushing through the crowd toward the hedge. Others, however, mistook where the missiles were coming from and attacked the crowd itself. Charlie Butterfield, for instance, grabbed one of the balls of frozen dung and threw it at a bald, heavyset man in the street, who roared joyously in response and crashed through the Blakes' front fence, kicking it over as if it were made of straw. Choosing John Roberts as the most vocal and therefore likeliest foe, he promptly head-butted him. This was the signal to all those who had gathered in the hope of a free-for-all to begin throwing whatever they could find—their fists, if nothing else. Soon the Blakes' windows were smashed, as well as those of their neighbors, John Astley and Miss Pelham, and men were shouting and tussling in the street.

In the midst of the mêlée Maisie stood, swaying from fear and dizziness. She sank to her knees just as Charlie Butterfield reached her. He put an arm around her and half-lifted, half-dragged her to the Blakes' door, where Mr. Blake still stood watching the riot, which had at least moved out of his garden. Maisie smiled weakly. "Thank'ee, Charlie," she murmured. Charlie nodded, embarrassed, then crept away, cursing himself for his weakness.

When Maggie saw the group of men approaching the hedge, she grabbed Jem's arm. "Run!" she hissed. "Follow me!" She bolted across the black field behind them, stumbling over frozen clods and furrows, across old vegetable patches, thrashing through dead nettles and brambles, stubbing her toes on bricks, tripping over netting meant to keep out birds and rabbits. She could hear Jem panting behind her and, farther back, the shouts of the rioters. Maggie was laughing and crying at the same time. "We got 'em, didn't we?" she whispered to Jem. "We got 'em."

"Yes, but they mustn't get us!" Jem had caught up with her and grabbed her hand to pull her forward.

They reached Carlisle House, the mansion at the edge of the field surrounded by an iron fence, and skirted it, coming out to the lane that passed in front of it and led to Royal Row, with its houses and the Canterbury Arms casting faint lights.

"Mustn't go there—people will see us," Maggie panted. She looked both ways, then scrambled over the hedge, cursing at the scratches and pricks from the hawthorn and bramble. She and Jem pitched across the road and dived over the opposite hedge. They could hear the huffs and shouts of the men following them, closer now, which spurred them on to run faster again through the new field, which was larger, and darker, with no Carlisle House to light the way—indeed, nothing but field all the way down to the warehouses by the river.

They slowed down now, trying not to crash about but instead to pick their way silently so that the men could not hear them. Above them, stars were pricking more and more holes in the blue-black sky. Jem breathed in the icy air and felt it draw like a knife across the back of his throat. If he weren't so terrified of the mob behind them, he would have appreciated more the beauty of the sky at this time of the evening.

Maggie was in the lead again, but was going more and more slowly. When she stopped suddenly, Jem bumped into her. "What is't? Where are we?"

Maggie swallowed, the click in her throat loud in the night air. "Near Cut-Throat Lane. I'm lookin' for something."

"What?"

She hesitated, then said in a low voice, "There's an old kiln somewhere round here, what they use to make bricks. We could hide in it. I've—it's a good hiding place. Here." They bumped against a squat structure built with rough brick into a kind of waist-high rectangular box, crumbling at one end.

"C'mon—we can both squeeze in." Maggie ducked down and crawled into the dark hole made by the bricks.

Jem squatted, but didn't follow her. "What if they find us here? We'll be cornered like a fox in a hole. If we stay out here at least we can run."

"They'll catch us if we run—they're bigger and there are more of them."

In the end the sound of the men crashing across the field decided Jem. He scuttled into the small, dark space left to him and pressed up next to Maggie. The hole smelled of clay and smoke, and of the faint vinegar of Maggie's skin.

They huddled together in the cold, trying to calm their breathing. After a minute they grew quieter, their breathing naturally synchronized into an even rhythm.

"I hope Maisie be all right," Jem said softly.

"Mr. Blake won't let anything happen to her."

"What do you think they'll do to us if they catch us?"

"They won't."

They listened. In fact, the men sounded farther off, as if they had veered away and were heading toward Lambeth Palace.

Maggie giggled. "The cabbage."

"Yes." Jem smiled. "That were a good aim."

"Thanks, Dorset boy." Maggie pulled her shawl closer about her, pressing against Jem as she did so. He could feel her shivering.

"Here, get close so I can warm you." He put his arm around her; as he pulled her to him she reached up and grasped his other shoulder so that they were encircling each other, and buried her face in his neck. Jem yelped. "Your nose be frozen!"

Maggie pulled her face back and laughed. As she looked up at him Jem caught the gleam of her teeth. Then their lips came together, and with that warm, soft touch all of the cold terror of the evening receded.

~ 7 ~

The kiss did not last as long as either wanted or expected, for suddenly a flaming torch was thrust toward them and a face loomed in from the darkness. Maggie screamed, but managed to cut it short so that it didn't carry more than a few yards.

"Thought I'd find you two here, gettin' cozy." Charlie Butterfield squatted on his heels and contemplated them.

"Charlie, you scared the shit from me!" Maggie cried, at the same time pulling away from Jem.

Charlie noted every move they made—their closeness, their pulling apart, their shame. "Got yourself a hidey-hole, have you?"

"What you doin' here, Charlie?"

"Lookin' for you, little sister. As is everyone."

"What were you doin' with those men at Mr. Blake's, anyway? You're not interested in any o' that. And why were you botherin' Mr. Blake? He's done nothing to you." Maggie had recovered herself quickly and was working hard to gain the upper hand over her brother.

Charlie ignored her questions, and gave up no ground, returning to the subject he knew made her the most uncomfortable. "Come back here, have you, Miss Cut-Throat? Funny place to bring your sweetheart—back to the scene of the crime. But then, this did used to be called Lovers' Lane, didn't it? Before you went and changed it!"

Maggie flinched. "Shut your bone box!" she cried.

"What—d'you mean you haven't told him, Miss Cut-Throat?" Charlie seemed to take great relish in repeating the nickname.

"Stop it, Charlie!" she shouted, heedless of the men hunting for them.

Jem felt her body shaking in the small space they shared. He said to Charlie, "Why don't you—"

"Perhaps you should ask your girl what happened out here," Charlie interrupted. "Go on, ask her."

"Shut up, Charlie! Shut up, shut up, shut up!" Maggie was screaming by the last repetition. "I could kill you!"

Charlie smiled, the torchlight twisting his face. "I expect you could, dear sister. You already showed me your technique."

"Shut up," Jem said.

Charlie laughed. "Oh, now you're startin'. I tell you what—I'll leave it to them others to decide what to do with you." He stood up and called out, "Whoo-wee—over here!"

Before he could think about what he was doing, Jem jumped up, grabbed a loose brick, and clapped it against the side of Charlie's head. Charlie stared at him. Then the torch in his hand began to dip, and Jem grabbed it just before Charlie himself staggered. As he fell, his head knocked against the side of the kiln, ensuring that when he landed on the ground he did not get up.

Jem stood still, clutching the torch. He licked his lips, cleared his throat, and stamped his feet, hoping Charlie would move. All that moved, however, was a trickle of blood down his forehead. Jem dropped the brick, squatted next to him, and held the torch in his face, fear clutching at his stomach. After a moment he saw in the flickering torch light that Charlie's chest was rising and falling slightly.

Jem turned around to Maggie. She was crouched in the shallow hole, arms wrapped around her knees, rocked with violent shudders. This time Jem did not get in next to her, but stood holding the torch and looking down at her. "What crime?" he said.

Maggie squeezed her knees tighter, trying to control the spasms that shook her. She kept her eyes fastened on the brick at her brother's side. "D'you remember when we'd lost Maisie in London and were lookin' for her, and you asked if I'd seen the man get killed on Cut-Throat Lane?"

Jem nodded.

"Well, you were right. I did. But it wasn't just that." Maggie took a deep breath. "It was a year and some ago. I was comin' back from the river down by Lambeth Palace, where I'd been diggin' in the mud at low tide. Found me a funny little silver spoon. I was so excited I didn't wait for the others I was with to finish. I just set off to find Pa so he could tell me what the spoon was worth. He knows that sort of thing. He was drinking at the Artichoke—you know, the pub on the Lower Marsh what I took you to when we met, where you met Pa and"—she jerked her head at Charlie lying prone— "him. It was foggy that day, but not so bad that you couldn't see where you was goin'. I took the shortcut up Lovers' Lane, 'cause it was quicker. I didn't think anything of it—I'd gone along there lots o' times. This time, though, I went round the bend, and round that bend there was a—a man. He was walking the same direction as me, but slowly, so slowly that I caught up with him. He wasn't old or nothing—just a man. I didn't think to hang back—I just wanted to get to the Artichoke and show Pa the spoon. So I passed by him, hardly looked at him. And he said, 'What you runnin' from?' And I turned and he—he grabbed me, and put a knife to my throat." Maggie swallowed, as if still feeling the cold metal pressed against the soft skin at the base of her neck.

"First he asked me what I had, and I gave him a penny—all the money I had on me. I didn't want to give him the spoon, though, as I'd spent so long digging for it in the mud. So I kept it hidden. But he felt in my pockets and found it anyway. And I should have given it to him to begin with—I shouldn't have hidden it, it was stupid of me, 'cause the hiding made him angry, and that made him—" Maggie paused and swallowed again. "So he dragged me— here." She patted the crumbled walls of the kiln.

Charlie's eyelids fluttered, and he moved a hand up to his head and groaned. Jem shifted the torch from one hand to the other, and picked up the brick. He was glad, in fact, for the excuse not to look at Maggie; relieved too that Charlie was not hurt worse. He did not think he would need to hit him again, but clutching the brick made him feel better.

Charlie rolled onto his side, then sat up, wincing and groaning. "Jesus Christ, my head!" He looked around. "You bastard!" he moaned when he saw Jem with the brick.

"You deserved it, Charlie. At least Jem's willin' to defend me." Maggie looked up at Jem. "Charlie found me, see, with the man. He was comin' along the lane and he saw us in here. And he come over, and he didn't do a thing! He just stood there grinning!"

"I didn't know it was you!" Charlie cried, then held his head, for shouting made it pound. "I didn't know it was you," he repeated more softly. "Not at first. All I could see was a muddy dress an' dark hair. Lots o' girls has dark hair. I didn't see it was you until you went and—"

"So you'd just let any girl in trouble get what was comin' to her, would you? Like you did with Maisie in the stables—you just walked away from her, you coward!"

"I an't a coward!" Charlie bellowed, heedless now of his raging headache. "I helped her just now!"

The mention of his sister made Jem think of her reciting Mr. Blake's song in the crowd. "I'd best get back to Maisie," he announced, "and be sure she's all right." He thrust the torch at Maggie, who gazed at him in confusion.

"Don't you want to hear the rest of the story?" she asked.

"I know it now—what the crime were."

"No, you don't! It wasn't that! He didn't get to do that to me, see! I stopped him! He had a knife, and when he was on top of me, fumblin' with himself, he dropped the knife and I grabbed it and I . . . and . . . I . . ."

"She stuck him in the throat," Charlie finished for her. "Right in the throat like a pig. Then she slashed him. You should have seen the blood." He spoke in an admiring tone.

Jem stared at Maggie. "You—you killed him?"

Maggie set her jaw. "I was defendin' myself, like you just did with Charlie here. I didn't wait around to see if it killed him—I ran. Had to throw away my clothes and steal some more, they were that bloody."

"*I* saw," Charlie murmured. "I watched him die. Took a long time, 'cause he had to bleed to death."

Maggie studied her brother, and something clicked in her mind. "You got the spoon off him, didn't you?"

Charlie nodded. "Thought it was his. Didn't know it was yours."

"Have you still got it?"

"Sold it. Was a caddy spoon, for tea. Got a good price for it."

"That money's mine."

The blow to his head seemed to have knocked the fight out of Charlie, for he didn't protest. "Don't have it now, but I'll owe you."

Jem couldn't believe they were discussing caddy spoons and money after such a story. Maggie had stopped shaking and grown calmer. Instead it was Jem who was now trembling. "I'd best get back," he repeated. "Maisie will need me."

"Wait, Jem," Maggie said. "Don't you—" She gazed at him, her eyes pleading. She was biting her lips, and Jem shuddered to think that a few minutes before he had kissed them—kissed someone who had killed a man.

"I have to go," he said, dropping the brick, and stumbled into the dark.

"Wait, Jem! We'll come with you!" Maggie called. "Don't you even want the torch?"

But Jem had found Cut-Throat Lane, and he ran along it, allowing his feet to feel their way home while his mind went blank.

~ *8* ~

The crowd was gone by the time he reached Hercules Buildings, though there was evidence all around of the recent brawl—bricks, dung, sticks, and other objects lying about, and windows all along Hercules Buildings broken. Residents had banded together and were walking up and down to deter thieves from taking advantage of the easy access afforded by the gaping windows. A carriage waited in front of Mr. Blake's house.

Miss Pelham's house was lit almost as bright as a pub, as if she were trying to chase every shadow of doubt from her rooms. When Jem went inside he heard his father's voice in her front room, and then her interrupting quaver.

"I am sorry about your daughter's health, but I cannot with any good faith allow revolutionary sympathizers to remain in this house even a day longer. Frankly, Mr. Kellaway, if it were not a cold winter's night, you'd already be out on the street."

"But where will we go?" came Thomas Kellaway's plaintive voice.

"You should have thought of that when you refused to sign the declaration, and in front of everyone. What will the neighbors think?"

"But Mr. Blake—"

"Mr. Blake has nothing to do with it. He will have his own price to pay. You did not sign, and so you will not remain here. I would like you gone by noon tomorrow. I shall be calling round to the Association in the morning, and I'm sure they will be very keen to help me if you are still here when I get back. Indeed, if they had not been so rudely attacked tonight, I expect they would be here now, rather than out chasing down ruffians. Where is your son, may I ask?"

Before Thomas Kellaway could mumble a response, Jem opened the door and walked in. Miss Pelham jerked her head around like an angry hen and glared at him. "I be here," he muttered. "Why d'you want to know?" There no longer seemed any reason to be polite to her.

Miss Pelham sensed his change, and turned both fearful and defensive. "Get out, boy—no one said you could come in!" She herself scurried to the door, as if obeying her own order. She was scared of him, Jem could see, and it made him feel briefly powerful. But there was no benefit to be gained from it other than the pleasure of seeing her cower—she was still throwing them out.

He turned to his father. Thomas Kellaway was standing with his head bowed. "Pa, Ma wants you upstairs," Jem said, giving him the lie he needed to escape from the room.

Thomas Kellaway looked at his son, his blue eyes tired but focused for once on what was in front of him rather than in the distance. "I'm sorry, son," he said. "I made a mess of things."

Jem shuffled his feet. "No, Pa, not at all," he insisted, aware of Miss Pelham listening greedily. "It's just we need you upstairs." He turned and pushed past Miss Pelham, knowing his father would follow. As they clumped up the stairs, Anne Kellaway popped her head out from the doorway at the top, where she had been listening. Their landlady, taking courage from their receding backs, came out into the hallway and called up, "Tomorrow by noon you're to be out! By noon, d'you hear? And that means your daughter as well. She's only got herself to blame, getting herself into trouble like that. I should have thrown you out two months ago when she—"

"Shut up!" Jem spun about and roared. Sensing in Miss Pelham the eagerness of months of pent-up curtain-twitching about to spill over, he had to use harsh words to stop her. "You shut your bone box, you poxy bitch!"

His words froze Miss Pelham, her mouth agape, her eyes wide. Then, as if a string were attached to her waist and had been given

a great tug, she flew backward into her front room, slamming the
door behind her.

Anne and Thomas Kellaway stared at their son. Anne Kellaway
stepped aside and, ushering her men in, closed the door firmly to
the outside world.

Inside, she cast her eyes around the room. "What do we do
now? Where do we go?"

Thomas Kellaway cleared his throat. "Home. We'll go home."
As the words left his mouth it felt to him to be the most important
decision he had ever made.

"We can't do that!" Anne Kellaway argued. "Maisie an't strong
enough to travel in this weather."

They all looked at Maisie, who was sitting wrapped up by the
fire, as she had been for much of the last two months. Her eyes
were bright from the evening's events, but not feverish. She glanced
at them, then gazed back into the fire. Anne Kellaway stared at her
daughter, searching for answers to the questions Miss Pelham's
words had raised. "Maisie—"

"Leave her be, Ma," Jem interrupted. "Just leave her be. She's
all right, an't you, Maisie?"

Maisie smiled at her brother. "Yes. Oh, Jem, Mr. Blake were
ever so grateful. He said to thank you and Maggie—you'll know
why. And he thanked me too." She flushed, and looked down at
her hands resting in her lap. At that moment Anne Kellaway felt,
as she often had in London, that her children lived in a different
world from their parents.

"I've an idea," Jem said suddenly. He clattered back downstairs
and reached the carriage next door just as the Blakes were stepping
into it.

PART VIII

July 1793

Maggie was sure she had heard the hurdy-gurdy player before; indeed, he was ruining the same song he'd ruined the last time he'd played at Hercules Hall, even down to the same wrong notes. Still, she hummed along to "A Hole to Put Poor Robin In" as she sat against the wall in Astley's field. With ten Dorset Crosswheels completed in her lap, she was thinking about starting on High Tops. Before she began another, she yawned and stretched, for she'd been out all night helping Bet Butterfield with laundry. Though Maggie had finally decided to trade in mustard and vinegar for laundry and buttons, she was not sure that she would stick at it. Unlike her mother, she found it hard to sleep during the day, for she always woke feeling that she had missed something important—a fire or a riot or a visitor coming and going. She preferred to remain half-awake at least.

The hurdy-gurdy man changed tunes to "Bonny Kate and Danny," and Maggie couldn't resist accompanying him:

> He took her to the river's side
> Bonny Kate and Danny
> He took her to the river's side
> And there he laid her legs so wide
> And on her belly he did ride
> And he whipped in little Danny.
>
> When forty weeks were come and gone
> Bonny Kate and Danny
> When forty weeks were come and gone
> She was delivered of a son—
> And she called him little Danny!

When he finished, Maggie sauntered over to the man, who was sitting on the steps outside Hercules Hall.

"You, you saucy cat!" he cried when he saw her. "Don't you ever stop prowlin' round here?"

"Don't you ever stop wrecking the same songs?" Maggie retorted. "And didn't no one tell you you're not to play those songs no more? You keep singin' 'Bonny Kate and Danny' and the Association'll take you away."

The man frowned. "What you mean?"

"Where you been? You're not to play bawdy songs, but the ones they've writ for you, about the King an' that. Don't you know?" Maggie stood straight and bellowed to the tune of "God Save the King":

> To sing Great George's praise
> Let all your voices raise
> Noble the theme.
> Britain has various charms
> Inviting to her arms
> God guards us from all harms
> Sacred His name.

"Or this?" She began to the tune of "Rule Britannia":

> Since first the Georges wore the crown,
> How happy were their subjects made—

She broke off and laughed at the hurdy-gurdy man's expression. "I know, it's silly, an't it? But I don't know why you're bothering to play anyway. Didn't you know Mr. Astley's not here? He's gone to France to fight. Came back from Liverpool this winter when the French King was executed and England declared war against France, and went straight off to offer his services."

"What use is his horse dancing against the French?"

"No, no—old Astley, not his son. John Astley's still here, run-nin' the circus. And I can tell you, he don't hire musicians off the street the way his father did, so you can just give yourself a rest."

The man's face fell. "What's old Astley doin' over there? He's too fat to ride or fight."

Maggie shrugged. "He wanted to go—said as an old cavalry man, it was his duty. 'Sides, he's been sending back reports from the battles, and John Astley reenacts 'em here. No one understands 'em much, but they're great fun to watch."

The man removed the hurdy-gurdy strap from around his neck.

"Wait—will you play me something before you go?" Maggie begged.

The man paused. "Well, you are a rascally little cat, but since you've saved me sittin' here all day playing, I'll do one for you. What'll it be?"

"'Tom Bowling,'" Maggie requested, even though she knew that hearing the song would remind her of Maisie Kellaway sing-ing it down by the warehouses along the river, back when she barely knew Jem.

As the man played, Maggie swallowed the lump in her throat and hummed along, though she did not sing the words. The mem-ory of Maisie singing fed the dull ache in her chest that had never entirely disappeared over the months since Jem had gone.

Maggie had never missed anyone before. For a time she had in-dulged the feeling, conducting imaginary conversations with Jem, visiting places they'd been together—the alcoves on Westminster Bridge, Soho Square, even the brick kiln where she'd last seen him. At the manufactory she'd met a girl from Dorsetshire and had got her to talk, just to hear the accent. Whenever she could get away with it she mentioned Jem and the Kellaways to her mother or father, just to be able to say his name. None of this brought him back, though; indeed, eventually it always led her to the look of horror on his face at the kiln that night.

Midway through the second verse, a woman with a lovely clear voice began to sing. Maggie cocked her head to listen: It seemed to be coming from either the Blakes' or Miss Pelham's garden. Maggie signaled thanks to the hurdy-gurdy player and walked back toward the wall. She doubted the singer was Miss Pelham—she was not the singing type. Nor had Maggie ever heard Mrs. Blake sing. Perhaps it was Miss Pelham's maid, though the girl was so cowed that Maggie had never heard her speak, much less sing.

By the time she wheeled the Astley barrow over to the wall, the hurdy-gurdy and the singing had stopped. Maggie climbed onto the barrow anyway and hiked herself up the wall to spy into the gardens.

Miss Pelham's garden was empty, but in the Blakes' garden a woman was kneeling in the vegetable rows near the house. She wore a light gown and apron, and a bonnet with a broad brim to keep the sun off. At first Maggie thought it was Mrs. Blake, but this figure was shorter and moved less nimbly. Maggie had heard that the Blakes had taken on a maidservant, but she had not seen her, for Mrs. Blake continued to do the shopping and other errands. Maggie had not visited no. 13 Hercules Buildings for months; with Jem gone she'd felt shyer about knocking on their door on her own—though Mr. Blake did always nod and ask her how she was whenever they passed in the street.

As she watched the maid work, she heard the sound of horse hooves clopping down the alley toward Hercules Hall's stables. The maid stopped what she was doing and turned her head to listen, and Maggie got the first of two shocks. The figure was Maisie Kellaway.

"Maisie!" she shouted.

Maisie jerked her head around, and Maggie scrambled over the wall and hurried toward her. For a second it seemed Maisie would jump up and run inside. She clearly thought the better of it, though, and remained crouched in the dirt.

"Maisie, what you doing here?" Maggie cried. "I thought you

were in Dorsetshire! Didn't you—hang on a minute." She thought hard, then shouted, "You're the Blakes' maid! You never went back to Piddle-dee-dee, did you? You been here all this time!"

"Tha' be true," Maisie murmured. Casting her eyes down to the rich soil, she pulled a weed from a row of carrots.

"But—why didn't you tell me?" Maggie wanted to shake her. "Why are you hiding away? And why did you run off like that, without even sayin' good-bye? I know that old stick Pelham was after you to go, but you could have said good-bye. After all we been through together. You could have found me and said that." Sometime during this rant, her words had been redirected at the absent Jem, and her welling tears as well.

Tears were always addictive to Maisie. "Oh, Maggie, I'm so sorry!" she sobbed, lumbering to her feet and throwing her arms around her friend. That was when Maggie got her second shock, for pressing into her stomach was what hadn't been visible when Maisie was kneeling: the solid baby she carried inside her.

The bump between them effectively stopped Maggie's tears. Still hugging Maisie, she pulled her head back and looked down at it. For a rare moment in her life she could not think of anything to say.

"You see, when Ma and Pa decided to go back to Piddle-trenthide," Maisie began, "it were so cold that they was afraid I weren't strong enough for such a long journey. Then Mr. and Mrs. Blake said they'd take me in. First we went off to stay with their friends the Cumberlands, to escape from those awful men who came to their door. The Cumberlands live out a ways in the countryside—Egham, it were. Even that short ride gave me a chesty cold, an' we had to stay there a month. They was ever so nice to me. Then we come back, an' I been here all this time."

"Do you never go out? I han't seen you at all!"

Maisie shook her head. "I didn't want to—not at first, anyway. It were so cold and I felt sick. An' then I didn't want Miss Pelham and others nosing about, especially not once I began to show. I didn't want to give her the satisfaction." She laid a hand on top of her bump. "An' those Association men had threatened to come after Pa. I just thought it were better to be quiet here. I didn't mean to hide from you, really. I didn't! Once, after we come back from Egham, you came to the door and asked Mr. Blake about Jem, d'you remember? You wanted to know where he were, when he had left. I were upstairs and heard you, and I so badly wanted to run down and see you. But I just thought it would be better—safer—to stay hidden, even from you. I'm sorry."

"But what do you do here?" Maggie glanced through the back window into Mr. Blake's study and thought she could make out his head, bent over his desk.

Maisie brightened. "Oh, all sorts of things! Really, they be wonderful to me. I help with the cooking and the washing and the gardening. And you know"—she lowered her voice—"I think it's done them good to have me, as it frees Mrs. Blake to help Mr. Blake more. He han't been himself since they come for him that night o' the riot, you see. The neighbors is funny with him, an' give him looks. Makes him nervous, an' he don't work so well. It takes Mrs. Blake to steady him, and with me here she can do that. An' I help Mr. Blake too. You know the printing press in the front room? I helped him and Mrs. Blake with that. D'you know, we made books. Books! I never thought I'd touch a book in my life other than a prayer book at church, much less make one. An' Mrs. Blake has taught me to read—I mean really to read, not just prayers and such, but real books! At night sometimes we read out from a book called *Paradise Lost*. It's the story of Satan and Adam and Eve, and it's so thrilling! Oh, I don't always understand it, because it talks about people and places I never heard of, and uses such fancy words. But it's lovely to listen to."

"Pear tree's loss," Maggie whispered.

"An' then sometimes he reads his poems aloud to us. Oh, I love that." Maisie paused, remembering. Then she closed her eyes and began to chant:

Tyger tyger, burning bright
In the forests of the night
What immortal hand or eye
Could frame thy fearful symmetry?

In what distant deeps or skies
Burnt the fire of thine eyes?
On what wings dare he aspire?
What the hand dare seize the fire?

And what shoulder, and what art
Could twist the sinews of thy heart?
And when thy heart began to beat
What dread hand? And what dread feet?

"There's more, but that's all I remember."

Maggie shivered, though it was a warm day. "I like it," she said after a moment. "But what do it mean?"

"I heard Mr. Blake say once to a visitor that it were about France. But then to another he said it were about the creator and the created." Maisie repeated the phrase with the same cadence Mr. Blake must have used. A stab of jealousy shot through Maggie at the thought of Maisie spending cozy evenings by the fire reading with the Blakes and listening to Mr. Blake recite poetry and talk to cultured visitors. The feeling vanished, however, when Maisie put a hand to her back to ease the strain of the baby's weight, and Maggie was reminded that, whatever period of grace Maisie was having, it wouldn't last. Guilt quickly replaced jealousy.

"I didn't realize that"—Maggie hesitated—"well, that you and John Astley had actually—you know. I thought we'd got back to you in time, me and Mr. Blake. I wasn't gone long from the stables that night. I came back as quick as I could."

Maisie's eyes dropped to the ground, as if to study her weeding. "It didn't take long, in the end."

"Does Jem know? Do your parents?"

Maisie's face crumpled. "No!" She began to cry again, great sobs that shook the whole of her ample body. Maggie put an arm around her and led her over to the steps of the summerhouse, where she let Maisie lay her head in her lap and sob for a long time, weeping as she had wanted to do for months but didn't dare to in front of the Blakes.

At last her sobs died down, and she sat up, wiping her eyes on her apron. Her face had gone blotchy, and was broader and fleshier than it had been months before. Her bonnet looked like an old one of Mrs. Blake's, and Maggie wondered what had happened to her silly, frilly Dorset mop cap. "What we going to do with this baby, then?" she said, surprising herself with the "we."

Maisie did not start to cry again—she had rid herself of the dam of tears and was now drained and weary. "Ma and Pa keep sending word for me to come back—say they'll get Jem to come up and fetch me." Maggie caught her breath at the thought of Jem returning. "I been putting them off," Maisie continued, "thinking it be better to have the baby here. Mrs. Blake said I could stay and have it. Then I could—could give it away and go home and no one would know. If it be a girl I could just take her round the corner to the Asylum for Female Orphans and . . . and . . ."

"What if it's a boy?"

"I don't—I don't know." Maisie was twisting and untwisting a corner of her apron. "Find some place to—" She couldn't finish the sentence, so began a different one. "It be hard staying here, what with him just next door." She looked fearfully up at the windows of John Astley's house, then turned her face and pulled her bonnet close so that no one from there could recognize her. "Sometimes I can hear him through the walls, and it just makes me feel—" Maisie shuddered.

"Does he know about this?" Maggie nodded at Maisie's belly.

"No! I don't want him to!"

"But he might help—give you some money, at least." Even as

she said it Maggie knew it was unlikely John Astley would do even
that. "Shame old Mr. Astley an't here—he might do something
for you, seeing as it'll be his grandchild."

Maisie shuddered again at the word. "Oh, he wouldn't. I *know*
that. I heard him with Miss Devine. You know, the slack-rope dancer.
She were in the same state as me—and by the same man. Mr. Astley were awful to her—threw her out of the circus. He wouldn't
help me." She gazed at the brick wall dividing the Blakes from
Miss Pelham. "Miss Devine were kind to me once. I wonder what
she did."

"I can tell you that," Maggie said. "I heard she went back to
Scotland to have her baby."

"Did she?" Maisie brightened a little at this news. "Did she
really?"

"Is that what you want to do—go back to Dorsetshire?"

"Yes. Yes, I would. Mr. and Mrs. Blake have been so good to
me, and I'm so grateful, but I miss Ma and Pa, and especially Jem.
I miss him dreadful."

"So do I," Maggie agreed before she could stop herself, so grateful to have someone else concur with her own feelings. "I miss him
dreadful too." After a pause, she added, "You should go home,
then. Your family'd take you in, would they?"

"I think so. Oh, but how would I get there? I han't any money,
and besides, I can't go alone, not when the baby be due soon. I
don't dare ask the Blakes—they be so busy these days, and besides,
though they've a big house, they really han't any money. Mr.
Blake don't sell much of what he makes because it be so . . . so . . .
well, difficult to understand. I think even Mrs. Blake don't understand what he means sometimes. Oh, Maggie, what do we do?"

Maggie was not really listening, but thinking. To her it was as
if a story had been laid out before her with its clear beginning and
middle, and she was now responsible for its safe passage to the end.
"Don't you worry, Maisie," she said. "I know what to do."

~ 2 ~

Maggie was not sure what a silver caddy spoon was worth, but she suspected it would more than cover two passengers by coach to Dorchester, with a bit left over to help Maisie.

She decided to tackle Charlie head-on. After leaving Maisie in the Blakes' garden, she headed for the pubs he drank in, starting with the Pineapple and Hercules Tavern, then moving on to the Crown and Cushion, the Old Dover Castle, and the Artichoke, before she had the idea to return to the Canterbury Arms. Charlie Butterfield had a weakness for one of the barmaids there, who had patched him up when Maggie led him in from Cut-Throat Lane the previous December. The Canterbury Arms was also discreetly anti-Association, those who worked there keeping men from that group waiting just that much longer before serving them, and then giving them sour beer. Charlie had kept his head low with the Association ever since the confrontation at the Blakes' house.

Maggie found him standing at the bar, chatting to the barmaid. "I need to talk to you," she said. "It's important."

Charlie smirked and rolled his eyes at the barmaid, but allowed his sister to lead him to a quiet corner. Since the night in Cut-Throat Lane, they had got on better, having reached a wordless understanding negotiated via Jem's blow and sealed as Maggie led her brother, bloody and dizzy, out of the dark and toward the pub's lights. Maggie no longer blamed him for what happened on Cut-Throat Lane, and he was no longer so cruel to her. Indeed, as painful as her confession to Jem had been that night, after it Maggie felt older and lighter, as if ridding herself of a pocket full of stones.

"I need that spoon money," Maggie announced when they'd sat down. She had found these days that it was best to be straight with him.

Charlie raised his eyebrows at his sister, both now scarred, for Jem's blow had left its mark. "What you want it for?"

"Maisie." Maggie explained what had happened.

Charlie slammed down his mug. "That bastard. I should've ripped his teeth out that night."

"Well, it's too late now." Maggie marveled at how quickly Charlie could get angry at just about anything. Even his attempts to flirt were laced with violence—usually boasts of which girl's sweetheart he would fight and how hard he could punch.

Charlie sat back and slugged his beer. "Anyway, I don't have the money now."

"Get it."

When he laughed, she repeated herself. "Get it, Charlie. I don't care how, but I want it tomorrow, or the next day. Please," she added, though the word held little currency with him.

"Why so quick? She's been here all these months—she can wait a little longer."

"She wants to have her baby back home. Wants it to be a Piddle baby, God help her."

"All right. Give me a day or two and I'll get you what you need for the coach fare."

"And a little extra for Maisie."

"And the extra." Though Charlie was no longer interested in Maisie—seeing John Astley's mouth on her breast had cured him of that—the ghost of his attraction seemed to encourage him to be generous for once.

"Thanks, Charlie."

He shrugged.

"One more thing—don't tell Ma and Pa. They won't under-stand, and they'll just try an' stop me, say it's a waste of money and none of my business. You can tell 'em once I've gone—where I've gone and why."

He nodded. "And when you're coming back."

Next Maggie booked two places on the London-to-Weymouth coach leaving in two and a half days, and hoped Charlie would have the money in time. Then she called on the Blakes to tell them, for she did not want Maisie to sneak away, after all they had done for her. Mrs. Blake seemed to know her business was serious, for she led her up to the front sitting room on the first floor, where Maggie had never been. While Mrs. Blake went to fetch her husband and some tea, Maggie peered at the walls, which were crowded with paintings and engravings, mostly by Mr. Blake. She had previously seen only glimpses of drawings in his notebook, or the odd page of a book.

The pictures were mostly of people, some naked, many wearing robes that clung to them in a way that made them look naked anyway. They were walking or lying on the ground, or looking at one another, and few seemed happy or content, as the figures Maggie had seen in *Songs of Innocence* were; instead they were worried, terrified, angry. Maggie felt anxiety rising in her own throat, but she could not stop looking at them, for they reminded her of echoes of feelings and remnants of dreams, as if her mind were a hidey-hole that Mr. Blake had crawled into and rummaged through before pulling the contents halfway out.

When the Blakes came in they had Maisie with them, though Mrs. Blake herself carried the tray that held a teapot and cup, which she set on a side table next to the armchair Mr. Blake gestured Maggie to. Maggie wasn't sure if she ought to pour the tea herself, and so left it, till Mrs. Blake took pity on her and poured out a cup for her.

"An't you having any, ma'am?" Maggie asked.

"Oh, no, Mr. Blake and me don't drink it—it's just for our guests."

Maggie stared at the brown liquid, too self-conscious to bring it to her lips.

Mr. Blake saved the awkward moment by leaning forward in the armchair opposite and fixing his big bright eyes on her—eyes that Maggie recognized now as being in many of the faces in the pictures on the wall; she felt as if there were a dozen pairs of William Blake's eyes all watching her. "Well, now, Maggie," he said, "Kate tells me you have something you want to say to us."

"Yes, sir." Maggie glanced at Maisie, who was standing against the door, her eyes already welling with tears when they hadn't even begun discussing her. Then Maggie laid out the plan to the Blakes. They listened courteously, Mr. Blake's gaze steady on her, Mrs. Blake looking into the unlit fire, not needed now in summer.

When Maggie finished—and it didn't take long to tell them she would accompany Maisie on the coach to Dorsetshire, and that they would leave in two days—Mr. Blake nodded. "Well, Maisie, Kate and I knew you would leave us eventually, didn't we, Kate? You'll be needing the coach fare, won't you?"

Mrs. Blake shifted, and her hand stirred in the folds of her apron, but she said nothing.

"No, sir," Maggie announced with pride. "That's taken care of. I got the money myself." She had never been able to say that before about something as significant as two pounds for two coach fares. Maggie had rarely had more than sixpence of her own; even her mustard and vinegar money had gone straight to her parents, bar a penny or two. The luxury of being able to refuse Mr. Blake's money was a feeling she would long savor.

"Well, now, my girl, if you'll wait a moment, I'm going to get something from downstairs. I won't be a minute, Kate." Mr. Blake jumped up and was out of the door almost before Maisie could get out of the way, leaving the two girls with Mrs. Blake. "Drink your tea, Maggie," she said gently, and now, without Mr. Blake's persistent eyes on her, Maggie found that she could.

"Oh, Maggie, can you really pay the fares?" Maisie knelt at her side.

"Course. I said I would, didn't I?" Maggie didn't add that she was still waiting for Charlie to give her the money.

Mrs. Blake was going around the walls, straightening the prints and paintings. "You will be careful, girls, won't you? If you start to feel ill or have pains, Maisie, you'll get the coachman to stop."

"Yes, ma'am."

"Have you been in many coaches, Mrs. Blake?" Maggie asked.

Mrs. Blake chuckled. "We've never been out of London, my dear."

"Oh!" It had not occurred to Maggie that she might be doing something the more experienced Blakes had not.

"We've walked out in the countryside, of course," Mrs. Blake continued, brushing the back of Mr. Blake's armchair. "Sometimes a long way. But always within a half day's walk of London. I can't imagine what it must be like to be so far away from what you know. Mr. Blake knows, of course, for he journeys far and wide in his mind. Indeed, he's always someplace else. Sometimes I see very little of him." She let her fingers rest on the ridge of the armchair's back.

"'Tis hard," Maisie murmured, "being in one place, and thinking about t'other so." Tears began to roll down her face. "I'll be so glad to see the Piddle Valley again, no matter what they think of me when they see me." She quickly dried her eyes with a corner of her apron when she heard Mr. Blake's step on the stairs.

He came in with two small, flat, identical packages wrapped in brown paper and tied with string. "This is for you, and that for Jem when you see him," he said. "For helping me when I most needed it." As he handed the packages to Maggie, she heard the sharp catching of Mrs. Blake's breath in her throat.

"Oh, thank you, Mr. Blake!" Maggie whispered in confusion as she held one in each hand. She didn't receive many gifts, and certainly not from someone like Mr. Blake; she wasn't sure if she was meant to open them now or not.

"Take good care of those, my dear," Mrs. Blake said in a tight voice. "They're precious."

That decided Maggie—she wouldn't open them just yet. Stacking them together, she slipped them into her apron pocket. "Thank you," she repeated, wanting to cry but not knowing why.

~ 4 ~

Another surprise awaited Maggie out in the street. Now that the Kellaways no longer lived at no. 12 Hercules Buildings, she never bothered to give the house more than a glance as she passed. This time, though, she heard Miss Pelham's raised voice and looked to see who was on the receiving end. It was a girl Maisie's age, rough in a torn satin skirt that strained against the protruding bump only a little smaller than Maisie's.

"Go away!" Miss Pelham was shouting. "Get out of my garden! That family was nothing but trouble when they lived here, and look—even now they drag down my good name. Who told you to come here, anyway?"

Maggie couldn't hear the girl's reply, but Miss Pelham soon supplied the information. "I'm going to have a word with Mr. Astley. How dare he send a tart like you round to me! His father wouldn't dare do such a thing. Now, away! Go away, girl!"

"But where do I go now?" the girl wailed. "No one'll have me like this!" As she turned from Miss Pelham's door Maggie got a better look at her and, though she'd only seen her once before, recognized the straw hair and pale face and unmistakable pathos of Rosie Wightman, Maisie and Jem's friend from Dorsetshire.

"Rosie!" Maggie hissed as the girl reached the gate. Rosie looked at her blankly, unable to distinguish Maggie's face from the long parade of characters she'd been involved with over the months since she'd briefly met her.

"Rosie, are you looking for Maisie Kellaway?" Maggie persisted. Rosie's face cleared. "Oh, yes!" she cried. "She told me to come to the circus, an' I did just now, but there be no Kellaways there no more. An' I don't know what to do."

Miss Pelham had caught sight of Maggie. "You!" she crowed. "Of course I'm not surprised to find you hanging about with tawdry trash like her. She's a fine example of what you'll become!"

"Shhh!" Maggie hissed. Passersby were beginning to take note of them, and Maggie didn't want to draw attention to yet another pregnant girl.

No one, however, could shush Miss Pelham. "Are you telling me to be quiet, you little guttersnipe?" she cried, her voice rising almost to a song. "I'll have you taken away and beaten till you're sorry you're alive! I'll have you—"

"I was only saying shush, ma'am," Maggie interrupted loudly, and thinking fast, "because you won't want to draw more attention to yourself than you already have. I just heard someone telling another that you'd a visitor—your niece." She nodded at Rosie Wightman. A man in the road carrying a basket of shrimps on his head broke his stride at Maggie's words and leered at Miss Pelham and Rosie. "She looks just like you, ma'am!" he said, to Maggie's delight and Miss Pelham's horror. The latter gazed fearfully about to see if anyone else had heard, then jumped inside and slammed the door.

Turning away in satisfaction, Maggie contemplated her latest surprise and sighed. "Lord a mercy, Rosie Wightman, what we goin' to do with you?"

Rosie stood complacent. It was enough for her to have got herself this far, even if ten months later than Jem and Maisie had expected her. As with the men she went with, once a course of action was set in motion, she was content to surrender. "Have you anything to eat?" she yawned. "I be so hungry."

"Oh Lord," Maggie sighed again, before taking Rosie by the arm and leading her to no. 13 Hercules Buildings.

~ 5 ~

It was rare for the Butterfields to sit down of an evening and eat together at home. To Maggie it was a miracle that this happened the night before she was to leave on the Weymouth coach. It was what she might have planned if she had thought she could manage it. As it was, she had expected simply to go to bed early and sneak out before dawn to pick up the girls. She had prepared several lies, if she needed them, for why she couldn't accompany her mother to a night wash (a vinegar girl had asked her to fill in the next day) or her father to the pub (she had a bellyache). In the end she didn't need either: Bet Butterfield did not have a wash to go to, and Dick Butterfield announced that he was staying in and expected a steak and kidney pie for supper.

Pie brought Charlie sniffing, and pulled them to the table to sit around the plate Bet Butterfield set down in the center. For a few minutes there was no sound as they tucked in. "Ah," Dick Butterfield sighed after several bites. "Perfection, chuck. You could be cooking for the King."

"I'd settle for washin' his sheets," Bet Butterfield replied. "Think what a lot o' money them palace laundresses must earn, eh, Dick?"

"What's the matter, Mags—you're not eatin' the pie your mam's taken such trouble over. Is that gratitude?"

"Sorry, Mam, I've a bit of a bellyache." Maggie used up one of her lies anyway. She was finding it hard to swallow, her stomach jittery with nerves about the next day. Her mother's talk of money made her feel even worse: She kept shooting glances at Charlie, who still hadn't given her the spoon money. She was hoping to pull him aside later. Now he was enjoying ignoring her as he reached for another helping of pie.

"Well, now, that's a shame," Dick Butterfield said. "Maybe you'll feel better later."

"Maybe." Maggie looked at Charlie again. He was sucking at a piece of beef fat, the grease glistening on his lips. She wanted to slap him.

Charlie smiled at her. "What's the matter, Mags? Not making you sick, am I? You're not feeling *poor*, are you?"

"Shut up," Maggie muttered, wondering now at Charlie's mood, which was not the sort in which he was likely to keep promises.

"What's this, what's this?" Dick Butterfield said. "Stop it, you two. Let's eat in peace."

When they'd finished, Dick Butterfield sat back and wiped his mouth on his sleeve. "I'm going up to Smithfield's tomorrow," he announced. "Goin' to see someone about some lambs comin' in from—where was they comin' in from, Charlie?"

"Dor-set-shire," Charlie answered, drawing out each syllable.

Maggie's throat closed so that she couldn't speak.

"You want to come, Mags?" Dick Butterfield's eyes rested on her. "It's easier to let Dorsetshire come to you rather'n you go to Dorsetshire, wouldn't you say?"

"Charlie, you bastard!" Maggie managed to get out, realizing now that he had never intended to give her the spoon money.

"Now, Mags," Dick Butterfield interjected, "don't blame him. He's just lookin' out for you. You don't think he's goin' to let you go off on a country adventure without tellin' me."

"I— Please, Pa. I'm just tryin' to help her."

"The best help you can give is to your mam with her laundry, not runnin' round Dorsetshire looking for that boy, under the ruse of helping his sister."

"I'm not doing that! I just want to take her home, where she wants to be, out of this—this cesspit!"

Dick Butterfield chuckled. "You think this is a cesspit, gal, wait till you get to the countryside. Things happen out there just as bad as here—worse, sometimes, as there an't so many people watchin' out for you. You forget that your mam and me is from the countryside—we knows what we're talkin' about, don't we, Bet?"

Maggie's mother had remained quiet throughout this exchange, concentrating on clearing the table. She looked up briefly from the last bit of pie she was moving to the sideboard. "That's right, duck," she agreed, her voice flat. Maggie studied her mother's face, and found in her frown a spark of hope, even as her father was saying, "You'll be staying here with us, Mags. You're a London girl, you know. You belong here."

Maggie lay awake most of the night, thinking of ways she might still get the money she needed for the journey. This included selling one of Mr. Blake's gifts, if they were valuable, though she hated the idea.

Then hope arrived. After a short doze, Maggie awoke to find Bet Butterfield sitting by her bed. "Shh. We don't want to wake no one. Get yourself dressed and ready for your journey. Quiet, now." Her mother gestured toward the other bed, where Charlie was sleeping on his stomach, his mouth open.

Maggie quickly changed and gathered the few things she would need, making sure above all that Mr. Blake's packages were safe in her pocket.

When she joined her mother in the kitchen, Bet Butterfield handed her a sack filled with bread and the remnants of the pie, and a handkerchief knotted around a bulge of coins. "This should get you to Dorsetshire," she whispered. "It's bits and bobs I've set aside these past months—all my button money, and other things too. Since you've helped me with 'em, some of it's yours. That's how I see it." She said this as if already rehearsing her side of the argument she would have the next day with her husband when he discovered Maggie and the money were gone.

"Thanks, Mam." Maggie hugged her mother. "Why you doin' this for me?"

"I owe that girl somethin' for lettin' her get in the state she's in. You get her home safe, now. And come back, will you."

Maggie hugged Bet Butterfield again, breathing in her smell of pie and laundry, then crept out while her luck still held.

$\sim 6 \sim$

Maggie remembered every moment of the journey to Dorsetshire, and long afterward liked to travel through it again in her mind. Bet Butterfield's money extended only to two passages inside the coach, and it took a great deal of persuasion for the coachman to agree to let Maggie sit up beside him for the reduced third fare. He was convinced at last by the state of Maisie and Rosie, with Maggie claiming she was a midwife and if she didn't go along the coachman might have to deliver the babies himself.

Maisie and Rosie caused a sensation everywhere they went together—at the inns where the horses were changed, at the dinner tables, in the streets where they took a turn to stretch their legs, in the coach itself, crowded with the other passengers. One pregnant girl was common enough, but with two together the double dose of fertility directed attention their way, offending some, delighting others. Maisie and Rosie were so happy to have each other's company that they barely noticed the tuts and smiles, but snuggled together in the coach, and whispered and giggled in the street. It was just as well, then, that Maggie sat on top of the coach.

Besides, from there she had a much better view of the vivid, unfamiliar landscape of southern England.

The first stage was not so surprising, as the coach passed through a string of villages that shadowed the Thames and looked back to London for their vitality—Vauxhall, Wandsworth, Putney, Barnes, Sheen. Only after Richmond and the first change of horses did Maggie feel they had truly left London behind. The land opened out into long, rolling hills in a physical rhythm unknown to someone accustomed to the chopped-up streets of a big city. At first Maggie could only look ahead over the layered hills to the horizon, which was farther away than she'd ever witnessed. After coming to terms with that spacious novelty, she was then able to focus on the landscape closer to hand, to take in the fields segmented by hedgerows, the sheep and cows sprinkled about, and the thatched houses, whose shaggy curves made her laugh. By the time they stopped for dinner in Basingstoke, she was even asking the coachman for the names of roadside flowers she had never taken any interest in before.

It would all have been overwhelming for a London girl if she weren't perched on the rattling box, detached from what she saw, passing by but not engaging with the countryside. Maggie felt safe where she was, squeezed between coachman and groom, and loved every minute on the road—even when it began to rain midafternoon and the coachman's hat dripped directly onto her head.

They stayed the night at an inn in Stockbridge. Maggie got little sleep, for it was noisy, with coaches arriving till midnight and the inn serving far later. Sharing a bed with two pregnant girls meant that one or the other was always getting up to use the chamber pot. Then too, Maggie had never slept anywhere other than at home and, briefly, in the Blakes' summerhouse. She wasn't used to such a public place for sleeping, with three other beds in the room, and women coming and going all night long.

Lying still after a day on the move gave Maggie time at last to think about what she was doing, and to fret. For one thing, she had little money left. The inn meals had been half a crown each, with another shilling to the waiter, and extra costs kept appearing— sixpence expected by the chambermaid who showed them to their room and gave them a sheet and blankets, tuppence for the boy who told them he must clean their boots, a penny for the porter who insisted on carrying their bags upstairs when they could easily have done so themselves, for they had few things. With her mea- ger fund of pennies and shillings rapidly eroding, Maggie would have nothing left by the time she reached the Piddle Valley.

She thought too about her family: how angry her father would be to discover she had escaped, how much grief her mother would have to suffer from him for helping Maggie. Above all, she won- dered where Charlie was right now, and whether he would find her one day and punish her for the revenge she took on him. For that morning, when she and the girls had reached the White Hart in the Borough High Street where the Weymouth coach started, Mag- gie had spied a soldier, taken him aside, and told him there was a young man at no. 6 Bastille Row full of enough piss to take on the French. The soldier had promised to visit the house first thing— the army was always looking for likely young lads to send to war—and had given her a shilling. It was nothing like the amount of the spoon money she never got off her brother, but it was every bit as satisfying—and even more satisfying to think of Charlie shipped off to France.

In the morning, though still damp from the previous day's rain, Maggie was keen to start—keener, indeed, than Maisie and Rosie, who were tired, flea-bitten, and sore from the previous day's bump- ing about in the coach. Maisie in particular was silent over the hurried bread and ale breakfast, and stayed in the coach at the changes of the horses. She ate little of her dinner at Blandford— which was just as well, for Maggie had only enough money for two dinners, split between the girls while she ate her mother's pie.

"You all right?" she said as Maisie pushed her plate to Rosie, who happily ate her way through the untouched potatoes and cabbage.

"Baby's heavy," Maisie replied. She swallowed. "Oh, Maggie, I can't believe I'll be home in a few hours. Home! It do feel like I han't seen Piddletrenthide in years, though it be only a year and a bit."

Maggie's gut twisted. Until now she'd been enjoying the trip so much that she'd managed to push from her mind what it was leading to. Now she wondered what it would be like actually to see Jem again, for he knew her deepest secret and had shown what he thought of it. She was not sure he would want to see her. "Maisie," she began, "p'raps—well, it's not far now, is it?"

"No, not far. They'll leave us at Piddletown—tha' be six miles from here. We can walk from there—another five miles or so."

"P'raps, then, you two could go on without me. I'll stay here and catch the coach on its way back." Maggie hadn't told Maisie of her money troubles, but looking around Blandford—a busy town, the largest they'd been through since Basingstoke—she thought she could find work briefly somewhere and earn her fare back. It couldn't be that hard to be a chambermaid in a coaching inn, she decided.

Maisie, however, clutched at Maggie. "Oh, no, you can't leave us! We need you! What would we do without you?" Even the passive Rosie looked over in alarm. Maisie lowered her voice. "Please don't abandon us, Maggie. I . . . I do think the baby's coming soon." Even as she said it she winced, her body tense and rigid, as if trying to contain a deep pain.

Maggie's eyes widened. "Maisie!" she hissed. "How long has this been goin' on?"

Maisie gazed at her fearfully. "Since this morning," she said. "But it an't bad yet. Please can we go on? I don't want to have it here!" She looked around her at the noisy, busy, dirty inn. "I want to get home."

"Well, at least you an't at the yelling stage," Maggie decided. "You could be hours yet. Let's see how we get on."

Maisie squeezed her hand gratefully.

Maggie did not enjoy that last leg of the coach journey, worrying about Maisie down below but reluctant to ask the coachman to stop so she could check on her. She could only assume that Rosie would rap on the ceiling if something were wrong. And the surrounding landscape—despite the greenness of the fields, the pleasing movement of hills and valleys, the bright blue sky, and the sun lighting up the fields and hedgerows—looked threatening to her now that she knew she'd soon be out in the middle of it. She began to notice how few houses there were. What are we going to do? she thought. What if Maisie has the baby out in a field somewhere?

~ 7 ~

Piddletown was a large village, with several streets lined with thatched houses, a handful of pubs, and a market square, where the coach let them down. Maggie said good-bye to the coachman, who wished her well, then laughed and cracked his whip at the horses. When the coach was gone, taking with it the clopping and jangling and rattling they had lived with for the last day and a half, the three girls stood silent in the street. Unlike London, where most passersby wouldn't even notice the girls, here it felt to Maggie as if every person was staring at the new arrivals.

"Rosie Wightman, look a' wha' you been doin'," remarked a young woman leaning against a house with a basket of buns. Rosie, who'd had many reasons to cry in the two years since she'd left the Piddle Valley but never had, burst into tears.

"You leave her be, you bandy little bitch!" Maggie shouted. To her amazement, the woman guffawed. Maggie turned to Maisie for a translation.

"She can't understand you," Maisie explained. "They're not used to London ways. Don't." She pulled at Maggie's sleeve to keep her back from the laughter that had spread to others. "It don't matter. Piddletowners has always been funny with us. Come on." She led them up the street, and in a few minutes they were out of the village and on a track heading northwest.

"You sure you want to leave town?" Maggie asked. "If you need to stop and have your baby, now's the time to say."

Maisie shook her head. "Don't want to have it in Piddletown. An' I be all right. Pain's gone." Indeed, she stepped eagerly along the track, taking Rosie's hand and swinging it as they entered the familiar landscape of hills that would take them down into the Piddle Valley. They began to point out landmarks to each other, and to speculate once again about various residents of their village, as they had done constantly over the past few days.

At first the hills were long and gently rolling, with a wide sky above them like an overturned blue bowl and a view for miles of green and brown ridges divided by woods and hedgerows. The track led straight alongside a tall hedgerow, with misty banks of shoulder-high cow parsley flanking the way. It was hot and still, and with the sun beating down, insects invisibly whirring and ticking, and the cow parsley floating her along, Maggie began to feel as if she were in a dream. There were no sheep or cows in the nearby fields, and no people about. She spun all the way around and could see neither a house nor a barn nor a plow nor a trough nor even a fence. Other than the rutted track, there was nothing to indicate that people even existed, much less lived, here. She had a sudden vision of herself in this land as a bird might see her from high above, a lone speck of white among the green and brown and yellow. The emptiness frightened her: She could feel fear gripping her stomach and working its way up her chest to her throat, where it held tight and threatened to throttle her. She stopped, gulped,

and tried to call to the girls, who were getting farther and farther
away from her down the track.

Maggie shut her eyes and took a deep breath, in her mind hearing her father say, "Pull yourself together, Mags. This won't do at
all." When she opened her eyes she saw a figure coming down the
hill in front of them. The relief that flooded her was tempered by
new concern, for as Maggie knew too well, a lone man could be the
danger that made the emptiness so threatening. She hurried to
catch up with the girls, who had also spotted the man. Neither
seemed worried—in fact, they quickened their pace. "Tha' be Mr.
Case!" Maisie cried. "He'll be comin' from the Piddles. Ar'ernoon!"
She waved at him.

They met him at the lowest part of the valley, just next to a
stream that ran along the seam of two fields. Mr. Case was about
Thomas Kellaway's age, tall, wiry, with a pack on his back and the
long, steady gait of someone who spends much of his time walking. He raised his eyebrows when he recognized Maisie and Rosie.
"You going home, you two?" he inquired. "I heard none about it
in the Piddles. They be expecting you?"

"No, they don't know—anything," Maisie answered.

"You back to stay? We missed your hand. I've had customers
ask specially for your buttons, you know."

Maisie blushed. "You be teasing me, Mr. Case."

"I must get on, but I'll see you next month, aye?"

She nodded, and he turned and strode off up the track they had
just descended.

"Who was that?" Maggie asked, gazing after him.

Maisie looked back at him fondly, grateful that he'd not said
anything or shown any surprise about the baby she carried. "The
button agent making his rounds—he comes to collect buttons
every month. He's off to Piddletown now. I'd forgot he comes this
day every month. An't it strange how quick we forget things like
that?"

The girls took a long time to climb the hill, panting and puffing, and stopping often, with Maggie carrying all of their bundles by now. As they rested she saw the telltale wince and tightening of Maisie's jaw, but decided to say nothing. They were able to go more quickly down the next hill before climbing slowly again. In this stop-start manner they made their way along the Piddle Valley, Maggie discovering that the stream they crisscrossed was actually the River Piddle, reduced to a trickle in the midsummer heat. This piece of information restored something of her old sense of humor. "River. River! You could fit a hundred o' them Piddlers in the Thames!" she crowed as she hopped onto a rock to cross it in two bounds.

"How d'you think I felt, seeing the Thames the first time?" Maisie retorted. "I thought there were an awful flood!"

Eventually they crested a hill to find that the track they were on intersected a proper road, which led down into a huddle of houses around a square-towered church, one side of it painted in gold light by the descending sun.

"At last!" Maggie said brightly, to cover her nerves.

"Not quite," Maisie corrected. "Tha' be Piddlehinton—next but one to Piddletrenthide. It be a long village, mind, but we'll be there soon enough." She gripped the stile they'd stopped by and leaned over it, groaning softly.

"It's all right, Maisie," Maggie said, patting her shoulder. "We'll get you help soon."

When the contraction had passed, Maisie straightened and stepped firmly onto the road. Rosie followed less certainly. "Oh, Maisie, what they going to say about us—about . . ." She glanced down at her own bump.

"There be nothing we can do about that now, can we? Just hold your head up. Here now—take my arm." Maisie linked hers through her friend's as they descended into Piddlehinton.

~ 8 ~

While on the track, they had met no one other than the button agent, and seen a man with his sheep on a distant hill, and another with a horse and plow. The road proper carried more traffic, however—workers coming in from the fields, horsemen passing through on their way to Dorchester, a farmer driving his cows toward a barn, children running home from an afternoon playing by the river. The girls slipped in among the others, hoping not to draw attention, but that was impossible, of course. Even before they reached the first house in the village, children began to appear and follow them. Each time they had to stop to wait for Maisie, the children stopped too, at a distance. "I bet they an't had so much excitement all week," Maggie remarked. "All month, even."

As they approached the New Inn—the first pub in the village—a woman called out from her doorway, "Tha' be Maisie Kellaway, don' it? Didn't know you was coming back now. An' like tha'."

Maisie flinched, but was forced to stop short with a contraction.

"You too, Rosie Wightman," the woman added. "You been busy in London, have you?"

"Could you help us, ma'am?" Maggie interrupted, trying to keep her temper in check. "Maisie's havin' her baby."

The woman studied Maisie. Behind her, two small boys appeared, peeking out at the newcomers. "Where be her husband? An' yourn?"

There was a silence during which Maisie opened her mouth and then shut it; the ease she'd developed in lying in London appeared to have deserted her.

Maggie had less trouble. "France," she declared. "They gone to fight the Frenchies. I been charged to bring the wives home." To counter the woman's skeptical look, she added, "I'm the sister of Maisie's husband. Charlie—Charlie Butterfield's his name." As she spoke she kept her eyes fastened on Maisie's, willing her to follow suit. Maisie opened her mouth, paused, then said, "Tha's right. I be Maisie Butterfield now. An' Rosie be . . ."

"Rosie Blake," Maggie finished for her. "Married to Billy Blake same day as my brother, just before they gone off to France."

The woman regarded them, her eyes lingering on Rosie's dirty satin skirt. At last, though, she said to one of the boys peeking around her, "Eddie, run up to the Five Bells—don't bother at the Crown, they've no cart there today. Ask if they can send a cart back to pick up a girl in labor needs to go up the Kellaways' in Piddletrenthide."

"We'll go along and meet the cart," Maisie muttered as the boy ran off. "Don' want to stay round with her lookin' at us." She linked arms with Rosie and started down the road, Maggie shouldering the bundles once more, the gang of children still following. Glancing behind her, she saw the woman cross the road to another who had just come out of her cottage; the first spoke to the second as they watched the trio.

As they walked, Maisie said in a low voice to Maggie, "Thank'ee."

Maggie smiled. "Didn't you say once you'd always wanted a sister?"

"An' Rosie married to Mr. Blake! Can you imagine?"

"What would Mrs. Blake say?" Maggie chuckled.

They passed from Piddlehinton into Piddletrenthide, though Maggie would not have guessed without Maisie telling her, as there was no break or change in the long string of houses along the road. She felt herself being sucked deeper and deeper into the Dorset village, and though it was better than being in the empty field, its unfamiliarity—the mud everywhere, the cottages with their peculiar straw roofs, the flat eyes of the villagers watching her— made her uncomfortable. A few called out greetings, but many said nothing, simply staring at the girls even though they recognized them. Maggie began to wonder if perhaps Maisie should have remained in Lambeth to have the baby after all.

Maisie's waters broke in front of the Crown, and the girls had to stop, for her contractions were becoming more frequent and more painful. They led her to the bench next to the pub's door. "Oh, where is that cart?" Maisie gasped. Then the publican's wife came out with a cry and a hug for both Maisie and Rosie. It seemed only to take that one well-wisher to turn the mood from judgment to joy. Others emerged from the pub and from neighboring houses, and the Piddle girls were surrounded by surprised neighbors and old friends. Maisie rolled out her new lie for the first time, calling herself Maisie Butterfield so casually and fluently that Maggie wanted to congratulate her. She's going to be fine, she thought, and took a step back from the crowd.

The cart arrived at last, driven by Mr. Smart, the very man who had first brought the Kellaways to London, and who was now taking part in another, more local adventure he could talk about at the pub later. Several women lifted the groaning Maisie into the bed of straw spread in the back, and Rosie and the publican's wife climbed in after her. Maisie turned to ask Maggie for something from her bundle and discovered her friend was not in the cart with them. "Maggie!" she cried as they began to pull away. "Mr. Smart, wait for Maggie!" She had to stop, however, when the strongest contraction yet turned her cry into a scream.

The only sign that Maggie had been there at all was the girls' bundles she'd been carrying, stacked on the pub bench.

~ 9 ~

Jem sensed something was different long before the cart appeared. As he worked outside the front door of the Kellaways' cottage, painting a chair that his brother Sam had just finished leveling, he could hear a distant buzzing in the air of the kind that occurs when people have gathered and are discussing a subject, punctuated by occasional yelps from excited children. He did not think too much of it, for he had heard the same earlier that afternoon when the button agent passed through, and though he was long gone, his visit might account for the renewed disturbance. Perhaps two women were arguing over the quality the agent had assigned their buttons, whether superior, standard, or seconds. Each Piddle woman was proud of her handiwork, and hated to be judged not up to the usual standard. A catty remark by another could start an argument that might run publically for weeks.

Jem smiled at the thought, but it was with resignation rather than appreciation. Aspects of village life appeared very different to him since his return from London, now that he had something to compare it to. He couldn't imagine his Lambeth neighbors arguing over the quality of their buttons, for example. Though he never told anyone, there were times when Piddletrenthide, like its river, seemed limited after Lambeth and the Thames. Some days he opened the front door to look out, and his heart sank at the sight of everything being the same as it had been the day before. There were no pineapples carried past, no sky blue ribbons dangling down girls' backs. This was the sort of thing he might have complained about to Maisie if she were there. He missed her; and he envied her the months she was spending at the Blakes'.

It had not been easy for the Kellaways to settle back in to Piddletrenthide, even though they had been gone less than a year. They arrived in the middle of a snowstorm, so that no one was out on the road to greet them, and walked into their old cottage to find Sam Kellaway and his wife, Lizzie, in bed together, though it was gone noon. It had been an uncomfortable start, and some of the family had not quite recovered.

Thomas Kellaway soon enough took up his old spot in the workshop, relinquished grudgingly by Sam, who had enjoyed his brief taste of being his own master. His father was slower making his chairs than Sam liked, and Sam was quicker to point this out than before. Though neither said anything, Thomas Kellaway sometimes wondered if he was really still master of his workshop.

Anne Kellaway found it hard to fit in as well, for she had come back to a daughter-in-law in her place. In the past, Anne Kellaway and Lizzie Miller had got on, for Lizzie had been a quiet girl who always deferred to her future mother-in-law. With marriage and her own home, however, Lizzie had grown into a woman with opinions, which she was reluctant to hand back when the Kellaways reappeared at the cottage she had begun to make her own. She had changed some things, bringing in some Miller furniture, hanging new curtains, moving a table from one side of the room to the other. Within an hour of their arrival, Anne Kellaway had moved the table back, sending Lizzie into a sulk that had lasted these seven months. As a result the two women avoided being alone together—not easy when their work kept them in the same room so much; indeed, Anne Kellaway ought to have been helping Lizzie wash the curtains, but chose instead to work out in the garden beyond the chair workshop. She did not sense what Jem did— did not catch the current of excitement that passed invisibly through the village when something new was happening. Instead she was weeding among the leeks and trying not to think about the stump of the pear tree at the bottom of the garden. It had been a year and a half since Tommy died, and she still thought of him several times a day. That was what being a parent meant, she had come to realize: Your children remained with you, alive or dead, nearby or far-away. She fretted too about Maisie, stuck in Lambeth. They must find a way to get her back.

Then she heard Maisie's screams.

Anne Kellaway reached the front of the house at the same moment as the cart. "God in heaven," she murmured as she caught sight of her daughter's bulk, and sought out her husband's eyes.

Thomas Kellaway took in his daughter's condition without

blinking. A determined expression crossed his face—one that had developed during the months the Kellaways spent in Lambeth. He gazed at his wife. Then, in full view of his neighbors who had come out to see what the fuss was about, Thomas Kellaway strode over and, calling to Jem and Sam to help, lifted his daughter down from the cart.

Despite Thomas Kellaway's gesture, Anne Kellaway knew that the neighbors would watch to see what she would do, and take their response from her. Looking around, she saw her daughter-in-law, Lizzie, studying Maisie with barely concealed disgust. Anne Kellaway closed her eyes, and an image of Miss Laura Devine swinging freely on her rope arose in her mind. She nodded to herself, opened her eyes, and joined her husband, putting her arm around Maisie while Thomas Kellaway propped up her other side. "All right, Maisie," she murmured. "You be home now."

As they led her into the cottage, Maisie called over her shoulder, "Jem, you must find Maggie—I don't know where she's gone!"

Jem started, his eyes wide. "Maggie be here?"

"Oh yes, we couldn't have come without her. She's been so good to Rosie and me—arranged everything and looked after us. But then she disappeared!"

"Where were she last?"

"By the Crown. We got on the cart and I turned round and she weren't there. Oh, please find her, Jem! She han't any money and she's scared out here." Maisie was pulled inside before she could see how fast her brother turned and ran.

~ *10* ~

Piddletrenthide was a long, narrow village, with far more than the thirty houses it had been originally named for stretched out along

the Piddle for more than a mile. The Crown was on the edge, just
before the village became Piddlehinton. Jem was out of breath by
the time he reached the pub. Once he got his breath back he asked
around, but no one had seen Maggie. He knew, however, that a
stranger could not get far in the valley without people noting it.

At the New Inn Jem spoke to some children hanging about,
who said Maggie had passed them half an hour earlier. Farther on
an old man confirmed he'd seen her by the church. Jem ran on in
the gathering dusk.

At the church he spied a flash of white behind the wall separating the churchyard from the road, and his heart beat faster. When
he peeked over the wall, however, he saw, sitting up against it in
the last patch of sunlight, a Piddle girl Jem recognized as a distant
cousin of his sister-in-law. She held something in her lap that she
quickly covered with her apron on Jem's approach.

"Evenin'," Jem said, squatting next to her. "Tell me, you seen
a girl walking this way? A stranger, older'n you. From London."

The girl stared at him with wide dark eyes that flashed with
concealed knowledge. "You be a Miller girl, don't you?" Jem persisted. "The Plush Millers."

After a moment the girl nodded.

"Your cousin Lizzie lives with us, you know. She's married to
my brother Sam."

The girl contemplated this. "She told me to find Jem," she said
at last.

"Who—Lizzie? I just been with her at home."

"The London lady."

"You seen her? What did she say? Where is she?"

"She said—" The girl looked down at her lap, clearly torn between concealment and revelation. "She said—to give you this."
From underneath her apron she removed a slim mushroom-colored
book, which had been wrapped in brown paper that was now un-
done. The girl looked at him fearfully. "I didn't mean to unwrap it,

but the string did come off, an' the paper slipped, an' I saw the pictures, an' I couldn't help it, I just wanted to look at it. I never seen such a thing."

Even as he reached for it Jem thought he knew what it was. When he opened it to the title page, however, he discovered that it was different from the book he'd seen. Instead of children clustered at their mother's knee, the colored drawing was of a young man and woman bent over the bodies of a man and woman laid out on a bier, reminding him of the stone statues lying on the tombs at Westminster Abbey. Above the picture were letters adorned with floating figures and curlicues of vine. He began to flip about in the book, seeing but not taking in page after page of words and pictures intertwined and tinted with blue and yellow and red and green. There were people both clothed and naked, and trees, flowers, grapes, dark skies, and animals—sheep and cows, frogs, a duck, a lion. As Jem turned the pages, the girl crept up to look over his shoulder.

She stopped his hand. "Wha's that?"

"A tiger, I think. Yes, that's what it says." He turned the page and came upon the title "London" under a picture of a child leading an old man through the streets, with the words he knew well and sometimes recited under his breath:

> I wander through each chartered street
> Near where the chartered Thames does flow

Jem shut the book. "Where'd she go—the London girl?"

The girl swallowed. "Can I see more o' that?"

"Once I've found Maggie. Where were she going?"

"Piddletown, she said."

Jem stood. "Well, you come to see your cousin one day and you can look at this. All right?"

The girl nodded.

"Get you home now. It be comin' on evening." He didn't wait to see if she did what he said, but hurried up the hill out of Piddlehinton.

~ *11* ~

Maggie was sitting on the stile overlooking the first valley the track passed through. Seeing her perched there was so incongruous that Jem almost laughed. Instead he swallowed the laughter and quietly said her name so as not to startle her. Maggie whipped her head around. "Jem," she said, her mouth tight, "who'd have thought we'd meet in a place like this, eh?"

Jem stepped up to the stile and leaned against it. "It be funny," he agreed, looking down into the valley, much of it purple with shadows now that the sun was setting.

Maggie looked back at the valley again. "I got to this point and couldn't go no further. I been sittin' here all this time trying to get up the nerve to go down there, but I can't. Look, there's not a soul anywhere about but us. An't natural." She shivered.

"You get used to it. I never give it any thought—except when we moved to London and I missed it. I could never get away from people in London."

"People's all there is, though, an't they? What else is there?"

Jem chuckled. "Everything else. Fields and trees and sky. I could be in them all day and be happy."

"But none of that would mean anything if there weren't people about to be with."

"I suppose." They continued to look at the valley rather than at each other. "Why didn't you come to the house?" Jem said finally. "You come all this way and then turn round at the last mile."

Maggie answered his question with her own. "The girls get there all right?"

"Yes."

"Maisie didn't have her baby in the middle of the road?"

"No, she got inside."

Maggie nodded. "Good."

"How did you find Rosie?"

"She found us, or the old stick, anyway." She told Jem about discovering Rosie at Miss Pelham's.

Jem grunted. "I don't miss *her*." His emphasis made it clear that there were things he did miss. Maggie felt her chest tighten.

"Thank'ee for bringing 'em back," he added.

Maggie shrugged. "I wanted to see this famous Piddle-dee-dee. And they needed someone to take 'em, in their state."

"I . . . I didn't know about Maisie."

"I know. You could've knocked me over when I saw her, I was that surprised." She paused. "I have to tell you something, Jem. Maisie's Maisie Butterfield now."

Jem stared at her in such horror that Maggie giggled. "I know Charlie's bad," she said, "but he's come in handy." She explained about the lie she'd invented, adding, "Rosie's married to Mr. Blake."

Jem chuckled, and Maggie joined him with the bark of laughter he'd missed over the months they'd been apart.

"How be Mr. Blake?" he asked when they'd stopped laughing. "And Mrs. Blake?"

"The Association still bullies him. Nobody can say a thing about the King or France, or anything unusual, without 'em pouncing. And you know how Mr. Blake says unusual things. He's had a bad time of it. Maisie can tell you—she's been around him the most."

"Did he give me this?" Jem pulled the book from his pocket.

"He did. Well, in a way." At a look from Jem, she added, "No, I didn't steal it! How could you think that? I'd never take anything from Mr. Blake! No, it's just—he gave me two of 'em, both wrapped in brown paper, and the same size. And—well, I mixed 'em up in my pocket. I don't know which is yours and which mine."

"They an't the same?"

"No." Maggie jumped down from the stile—now she was on one side, with Jem on the other—picked up her bundle, and dug out the other book. "See?" She opened it to the title page, where the two children were reading a book at a woman's knee. "*Songs of Innocence*," she said. "I remember it from before. I didn't know what the other said, so I chose this one. What's that one called, then?"

"*Songs of Experience*." Jem opened his to the title page and showed her.

"Hah! Opposites, then." They smiled at each other. "But which is yours, d'you think, and which mine? I mean, which do you think Mr. Blake meant us to have? He was very particular about one being specially for you and one for me."

Jem shook his head. "You could ask him."

"Oh, I couldn't. He'd be disappointed I got 'em mixed up. We'll have to decide for ourselves."

They contemplated the books in silence. Then Maggie spoke again. "Jem, why'd you leave without saying good-bye, back in Lambeth?"

Jem shrugged. "We had to leave quick 'cause of Miss Pelham."

Maggie studied his profile. "You could've found me to say good-bye. Was it 'cause you couldn't—can't—forgive me for—for doin' what I did, what I told you about, at Cut-Throat Lane? 'Cause when that happened to me—well, for a time I thought the world would never be right again. Once you do summat like that, you can't go back to the way it was before you did it. You lose it, and it's hard to get it back. But then you and Maisie and Mr. Blake came along, and I felt better, finally, once I told you—except I'm scared of the dark, and of being alone."

"It's all right," Jem answered at last. "I were surprised, is all. It made me think of you different. But it's all right."

They looked down at their books in the coming dark. Then Maggie leaned over the page of Jem's book. "Is that a tiger?"

Jem nodded, and peered at the words. "'Tyger tyger—'"

"'Burning bright,'" Maggie joined in, to his surprise,

> In the forests of the night
> What immortal hand or eye
> Could frame thy fearful symmetry?

"Maisie taught me that," she added. "I can't read it—yet."

"Maisie taught you?" Jem pondered this, wondering how much his sister had changed from her stay in London. "What's 'symmetry'?"

"Dunno—you'll have to ask her."

Jem closed the book and cleared his throat. "Where you going now, in the dark, all alone?"

Maggie tapped the book against her palm. "I was going to catch up to the button man in Piddletown, and offer to make buttons for him to raise my fare back to London."

Jem wrinkled his brow. "How much do it cost?"

"A pound all in on the stage if I ride up top, less if I get a wagon."

"Maggie, you'd have to make a thousand buttons at least to pay your fare!"

"Would I? Lord a mercy!" Maggie joined Jem's laughter. It released something, and soon they were laughing so hard they had to clutch their stomachs.

When their laughter at last died down, Jem said, "So what were you going to do, stuck on this stile—stay here all night?"

Maggie ran her fingers over the cover of the book. "I knew you'd come."

"Oh."

"So if I'm on this side o' the fence, and you're on t'other, what's in the middle?"

Jem put his hand on the stile. "We are." After a moment Maggie pressed hers over his, and their hands remained sandwiched that way for a time, each warming the other.

The valley before them was darkening now, the river and trees at the bottom no longer visible.

"I can't stay here, though, Jem," Maggie said softly. "I can't." She shed some tears, but soon wiped them.

"I'll walk you to Piddletown if you like," Jem said after a while.

"How can you? Look how dark it is!"

"Moon'll be up soon—we can see by that."

"Will it? How do you know that?"

Jem smiled. "Tha' be the sort o' thing we know out here. We don't have lamplighters going up and down the streets." He handed her his book while he climbed over the stile. When Maggie held out *Songs of Experience* for him to take back, Jem shook his head. "You keep it with t'other. Look how they fit together in your hand. They be just the same size."

"Oh no, I couldn't! No, *you* keep 'em. Otherwise you'll never see 'em."

"I could come up to London to see them."

"No, that's not fair. No, you keep 'em and I'll come to Piddle-dee-dee to visit."

Jem laughed and took her hand. "Then you would have to learn to cross this field alone."

"Not if you came to meet the coach."

They argued about it all the way to Piddletown.

SELECTIONS FROM
WILLIAM BLAKE'S

Songs of Innocence

AND

Songs of Experience

Songs of Innocence

Introduction

Piping down the valleys wild,
Piping songs of pleasant glee,
On a cloud I saw a child,
And he laughing said to me:

'Pipe a song about a Lamb:'
So I piped with merry chear.
'Piper pipe that song again;'
So I piped, he wept to hear.

'Drop thy pipe, thy happy pipe;
Sing thy songs of happy chear.'
So I sung the same again,
While he wept with joy to hear.

'Piper, sit thee down and write
In a book that all may read.'
So he vanish'd from my sight
And I pluck'd a hollow reed

And I made a rural pen,
And I stain'd the water clear,
And I wrote my happy songs
Every child may joy to hear.

The Lamb

Little Lamb, who made thee?
Does thou know who made thee?
Gave thee life & bid thee feed
By the stream & o'er the mead;
Gave thee clothing of delight,
Softest clothing wooly bright;
Gave thee such a tender voice,
Making all the vales rejoice;
Little Lamb, who made thee?
Does thou know who made thee?

Little Lamb, I'll tell thee,
Little Lamb, I'll tell thee:
He is called by thy name,
For he calls himself a Lamb:
He is meek & he is mild,
He became a little child:
I a child & thou a lamb,
We are called by his name.
Little Lamb, God bless thee.
Little Lamb, God bless thee.

The Chimney Sweeper

When my mother died I was very young,
And my father sold me while yet my tongue
Could scarcely cry 'weep weep weep weep,'
So your chimneys I sweep & in soot I sleep.

There's little Tom Dacre, who cried when his head
That curl'd like a lamb's back was shav'd, so I said:
'Hush Tom, never mind it, for when your head's bare,
You know that the soot cannot spoil your white hair.'

And so he was quiet, & that very night,
As Tom was asleeping he had such a sight,
That thousands of sweepers, Dick, Joe, Ned & Jack
Were all of them lock'd up in coffins of black,

And by came an Angel who had a bright key,
And he open'd the coffins & set them all free.
Then down a green plain leaping laughing they run
And wash in a river and shine in the Sun.

Then naked & white, all their bags left behind,
They rise upon clouds, and sport in the wind.
And the Angel told Tom if he'd be a good boy,
He'd have God for his father & never want joy.

And so Tom awoke and we rose in the dark
And got with our bags & our brushes to work.
Tho' the morning was cold, Tom was happy & warm.
So if all do their duty, they need not fear harm.

Laughing Song

When the green woods laugh with the voice of joy
And the dimpling stream runs laughing by,
When the air does laugh with our merry wit,
And the green hill laughs with the noise of it,

When the meadows laugh with lively green
And the grasshopper laughs in the merry scene,
When Mary and Susan and Emily
With their sweet round mouths sing 'Ha, Ha, He,'

When the painted birds laugh in the shade
Where our table with cherries and nuts is spread,
Come live & be merry and join with me,
To sing the sweet chorus of 'Ha, Ha, He.'

Holy Thursday

Twas on a Holy Thursday, their innocent faces
    clean,
The children walking two & two in red & blue &
    green;
Grey headed beadles walkd before with wands as white
    as snow
Till into the high dome of Paul's they like
    Thames waters flow.

O what a multitude they seemd these flowers of
    London town!
Seated in companies they sit, with radiance all
    their own.
The hum of multitudes was there but multitudes
    of lambs,
Thousands of little boys & girls raising their
    innocent hands.

Now like a mighty wind they raise to heaven the
    voice of song,
Or like harmonious thunderings the seats of
    heaven among.
Beneath them sit the aged men, wise guardians
    of the poor;
Then cherish pity, lest you drive an angel from
    your door.

Infant Joy

'I have no name;
I am but two days old.'
What shall I call thee?
'I happy am,
Joy is my name,'
Sweet joy befall thee!

Pretty joy!
Sweet joy but two days old.
Sweet joy I call thee;
Thou dost smile,
I sing the while,
Sweet joy befall thee.

Songs of Experience

Introduction

Hear the voice of the Bard!
Who Present, Past, & Future sees;
Whose ears have heard
The Holy Word
That walk'd among the ancient trees,

Calling the lapsed Soul,
And weeping in the evening dew:
That might controll
The starry pole;
And fallen fallen light renew!

'O Earth O Earth return
Arise from out the dewy grass;
Night is worn,
And the morn
Rises from the slumberous mass.

'Turn away no more:
Why wilt thou turn away?
The starry floor,
The watry shore
Is giv'n thee till the break of day.'

Holy Thursday

Is this a holy thing to see,
In a rich and fruitful land,
Babes reducd to misery,
Fed with cold and usurous hand?

Is that trembling cry a song?
Can it be a song of joy?
And so many children poor?
It is a land of poverty!

And their sun does never shine,
And their fields are bleak and bare,
And their ways are fill'd with thorns:
It is eternal winter there.

For where-e'er the sun does shine,
And where-e'er the rain does fall:
Babe can never hunger there,
Nor poverty the mind appall.

The Chimney Sweeper

A little black thing among the snow:
Crying 'weep, weep,' in notes of woe!
'Where are thy father & mother? say?'
'They are both gone up to the church to pray.

'Because I was happy upon the heath,
And smil'd among the winter's snow:
They clothed me in the clothes of death,
And taught me to sing the notes of woe.

'And because I am happy & dance & sing,
They think they have done me no injury,
And are gone to praise God & his Priest & King
Who make up a heaven of our misery.'

The Sick Rose

O Rose, thou art sick,
The invisible worm,
That flies in the night
In the howling storm:

Has found out thy bed
Of crimson joy:
And his dark secret love
Does thy life destroy.

The Fly

Little Fly
Thy summer's play
My thoughtless hand
Has brush'd away.

Am not I
A fly like thee?
Or art not thou
A man like me?

For I dance
And drink & sing:
Till some blind hand
Shall brush my wing.

If thought is life
And strength & breath:
And the want
Of thought is death;

Then am I
A happy fly,
If I live,
Or if I die.

The Tyger

Tyger, Tyger, burning bright,
In the forests of the night:
What immortal hand or eye
Could frame thy fearful symmetry?

In what distant deeps or skies
Burnt the fire of thine eyes?
On what wings dare he aspire?
What the hand dare seize the fire?

And what shoulder, & what art,
Could twist the sinews of thy heart?
And when thy heart began to beat,
What dread hand? & what dread feet?

What the hammer? what the chain,
In what furnace was thy brain?
What the anvil? what dread grasp
Dare its deadly terrors clasp?

When the stars threw down their spears
And waterd heaven with their tears:
Did he smile his work to see?
Did he who made the Lamb make thee?

Tyger, Tyger burning bright,
In the forests of the night:
What immortal hand or eye
Dare frame thy fearful symmetry?

The Garden of Love

I went to the Garden of Love,
And saw what I never had seen:
A Chapel was built in the midst,
Where I used to play on the green.

And the gates of this Chapel were shut,
And 'Thou shalt not' writ over the door;
So I turn'd to the Garden of Love,
That so many sweet flowers bore,

And I saw it was filled with graves,
And tomb-stones where flowers should be:
And Priests in black gowns were walking their rounds,
And binding with briars my joys & desires.

London

I wander thro' each charter'd street,
Near where the charter'd Thames does flow
A mark in every face I meet
Marks of weakness, marks of woe.

In every cry of every Man,
In every Infant's cry of fear,
In every voice; in every ban,
The mind-forg'd manacles I hear.

How the Chimney-sweeper's cry
Every blackning Church appalls,
And the hapless Soldier's sigh
Runs in blood down Palace walls

But most thro' midnight streets I hear
How the youthful Harlot's curse
Blasts the new born Infant's tear
And blights with plagues the Marriage hearse.

A Poison Tree

I was angry with my friend:
I told my wrath, my wrath did end.
I was angry with my foe:
I told it not, my wrath did grow.

And I waterd it in fears,
Night & morning with my tears:
And I sunned it with smiles,
And with soft deceitful wiles.

And it grew both day and night,
Till it bore an apple bright,
And my foe beheld it shine,
And he knew that it was mine,

And into my garden stole,
When the night had veild the pole:
In the morning glad I see
My foe outstretched beneath the tree.

Acknowledgments

There are many—too many—resources on William Blake in the world. A few that I found most useful:

The Life of William Blake by Alexander Gilchrist (1863, and recently reissued)
Blake by Peter Ackroyd (1995)
The Stranger from Paradise: A Biography of William Blake by G. E. Bentley, Jr. (2001)
Blake Records (2nd edition) edited by G. E. Bentley, Jr. (2004)
William Blake (Tate Britain exhibition catalog) by Robin Hamlyn et al. (2001), particularly the section on Lambeth by Michael Phillips
William Blake by Kathleen Raine (1970)
William Blake: The Creation of the Songs by Michael Phillips (2000)
"Blake and the Terror, 1792–1793" by Michael Phillips, in *The Library*, sixth series, vol. 16, no. 4 (December 1994), pp. 263–97
"No. 13 Hercules Buildings, Lambeth: William Blake's Printmaking Workshop and Etching-Painting Studio Recovered" by Michael Phillips, in *The British Art Journal*, vol. 5, no. 1 (Spring/Summer 2004), pp. 13–21

The most comprehensive Internet resource on Blake is undoubtedly the William Blake Archive at www.blakearchive.org.

I am going to list only the most entertaining of the myriad works that have helped me to re-create eighteenth-century London, as well as a selection of resources useful for more specific topics:

The Autobiography of Francis Place edited by Mary Thale (1972); also the archive of Francis Place held at the British Library

London Life in the 18th Century by M. Dorothy George (1925)

On Lambeth Marsh by Graham Gibberd (1992)

A to Z of Regency London (1985): a remarkably detailed map made of London by Richard Horwood from 1792 to 1799 (with subsequent updates); also available online at www.motco.com

The Shadow of the Guillotine: Britain and the French Revolution edited by David Bindman (1989)

Astley's Amphitheatre and the Early Circus in England, 1768–1830 (Ph.D. thesis) by Marius Kwint (1994); also the archive of Astley's cuttings from newspapers held at the British Library

Buttony by Mervyn Bright (1971)

The English Regional Chair by Bernard D. Cotton (1990)

The punctuation Blake used in reproducing his poems was erratic and confusing; I have taken the liberty of stripping it away so that it can be read aloud more easily; readers who would like to see it as he printed it should refer to *The Complete Poetry and Prose of William Blake*, newly revised edition, edited by David V. Erdman (1988). Additionally, for similar reasons, the poems included at the back of the text were taken from the Penguin Classics edition, *Selected Poems* by William Blake (2005). I am aware too that Blake's poem "London" would likely have been in an earlier draft when Jem hears it in Bunhill Fields, but I've used the final version so as not to confuse everyone.

I would like to thank the following people who helped me during the making of this book:

Robin Hamlyn, curator at the Tate Collection, London; Chris Fletcher and his successor, Jamie Andrews, at the British Library, who allowed me to handle Blake's notebook without flinching;

Greg Jecman at the National Gallery of Art and Daniel De Simone at the Library of Congress, both Washington, DC; Sheila O'Connell at the Prints and Drawings Room of the British Museum; Tim Heath, president of the Blake Society (UK);

Marius Kwint, expert on Philip Astley, whom I hope will write a biography about him, for Astley was probably even more outrageous than I have portrayed him;

Mike and Sally Howard-Tripp, who first introduced me to the joys of Piddletrenthide;

Thelma Johns of the Old Button Shop in Lytchett Minster, Dorset, for sharing her knowledge and her Dorset buttons;

Guy Smith of Dorchester, for help with Piddle Valley pub names;

Lindsey Young and Alexandria Lawrence for their able assistance; Zoë Clarke for capable copy editing; Jonny Geller and Deborah Schneider, star agents; and editors Susan Watt and—new to the team, and what would we do without her—Carole DeSanti, pushing me to flex muscles I didn't know I had;

Laura Devine, who bravely bought the privilege of allowing me to name a character after her, at an auction to raise funds for the Medical Foundation for the Care of Victims of Torture (UK).

My single greatest debt, however, is to Blake scholar Michael Phillips, whose groundbreaking, attentive, and blessedly commonsensical work on Blake during his Lambeth years inspired me to focus on this period, and specifically on 1792 and 1793. His biography of Blake in Lambeth during the anti-Jacobin Terror in Britain is nearing completion, and will do much to help us understand this most complicated, unusual man. I eagerly await it.

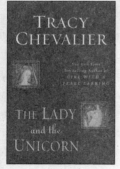